Pra

taking the joke just a little too far...

By
HAG HUGHES

Pen Press Publishers Ltd

Copyright © Hag Hughes 2008

All rights reserved

No part of this publication may be reproduced,
stored in a retrieval system, or transmitted
in any form or by any means, without
the prior permission in writing of the publisher,
nor be otherwise circulated in any form of binding or cover
other than that in which it is published and without a similar
condition including this condition being imposed on the subsequent purchaser.

All characters in this book are fictitious; and any resemblance
to actual persons, living or dead, is purely coincidental.

First published in Great Britain by
Pen Press Publishers Ltd
25 Eastern Place
Brighton
BN2 1GJ

ISBN13: 978-1-906206-93-2

Printed and bound in the UK

A catalogue record of this book is available from
the British Library

Cover design by Hag Hughes

For Bradley and Lara, my best friends.

"May any shadows of doubt and uncertainty be forever bleached from your mind by the brightness of your character, the confidence of your ability, and the unbending strength of your own self belief.
You are the most perfect person you will ever know."

Dad.

thank you, thank you, you're far too kind...

I would like to thank the following people for their help and guidance in making this all possible...

Jerry Woods.
For unending proof reading, advice and cups of tea.

Cassie Gledhill.
For fixing the body to allow the brain to work properly.

Charles Moore.
For fixing the brain, to allow the body to work properly.

Paul Sonvico.
For insight into the shoot.

Hag Hughes was brought into the world as the sixties were drawing to a close. A magical time indeed, when love was free and drugs made you happy. The colourful suburbs were interspersed with parks and trees and the only people to have guns were the soldiers.

A stark contrast indeed to the streets in which we find ourselves today.

His experience is drawn not only from a mis-spent youth of drugs, alcohol and anarchy, but the sobering real life surroundings of motorcycle racing at every level. As a rider he has competed in motocross and road racing in various championships, favouring now the uk endurance series, finishing 3rd in 2006, and still continues to chase that elusive number 1 plate. As a mechanic, manager and team owner, he has also competed in various capacities at World Endurance, British Superbike and World Superbike, but thinks that those number 1 plates may be a little more elusive!

Hag has also worked as a test rider, journalist and race product designer throughout the motorcycle industry, as well as graphic design in other fields and now studies various aspects of psychology and behaviour, usually of the female species in various bars around south London.

Having lived in Surrey since birth, he continues to do so with his two little angels Bradley and Lara. He has no plans to disappear off to anywhere warmer yet, not till the inland revenue catch up, anyway...

"Prank!" is Hag Hughes' first novel, his second "Destdenied" is due to be released in early 2009. For advanced notification, please register at; www.haghughes.com

Chapter 1

Smashing!

taking the joke just a little too far...

A numb consciousness gradually ekes its way into my weary brain. I slowly and painfully begin to open my left eye.

It's still dark.

I'm horizontal, next to somebody else's wife.

I'm in the shit.

This much I know for sure, the true depth of it I am yet to fathom. I draw the duvet back from my side of the sofa, and as I swing my lead-filled legs around to the floor, my pounding head notices my penis has stuck itself to the inside of my boxer shorts.

This is a good sign, of course; if I hadn't managed to make it out of my boxers the night before, the chances of me having been unfaithful are greatly reduced. The fact is, I can't remember. I gently peel him from his fabric straitjacket, and give him a little wiggle to perk him up a bit. Tess then stirs, mumbling, 'Not again, soldier, come back and cuddle.' She reaches out and starts to stroke it. The alarm bells ring so loudly in my head I'm incapable of thought. I leap to my feet, gather my clothes and rush to the bathroom. After a moment's rummaging I find a small but neatly folded tin foil package in my shirt, then set about chopping and snorting its contents on the toilet cistern. A couple of hits later, I stumble backwards and land on the wooden floor with my back to the wall.

It takes me a moment to regain focus, with both my raging hangover and lack of sleep. I struggle to clear my mind enough to recall the last few hours' events.

The clues are all there: hangover, cocaine, sticky boxer shorts and my mate's naked wife with her hand on my cock. It certainly tips the odds slightly against me in the infidelity stakes, but I still can't quite piece it together. I dress somewhat awkwardly as my back complains of the night's choice of bed. I try to ignore it.

After running my head under the tap for a moment I brush my teeth with her toothbr… Euuuuggghh! I spit the toothpaste into the sink and rinse my mouth. As I was brushing I realised I was using *his* toothbrush, not hers. It feels disgusting and vile, even though a short while before I was inspecting his wife's dentistry with my tongue. It seems impossibly wrong to be using his toothbrush; strange, I know, but wrong all the same. I throw it in the sink and make a beeline for the front door.

Whilst clumsily grappling with the unfamiliar latch, I glance over my shoulder to see Tess still on the sofa. She's engulfed in a blue king-size duvet, all pouty lips and deep eyes, deep black and blue eyes, thick lipped with a swollen cheek.

My jaw falls open as the hairs on the back of my neck spring to life. I stand in stunned silence as she nestles back down in her duvet, breaking the spell.

I make my way uneasily towards her, feet hardly moving, but my brain racing a million miles per hour.

I touch the top of her head, stroke her hair, and desperately try to remember what she had told me the night before. She remains in the fully snuggled tuck position, so I bend down towards her, heavily breathing in the wonderful scent of her perfume. I then rest my lips and nose on her head for what seems like an eternity.

Snapping out of my trance, I stand, about face, then roll towards the door like a cartoon character whose body is forever trying to catch up with the overly heavy head at some 45° in front.

Once outside, the cold attacks me like a swarm of hungry piranhas, my flimsy shirt doing little to ward off the morning chill. I stagger over the road, then make my way through the field opposite, managing only to fall twice before reaching the footpath at the other side. The path is cloaked in darkness as the moonlight struggles to squeeze past the trees that have only partially spread their leaves. I manage to walk head-first into a branch, but I don't think I injured it.

Reaching the end of the path, the humming yellow glow of the streetlight welcomes me into the back entrance of the pub car park.

After fumbling around in my pocket for a moment, I eventually retrieve my keys and thumb the alarm zapper. Two swift blinks of the indicators and a glow emanates from the interior light. The subtle lines of the black Porsche's front wings appear almost green under the artificial light; this, mixed with the orange glow on the horizon, heralds the dawn of just another day under the dim-witted haze of yet another hangover.

I climb in, start the motor, and indulge in a quick zip of go-go dust. The engine's revs rise and fall with hypnotic harmony as it struggles to warm up. The initial hit from the coke numbs me within seconds. A further snort serves to just dilute the hit, and bring a warm welcome glow to the anaesthetised mush behind my tired eyes. I sit for a moment, tranquil, then with first selected, I lift the clutch, and slowly whoosh out onto the main road.

Once underway I realise how light-headed I still feel. The corners begin to flow within a mile or so, and with this, the stereo grows louder and louder. Linkin Park's 'Somewhere I Belong' throws itself from the speakers, filling the car with a demonic beat, intensifying by the second. As my speed increases, my concentration replies with an equal but opposite effect.

I negotiate a roundabout at a good 15 mph faster than I should, thumping the inside kerb with one of my rear wheels.

'Fuck it!' I shout as I envisage a new scar on my previously pristine alloys. I glance over my shoulder as I hear the resulting crash of Becks bottles falling from the back seat into the rear foot wells, and see them rolling around messily together. Reaching back to grab one of the bottles, a massive shot of cramp fires its way along the entire length of my left arm. The pain is so intense I close my eyes and grit my teeth, not a good idea as I am rapidly approaching a deceptively tight bend in the road.

Entering the corner, eyes now open, the car slews violently to the left, and I'm far too dramatic with my one-armed steering efforts so swerve across both lanes in a lazy zig-zag fashion. I correct with some opposite lock, only to exaggerate the problem. Eventually my addled brain registers which direction the steering wheel ought to face, and aims it accordingly. The following straight is some two miles long, with a stream to one side, and a tree-lined ditch the other. With the car now settled, I squeeze the accelerator firmly to the carpet and watch the speedo as it purrs its way around to 110.

I buzz the window down to draw a noseful of crisp dawn air. The bottle of Becks I had managed to retrieve from the back is now sitting comfortably between my legs. I pop the cap, and with a quick spuff of foam, guzzle a couple of mouthfuls. Suddenly, I'm aware of a dull thudding growing slightly louder. I crane my neck to listen out of the open window whilst reaching for the volume control on the stereo.

BANG!!

The rear tyre explodes, causing the car to veer violently to the left, snapping the steering wheel from my hand, breaking two of my fingers. I struggle to control the wayward beast with my other hand, but it's too little too late. The nose of the car ploughs through the stream, up a bank, and with the aid of a drystone wall, pirouettes onto its roof and back onto its wheels, albeit travelling backwards. The deafening screech from the tyres trying to turn the engine backwards at 100 mph is almost as loud as my own screams of absolute horror and dread of the next impact.

The back of the car instantly drops 6 ft as it heads airborne into the ditch below. The ensuing impact renders me unconscious as the car compresses its way into Mother Earth, rebounding over onto its roof again, finally resting in a bramble hedge that borders a field.

As I come to, a man – who appears upside down – fights to unclasp my seat belt. Being a five-point racing type of harness he is certainly having a little difficulty. I depress the release button he has been frantically searching for and promptly fall straight on my head, for it was I who was inverted, not he.

'Come on, we must hurry, before she goes up!' he pleads in a pure New York squawk, as he frantically drags me from the smouldering wreck.

'Come on, come on,' he insists. I struggle to help him as I'm both somewhat disoriented, and barraged with pain.

Eventually we're clear and I collapse in a heap, breathing as heavily as I dare with the broken ribs I have just sustained. Helplessly I watch the amber glow from the engine bay grow steadily, then burst into a raging inferno before I pass out.

Apparently it exploded, but my head was miles away, dancing with the fairies by then.

Chapter 2

Introductions

taking the joke just a little too far...

Four years earlier, a Tuesday in May.
I woke early, and after a breakfast of cornflakes and toast set out to meet my Uncle Jack. He was head of special effects at Shepperton Studios, and had worked on everything from Michael Benteen's *Potty Time* to *Terminator 2*.

Jack was well and truly part of the furniture at the Shepperton site, with his bright white swept-back hair, and the wispy thin moustache that graced his top lip. At 67 he was well overdue for a villa in Spain, but was quite happy where he was, thank you very much.

He worked alongside a friend of mine, whom I had known for some time, also named Jack. The pair had been there for nearly 20 years and, despite the near 30-year age difference, were almost like a married couple, pre-empting what the other would say or do, putting the kettle on just seconds before it was asked. A true partnership.

Ironically, I had only in later years become close to my Uncle (big) Jack through my friendship with Little Jack. Little Jack – ridiculous as it may seem, being 6 ft 8 – and I had met at a friend's party some five years previously. As most people I meet are focussed on either what colour bike they are going to buy next year, or how they'd love to entertain the blonde Doris at the bar who was trying her best to mimic Jordan or Posh, it was a breath of fresh air to talk about something other than this or the current championship standings. Little Jack spoke of R2-D2s and explosion rigs, of aerial ropeways, animatronic models and, of course, his boss, my Uncle Jack.

I arrived at the gate as the heat of the day ahead was just starting to nose its way around the back of my collar. I began to question my sanity for not choosing shorts, noticing my Betty Swollocks sliding gracefully against my inner thigh as I stretched out of the van window in an attempt to decipher what the clipboard Nazi was mouthing at me from behind his Perspex bubbled guard hut. The balding self-important geek then lowered himself to actually open the window and let some of his valuable portably air-conditioned air waft out of his little plastic castle.

'Who do you have an appointment with, and what time does it start?' squeaked the 6 stone uniformed nerd.

'My uncle, Jack Klein, anytime today,' I replied. Mr Nazi then retreated back into his bubble, carefully closing the double-hermetically sealed window behind him. He then flicked the automatic barrier switch to allow me in. The van made forward progress with a lurch, and then trundled through the maze of stages and stores. I narrowly missed a collision with a milk float that came careering around one corner, carrying the hand and forearm of what must have been a 50 ft high gorilla strapped to the back. 'Ho-hum,' I thought to myself, 'another remake of *King Kong* on the way then.'

No sooner had I avoided this than I nearly wiped out Mel Gibson pedalling frantically on a kid's BMX bike, dressed in what I can only imagine as a nineteenth century chimney sweep's attire. He tipped his ferret fancier's flat cap, rang his bell, and then disappeared around another corner. This, coupled with the odd horse-drawn cart, alien invader and a few cheerful, but blood-soaked infantrymen, was enough to disorientate anyone.

I found the special effects department eventually, after asking directions from several green fish and the back half of a panto horse. As I walked through the door I was greeted almost face-to-face by a rather delightful little blonde-haired angel called Sally.

'Do you know where I can find Jack please?'

'They're over there,' she replied, pointing to the far end of the vast high-ceilinged building. I threaded my way through the maze of work benches and half-built models, ducking under a life-size whale to eventually meet the pair of them working on a golden chariot, apparently returned because of a problem Boadicea encountered with it whilst trying to run over a few Romans or something.

'Hello boys.'

'Good morning, my old son, and how are we today?' Uncle Jack started, patting me on the back and shaking my hand with the vigour of a ten-year-old.

'You know Little Jack here, don't you?'

'Of course I do, we met yonks ago. You must be going soft, Jack, I tell you that every time,' I responded.

'And Tess, I presume you have met the adorable Tess before?'

'No,' came my reply, 'I don't believe I have.' A breathtakingly beautiful woman then appeared from behind a 12 ft tall Roman column.

'Hi, how are you?' she said in a bright and breezy manner. 'You must be Hazy, Big Jack's nephew.'

'That's right, Paul's the name, but most just call me Hazy.'

She was blonde by bottle, deep-blue eyed, and a little scatty to say the least, but after a few years of inhaling fibreglass resin, who wouldn't be?

'We're just knocking off for morning break, why don't you join us for a cuppa?' Uncle Jack asked. We both said okay in unison.

Once seated at a rickety table in the corner of the dark but cosy canteen, the four of us roared like a house on fire for over an hour, laughing and joking like true old friends.

'I have a mate that I'm sure would love to meet you,' I mentioned to Tess. And love to meet her he certainly did. Not six months later, they were engaged to be married. That meant that as the best man, I had one hell of a stag do to organise.

Thankfully it lived up to the hype, and then some… Read on, dear reader, read on.

Chapter 3

Dublin

taking the joke just a little too far...

Five months later, 8:17 a.m.
Wednesday 27th October, to be precise.
M23 towards Gatwick...late.
The Aer Lingus ticket said check in one hour before your departure time. Simple enough, I had thought, checking the ticket again – 9 a.m. departure.

8:33 a.m.
M23, stationary...later.
'Its not my bloody fault the traffic's backed so far up its own arse I can still see Croydon in the mirror!' came the heated and overly aggressive snap from the driver's seat, which was occupied by Patrick – a chauffeur by trade, who was glowing that colour of fuchsia that is usually reserved for the gaudy lip gloss of the overperfumed and utterly obnoxious elite that he usually ferries between Champneys and Harrods.

Today the 'Yes, m'lady' facade had slipped, and the usual scent of fresh new leather had been overpowered by the stench of stale beer breath and flatulence from the previous evening's late-night curry.

Beads of sweat appeared on Patrick's forehead. He wiped them away with a swift flick from the back of his hand, but they re-appeared, much to his annoyance, almost immediately.

The stress was getting to him, and his agitated state had become increasingly obvious. This, however, encouraged nothing but banter and piss-taking from the occupants of the overloaded rear seat.

He drummed the steering wheel with ever-increasing ferocity. Nobody noticed, the jibes were still coming thick and fast.

Finally, he snapped.

'Fuck it!' he announced as he tugged the wheel left whilst simultaneously burying the accelerator into the carpet. The Merc lurched diagonally with the grace of a cruise liner running aground. Cheers, jeers and screams filled the car as it hurtled down the hard shoulder full of half-pissed, half-hungover lads on their way to the ultimate stag weekend in Dublin. A chorus of 'Ere we go, ere we go, ere we go... Ere we go, ere we go, ere we gooo-ooow...' broke out from the back seat.

'WILL YOU ALL JUST SHUT THE FUCK UP!' came the response from the driver's seat. The ensuing explosion of laughter from the back had even me in fits. We didn't care if we made the plane or not, we were going to have a riot wherever we were!

8:49 a.m.

The Merc screeched to a halt in the last available spot on the fourth floor of the short-term car park. We knew we had missed our check-in slot and would have to catch a later flight, but we ran all the same.

What is it about going away? No matter how short your intended visit or what the weather is doing, you always take the largest, heaviest coat in your possession. Usually it's stuffed on top of your bags and cases that you've balanced precariously upon your trolley. Then, apart from really pissing you off every time it slides to the floor as you negotiate your trolley around the sprawled mess of the cafeteria (whilst carrying an overly laden tray, spilling Coke all over your bags in the process), you do not have any further use for it until you return to the airport two weeks later... You think we'd learn, wouldn't you?

Anyway, back to the six of us sprinting down the corridor and into the terminal building, looking more like extras from the film *Braveheart* than the lean mean drinking machines our deluded brains thought we were. Beaker got to the check-in desk first, named quite unsurprisingly because he is a bit prone to flipping his lid – no honestly, I've been to visit him several times when things get too much and the nice men in white coats take him away... Ugly...but then, I suppose when you are in that frame of mind it's the best place for you. I had, on occasion, visited my dad in similar places too, so I guess someone will be paying *me* a visit there sometime in the not too distant future.

The perfectly proportioned 6 ft tall – but still a size ten – flight attendant smiled at us from behind her counter, and said in her super-sexy smooth-as-a-cashmere-codpiece low-pitch Irish voice, 'I guess you lads will be pleased to know your flight has been delayed by 30 minutes due to an electrical fire in the control tower.'

'That's a new one on me,' I thought to myself, but we were grateful none the less as it provided an opportunity for most of us to stuff our faces with some much needed sausage and egg McGunge. We hooked up with the rest of the party in the lounge. Beaker, Patrick, Sully (a ridiculously overweight footie hooligan) and Ed (the stag himself) opted for the liquid breakfast, by way of a swift pint.

The airport had the same stale hum we have all come to expect. I truly believe that airports are a cunning time void placed here by aliens to confuse us. Where else on earth (except a prison cell) looks exactly the same at 3 a.m. on a dismal rainy Tuesday in January, or in the midday sun on a Saturday afternoon in July? Where else can you arrive on a Friday morning at 6 a.m. – angry, stressed, and verging on a nervous breakdown, dragging your thoroughly pissed-off (and boy does she let you know it) wife and two screaming/bickering/fighting children through the rigmarole of check-in, Customs, Passport Control, and then the obligatory two-hour departure lounge fiasco, where all you have for comfort is a selection of pay phones (do you know anybody who doesn't have a mobile phone these days?) and broken Coke vending machine.

The oh-so-nice stewardess gives you the same line she remembers from her ingrained flight school education: 'I'm sorry, sir, we are experiencing some delays, but I'm sure all will be fine and we can board in the next ten minutes or so.'

Bollocks! What she actually means is, the leak in the fuel hose to the number three engine is now so bad, it's pissing fuel onto the underside of the wing so the pilot daren't spark her up for fear of torching the whole terminal!

We then return two weeks later with a completely metamorphosed family. Tanned, happy, and eager to see their pals after what seems a lifetime of low-stress vacationing. Your son's tales of crab fishing in the jagged and treacherous rocks of the Marbella pier, or your daughter's first kiss from Pedro, the local super hero who pulls wheelies past the Athens youth club on his ten-year-old shit-heap of a moped, whose only real goal in life is to shag as many gullible blonde English teenagers as possible. Or the awesome 'I'm a hero' for snowboarding down that ice field stacked black run, with those stupid white panda-eyed suntans and neon carcinogenic lipstick.

Your new trophies being either a stupid Mexican hat or a Swiss horn that displace the now redundant jacket you still struggle to keep on your trolley as you battle your way through terminal two.

Our party, by contrast, arrived at the airport alive, excited and champing at the bit. Eager to be as bold as swollen bull's bollocks, with the loud echo of overly enthusiastic piss-taking, charged by raw adrenalin and a rather large dose of Red Bull to the system, only to return in under a week exhausted, hungover, partied out and in desperate need of a nice quiet nap.

As I bit into my sad – and sorry, looks nothing like the picture – egg & hoof Mc-thing, it oozed grease and egg yoke shite all down my arm and into the sleeve of the only shirt in my possession. I heard a scream emanate from Murphy's Tavern (the in-lounge bar), from whence Beaker came bowling out, laughing hysterically as tears rolled down his cheeks, followed closely by Ed, running with a face like thunder and the leg of a wooden table held high above his head. Beaker had apparently pulled the old 'removing the bar stool whilst someone is about to sit on it' gag to Ed, not realising that as he fell, Ed took a couple of staggered steps back, causing him to tip over the balcony they were on, and land flat on his back, smashing a table on the level below.

He chased Beaker round our Mc-table three times before deciding a change of direction would prove less effort. He stopped, span around on the spot, but before he had a chance to react, was barged to the floor by the high-speed alcoholic he was chasing. The momentum the two of them carried took both me and Glynn (A top lad, short but stocky, with thick jet-black swept-back hair, stubble to strike a match on, and what seems to be the obligatory Irish knee-length black leather coat. He grew up in Belfast during its most troubled times, but seems to have evolved for the better, having the most level head of the assembled mess we represent, and whilst being a massive Tommy Cooper fan, is never short of a gag or a one-liner for any occasion.) with them to the floor, with Mc-fookin hot coffee and trays laden with granite-hard hash browns and Fisher Price-like scrambled egg that showered us from every direction. Thankfully, I landed under Glynn, and his bat cape of a coat did a sterling impression of a leather marquee and saved the two of us from a right dousing. Beaker, however, was not so lucky. He stood to display a coffee stain that resembled a sawn-off shotgun wound, stretching from his kidneys right up to the neck of his recently acquired white Oakley T-shirt. He screamed, 'Fuck-fuck-fuck! Hot...hot as fuck! Fuck!'

He danced and jumped around like a manic cokehead at a rave holding his shirt off his now scorched skin. This appeared to have released any tension between him and Ed, who was now, with everyone else, in absolute fits of laughter.

Beaker then made a swift duck and leggit manoeuvre, as airport security had now been woken from their standing slumber by the commotion, and were making a beeline for our table.

I checked the time, and saw that there was more than enough for me to both answer nature's call, and ensure that Beaker was okay whilst I was there. I made my way to the gents'.

Mistake number one: as I entered, I saw Beaker washing himself down in one of the sinks. His T-shirt was off, and I could see the massive red mark the burning coffee had left on his skin, resembling a claret birthmark. I smiled and said, 'I bet Ed's back is a bit more painful, you are a twat!' He turned and laughed. 'Anyway, top start to the piss-up,' I said, as I disappeared into one of the lock-ups for a trouser ankle interface meditation session...

Before my belt had hit the floor, I knew that I was in trouble. My stomach felt as if I had been swallowing helium balloons all morning and now was the time to let rip!

The first gust tore its way out, taking me quite by surprise, before my cheeks had even touched the seat: BRAAAAP... SPLATT! BRAAAAP...SPLATT-SPLATT! DRIP-DRIP. BRAAAAAP...SPLAT-SPLAT-SPLAT! DRIP... and so it went – on and on and on. Twenty minutes in fact, and I cursed every Indian restaurant from here to Bombay throughout.

The cleaning-up process was also quite a delicate affair, summoning up the courage to attack my now swollen and red-raw ringpiece with the 'not quite Andrex' quilted luxury sandpaper, supplied by the ever cost-cutting 'where can we scrimp a bit' airport service providers.

After cleaning up, I suddenly felt 'the urge' sinking through my bowel again, so sat for a few more moments to make sure all the shite had been shat.

I then heard the outside door bang as it was swung open, its handle deepening the dent in the wall that it was hung upon. This was followed by the door of the lock-up next to me whining closed. After the clink of a lock and a scrabble of paper to clean the seat, my new neighbour's belt buckle clanged onto the tile floor. BRAAAAAP...SPLAT! Trickle trickle, SPLAT!

My arse was on fire again as the brown mush jettisoned itself into the bowl. After a moment's silence, a voice emanated from the next cubicle, 'Hello.'

I wasn't sure whether to respond, so hesitated a moment before he repeated, 'Hello...are you there?'

Not wishing to be rude, but equally a little embarrassed at the whole scenario, I felt I should respond. 'Err...hi, how are you?' I said, a little sheepishly.

'Fine, fine. Listen, I think we should get together, I'd love to see you, we could do dinner at Franco's.'

Oh my God, my hair rose with fright as I realised I was being picked up by a weirdo in a gents' toilet!

'Listen, mate,' I responded, somewhat vigorously, 'I'll have you know I'm not into all that, you filthy little pervert. Can't a man even take a crap in peace these days without being harassed by some seedy little vermin shitebag?' I banged my fist on the dividing wall in disgust before reaching down for the last of the loo roll.

'I'm sorry, dear,' he said, 'I'll have to ring you back, there's some violent lunatic shouting in the cubicle next to me. I'll call you when I'm at Charles DeGaulle.'

Bleep.

I left the gents' toilet a little thinner and far more carefully after my rather unpleasant chicken vindaloo extraction, only to find the table we had occupied for breakfast now devoid of any familiar faces. As I sauntered down to the departure gate, I heard my name being called over the public address system. Could I make myself known to a member of staff, was the request. I duly did so, to a rather thin bleach-blonde and obviously ravingly left-footed member of ground staff, proudly wearing the name 'Andrew' on his badge.

'Oooooo sir, we are a little late, aren't we?' he spurted in his finest scouse Lilly Savage accent. I smiled and replied with a wink, 'Better late than never.'

'Oooooo sir, if you say so, sir, I'm afraid we'll have to take the back way, as you are sooooo behind,' he replied with a matching smile and a healthy dose of sarcastic piss-take in his voice.

I followed Andrew down the corridor, and through an 'employees only' door for which he used his swipe card, held around his neck with an enclosed ball-type chain.

With the plush purple and blue underlaid carpet and the framed futuristic works of obscure art – that I'm sure my five-year-old son could better – left behind, we had now entered the aluminium checker-plate floored and plywood walled bowels (excuse the terminology!) of the airport the public never normally see. Down two flights of stairs, more barren corridors illuminated by just enough flickering strip lights, and we were out on the tarmac.

The sweet aroma of jet-engined aircraft fuel filled my nostrils, and was as intoxicating as any girl's perfume. The Avgas smell reminded me of the hundreds of times I have refuelled superbikes on their 30-second pit stops during my time as a mechanic in World Endurance Championship teams.

The smell in fact stopped me dead in my tracks, and as I closed my eyes to drink in the addictively sweet fumes, I imagined the pit lane of Circuit Paul Ricard in the South of France.

The weak September sun would have been warming my bones with the last memories of a summer past, traditionally the season's end, signalling a two-week break in the cost-a-shitload towns surrounding the circuit.

The smell, the noise, and not least the heat from the Boeing 747 engine had me riveted to the spot for what seemed like eternity, broken only by my escort's quite effeminate voice.

'Sir…sir…is everything all right, sir. We are awfully late, sir…if you wouldn't mind…'

'Sorry, I was just having a moment…I doubt you'd understand. No, actually you probably would, but I can't go into it right now, so where the hell's my plane so you can get back to your job.'

He rushed me across the tarmac, hailing, 'Cooooo-eeeee, Bo-ob, over heeeeere,' whilst waving frantically at a baggage handler driving one of those weird squashed-looking vehicles. Bob obliged, although seeming a little reluctant, and this was confirmed by my escort, Andrew, who turned to say, 'Ooooooh Bob's suuuch a hunk, but we've had a bit of a tiff, so smile and be nice!'

We jumped onto the back of this rather odd-looking vehicle, and after a brief confab with said driver we were underway to gate 12.

When we arrived, the usual concertinaed walkway had been retracted, and there was nothing but a glorified ladder leading to the fuselage of the Aer Lingus plane occupied by the rest of the motley crew I was about to spend the next few days with. I was deposited at the base of the ladder by Bob, who grunted his disapproval and left with Andrew clinging on to his grappling holds as they sped off into the distance.

The ladder, to be truthful, wasn't the most confidence inspiring piece of British engineering I have ever had the pleasure to use, but in its own wobbly way it did the job.

I entered the plane, head held low. The occupants had already waited a half an hour for my arrival, and as I boarded to a slow, sarcastic clap, I was greeted by the captain announcing over the public address system that we had missed yet another runway slot and he would do all he could to get us on the next one available. I took the last remaining seat on the plane and waited.

After what seemed like an eternity, the Tannoy crackled and hissed its way into life. After clearing his throat, the captain announced, in a 'Tally ho chaps' voice, 'The wunway'z all cleeer fooor thake off, so pleesthe fasthen wore sheet belths and pwepawe for take offff.'

At which point the stewardesses started their usual show of being overly nice as they checked that everyone was capable of pulling the seat belt across their bellies and clipping the little buckle in.

Of course there were the few tossers who, no matter how many times they had flown, or indeed how many times they had been told that morning, thought they were somehow above the rest of the passengers and waited to be told personally that the 'no smoking' sign really does mean no smoking, the 'fasten seat belts' sign really does mean you too, and a chair in the upright position does not mean you are lying at 45° with your headrest wedged firmly up the nose of the mum in the chair behind you, who is frantically trying to calm down her newborn offspring that you have just sandwiched between her lap and the flimsy plastic fold-up tray on the back of your seat.

The plane lurched backward from its departure dock with the grace of one of Patrick's lane changes, stopped momentarily, then trundled its oaf-like way to the runway. The stewardesses were now all fully in the swing of their dance routine – sorry, I mean safety procedure display – and struggled somewhat as the plane swayed left and right with little warning. This sent them shuffling from one leg to the other, whilst smiling radiantly and trying their hardest to look completely unstressed and Barbie-doll perfect. Especially the one nearest me, who also had the added distraction of a yobbo in aisle 14 leering and making suggestive comments and gestures throughout the entire demonstration. I later realised that said yobbo was actually Beaker – sat, of course, in the wrong seat.

Shortly after take-off the seat belt sign was extinguished, and as expected, Beaker was on his toes hot footing it to the back of the plane to turf out the poor unsuspecting punter occupying his seat. The mix-up had occurred as Beaker had only boarded moments before me, after being thrown out of the airport bar, half-cut and slurring.

The man occupying his seat, it transpired, had also been in the bar drinking with Beaker at the time. Said accomplice, after flying in on an all-expenses-paid first-class flight from Phoenix, Arizona, had just secured an extremely lucrative business deal for his employers, the O'Grady & Booth soft luggage company in Wexford, just south of Dublin. The lad, 25 years of age and Dermot O'Brannigan by name, was, as one would expect, completely wankered.

After a brief and barely decipherable exchange, it was decided that there had been some confusion over whose boarding pass was whose in the bar. The arm rests then went up and Beaker plonked himself down amid the rest of the lads. A cry came out from Dermot, 'Champagne for the whole plane!!'

This prompted a massive round of cheers and shouts from the other passengers, only to be doused by the stewardess announcing they only keep one bottle on board as it is indeed a rare occasion that anyone even orders a glass of champagne on the mostly commuter based 9 a.m. flight from Gatwick to Dublin, let alone order the 20 or so bottles it would take to service the whole plane.

Enthusiasm dwindled, and as the bottle made its way down the line of eager stag-goers it was drained completely by halfway. What now? the question posed to nobody in particular. A rush of beer orders followed, and before we touched down on the Emerald Isle we had managed to drink the plane dry.

Dublin airport was a haze; all anyone can remember is throwing Dermot O'Brannigan into the first cab that came along and wishing him good luck. He was due back in work at lunchtime, though we all doubted he'd see daylight again until tomorrow once he'd reached home – or his local, whichever was closer.

The next cab in the rank pulled up, and thankfully it was one of those people carrier type jobs with plenty of space and loads of seats. Unfortunately, however, although all 13 of us would have gladly crammed ourselves in, the driver wasn't too keen on having bodies piled up on the floor of his nice new motor, so we opted to take a selection of cabs instead.

I was lucky enough to remain in the people carrier with Glynn, the lad from Belfast, Gandhi – also known as the fat northerner, even though he comes from Nottingham (it's all north from Watford up if you live in Surrey) – Ron, 6 ft 3, stocky with short-cropped hair. Blunt and in your face, but smart and well-read all the same, loves his kids more than life itself, so we had all been quite amazed to see him on the plane. Most assume with his forward approach and manner that he is German, but he is actually half-Irish. And finally Beanie, a quiet office type with a meek and mild persona, until riled. He has an outstandingly abysmal driving record (his first six cars all went to the scrap heap), but has a certain cool about him. He's the first to wear a soon-to-be-trendy label, or plays a soon-to-be-famous band, always immaculately dressed and never without his gadgets. Kind of brains from *Thunderbirds* crossed with Keanu Reeves, with a little Rowan Atkinson thrown in!

'All on board,' the cabby squawked from the front, and bugger me if it wasn't Eric Idle himself, he of *Monty Python* fame!

Okay, I admit it; it wasn't the Lord God of Python Idle himself, but a closer double you would never find.

He spouts, in his deeply smooth southern Irish accent, 'How ya goin' laaaadz, welcome to the European stag capital of the wurld, if ya can't get shaagg'd senseless by the time ya leaves no matter how short yer stay is, then ya may as well accept you're a raging fudge paaacker!'

The sound echoed around the cab like a cry for help in a deep and dark mountainside bear cave. It was Glynn who finally broke the ensuing silence, by saying, 'So whilst on this magical mystery tour, when are we going to discover the whereabouts of our hotel?'

Eric (so now named) threw the motor into first and rolled off in search of the Amber Lane Hotel.

As we filtered through the streets of Dublin at a rather sedate pace, I couldn't help but notice the change in aura that surrounded us.

Gone, it seemed, were the 'Get out of my way you underling!' red-faced businessmen that are far too important to say excuse me as they barge past you, late for their next meeting after devouring half an undercooked cow and several glasses of port at 'Pascal's Bistro' down that little side street that nobody knows about. (In reality everybody knows about it, but nobody else goes there because it's a bloody rip-off.) Gone were the stuck-up pretentious Sloane rangers who quibble over what tone of mink happens to be 'in' that season 'darling', whilst sipping £5 coffees on the Kings Road, their Range Rovers dumped diagonally across any square inch of London territory that doesn't wear a double red line or a 'disabled only' sign.

These seemed to have been replaced by what can only be described as the more laid back 'don't have a care in the world' type of persona, or so it seemed. That perception was all too quickly dissolved before the end of the evening, but more about that a little later.

We crossed the Liffey, and had the Guinness factory pointed out to our right. Eric couldn't resist the temptation to bolster his fare with a little side tracking through the more picturesque parts of the city, and to be honest nobody was that bothered if it meant putting off lugging our luggage for another ten minutes, so we all played along.

'Here we goooo laaaads,' announced Eric from the driver's seat, as we drew up to our palatial residence. 'Dat'll be tweeeeelve euros please laaads.'

Split between the five of us was about two and something each. Beanie, ever the accountant, was still doing the arithmetic long after the driver had pulled away, having been chucked three euros each by the four of us who didn't really care.

The second cab rolled up and out spewed Beaker, laughing hysterically at the vile waft emanating from the taxi, as he let another roaring trouser trumpet rip. He stumbled to the floor with a perfect stuntman double roll, finishing upright and perfectly balanced, with his heels tight together. He then bowed, arms outstretched, to a fake drum roll through clenched teeth, and ended, smiling, with the chink of a make-believe cymbal.

Ed threw himself from the cab, gasping for air, along with Sully and Patrick, all equally poisoned from the contents of Beaker's intestinal stench. Even the cabby came out for air!

The third and final cab of revellers then arrived, comprising of Gimp – so named for his absolute adoration and subservient nature towards Ed, his 'hero'. He's somewhat effeminate, and seems to need a focus in life to disguise his own reason for being. Tall, with dark hair, but skin of a rather pale complexion, 40-something and single. A great laugh to have around, but seemingly reserved in most situations.

Also on board were the twins, A and B. Nobody can really tell them apart, they are to all intents and purposes identical, which can prove a little distracting when you are talking to both of them. Frequently, whilst down the pub, nature inevitably calls, so you nip off for a swift slash, only to return and not know which one you were talking to as they are standing only inches apart; they do it on purpose, I'm sure.

Finally, the last member of our party to disembark was Coco the Clown, so named for his quite unbelievable cocaine distribution network, whilst he appearing to be such a numbskull. Also the fact that he's a dumpy 5 ft tattoo-covered prankster, with a ponytail halfway down his back and a smile like a Jewish jeweller.

So the ensemble was complete, and if the devil should cast his net, I think he'd ask for a refund!

The dirty (baker's) dozen strode into town, well the Amber Lane Hotel to be precise, and were greeted by a hippy chick that obviously believed what her mother superior had told her about the evils of personal hygiene.

This scrawny, undernourished, smelly seventeen-year-old confirmed our booking. Then, through her vile matted hair that was draped across her face like a mop on a basketball, said that she would show us to our room.

'Room?' I inquired. 'Surely as there are 13 of us the plural should be used?'

'No,' she assured me, 'we keep a tight ship, with no space wasted.' She was certainly right; upon arrival at our room we all stood, stunned in disbelief at the exemplary design of the 25 ft x 25 ft (go on, pace it out for yourself) room with a large floor-to-ceiling sash window and no less than 14 beds, arranged in what I can only describe as a spiral staircase fashion.

Two large pillars rose from the floor, each supporting seven beds around its circumference. The beds were only about 18 inches above one other, but as they were arranged in this spiral way, didn't feel the slightest bit claustrophobic. The lower bunk was only overshadowed by the one directly above it from the waist down, then the one above that was rotated likewise, and so on, so by the time a full circle was complete, the bunk directly above you was over 4 ft higher than yours. A brilliant design, and the subliminal message I took from this, albeit several years later, was no matter how restricted you feel (how would you have fitted 14 beds into a 15 ft x 15 ft space?), there is always a solution to any problem, you just need to adapt your thinking to an entirely higher dimension.

Anyway, we all settled in. I managed to get third bed up on my spiral, which suited me, fine. Directly above me was Patrick, followed by Beanie, Beaker, and Gimp at the top. Below were Ron and Gandhi.

The other spiral featured the rest of the mob, namely A and B on the lower two bunks, Ed on number three, Glynn on four, Sully above him (poor Glynn) and Coco topping off the 'room for one more' spiral.

Our scrawny host gave us a brief 'if you see a fire, RUN!' kind of safety speech and pointed towards the end of the corridor where apparently the mixed showers could be found. All of a sudden the whole cast turned, and as if by magic were then hanging on the hippy chick's every word. We all agreed it would be a great time to freshen up, and like a bunch of school kids, we all raced towards the shower room.

Only disappointment greeted us though. The showers themselves were all individually cubicled off, so no eye candy for the lads just yet!

We all returned to the room one by one, and after a quick whip-round sent the twins off in search of an offie.

With us all settled in, unpacked and raring to go, murmurs began for the continuation of alcohol consumption. Fair enough was the consensus; after all, it was nearly midday.

As luck would have it, there was a pub parked directly opposite our new residence. So, thinking it would be rude not to, we all set off for the so-called 'Puffing Griffin'.

The old boy sat on a stool behind the bar greeted us with a broad but thin-lipped smile as we all dragged our weary 'haven't had a drink for a couple of hours and the last one's wearing off' bodies through the door and up to the desolate bar.

The long and narrow room was paved with an intricate mosaic pattern of brick red, black, and an ivory white, which echoed underfoot. The complex pattern it portrayed of arches and columns looked almost Roman, save for the lack of grapes and nudes.

The bar itself was a heavy oak item, which had no doubt been there since the turn of the (last) century, was stained a dark brown, and had a gloss varnish upon it to shame any yachtsman this side of Cowes.

There were a few booths to our right, but far from intimate as each one had a rather large stained glass window on the wall it rested against.

The sun shone in through these windows, illuminating the room as you might imagine an enormous Tiffany lamp would, reminiscent of the first rays of spring through the stained glass church window on Easter Sunday.

The rays of light brought peace and happiness with them into the pub, highlighting the speckles of dust in the air and provided a warm glow to any that stood in its path. A stark contrast to the bright, but bitterly cold winter's day outside.

A line of freshly half-poured Guinnesses was being balanced precariously in the drip trays under the taps, looking as if the slightest knock would have them all cascading to the harsh floor in an instant.

A swift nod to the barman and 11 pints of the black stuff were brimmed, and then served to our goodselves.

It then occurred to me the reason for the half-filled pints under the bar. We were served 11 pints in the time it would normally take to pour just one properly. For those who are unfamiliar with the art of Guinness pouring, here's my take on the way to do it:

Firstly, you pour to the halfway mark. Then after five minutes' settling time, you displace three quarters of the remaining air in the glass with the road tar-like liquid. Then, after only another five min's can you top the pint off, scrolling a shamrock in the top with the stream of tar – sorry, I mean Guinness – from the tap. (Though if the truth be known, the shamrocks that I used to present to punters whilst enduring the misfortune of working behind a bar more closely resembled the typical cartoon image of a gent's genitals.)

No sooner did we have our pints delivered, the landlord was back at it. Loading up those glasses, balancing them in the drip trays again, highlighting to me that in Dublin they do sell a whole load more Guinness in a day than an average English bar sells in a whole year.

With the first pint downed, we were all well and truly up for it. The second round comprised of not only pints, but a round of tequilas to chase.

A and B appeared some time later, both smiling in their own slightly overweight way, with cheeks bulging like a couple of well-fed chinamen, slit-eyed and dressed in black.

Upon arrival they were both several pints and several shots in arrears, but then I suppose you always need a sober one or you would never eat.

Lunch was taken at a rather sedate pace in a pub whose name unsurprisingly escapes me. It overlooked the river Liffey, which incidentally runs the length of Dublin, and then some. I was amazed, upon reflection, that none of us ended up swimming in said river during our brief, but entertaining stay.

4 p.m., back at the pad.
The booze had taken its toll and most of us had crashed out. The rest of us enjoyed our time alone, away from the other half, by doing the things that usually wound her up, like nail trimming, nose picking, or just trying to fart as loudly as possible.

5 p.m., we started to stir...
Compulsory Red Bull vodkas all round, followed by a short line of angel dust (for those who partook) and we were set for the evening.

Our first bar was a bit naff I must admit...15-year-olds in skin-tight minis, too much of mum's perfume, dancing to Kylie and S Club. A swift pint then on.

Next we found ourselves in the most superbly babelicious letch den, wall-to-wall 20-somethings, as eager as you have ever seen!

The entrance was strangely deceptive; from the outside it appeared to be just another Dublin pub, the only exception being a pair of fat bastard bouncers on the door, in their Top Man suits and Oakley shades...at night.

Once across the threshold though, it became obvious we had arrived in a reveller's paradise!

The pub had been fully 'Alan Titchmarshed' with a multi-level landscaping operation, performed in your finest timber decking, joined by a series of rope and plank bridges that even Indiana Jones would have been apprehensive of.

The ceiling above us was some 40 ft high, and the multiple levels rose in a staggered fashion up to a wooden balustraded dance floor on the highest level, which resembled an old court house.

We made our way through the surging masses, up the rather flimsy staircases, reaching the top level with our pints almost intact.

'Rockin'' is the only way to describe the atmosphere in this little den of iniquity. There was a rather healthy number of uni graduates celebrating something or other, so as the music pumped, the wooden floor rose and fell by at least 8 inches. A rather worrying sensation when you are some four storeys above the pavement!

As the evening zipped along, the pump and grind got louder, the beers sank quicker, and we all got pisssssster.

The grads were now dancing on the tables, some of them topless, much to the roars of appreciation of the assembled mob.

Gimp was going for gold (or a kick in the nads) with his pelvic thrusts, whilst also topless, on one of the tables. The girls were all either ignoring him, or failing to notice his overly suggestive moves.

Ron and Gandhi had nipped out for a spliff with Coco, and I was getting on down, dancing like a harpooned squid to the inane pumping in my ears, as were Glynn and Beanie. Ed and Sully were having a talk (don't ask) outside the gents', and Patrick was attempting to score some wildlife at the bar. Beaker had done the Houdini, and I hadn't a clue where the twins were.

1 a.m., absolutely battered.
We left the bar and strolled northwards as I presumed this was the correct direction for both food and bed... Wrong!

Whilst navigating (badly) through the southern streets of Dublin, we (myself, Glynn, Ron and Gandhi) bumped into Coco, Ed, Sully and Beanie. The conversation went something like this:

Ron: 'Waaaaa-aaaaay lads.'
Ed: 'Waaaaa-aaaaay back, watchupto lads?'

Me: 'Tryin ta score some scoff mate…watchupto?'
Ed: 'Same like, where ya bin?'
Ron: 'Oooo, roundn'bout, no scoff, but no punch-ups either, so job's a goodun!'
Sully: 'There's fuck-all up that way, 'cept tramps and smackies.'
Me: 'U-turn?'
All: 'U-turn.'

We headed back the way we had come, and being as blokes in (and full of) high spirits are, we ran, barged and climbed anything in our way, laughing, joking and each generally acting the twat as we went.

2 a.m.

'Where on earth are we?' asked Sully.

'Dublin, you twat,' came the general answer from nobody in particular. We were lost, plain and simple. None of us had the slightest clue where on earth we were.

'Nosh!' shouted Ron, as he barged through us like a man possessed towards the faint glow of a kebab shop's illuminated sign.

We entered.

There was a jostling mass of piss-heads all vying for pole position at the counter of 'Sultans Delight', the imaginatively named salmonella emporium in which we found ourselves. Ron steamed ahead, parting the masses as if they were the sea that Moses strolled through that Sunday afternoon, around 1400 BC.

'Large donner, cheeseburger and a double large chips, mate,' he spouted with a nod, a wink, and a thumbs-up to Stavros, the man sporting the not exactly Daz-white T-shirt with a nice pair of yellowy-brown rings about the armpit, denim shorts, and a pair of flip-flops made from camel hair and yak dung.

Stavros then nodded to Spyros, a similarly attired gentleman who made himself busy preparing the burger and fries.

Stavros was wielding one of those newfangled electric kebab carvers that resemble an oversize hair trimmer, and Spyros was now picking his nose whilst standing over the grill flipping burgers and pitta breads.

Stereos, another brother, then appeared through the sixties-style strips of coloured plastic that hung from the top of the doorframe leading to the dimly lit and no doubt vile back room.

A few donners, one or two shishes, some chips and veggie pitta bread later, we were all happy again.

Three bites into my large chicken with double chilli sauce found me yakking and retching down the nearest drain. The liquid forced itself up from my stomach with such violence it had me doubled up in agony, lying on my side in the gutter. The puke was obviously not finding my mouth adequate for ejecting its evil acidic-burning self, so also found exodus through my nose. The burning was almost intolerable as this thick lumpy liquid jettisoned itself from my body at an alarming rate.

Then silence.

I staggered back into the kebab house in search of water.

'Sorry, sir, we only has Coke, Fanta or 7UP.'

'You're avin' a fuckin' giraffe, mate,' I slurred. 'All I want is some water, just turn the fuckin' tap on!'

'Sorry, sir, all we have is Coke, Fanta and 7UP.'

I lost my rag. As I reached over the counter to grab a handful of water from the tap, Stavros thought I was going for the till, and lashed out with his electric kebab trimmer. It caught the back of my hand and tore out a neat patch of skin. This really pissed me off.

I leant over the counter and simultaneously grabbed both his throat, and the handle of the carving thing he was using for a weapon. I pinned him to the counter with my elbow, and overpowered his grip on the trimmer. I yanked the flex to give me more agility, but in doing so caught the tool on Stavros's moustache! He laid, flat on his back, legs kicking like a decapitated chicken, screaming and desperately trying to pull the rogue trimmer from his face. I retreated. The rotating blades had dug in good and proper, not only devouring his hairy handlebar slug, but it also appeared to be eating his top lip. His gums were now visible as he frantically pulled at the machine that was rapidly devouring him. We were all riveted to the spot in horror. The quick-thinking Stereos took a swan dive to the floor, arms outstretched, and crashed into the wall, nose pressed to the skirting board, and flicked off the power to the trimmer, while the rest of his body caught up and concertinaed him Tom and Jerry style.

We all turned and ran.

I glanced behind as we took a left turn up an alley. Spyros and Stereos were closing in, Stavros a little further back, but making good time. It wouldn't take him long to catch up at the pace he was going.

Down the alley, faster and faster, I could taste the sour bile in my mouth as I gasped for air, a stitch grew across my stomach and I began to lag behind the others.

My sense of urgency returned, however, when I glanced back once again to see that the Greeks were even closer. Reflected in the poor light was the white glow of a carving knife's blade held high above Spyros' head, and the demented look of rage on his face. This was all the encouragement I needed to push the pace faster than I had ever run before. My eyes became blurry, my head thumped, and that damn taste of bile surged up into my throat again. We beat them though; a couple more blocks and they were nowhere to be seen, thank God.

Out onto a main road again, we ran across its four lanes with little concern for our own safety, then hopped over an iron railing and into a park.

The moon lit our way as we staggered quietly (except for the overly exaggerated 'Shushhhhh') across the lawns, then followed a path around a lake, with its hauntingly illuminated weeping willows draped like a sobbing widow's hair, dipping only their very ends into the otherwise still water.

The park benches beneath these proved just far too appealing to both Sully and Coco, who promptly stretched out across them and settled down for the night.

This was, of course, an extremely short-lived experience as within seconds the rest of us realised the benefit of a couple of horizontal headrest stations. They were swamped by cascading drunks shouting 'BUNDLE' at the tops of their voices, followed by more overly exaggerated shushes. We all fell to the floor, tipping one of the concrete framed benches flat on its back, then scrabbled to our feet and ran like men possessed, scattering to the four corners of the park in a state of sniggering adrenalin.

I came to rest beneath an enormous oak tree, surrounded at its base by a sprawling mass of unkempt ferns. 'Ideal for a hideout,' I thought. Unfortunately so did Sully as he hurled his grotesque mass through the air towards me.

I had little time to react, and all my personal defence mechanism could muster was a little muscle tightening to help absorb the impending impact. He hit me like an unripe pineapple would smash Jerry – your daughter's favourite gerbil – at 80 mph... messy.

As he made contact, in a full body slam kind of way, he added insult to (copious) injury by vomiting a mixture of warm beer and diluted donner over me. Thankfully his convulsions were so violent he managed to clear me on the initial ejection, and only make contact with my only (and now well-soiled) shirt with his latter and less forceful retching. He muttered a form of apology and made a show of dabbing down my puke-sodden trousers with a pink frilly hankie. (No, nor does he know how it ended up in his pocket either!) We re-grouped next to the statue of James Joyce and decided to make a concerted effort to get back to the digs before sun-up.

* * * * *

Day two, sometime around 8 a.m.
The lank hippy chick knocked on the door, leant in, and chucked a dozen white paper bags on the floor.

We ignored them.

Ten o'clock, the brave started to surface, and by midday we were all set. The mob dissipated for a day's leisure and agreed to meet up at a bar called Caspers at 7 p.m. that evening.

Following Caspers, we ended up in a kind of 'Thank God it's Tuesday' type place, serving overpriced burgers and featuring hot and cold running 17-year-olds. This suited Ed, and Gimp, but the rest of us grew restless after a pint or so.

The party then split. Glynn, Ron, Gandhi, Beaker, Patrick, Beanie and myself opted to move on to a more sophisticated letch den, whereas Ed, Sully, Coco, the twins and Gimp remained in teenysville. We were all to reunite at a club called Lilies Bordello on Grafton Street at midnight.

My troop dug in at a rather dingy dump to start with. The pub was long, thin and down a flight of stairs, sporting exposed brickwork and the odd fake blackened beam here and there. It was lit like the blitz, and seemed to contain more 50+ fat bastard businessmen than 25+ fit and firm delectable girlies. Still, we put a brave face on and made it our mission to get completely bladdered.

The barman, Françoise, took an instant dislike to us. Not surprising really, we were being fairly loud and weren't the slightest bit interested in the wine list. He ruffled his 'I'm a sad bastard' permed shoulder-length bob in disgust whilst checking his fake Mediterranean tan hadn't washed off yet in the mirror behind the bar, then set about ignoring us for as long as possible.

After he had shuffled the menus, arranged the olives, checked the dips, and sliced half a dozen lemons, he eventually took our order.

'Seven pints of Stella please.'

'Zorry zir we only aaave, awyooouwsay…eeeeer, boooooutles of laaaaager.'

'Fuck this place, I'm off to find a proper pint,' croaked Beaker.

'I'll go with that,' concurred Glynn. The pair of them lurched in unison towards the staircase, over the Yorkstone paved floor like members of the Addams Family. Both with hunched shoulders, dropped heads, knee-length black coats and pasty 'Have you seen the sun? No, buggered if I know where it is' type complexions that reflected off the cheesy flickering light bulbs in this quasi dungeon.

The next time we would see them they would be completely transformed. Patrick then took command of the drinks order and requested, 'Five bottles of Becks with tequila chasers.' This same order was then continued throughout the evening until we had all bought a round.

We drifted from bar to bar en route to our final destination on Grafton street, picking up a few hangers-on along the way. The queue for Lilies was quite substantial by the time we arrived, but I guess we all benefited from a nip of fresh air to help sober us up a touch.

We saw them from quite a way off, dark figures making their way towards us like sharks approaching a shallow bay. Veering left and right with little warning, snapping at any that would dare enter their space. The constant changing of direction seemed purposeful and calculated, slicing through the public with surgical precision.

This is all bollocks, of course, it was just Glynn and Beaker swerving in their pissed state through the masses whilst trying not to lose their latest female (just) acquisitions.

Beaker's catch (probably quite literally if things progressed any further) was quite fitting with my earlier notion of an Addams Family simile. The tall, long-black-haired, but white-as-a-sheet skin tone glowed in the half-light of the mock Victorian street lighting, like a fisherman's glow-stick on the bank of an inky black lake. Her attire was somewhat fitting with the 'am I dead yet?' image she wished to portray, being predominantly black with the odd splash of burgundy velvet. She was also wearing a jewellery collection to rival Keith Flint's. Quantity, not quality, that is, and this was mostly shared between her nose, lips, and ears.

Glynn's find, however, could not have been a more stark contrast. Laura by name and Ashley by nature, was she.

A petite 40-something, whose nice summery dress really did resemble a re-trimmed version of your Aunt Wendy's curtains. You know the ones, tucked away in her conservatory, faded, floral, and just a bit too seventies. Glynn couldn't give a shit though. He and Beaker had been lapping the scotch since teatime, so now some six hours later they were both on fast forward to Never, Neverland. Me and the lads had all decided to steam the local Burger King, located as if by magic, next to Lilies' punter queue.

Several flame grilled carcasses later and we were in pole position for the door of the club. The doormen (again sporting cheap suits and expensive sunglasses) sussed us immediately, offering entry to only those who appeared to have consumed just half a brewery, leaving the absolutely annihilated Glynn, Beaker and Coco behind. My strongest memory of that evening must be the sight of Beaker and Glynn hailing a horse-drawn carriage, standing with Laura, Death-bird and Coco at their side. A truly bizarre vision, sort of *Time Bandits* dwarf

(Coco) drags mediaeval witch through time to her destiny with two millennium matrix-esque executioners, witnessed by seventies housewife in Victorian Dublin! (Do I take too many drugs? Best not answer that one.)

The club was, as per usual, expensive and not really worth it. We all decided to go Dutch as ten rounds in this place would have us resorting to soup kitchens for the remainder of our stay. Still, a few bottles of booze and a great time was had by all. I think we left at about 3 a.m.

* * * * *

Day three, 8 a.m.
The now familiar image of the scrawny bird chucked us our breakfast bags through the door the way a lion tamer might lob a rack of ribs into the cage on a bad day.

A murmur, followed by several triumphant heralds of male flatulence later, and we were all sitting at our bunks feeling decidedly dodgy. I, of course, waded in to the muffin and yoghurt breakfast, consuming any unwanted leftovers with the voracity of a hyena at Mr Gerbil's barbecue. Then the piss-take started:

'Go on then, what was she like?' hails Sully from his pit, towards Glynn.

'Great, till her wig fell off that is.'

An eruption of hysterical laughter ensued.

'No, no seriously, we were on the job like, and I went to run my fingers through her hair, but it...sort of...came off in my hand! I didn't know what to do. I mean, it's not every day you're on the job, and you get jumped on by a rogue rug, is it now boys?'

The laughter didn't calm for at least five minutes.

'What about you then?' prompted Gandhi, towards Beaker's general direction.

'Shit out of luck and I don't want to talk about it. I need a piss,' was the gruff reply. He jumped from his bunk, misjudged the distance and landed with a thud. He was straight back up on his feet though, as if through embarrassment, and after a quick clearing of the head by way of a swift shake, he was off.

The door slammed behind him.

Group sniggering.

'I wouldn't pursue that one,' offered Glynn, to nobody in particular.

'Sounds like prime piss-take target has been set for the day then!' smirked Ed from his bunk, whose spiky peroxide white hair was at odds with both gravity and style as it sprang into life off the pillow. His tattoo 'need for speed, pain for gain' in black Biblical text was now clearly visible as he sat up. It ran along the length of the 6 inches scar that had given the doctors access to fit their titanium plates and screws to his once shattered collarbone.

Ed, the celebrity amongst us, had raced all manner of bikes from the age of eight, and had progressed at the ripe old age of 33 to the very top of his game. As a factory paid Grand Prix star, he now rode for Team Vertex as their number two rider, but was under a great deal of pressure. His team mate Tahido Kayagami had been the first Japanese rider ever to have won the world championship in the premier class, and had done so the previous year for Team Shinzui, but had switched teams in the off season, taking the number one plate with him to Vertex. This meant Ed had been in the most impossible of situations. He was expected to achieve top results, yet also ride shotgun for the defending champion. This meant that, frustratingly, he had only been allowed to win if his team mate had no chance of doing so, and as the season wore on, this became increasingly difficult.

Kayagami would often only achieve a mediocre start, and Ed had become increasingly frustrated with missed overtaking opportunities. Eventually he had become ragged in his riding style, causing a loss of concentration as he followed his team mate like it was just a high-speed fairground ride, causing, ultimately, missed apexes and eventually crashes. The greatest source of frustration had come from following 'team orders' only to watch Kayagami crash out after three-quarter distance, not leaving him enough time in the race for a charge to the front.

Given a free rein he would certainly have had the beating of Kayagami, and would have a damn good shot at the title. Sadly though, the sponsors who signed the wage cheques were mostly oriental, and were, quite understandably, rooting for their own guy.

Rapturous laughter found its way through our door, as Beaker (who else) burst in clutching a towel. There was the high-pitched cackle from several of the (female) Rumanian students, who were enjoying the hospitality of Amber Lane's finest, next door. This was followed by Gimp running in, stark naked, cursing Beaker for his 'rip the towel off a fully grown (and he certainly is!) naked male in a corridor' type of prank.

Gimp recovered his towel, and then larruped Beaker around the top of the head. The effect was minimal though, as the communal showers and corridor full of scantily clad females had lifted his spirits no end!

The morning took its usual form of hunting and gathering as we trudged ourselves through the sprawling metropolis that is Dublin city centre.

'Fuck me! We've got to 'ave a bash on that,' spurted Ron as a rather odd vehicle swerved its way past us. The exceedingly large, bright yellow World War Two amphibious vehicle, crammed to the rafters with tourists wearing cheap shite, plastic-horned Viking hats roared past with a collective Raaaaarrrrrgggggh!!!!! from the occupants, who waved their plastic axes with the vigour of a mass murderer at the auditions for another teen slash movie.

We downed our bacon sarnie breakfast, from the only cafe in a van we could find, served, incidentally, to us by a rather cunning looking Buster Edwards type (nice as pie, I am, till I smash yer face in with this 'ere lead pipe that is, my darlin') kind of east end of London meets the sly fox who slipped out through the 'smarmy pipe' only to land in the school of hard knocks.

White paper wrappers in bins, and we were off, hot on the heels of the Dublin Viking Splash tour bus.

Eventually we found our way to Patrick Street, which not only served as the base camp for Viking Splash Tours, but also provided a children's playground for us to entertain ourselves in whilst we waited.

Glynn was first, playing on the swings whilst reciting in his deep Belfast accent one of the oldest jokes in his book:

'A man called Bob was woken in the middle of the night by a knocking at his door. He got out of bed and opened the upstairs window. There was a man standing below him at the front door, so Bob shouted down, "What's the matter?"

'The man at the door replied, "I was wondering…would you be able to give me a push?"

'"Piss off, it's gone one in the morning," came Bob's reply.

'He slammed the window and returned to his bed. After a while his conscience gnawed away at him...

'A short time later, there was another knock at the door. Enraged, as sleep had just taken hold of his weary body, Bob stormed to the window and thrust it open.

'The same man was still stood below, and in his pathetic way cried, "Please, please, I only need a push. I would really appreciate it."

'Bob, now with steam pouring from his ears, screamed, "Piss off! And don't you dare ever come back and disturb me again."

'Bob slammed the window and stomped back to bed. Jessica, Bob's wife, then turned to him and said, "That was awfully mean, Bob, the poor chap is probably stranded. Imagine if you were in his shoes."

'Bob's conscience was driven into overdrive; the guilt became just too much, so he threw on his robe and made his way down the rickety staircase. After negotiating the dark hallway, he opened the front door, but to his surprise there was not a car in sight, so he called out, "Hellooooo…do you still need a push?"

'"Oh great, it's awfully kind of you," came the polite reply.

'"Well come on, man, whereabouts are you then?" gruffed Bob, fully awake as the cold, cobbled pavement draws the last remaining warmth from his bare feet.

'"I'm over here, on the swing!"'

A collective groan emanated from the assembled mass as we all started to stretch the boundaries of both our semi-sober balance skills and the inherent strength of the children's playground. I was first up the top of the gaudy yellow and fire-truck red climbing frame, with Gandhi in hot pursuit. He was followed – all too closely – by Ed, who was pulling at the bottom of Gandhi's jeans to slow his progress. Ed tried to flank him, and swung by one hand around to the other side of the climbing frame, only to make full contact with Beaker. The pair of them crashed to the ground after freefalling the six or so feet to the scattered woodchip below.

Beaker was first to rise, his white T-shirt had grown a brown skid mark from the bark chips on his chest, and a few drips of claret had also leaked onto his shoulder from his now torn left ear. He looked a mess, again.

Ed appeared, as any normal person would from such a minor incident, both unscathed and mystified as to how Beaker had managed yet again to end up in such a state.

I, by contrast, was balancing, arms outstretched, as if tightrope walking, along the uppermost section of the A-framed swings, some 8 feet above Glynn, who was still rocking gently back and forth.

I snorted deeply through my nose with a revolting phlegm rasp as my mouth filled with oyster-esque slobber. As I rolled it over my teeth in a vile 'I'm gonna getcha' type way, Glynn stepped off the swing below and shot me a 'Don't you fucking dare' kind of glare. The intent was never there, but in the absence of a rod and a river I guess I was just fishing for a reaction.

'Hey, you! You should know better,' came the high-pitched squawk from the ill-befitting Irish park keeper. A fat old git with what looked like the remains of a steak and kidney pie down his front.

'Bugger off the lot of you before I call the garda.' (Irish for cops.)

We then sauntered down to where the Viking Tours commenced, and sat sucking our Ribena cartons, generally feeling a bit below par. The excesses of the prior evening had started to take their toll as, one by one, we all had a sneaky yawn, and tried to keep our eyes closed for as long as possible without being noticed.

With a screech, a boom and a hiss, our chariot arrived. The 'Duck' as it was so named, towered above us some 12 foot high, yellow, and pleasingly anarchic looking.

We rose to our feet and all filed our way up the steps to board the vehicle.

After we had all settled, the rather unconvincing Viking tour guide handed around the twin-horned plastic hats and axes for the princely sum of six euros a pop. We all indulged, and set off about Dublin for the educational segment of our trip.

The World War Two amphibious vehicle lurched into life with the grace of a frog vomiting up a half-digested dragonfly, then after a short roll to the end of the street took a left turn.

The tour had begun.

We passed endless bronzes and sculptures of lord this and lady that, but nobody paid attention; that is, until the figure of the famous Molly Malone was come upon. The fine looking buxom lady was as famous a Dublin landmark in her time as a pint of Guinness is now. She pushed her cart through the streets of the city stacked high with all types of fresh fish, and no doubt out-selling her peers tenfold by what can only be described as an amazing foresight into modern advertising.

Yes, boys and girls, with her overly generous top half, and just the right amount of buttons on her blouse missing, she single-handedly moulded the focus of the Saatchi and Saatchis of the world to come; she discovered that sex sells!

With our interests now stimulated, we all woke up a bit and started to pay some attention. Next up was Trinity College. An impressive building, to say the least. Its vast columns reached to the sky some 60 feet above terra firma, with elegant 6 foot high windows present on all four storeys, the entrance being a totally over-the-top 18 foot high pair of arched wooden doors, nearly 6 inches thick.

A couple of bronzes graced the lawn, but I hadn't the slightest clue as to who they might have been. One thing I did take note of, however, was the large Wedgwood-blue clock at the very top of the building, showing half past twelve.

'Beer, lads?' I queried. A collective of nodding donkeys followed. Glynn was voted as man most likely to persuade the driver that a swift offie pit stop was in order. Our host, however, was having none of it.

'Sit back down in your seat and remain there until the tour has concluded, young man!'

The pseudo Viking was wearing one of those neck-mounted voice-activated microphones, so the entire party of sightseers-come-piss-heads heard the bollocking loud and clear over the crackly old intercom system. Glynn retreated with his head bowed and his tail wedged firmly up his own arse. Moments later, a plan was formed. Sully rolled his bulk into the aisle and made his way to the rear of the vehicle. As soon as an offie was in sight, Beaker began a kind of deep breathing and belching ritual whilst looking skyward, whilst Gimp sauntered in his effeminate way to the front.

We were set.

A few moments later Gimp gave the nod. Beaker responded with a frantic dash up the aisle, hand over mouth, imploring the driver to stop!

Simultaneously, like a well-oiled machine, the crew flew into action. The driver slammed on the brakes, sending Beaker unexpectedly crashing into the windscreen. Sully jumped from the back of the vehicle, but landed in a mess down below. He pre-empted the halt a little too soon and hit a moving pavement at some 20 miles per hour (poor pavement), but thankfully he was not injured enough to compromise the mission. Struggling to his feet, he then made the ten-yard dash to the offie at the side of the road.

Beaker then announced that he was going to be sick and threw his torso over the side of the vehicle.

Gimp immediately put his arm around Beaker to console him as he pretended to retch and convulse over the side.

'Is yer man okay there?' the driver asked as Beaker was going for an Oscar.

'He gets a little motion sickness; he'll be fine in a moment,' Gimp replied.

Meanwhile, Sully was drumming his fingers on the case of Stella he was now sporting on his left shoulder, as the queue at the cash till was frustratingly slow.

Sully glanced out of the window to check that Beaker was continuing his ruse of vomiting over the side, but how long was it going to be before the driver sussed?

Sully started to get agitated.

'Get a fuck'n move on, will you.'

'You talkin' to me?' came the reply from the 5 foot 6 Taikwondo expert in front.

'Yes you spud picking twaaaaa...' almost came his response as the chap buried his heel into Sully's throat. The plastic Viking hat went into orbit as he crashed backwards through a pyramid of special offer Fosters cans, then ended up as part of the window display.

Back in the Duck

'You're having me on,' barked the driver as he stood, causing a metallic groan as his mike passed a little too close to a speaker. He'd spotted the action in the offie and sussed the gag. Beaker, thinking on the hop, then stuck his fingers down his throat as he turned to greet the driver with a cascade of warm tea and toast, accompanied by some partially digested bacon rasher – nice!

The driver fell back into his seat in disbelief.

With the Viking now distracted, mopping his face down with his fake orange beard, Ed and I jumped ship to rescue Sully.

Mr Taikwondo had paid up as Sully was just regaining consciousness in the window. We grabbed a fresh case of beer from the stack, threw 30 euros on the counter, and left in hot pursuit of our tour bus.

Once back on board, I noticed Gimp doing his best impersonation of a concerned mother as he dabbed the vomit off the Viking, saying, 'There there, we'll have this off in no time,' in a tone that could calm a weapons inspector entering a Baghdad armoury at gunpoint.

Job done, and we slid back into our seats unnoticed. Beaker retreated as swiftly as possible, and had (quite unbelievably) planted himself next to the most gorgeous blonde on the bus.

Not only that, but the pair of them were getting on like a pair of pyromaniacs on bonfire night.

The Viking, bemused by the last few moments' events then lapsed back into tour guide mode, lurching the Duck forward to the crackling sound of his chest-mounted mike announcing an apology for the delay. To our right we could see a shining tower of glass apartments, apparently built for the yuppies by Bono, that sell for half a million per corner of each floor. At 18 floors above the designer quayside it sat on, it made for a rather grand wad of lolly!

The driver then pulled up at the slip that adjoins the quay, yanked the hand brake with the voracity of a terrier on your trouser leg, then launched into his safety procedure demonstration, urging us all to don life jackets as the Duck was about to go aquatic.

Life jackets on, and after some whirring, scraping and groans from the antiquated chassis of the yellow beastie, she was ready to take us swimming.

We rolled down the slip, and as the buoyancy exceeded gravity, we slowly began to float, nose-first, causing more groans of complaint from the rear suspension until we cleared terra firma and continued our journey into the unknown.

We bobbed and chugged like the African Queen with a misfire across an open stretch of water. Then, after having Bono's riverside recording studios pointed out to us, returned to the slip we had entered by.

Moments later, we had retraced our steps, then began heading north towards O'Connell Street. (Not forgetting to wave as we passed the nice man in the off licence window, rebuilding his tower of Fosters cans. He returned a gesture, but I don't think it was a wave!)

Sully, chief beer distributor, then began doshing out the tinnies. For those that were out of arm's length, he and one of the twins – it could have been A or B for all I knew – developed a system whereby Sully would roll a can forward, down the centre aisle. The twin would stop it with his foot, then either pass it to a person on his side of the Duck, or hand it across the aisle to Coco, who in turn would distribute it on his side of the vehicle. It must be said that more than a few cans resulted in a little spuff of foam ejecting onto the opener's lap after its journey down the aisle, but stinking of beer was only a secondary concern to drinking it, so I guess a few of us got a little damp and smelly. Just when things were starting to go swimmingly, disaster struck.

Sully, having consumed the contents of his hip flask, had become ever keener with his rolling of cans, some of them not even touching the floor more than a couple of inches away from the twins' feet. This caused much amusement to all at Sully's end of the Duck, as the foam explosions from the ring pull of the shaken cans grew ever larger.

Can by can the rolls became faster, developing into throws, before eventually ending in full-on baseball type pitches down the length of the vehicle.

A, or was it B?...whatever... managed to let one by. It ricocheted off some poor unsuspecting punter's swede, then disappeared down into the foot well.

After a swift round of applause from the alcoholics, it was quickly forgotten, until the beer ran out, that is…

There I was, down on all fours in the middle of the aisle twisted and contorted, with my head wedged firmly between the damp floor and the steel frame of the seat that was preventing me reaching the last tinnie on the Duck.

It never ceases to amaze me the lengths people (myself included) go to after a wee taster, to further the rush of ring pull induced nirvana. Tell me honestly – how many 35-year-old men would be fishing around in a rusty old shit heap, sodden with the dregs of the Liffey swilling around on the floor (they obviously aren't as waterproof as they were during the war), trying desperately to reach that last inch with outstretched fingers, unless the Holy Grail I was so close to reaching contained a wee snippet of alcohol?

I had managed to get two fingers to it, and was rotating it around to face me so as I could then coax it into rolling back in my direction. We were stopped at a set of lights and I could hear the antiquated tick plunk tick plunk of the overworked indicator relay telling me we were about to turn. This, of course, could work superbly in my favour. If we turned left, the lurching of the Duck on its antiquated shock absorbers would roll the can directly into the palm of my hand. If, however, we turned right, the can would wedge itself further under the seat it was hiding below. The revs rose, the gears scrunched repeatedly under protest of the Viking's efforts to select first. It sounded like three ducks fighting in a coal sack. (Ahhh! Maybe that's how they got their name.)

'Ya fookin' moother fooocker, get tha foook in, wills ya!'

Eventually after a whurr, a klunk, and a thump (accompanied by a few more 'fooocks') and a 'bejazus' we were off again. The Duck lurched to the left, and as if by magic, the can began rolling my way. Closer, closer...I had it! I started to shuffle backwards, a smile on my face, arse pointing straight up, and my back arched like the big dipper, when suddenly, BANG! Twenty stone of Sully impacted me from above. He grappled with me for the can, but it popped from my hand like a well-greased ferret, sending it skating down the aisle as it disappeared again under the row of seats. There followed a chink, chink ping! noise of a pinball table as it danced its way towards the front of the Duck. I thumped Sully on the cheek with my elbow – he didn't retaliate. He knew he'd been a twat. After holding each other's stare for an uncomfortably long time, he retreated.

I peered beneath the seats again, and saw the glistening gold top of the rogue Stella can balanced precariously on a ledge, just behind the driver.

Simultaneously three things happened.

Firstly, the neck-mounted microphone the Viking tour guide was wearing crackled back into life. Secondly, the whole vehicle took a change in attitude as we crested a steep hill, and then tipped steeply downwards.

'This, ladies and gentlemen, is Broom Hill, and directly in front of us, youse can see the elaborately decorated former private residence of the governor and his good lady, which dates back to 1832.'

I'm sure you've guessed the third thing to happen by now. The beer can fell forward out of view. Slow motion then seemed to invade my space like the claustrophobia of being in a closed coffin. The loud speakers rattled and vibrated in protest at the screams of the petrified driver.

'Jaeeeezus fooockin' Christ, ay caaan't, caaan't, fooockin' staaaaap...Holy Mooother of Maary...' SPUFFF!!!!!!!!

The beer can finally exploded under the repeated pressure of the brake pedal being forced upon it. White foam erupted from the floor, covering both the Viking and the windscreen with white beer froth.

An eerie silence filled the air; people were screaming, shouting and waving their arms hysterically, but I couldn't hear them, nor the screech of brakes, or smell of fear from uncontrolled bladders. Bags and children flew through the air as the Duck lunged onto its side after clipping a kerb. We slid along for what seemed an eternity. I guessed this must be what a plane crash is like, slowly waiting in calm surreal oblivion of the impending fate that is on fast forward to greet you at any second.

I don't remember the impact.

I came round on the floor, wedged below the dashboard. The crash had sent me hurtling the length of the duck, and I had obviously blacked out for a time.

The vehicle had righted itself (or rolled all the way over, I had no way of knowing) and was now back on its (flat) tyres.

The first thing my beer-addled brain registered was Glynn repeatedly saying, 'Come on, come on,' whilst dragging me out by my shoulders, 'we have to get scarce before old Santa over there wakes up.' I looked up at what was previously our Viking tour guide, who now resembled every child's winter dream. He must have hit his head during the impact because the blood from it had dripped down onto his tunic and dyed his belly red. This, coupled with the white beer foam splashes over his beard, and now exposed bald scalp, due to his horned hat being jettisoned into the old governor's living room, along with a 16-ton World War Two amphibious vehicle, had completed the transformation.

We ran as if the Devil himself were chasing us. Whilst running, I felt a pang of guilt. My feeble mind slowly registered the enormity of pain and destruction we had caused, all for a beer. None of us looked back, but eventually slowed to a brisk walk, followed by a slow walk as both our adrenalin and our energy petered out. We collapsed on the first stretch of grass we came to.

We all lay a while in silence, no doubt analysing and justifying what had just happened.

Gandhi was the first to speak.

'Why don't we all take five and hide out in that cinema over there?' He pointed across the square at one of those new 400-screen multiplexes, with everything from laser dominoes to self-will writing machines on site. We strolled in like a gang of horse rustlers in a western town; bold as brass bull's bollocks, but feeling somewhat unwelcome.

We all opted for a Robert De Niro and Billy Crystal gangster psychiatrist movie, but with half an hour to kill before the movie we all grabbed a pint in the sports bar conveniently located about ten feet from the foyer.

It didn't take long, however, for it all to kick off again. Patrick appeared with a bucket of popcorn, salted.

He slotted himself next to Beaker in one of the booths. Beaker took a large handful of said popcorn, and crammed it in his mouth. This was almost immediately followed by an explosion, as the contents of Beaker's mouth was then showered with great velocity amongst all of us.

Salted...salted you wanker. I said sweet,' barked Beaker with his index finger rammed in his mouth trying to eject the last remaining bits from between his teeth. Ed, Coco and Gimp were all sitting opposite, and began picking the remains of the popcorn from each other's hair. (And here we see the rare, lesser-washed beer monkey in its natural habitat, feasting from crumbs plucked from his mate's matted hair...) The table looked like a chimp's tea party, and we'd only been there five minutes. Food was ordered then eaten, and after a couple of hours' escapism we all emerged from the cinema fully recharged.

This was our last night, so we were going BIG. We started off at an amusement arcade. Then, after the usual rounds of Grand Tourismo, shoot the baddie and that helicopter game in the gyroscope that's guaranteed to make you spaff your chips, we all headed out in search of eye, nose and throat candy (girls, coke and beer!)

We started at O'Flannagans. This time queuing like a coach party outside the only lock-up toilet for each of our turns on the angel dust. I was fifth in line, and passed Sully on his way out, wearing a demented grin and frantically rubbing his gums. I could certainly feel 'a bit of a night' coming on. My turn came. In I went, locking the door behind me. Coco was there, Stanley knife blade in hand doing his best impersonation of Jamie Oliver as he sliced and diced my entree on the porcelain lid of the cistern. He was hopping from foot to foot in a nervous, agitated way.

'Come on, hurry up, I've got loads more to do, and you're up to a hundred quid's worth now.' I glared at him with that 'a discussion for later' type of look. A sniff, a snort and a rub later, I was on my way. I cracked open the door to see Beanie's beaming gob looking straight at me. I breezed past him and whispered, 'Hope you enjoy the ride!' With an inane smile on my face I rolled back into the main room and collected my pint with tequila chaser from the bar. The shot burned as I necked it. This, coupled with the still nauseatingly ammonia-smelling aftertaste from Coco's crap, cut with Ajax, coke, sent me into a frenzy to throw my pint down my neck in record speed. Half an hour later I suddenly felt a twang.

The combination of a (foookin' long) line of coke, followed by a swift succession of alcoholic beverages (and no doubt a lack of sleep) suddenly sent my head spinning into an echoey dream world. My ears popped, and I had a problem standing. I reached out for the bar, but missed it, which left me staggering forward like a drunken fool.

I came to an abrupt halt when my right hip made contact with the solid oak pillar that marked the end of the bar, and I clung onto it for fear of falling to the ground, as my legs seemed to have joined my head in a distracted state of apathy. A dampness then made itself apparent as I noticed I was now wearing half the contents of my fourth pint.

I began breathing heavily, the blood thumped its way through my head as if it were the consistency of syrup. Beaker then stuffed his face in mine, and with a grin to shame a Cheshire cat's, sings, 'EEEEs are good, EEEEs are good, Ebeneeezer good!' His eyes were millimetres from mine, and his head skewed at an angle.

'You bastard!' was all I could muster. I closed my eyes and waited for the hit to mellow. The spinning in my head slowed, and after a few moments at the bar on my own I started to surf again.

The 'E' that had been slipped into every one of the first round of beers was planned perfectly. Nobody even tasted it after their tequila shots, and coke snorting had annihilated any hope of taste recognition. Beaker sat back on a bar stool and smiled at a job well done. For good measure, he had actually done three Es and two lines of coke himself, so there will be far more on his behavioural disorder tonight later on in this chapter!

The gaff we were in was a bit of a spit 'n' sawdust type, with the girls appearing to hail from the Dublin equivalent of Essex: all white stilettos and leopard skin Lycra, with screechy voices and boyfriends called Darren.

Once we had all sussed the gag, and were surfing about 3 inches away from the ceiling, we collectively grouped, and decided to do the off in favour of a beer cellar with a little more prime time totty to leer at...

Before we knew it, we were out on O'Connell Street in the heaving mass that is Dublin on a Saturday night. We managed to stay together long enough to sneak into the next watering hole.

As luck would have it, we managed to find the top bar of choice from the first night – you remember, the one with the rope decking and wall-to-wall uni grads.

We headed to the bar. Sully barked at the 4 stone barmaid, with jet-black arse-length hair. 'Fifteen pints of Stella please, luv.'

She immediately stopped pouring the pint of Ruddles for the innocent lad next to us, and with a look of absolute terror at the vastness of Sully, timidly got on with our order. Sully had downed a pint in the time it had taken the bar girl to pull the other 14, and we all stood in our collective groups waiting for the evening to progress.

Ed, Coco and Gimp all retreated to the gents' for a swift pick-me-up; the twins stood together, looking...twin-like, and were talking with Beanie and Gandhi about the physics of riding a mountain bike off a garage roof. Ron was ear-wigging the

53

banter, but not (unusually for him) partaking. The conversation, from a by-stander's point of view, began to take great shape. Suddenly, you had all variable angles covered. Beanie, the mathematician, trying to understand the physics in doing such a thing; the twins, both Grand Prix mechanics, were used to people doing daft things, but still questioning the sanity of it; and Gandhi, who would probably do it, because at 33 he still could – albeit with a bad back the following week!

Ron then jumps in (I didn't think it would take long), 'Well, what the fuck do you think the flat roof was invented for then, if it wasn't for jumping off.'

'That's not the angle I was coming from, actually,' retorted Beanie.

'Straight down is the angle you would be coming from,' Ron returned with a wry smile.

'If you are going to replace the sciences with the worst case of a Darwinian reversal of logic, then you really do have the intellect of pond life!'

'Nuther beer anyone?'

The 'E's were winding their evil way through our bodies. Coco scurried amongst us offering a top-up for only a fiver. I decided to go with it.

Another pill down, and I waited for the kick. It came, however, from behind, by way of an Oakley-wearing meathead who had been summoned by the serving Doris whom Sully had conveniently forgot to pay for the 15 pints in the first order.

The impact took me completely unaware, felling me instantly. I noticed Sully and Ron had been given the same treatment simultaneously. Looking up from the floor I was amazed to see Sully was still on his feet and holding two pint glasses, albeit with half their contents now sloshing around on the floor.

The bouncers were obviously not too bright. Any 23 stone lunkhead that orders 15 pints of Stella for an opener is hardly going to be easy to evict now, is he? Let alone with his 12 buddies. No sooner had the bouncers cast their first kicks, it all went off!

Ron grabbed an iron-legged barstool, and whilst swinging it around his head, narrowly missed the Doris Beaker had been chatting up. It then connected with bouncer number one's forehead, sending him stumbling backward, blood spurting as he collapsed over the table behind us.

Sully had bouncer number two, and started to crush his head between his gammon joint sized hands. The bloke called out for mercy, so Sully released his grip, only to grab the back of the bouncer's collar and straining leather belt.

He lifted him up, above the height of his own head. Then, holding him there a moment, grinning dementedly as if he was a modern day urban gladiator waiting for approval from the crowd, he slammed the bouncer's face at full speed into the top of a table.

Messy. The bouncer's head violently snapped back with a loud cracking noise that could be heard clearly above the thumping of the in-bar sound system. Blood erupted from either side of his nose, and he fell like a rag doll to the floor. Slowly a pool of crimson liquid made its way from under his body to soak the surrounding unvarnished floorboards.

The third bouncer just stood there; all the colour appeared to have drained from his face, as if in sympathy with his two buddies who were also draining, quite literally, of colour, lying face-down and motionless in front of him.

He went down on one knee and felt Mr Face Plant's neck for a pulse. Ed gave the nod, and we all cleared off, sharpish. We marched at a brisk pace, but never quite broke into a run, the last thing we needed was to attract any unwanted attention. Every police car that passed caused clenched fists and quickened heart rates. Thankfully after only ten minutes we spotted a nightclub doing early doors, so we headed towards it.

The door thug to the left offered, 'Got tickets 'ave you ladz?'

'No, but you'd better fu–'

Glynn swiftly slapped his hand over Beaker's face before he could utter another word, and interjected, 'No, but we was wonderin' if maybe a sixteenth of blow and a large smile might distract you for long enough to allow us to just slip by?'

'Guess it might if it were to be followed up by a couple of beers,' was the reply. A nod, a wink, and a shake of hands later we were descending the steps to the bass-pumping murk.

From the unassuming entrance – a single door between two quite forgettable shops – you would never have imagined a place such as this lurked below. It was entirely decked out (excuse the pun, I couldn't resist) like an old galleon. Absolutely massive it was, with all old oak wooden sides drawn up in a curve, to truly resemble the shape of the vessel it mimicked. The whole place was on three split levels. The central, main deck had dummy apertures for gun stations. Some of which even had reconditioned cannons strapped to them. Next to these were bench seats and tables running some 15 foot at a time in length, all with several flickering lanterns on.

Fixed to the back wall of these were portholes, each showing a different, yet typical scene. Some of the Battle of Waterloo, some of a treasure island, and others depicting anything from the high seas to a neighbouring pirate ship trying to invade, spewing grappling hooks 'n' all!

Above this, to our left and right respectfully, were the bow and stern of the ship. The former being a stage to allow live bands, DJs and the like to be centre of attention without being too overpowering. The latter, being where one would expect to be the map room and captain's quarters, was in fact both a bar and a flame-grilled burger servery. Perfect!

We stampeded towards the food like a herd of malnourished buffalo, screeched to a halt, and all babbled simultaneously,

'Double chilli burger with extra chilli and a portion of fries,' to the geek behind the counter.

Fifteen burgers later (don't forget Sully is on a three-for-one diet in whatever he consumes. He's trying to get up to 40 st before Christmas…) and we were ready for a top session.

A few beers in and we were all completely off our trolleys. The combination of a couple of 'E's, a few lines of fast forward, and about eight pints since teatime certainly had us rolling on the high seas. I stood, leant against the wooden balustrade that overlooked the centre of the club from just in front of the bar, and took a moment to just observe. Here's the lowdown:

Patrick and Beaker had gone on another munter hunt, and seemed to have harpooned some wildlife at the bar. Sully was moaning because there wasn't a darts board. Ed, Gimp, Coco and Beanie were all sprawled across a table in the mid-ship, engrossed in a fevered conversation. The twins had both gone to deliver the bouncers their beer, which left Ron, Gandhi and Glynn to head downstairs and check out the talent down below. Mellow moment over, I followed the back of Ron's thinning head.

We threaded our way down the spiral staircase to the lower decks, and found another bar. In earlier times, this area would have been reserved for black slaves pumping oars, or in later history, white steerage pumping whores. We seemed to blend right in and feel quite at home. Looking above, we could see, through the steel grates set into the ceiling, the party going on above us; but unlike our ancestors we were taking the opportunity to look up young girls' skirts as opposed to the short supply of sunshine that would have previously hailed from such an aperture. We all scored some more Stella, and set about a munter hunt of our own!

Ron and Gandhi were chatting to a quite stunning young thing, with hair in a chestnut-coloured bob, and a fair pair of chestnuts on display through her nicely tight plain white

T-shirt. I chewed the fat with Glynn for some time then made a move of my own.

Blonde, late twenties, wearing a perfect figure, pierced navel and just a hint of a tattoo on her left shoulder.

Perfect target practice! I ran over a few openers in my mind, but none seemed appropriate. I stood, desperately trying to come up with the all important line that would have led to a flowing and fulfilling conversation, that in turn would lead me to a flowing and fulfilling night of wild and passionate naked jelly wrestling, but it didn't come.

I stumbled towards her, tenth pint in hand, frowning hard with undivided concentration in an effort not to fall over before actually reaching her. I was closing in, 20 ft to go; I took my left hand out of my pocket, pulled my T-shirt out, then let it ping back to rest on my chest in an effort to make it a little baggier, disguising my ever-growing beer gut.

Fifteen feet to go; I removed my sweaty left hand from my pocket again, and after cupping it and blowing into it to check my breath, I wiped my nose with the back of it, checking it for evidence of blood or coke powder; all clear.

Ten feet to go; I removed my hand from my pocket yet again, and wiped my nose again…just checking; whoever said coke makes you paranoid?

Five feet to go; should I check my nose agai…

She turns towards me and says, 'Hiii-iiiyyy, I was wondering when you were going to come and talk to us; we've been watching you guys all night, and you certainly seem to be enjoying yourselves. My name's Kerry and this is Lilly, Amy and Sue.'

I was stunned. Lost for words. This doesn't usually happen, does it?

'What are you here for, a stag night?'

'Yes, as a matter of fact we are, been here a couple of days so we're well into the groove.'

'I can see that, you naughty boy!' Kerry smiled as she put a finger to the side of my nose, and then wiped it across my cheek. She held it up to the light, inspecting the remnants of white powder it had collected, before making an overexaggerated play of licking it off her long and sensual digit.

'Yummy!' She then smiled, winked, and took me by the hand. We weaved our way through the masses; she drew me nearer and asked, 'Who's your chemist then?'

'Coco the Clown...don't ask, it's just a nickname. That's him over there, let me sort something.' I nodded towards the dwarf who was occupying a corner, eyes closed, back hunched, ponytail swaying. He was dancing like a Red Indian, thousand yard stare and rhythmic hopping from one foot to another as he swayed his head completely out of time with the music... not a good advert for drugs.

'I need a couple of lines, mate.'

'Eeeeee wants sssome druuuuugggs, mate, eeeee wants sssome druuuuugggs, cost ya aaa miiiiint mate, coooost ya aaa ayyyyy miiiinnnnttt.'

'Fuck off, Coco, or I'll twat you.'

He sobered up.

'Okay, here ya go, call it 150 running total.'

'ONE FUCKIN FIFTY, YOU CHARLETAN! WITH DOUBLE FUCKIN' LOADED FLINTLOCKS, YOU BASTARD'

'Eeeeeeh, a boyyyyz got to get byyyyy,' he answered in his best Hatton Garden accent.

'Got to pick a pocket or two ta fuckin' pay for it then,' I retorted.

'Here we are, maaaa boy,' he said as he passed me some ready-cut in tin foil. I took Kerry's hand again and we headed off towards the gents'.

We entered the room, and following a few cheers and sniggers we scored a cubicle. Once inside, no time wasted. She grabbed her T-shirt with arms crossed over her chest and pulled it inside out over her head, forcing her pert breasts into my waiting mouth. I curled my arms around her waist and began to suck her nipples. My hands found themselves lower, over her hips, and down to her tight little bum; she pushed herself forward in a thrusting motion. I moved down from her chest and wound my tongue around the twin-ended stud that was pierced through her belly button.

I reached into my pocket and produced the folded tin foil. She rubbed her crotch up and down my thighs with hypnotic regularity as I slowly unwrapped the package, her breasts just millimetres from my face, teasing. She drew both hands up each side of my head, and ran her fingers through my short-cropped hair whilst letting out a muted whimper. I unfolded the packet fully and carefully formed it into a channel.

Her hands moved down from my head, over my shoulders as she leant backward, wrapping her legs around me as I leant forward and filled her belly button with angel dust. I closed one nostril with my finger and drank in the rush. I finished by licking the remains of the powder from her belly, making quite a meal of it, I must admit! She giggled with that schoolgirl kind of titter, before taking control and sitting back upright. Kerry leant forward and put her tongue on my lips, forcing it in my mouth, and explored like Captain Cook in a Tahiti brothel. Her lips and hips moved slowly but purposefully to release some early dampness from my overinflated ego, She moved further down, all the way in fact, until she reached my belt, which she unbuckled with her teeth. Boxers lowered to just below the buttocks and we were ready for take-off. She took the foil wrap and unravelled it again, then took my erect penis in her hand and put her mouth over it. Down the shaft until she gagged, then swiftly back up again; I was lubed and ready for action.

She then sprinkled the coke liberally on my knob, and set to work, paying particular attention to the crest of the helmet by licking furiously. The tingling sensation it gave was like the old space dust you used to eat as a kid, so God only knows what Coco had cut it with this time! Before I had a chance to comment though, she placed her pouting lips over it and glided all the way to the basement.

She sucked hard as her tongue did the polka in the mid section, followed by a lip withdrawal, only to repeat the exercise several times over.

On about the tenth sinking, I started to get the most awful head spins. The rising and falling of her barnet in my lap continued for a time, but the ecstasy downstairs was rapidly being rivalled by the ecstasy upstairs. As the juices were on the move from the testicles to the little head, so too were the juices from the intestinals to the big head. I clenched my teeth and swallowed hard, forcing the sickly taste of rising bile back to where it had come. Closing my eyes, I felt a quiver run down my spine, as I unloaded in her mouth. She was also swallowing hard, but thankfully she didn't join me in clenching her teeth!

She took her time to lick me clean, and with a job well done, kissed the top of my helmet, swiftly followed by a peck on my lips.

Before I knew it she was gone. I sat, with legs spread and my trousers around one ankle, on a closed bog seat with the open door slowly starting to close. I guess I had just learned a new meaning for the term coke head!

I made my way as best I could back to the bar, swaying and bumping as I went. Sully, Ed, Gimp, and Beanie were all downstairs; Glynn and Beaker had managed to find Laura and Death-bird, and were at the upstairs bar with Ron and Gandhi. The twins were stood in the corner but I couldn't see Patrick or Coco.

As I made my way over to Ed's congregation, I noticed another bloke standing with Death-bird. He was tall, maybe

6 ft 6, long shoulder-length ginger hair in loose ringlets and facially quite similar to the lead singer of that seventies band Wizard. He was heavily built, and wore a multi-coloured horizontally striped knee-length cardigan, all yellows, blacks and greens. Definitely a herbivore.

'Wassssuuuuupppp,' Sully shouted.

'Wassssuuuuupppp,' I returned. We then indulged in a little male slapping and punching. I opted for the dodging tactic as opposed to the attack. I'd found out the hard way, on more than one occasion, that he doesn't feel pain. Not my pathetic attempts at dishing it out to him anyway. Still, despite my best efforts, he managed to cuff me on the jaw and send me floundering to the deck.

When I looked up, he was stood, cartoon like, ankles together with his hands up to his mouth, tips of his fingers over his lips and eyes so wide that they were rounded into perfect circles. He resembled a school kid caught with his first fag.

Sully offered his hand to help me up. I took it, and then tried to pull him down to the floor with a swift yank. How stupid of me, at 10 st heavier, the laws of physics did their bit and I just found myself rising faster. A pat on the back, a pint on the bar and it was all forgotten about.

The evening rolled on and I started to feel somewhat drained. The swaying masses of the crammed club did little to help my onslaught of head spin and nausea. I'd totally overdone it, and clung to the bar in a vain effort to disguise the fact that I was completely bombed.

Having decided to go outside for a breath of fresh stuff, I trod my way up the wooden stairs, stopping momentarily to take a last look back at the superb club that had served as our refuge for the preceding few hours, only to see Ron shinning up the central mast in hope of reaching the crows' nest some 15 foot higher. I then left by the now closed front door.

Once out on the street, I could see my misty breath in front of me as Jack Frost made himself known with a chill down my spine that remained in my chest till I shook it out. Then, with chattering teeth and a shivering body, I set about a walk around the block to clear my head.

'Oi, part timer, where do you think you're off to?' I saw the cherry of a lit cigarette from the shadows between two wheelie bins. A figure stepped forward into the light.

'Christ, you made me jump!'

'You shouldn't be sloping off early then, should you?' replied Ed, zipping up his flies as he walked towards me. Kerry's friend Amy then followed him out from the shadows.

'You and your friends seem popular tonight,' I said, but Amy just smiled and scuttled back into the club. 'I'm just taking a quick breather, once round the block and I'll be back in.'

'I think I'll join you then, but first, best sneak a little perky, hadn't we?'

Ed produced one of Coco's tin foil pouches, and just buried his nose into it, snorting hard. He then stuffed it under mine in a 'don't argue' kind of way, so I obliged with a swift intake. We headed towards the end of the street, and before long, the top-up of coke and the fresh air had worked wonders. We walked (remarkably) in silence, but my brain raced at 300 miles per hour. We bumped into each other several times, as our balance was certainly not up to par, and eventually Ed connected head-on with a lamp post. The metallic dong rung out as he staggered back several paces then landed flat on his arse in the gutter.

He sat up almost immediately, rubbing his forehead as I awkwardly stumbled my way down to his level.

'Bit of a fookin' twang, that!' I said in my best Jordie piss-take accent. He just rubbed his head and grinned with the pain of it.

'Fuck it, better have another perk up.' He slipped the silver foil out again, but this time I declined. We sat in comfortable silence, as only old friends could.

'You must love her, Ed, if you're marrying her that is.'

'Of course I do, you wanker.'

'You know what I mean, *really* love her, till death do you part an' all that.'

'Yeah, I suppose I do, it's for the kids as much as anything though, you know. Becky starts school this year, and it just makes it all a little easier.'

'Yeah, I suppose.'

'That Amy bird gives fuckin' good head though!'

We pissed ourselves laughing for what seemed like an eternity, then continued our silence, both staring into oblivion, wondering where our lives were taking us.

'It's snowing.'

'Bollocks it is,' I replied, 'you've not done any acid have you?' As the words left my lips, the first flakes of snow landed on my cheeks. Ed just smiled as the flurry of white poured down gently on our shoulders.

'Well fuck me, you're right.'

'Best we shake a leg, don't want to catch pneumonia before the big day.'

We rose slowly to our feet and set off for the club. Threading our way back though, it became increasingly obvious that the fallen snow had completely camouflaged our return route, to the point that we had become completely lost.

'We turned left here, didn't we?' I questioned.

'No, bollocks, we came from over there.'

'Fuck it, I'm going this way.'

We made our way through downtown Dublin without a clue or a care. Whilst entering a brightly lit area, all posh shops and coffee bars, we happened upon a Dutch style pancake and waffle van.

'One large waffle with double chilli sauce,' I asked.

'This is a waffle and pancake sweet delicacy stall, sir, we do not have chilli sauce; maybe you have mistaken us for a less reputable vendor of ill-cooked meats, cloaked in a pungent spicy sauce, to hide its incompatibility with the human digestive system, served on a stale pitta bread with brown decaying lettuce. What we offer will marvel the taste buds and truly put the once forgotten spring back into your step, sir! Available with squirty cream, or for just one euro more, real dairy ice cream in a choice of three flavours: strawberry, chocolate, and, fresh as a spring daffodil, vanilla!'

'Fuckin'ell, I'll have two large waffles wiv squirty stuff and a double pancake wiv chocolate sauce and all three flavours of ice cream,' came the surprising but familiar voice of Sully, who had unbeknown to us fallen in behind.

'Hello mate,' Ed and I replied in astonished unison.

Sully grinned back inanely, swaying in a circular motion with his plastic Viking hat slewed at a 45° angle on his head.

'Where'dya find that, I thought we'd lost them all hours ago?' Ed asked.

'I nicked it off the head of a Japanese tourist who foolishly asked me for directions. I've got another one here that his wife was wearing, if there's any takers?'

Sully produced another plastic Viking hat as if by magic, and then stuffed it squarely on my head.

'There you go, Hazy, you can look a twat too, albeit a slightly less fat twat than myself, but a twat all the same!'

'Thanks,' I said, 'any idea where we are, and although truthful, Dublin is not the answer I'm after.'

Sully scratched his chin and shrugged. We ate our waffles and moved on. The snow, having eased, began to decompose into slush on the popular thoroughfares.

The city had a magical charm about it once a fresh coat of white had illuminated the blackness of its grime. This, coupled with the myriad of narcotics and alcohol that were coursing through my veins, gave me a safe, warm buzzy feeling. I don't know if it was the cold making me numb or the drugs, but I hadn't been able to feel the outer skin on my arms, legs or face for a couple of hours, and couldn't fathom if that was a good or bad thing.

We wound our way back to the river and walked until we found a familiar bridge, recognising also a Parisian style cafe on the corner of the road we needed to take. Outside it on the pavement, but protected from the elements by a large maroon and cream striped canopy, was an array of tables and chairs; even though the bar had closed hours before there still remained two customers – a man and a woman.

After drawing closer, we noted that it was Glynn and Laura, the latter being sat on Glynn's lap, and whose tongue was gently roaming where only dentists dare to go. Glynn, slightly less delicately, had a couple of fingers sunk to the knuckle, where only gynaecologists dare to go!

'Oiiiiiyyyyy!!!!' announced Sully. Glynn tutted as they broke their embrace.

'Not a fucking moment's peace with you wankers around.'

'Nice to see you too, mate; what have you done with Beaker, or is he hiding up Laura's skirt too?'

'Piss off will you, he disappeared with Death-bird and a bloke called Bongo.'

'The ginger-haired twat at the bar you mean?'

'That's the one, now if that's all, can you bugger off and leave us alone.'

He sounded irritated and flustered. I guess the coke had worn off a bit. He then unplugged his fingers from Laura, to show us his middle one in an otherwise clenched fist as we left. We all returned the salute. Sully, ever the shy retiring type, followed it up by dropping his trousers and boxers to the floor, then relieved himself in the middle of the pavement towards the loving couple, whilst thrusting his hips back and forth. His Viking hat came loose and fell to the floor in front of him. He just kept on urinating on it without a care. Once finished, after a quick shake, he then placed it proudly back upon his head. Eyyyyuuuuggghhh!

The three of us then made our way back without further incident, managing to eventually get our heads down by half-three in the morning.

* * * * *

BANG BANG BANG!
'It's the Garda, open up!'
BANG BANG BANG!

'What the fuck do the police want,' grumbled Gandhi as he dragged himself to his feet and squinted through the crack as he opened the door a couple of inches. Two police officers were stood outside, and were most insistent on coming into the room. They both wore full uniform, and flicked the lights on as they entered. My watch had informed me it was 5.30 a.m. The slightly taller one with short-cropped black hair spoke loud and clear, as only a copper knows how, pronouncing every syllable with exaggerated emphasis.

'Would any of youse guys know of an attack that occurred last night as a result of a mugging incident that was reported to us in the wee hours of this morning?'

A collective mumbled negative groan had come from those whose eyelids had surrendered to the bright lights.

'Right then, I thank youse for wasting valuable guards' time and we bids you good morning, gents.'

With that they left, making sure to slam the door as hard as possible behind them.

Eight o'clock. The door swung open and the usual 13 white bags skated their way across the floor. The door slammed again.

Ten o'clock. I counted the sound of 13 'pssssttt's.

'Here, drink this… Here, drink this... Here, drink this… The smell of Red Bull filled the air again and immediately shocked me into jaded memories of the previous night's fun.

I recalled when I first spoke to Kerry, my brief companion for the evening, all I could smell was the Red Bull on the breath of her and all her buddies. This made me smile as I lifted the sheet to see if my chap still smelt of it, but it was impossible to tell with the vast quantity of natural gas that I had emitted during my sleep. Gandhi eventually reached me, and with a 'Here, drink this' he thrust a can of Red Bull and four Nurofen into my waiting hands.

I guess we dozed for about half an hour after this, and eventually all came to. Tales of whit skill and bravado flowed like that of returning fighter pilots from hostile missions. Laughs, shrieks and groans were fed out ten to the dozen, when suddenly silence fell – quite literally – after a loud thud!

Beaker, who had been sleeping on the top bunk of my spiral, fell gracelessly to the floor.

Everyone just stared in shock. He rolled slowly onto his back, revealing his blood-soaked shirt and jeans. His face was black and blue with bruises and filthy dirty with what appeared to be soot.

He wore only one shoe and his clothes were randomly torn, some sodden with blood, others just simple tears. His face was pale, and he was not smiling. All of a sudden a barrage of questions as half the congregation gathered around to help him up into a sitting position: 'What happened?' 'Who did this to you?' 'Where were you?'

'Water, get me some fuckin' water,' came the reply. Ron then shot out of the room, to return a few moments later with a Red Bull can full of water. Beaker had taken a long drink as we all hung in anticipation. He coughed, rubbed his bloodshot eyes, and then cleared his throat by hacking up a phlegmy into the now empty can.

'Well, it all started like this…'

Chapter 4

Beaker's Tale

taking the joke just a little too far...

'I got this text message from Corrie, you know, Death-bird, at about nine, saying she wanted to meet me for drinks and a little après-beer quim quivering. I, of course, replied in the affirmative, and set about arranging a meet.

'She was indisposed for a time, but arranged to meet us at the galleon bar, where we had already dug in for the night. So far, so good, I had thought.

'I was stood at the bar, with Ron and Ghandi, who both were taking it in turns to get a mouthful of tongue off this short but sweet bird who looked a little bit Navajo to my eye – you know, all straight black hair and tasselled boots, slightly slanted eyes, and dark skin. Shows what I know; she came from Croydon as it happened.

'Corrie turned up about ten o'clock with this geezer in tow, hippy type, but quite a laugh. Bongo was his name, and as I recall acquired it for his quite spectacular collection of bongs. We spent the evening getting more and more wrecked. There was plenty of extended eye contact going on with me and her, but nowt that would signify a grope; still the offer seemed to be there, but just not for nows.

'When the urge to empty my bladder arose, I nodded my head in the general direction of the bogs with raised eyebrows, but was only met with a frown and subtle shaking of the head by Corrie. I still pinched her arse as I pushed past her, only to be returned by a wandering hand of hers over my crotch as I made my escape.

'Whilst standing there, plonker in hand, splashing away, it suddenly dawned on my addled brain that as we were in a country so deeply set in their religious ways and so obsessed with public correctness, this poor lass didn't dare show off the fact she had been cavorting with the opposite sex to this ginger-haired hippy that must have been her brother! There was no other explanation for her sudden withdrawal of public affection that I could fathom, so I drew this to be the correct conclusion. A shake of the whistling weasel later and I was back on board.

'I sneaked up behind Corrie and with one hand on her arse cheek shouted in her ear above the row of The Prodigy's 'Firestarter', "Sussed it, don't worry, save it for later." She thrust her arse back at me, and shot me a wide grin over her shoulder.

'The hours rolled by. Ron and Gandhi had disappeared into the gents' for a love triangle with the Croydon Navajo and the only other members of the crew I could locate were Glynn, who had a faceful of Laura in the corner, and Coco, who was trying to pedal his wares on a couple of teenies.

"Time to move," I had thought. We left the club at about 2 a.m. and started walking. Fuckin' cold it was, so Bongo hailed a cab. The four of us piled in – sorry, I forgot, Bongo had a mate called Simon, who had joined us in the club.

'Anyway, we all rolled up at this fuck-off type of sky-scraper, all mirror glass and chrome, on the side of this marina I recognised from our Viking tour. We stumbled inside after

Bongo coughed for the cab and took the smooth-riding elevator to the 18th floor.

'Once inside Bongo's pad, I crashed on the vast leather sofa and marvelled at the view before me. The whole outside wall was glass, divided only by a single vertical strengthening bar from top to bottom midway between one wall and the next. The view over Dublin was spectacular.

"Built by dat Bono of U2, you know," said Bongo, as he re-entered the room from the kitchen, wine bottle in hand.

"Yes I know, the Viking tour guide told us."

"Fuuuuuck, didjyas hear about all that theres in the news tonight then?"

"No," I replied.

"Some English fookin' eejits hi-jacked one of those amphibious Viking tour things and ploughed it straight into the governor's front drawing room as a mark of total disrespect for our independence."

"Err... It wasn't actually like that..."

"What... you was there... you was involved like?"

"No, no, no, I...I... I only overheard some people discussing it in the bar."

"Oh, 'cos if youse was a party to that kind of disrespect in my house, you'd be leavin' byse that there window, my friend."

'I then checked out the pattern of the carpet under my shuffling feet, and changed the subject. Bongo, true to form, sparked up one of his bongs, and then sat with Simon on an adjoining sofa.

'Corrie was sat next to me, but with no physical contact present seemed almost out of reach, even though there was barely an inch between us.

'The hours passed, and we all got a tad stoned. Corrie had begun to show me what may be construed as a little affection, as she lolled onto my shoulder, but I was ever aware of her brother's beady eye. I passed it off with a shrug and propped her up again, only for her to loll back to the same state of semi-uprightness moments later, to match her state of semi-consciousness.

'I think I passed out for a time, 'cos the next thing I remember was being alone in the room with Corrie. We were both sat back on the sofa, muntered.

'Once awake, and after a quick beak, I decided we were indeed alone. The old chap downstairs had drawn to attention, and I found myself having a good old go on her tits. Her head turned up towards mine and we started to kiss, not subtle like, but full on hammer and tongues. My attention was then drawn a little lower as I then set to work between her thrusting hips, my fingers all in a flurry. The light then suddenly came on, and I was caught, literally, with her pants down.

"Get thes fuck into yourse room, you fuckin slut, bejasus, before I fookin' kills ya!" Bongo shouted as he stormed across the room. He had a wine bottle in his hand, held, business-like, by the neck.

"I'll foookin' teach yas t' try an foook maaay foookin' girlfriend, ya foookiiin cooonnnt.'

'He swung at me, but I ducked and he lost his grip. The plate glass window cracked as it made friends with an unopened Pinot Grigiot, 1984.

'We then wrestled on the floor, until such time when the chemicals and alcohol in my body gave up the fight for life and I resigned myself to a right good kicking. Just call me Mr Punchbag. I was beaten head to toe before old Ginge-mop decided to pick me up, swing me around his head to gain momentum, and then lob me straight at the plate glass window.

'As I flew through the air, my short but eventful life flashed before me (in a disappointingly brief amount of time), followed by the panoramic view of Dublin.

'I closed my eyes, and then registered a loud smashing sound as I passed out. I presumed this was a self-defence mechanism to prevent me seeing the ground rushing towards me for the remaining 17 storeys, but being wrong, as usual, the smashing noise was in fact my nose as it impacted with the separating bar between the windows, which rendered me momentarily unconscious.

'I must have been out for a while, as I came to on the floor of the lift with Corrie half on top of me, covered in blood; she was either unconscious or dead, I didn't hang around to find out which.

'I stumbled along a couple of roads until I found myself back at Trinity College, where some fucking cunt of a mugger then has the audacity to stab me as I was no longer in possession of my wallet that had been either pick-pocketed or lost at some point during the evening's proceedings.

'I then trudged my way back through the snow-lined streets to our hostel, only to find, upon arrival, that the door was well and truly locked.

'After what seemed like an eternity of hammering and shouting, one of the student types that ran the place peered through the plate glass window adjoining the door, and yelled, "Piss off, you old tramp, we don't need your sort in here."

"No...no, I'm a resident." I pleaded.

"Yeah, right, now get lost before I call the Garda."

'I caught my reflection in the window, and instantly understood where she was coming from. My hair, what's left of it, was matted to the side of my head with blood, my clothes were ripped, blood-soaked and filthy. My face as you can see was not only swollen and bruised, but also blood-spattered and my hands looked as if they had not been washed for a week.

"Fuck this, I'm calling the guards," she said, as she disappeared back into her office.

'I slouched on the pavement and nodded off, despite the sub-zero temperatures, and the snow falling ever harder on my weary limbs. I was woken with a start some time later as two police officers lifted me from under the arm into the foyer of the hostel.

'Moments later, my booking was confirmed, and after a gush of apologies from the scrawny bird I find myself back in our room.

'Next thing I know, you bastards are waking me up – no peace eh!'

Chapter 5

Departure

taking the joke just a little too far...

Once showered, Beaker scrubbed up well. He looked as if he had only been run over by three cattle trucks, not ten. We had all donated a garment of clothing and a couple of quid to allow him to feel human again.

Following a swift bacon buttie from down the road, we collected our bags and set about killing a couple of hours until our plane left. We paraded around the shops a while, for that little something for that little somebody, decided our bags were too heavy to cart around, so Sully declared a farewell drink was in order.

We entered the bar, a quite glum and moody affair on the second floor of a rather old but important looking building. Dark-stained wood lined everything – bar, floor, walls, stairs – whole damn lot. In fact the only thing that wasn't wooden was the atmosphere.

The beer worked its usual magic, three pints in and we're off (yet) again. The time was 1 p.m. After a brief exchange of text messages, the Croydon Navajo that was entertaining Ron and Gandhi showed up, as did a rather pert little accomplice. She was introduced as Lucy. Ed and Lucy immediately hit it off, and were ensconced in full eye-to-eye flirting, some 3 inches from each other. Ron and Gandhi took turns to provide the Navajo with both a full mouth and a fondled breast, whilst the rest of us had set about draining the bar.

Beanie called time on the proceedings by announcing, 'Our plane won't wait, and is but two hours from take-off.'

Sully, ever the smart arse, then pointed out that this no doubt meant it was still sat on the tarmac at Heathrow. The group was dividing. The majority (just) opted for the return flight. The minority – being Beaker, Ron, Gandhi, Glynn, Ed, and Sully – decided to stay.

I must warn you, I am prone to laughter fits, and once one takes a hold, it is impossible to shake until nature takes its course. I stood, back to the stairs, hand in pocket, chatting away to Glynn. Beanie brushed past me in search of a signal for his mobile phone, then disappeared down said stairs and out the door. The flight of wooden steps levelled off at the street, where there was an open door to the left. It then continued down another half-flight in stone to where the toilets could be found.

I sensed Beaker approaching. He stumbled directly into my face, and with the style and grace of a sewer rat, belched at me with his alcohol rancid breath, then slurred, 'Don'tchu worrrrry, if you've gottchu get back, I'lllll look after Ed.'

He then missed the barstool he was attempting to lean on, and fell squarely onto his arse. I immediately lapsed into almost coma-inducing fits of hysteria, lost my balance, and fell backward down the stairs. The irony of Beaker trying to look after anything other than a cactus was just too much for me to handle.

I plunged down, rolling head over toe until I eventually reached the bottom. My laughter was such that my eyes were streaming, my bright crimson face contorted as my muscles spasmed like they were pulling 12 Gs. I was curled into a ball, clenching my chest and stomach. Even my legs had started to jitter. I was having trouble breathing as the convulsions of laughter came and went.

Before I knew it Beanie had me in the recovery position, piece of wood retrieved from the pavement between my teeth, and was calling 999 on his mobile phone to report an epilepsy-induced cardiac arrest.

Beaker rose to his feet, sniggering, then barrelled down the staircase to check I was okay. His size 13 feet obviously weren't designed for gallivanting down pokey little staircases, as he lost both balance and rhythm simultaneously.

He appeared to surf down half the staircase before performing a cartwheel as his leading foot caught grip, which catapulted him out the door and into the main road. This didn't pose any immediate problems, until that is, he rose to his feet and was run over by a taxi.

The cab screeched to a halt, and out popped a fat little Italian. He ran over to where Beaker was now rolling in the gutter and began shouting and screaming about the fresh dent in the front of his cab that was undeniably Beaker-shaped.

Beaker then dragged himself to his feet once again, and punched the Italian squarely on the nose, sending him flying backwards. The Italian reacted, after rising to his feet, with a barrage of fists and insults with various colourful references to Beaker's mother and sister. This certainly didn't help my plight, the Laurel and Hardy-esque scene unravelling before me had me in such fits of laughter, I honestly didn't know which one of us the paramedic was going to identify as the primary concern upon his arrival!

Beaker, working at swinging his punches as well as his return of insults, was unfortunately quite clearly losing. The sporadic bathing of blue lights filled the scene as both the Garda and an ambulance turned up in symphony. Sadly though, the ambulance crew sided with the Italian and the guards arrested Beaker.

At this point, our stay of evacuation ended. Beanie, like the Mad March Hare, herded us all towards the end of the road in his ever-flustered way, claiming that the next flight would cost not only hundreds of euros and our marriages, but also a healthy slice of our sanity.

We managed to hail a cab at our first attempt, amazing really considering the state of us, and blow me down with a steel wrecking ball if it wasn't our old pal Mr Idle from our outward trip.

'Joomp in laaadz, ya looks asif ye could do with a hand to the airport; don't tell me, youse only got ten minutes before yourse flights iz due to take off, I'd expect not'in less of youse scallywags, out at all hours with no regard for those thats are sleepin'. Baaaaastards, the lot of you, I'm only jealous of course, 'cos I'm too olds now, but I'll be tellin' ya, in my day...'

His voice droned on, and on, and on... Before we knew it we were stood at the check-in desk, glumly dumping our bags on the conveyor belt before they disappeared down the black hole. I wondered if I would ever see mine again. They were probably embarking on a trip to Antwerp for all I knew or cared.

A swift final round of Guinness was called for. We sat in the departure lounge, as an extremely sweaty Ron and Gandhi appeared, sans Navajo. They had thought better of staying on and had run the four miles to the airport with their bags on their backs.

Moments later we were sat on the plane. I was alone, in a window seat, listening through headphones to the in-flight entertainment. With a bit of tongue in cheek irony, the cabin steward selected the U2 album *All That You Can't Leave Behind* as our departure anthem. The engines roared, and as we made our dash for the sky, Dublin was history.

Roll on chapter six, old boy, there's plenty more joviality where this came from!

Chapter 6

Edinburgh

taking the joke just a little too far...

The Great North Eastern Railway. What a fine, long established, national company. A pillar in our society, a reflection of all that is good, proper, efficient and above all, British. Offering tradition, quality, and service beyond question.

What an absolute load of bollocks!

I sat at Euston fucking station for three fucking hours waiting for our fucking train to arrive. When it did, the dozy fucking booking agent had double fucking booked my fucking seat. Some dippy old fucking bat was sat in coach 7, aisle 12, seat D doing her fucking knitting.

I pointed out to her in the politest way possible that my ticket was emblazoned with the details pertaining to the fact that I had indeed booked coach 7, aisle 12, seat D for my lazy arse to sit in during our journey.

She had also booked coach 7, aisle 12, seat D, to rest her sorry arse in whilst 'journeying up country to see the grandchildren' as she put it.

Bollocks.

Some hours later, whilst feeling guilty for being so rude, I decided to get the old bat a glass of sherry.

After battling my way through the millions of kids playing 'it' in the aisles, whilst carefully trying not to wake the slumped businessmen, asleep with their Financial Times over their face, and legs sprawled as inconveniently as possible, I managed to make it to the buffet car.

Upon arrival, I then queued for what seemed like seven hours. I was then greeted by Pascal, who didn't speak a word of English, but had the smile of a politician on a toothpaste advert. I have never learnt the art of sign language, but Mister fucking Pascal the fucking waiter soon understood exactly what the fuck I wanted.

I returned to coach 7, aisle 12, seat D with four cans of Stella, a tube of Pringles and a nice little sherry. The old bat thanked me for my trouble, and then asked what time we were due to arrive in Daventry.

'Excuse me?' I questioned.

'Daventry,' she replied, 'what time do we arrive in Daventry? You really should get those ears of yours de-waxed if you can't hear what people are saying to you. It's quite rude, you know, to keep repeating yourself, and I would rather not have to do so, so please pay attention, young man, and answer the question.'

'The only fucking question I have is why the fuck you want to know when we are arriving at fucking Daventry, when you are sat on a fast fucking train to fucking Edinburgh.'

'Oh,' she replied, 'I thought it was taking a little longer than usual.'

'No fucking shit, so the coach 7, aisle 12, seat D that your decrepit fat arse is meant to be occupying is about 200 fucking miles south of here, not rapidly approaching the land of the sporran bag-piped fucking Haggis.'

'Err, no…sorry!'

'So, I've stood all the way to fucking Scotland because you are incapable of reading a fucking train ticket, am I right?'

'Err, yes dear, I suppose so.'

'Fucking marvel bloody fucking tastic. Where's my fucking beer.' I retreated to the back of the coach, fuming.

When we arrived at Edinburgh central, I spotted the missus easily, and my son Brads. They had flown up earlier in the week to catch a little R&R before the big weekend. My missus, Claire, was a couple of months gone, but you wouldn't really notice, midwinter, what with the clothes an' all. My lad was a bright little spark of a 3-year-old, with a football permanently at his feet and a grin cheesy enough to shame a game show host.

We hugged as we greeted each other, then grabbed a cab for the picturesque 100-mile cruise through the Trossachs National Park, around Loch Lomond and on to our final destination, the fabulous Loch Awe.

You've got to love Scotland, even the cabbies phone for directions! We arrived at Taychreggan Castle just as the sun was setting. I unloaded the bags and drew a deep, deep breath. It was certainly a bit Pearl Harbour. (Nip in the air...keep up at the back will you.) The gravel crunched underfoot as I stared in awe at the enormous looming towers above us, half expecting a fire-breathing dragon to come lolloping around the corner at any moment.

Once inside the 12 foot high solid oak doors, we were greeted by a long burgundy-carpeted entrance hall, illuminated through its entire length by the flicker of flaming torches fastened to the wall by rusting iron straps. This in turn led us to an open gallery, whose domed ceiling must have been 25 foot high. Ahead I spotted the solid 200-year-old mahogany check-in desk, no doubt used to sacrifice virgins on in the good old days, and behind it sat a bonnie wee Scots lass.

After a swift pint in the dimly lit gallery we were checked in. Why on earth in this day and age they can't just email the forms for our computers to auto-fill in and return is beyond me.

We were then greeted by some of the fellow wedding goers: Sully and Mrs Sully – Lucy to be precise. Ed and Tess, the bride-to-be, were also there greeting friends and family.

A dinner had been arranged in the Great Hall that evening as a kind of pre-wedding piss-up, as if we had needed any encouragement.

The castle itself held about 20 bedrooms, of which five were suites. The best pad was secured by Ed and Tess, of course, but another couple – Dosh and Pecks (you know them, I'm sure) – beat us to the number two. We settled for a nice little number overlooking the lake – sorry, Loch.

Me and Brads began our usual ritual of jumping on the bed until it either collapsed, or the neighbourly complaints became too much. Claire set about bathing and applying the evening's war paint. The babysitter arrived around half-seven, by which time I had well and truly laid in to the complimentary jug of Scotch that had been left for us on the coffee table.

* * * * *

The Great Hall left nothing to the imagination in its title. Like everything else in the castle, it had been well and truly built to impress. From the ornate arched ceilings to the hand chiselled granite statues, this place just reeked of history, an absolute American tourist's orgasm of detail and architecture.

The evening passed somewhat uneventfully, but generally a good time was had by all. That was, of course, until most of the women had gone to bed… Then things began to slip.

We had on board the entire Dublin crew, mostly with their wives, girlfriends, and other halves in general. There were also some old faces that had skipped the Dublin trip, most notable of all was Little Jack of Shepperton Studios fame.

After dinner we found ourselves sunk in the ever-sumptuous burgundy and gold-stitched sofas, nursing that one pint too many. Beaker stood and made for the bar, he misjudged the distance required to safely limbo past the coffee table and caught the sharply angled brass edge of it with his shin. A shriek of pain, followed by an explosion of expletives blasted their way into the room via the crimson-faced fool, who was now stooped, clutching his bloody shin up to his chest and standing, as a flamingo might, on one leg. This caused an imbalance in his small but perfectly pickled brain, resulting in a loss of both balance and grace. In turn (as your physics teacher would have told you, had you not been bunking off round the back of the bike sheds for a fag...) this leads every action to have an equal but opposite reaction.

The wounded Beaker replaced forward motion for backward, his upper body weight carried too much momentum so his un-injured leg was unable to keep pace with his torso. The wounded leg, shin to be precise, aided by the rearward motion of the entire body, now came across at an acute angle and hooked under the table in an effort to regain control. This caused the table to lift as Beaker crashed to the floor, and with his good leg now extended, flipped the coffee table upside down, showering the many pint glasses residing on it into the air, and over all of us.

'Fuck, fuck, fuuuuk!!! Fuckbollocksfuck,' was all Beaker could muster. He rolled around a while, then stood up and made a swift (well, as swiftly as you can with a limp!) exit.

I followed.

Eventually I caught up with him halfway down the dimly lit gravel driveway, quite some distance I might add.

'What the fuck's up with you?'

'Everyone thinks I'm a cunt, I can't even keep it together for one fucking night. Not only that, but I don't even have the money to replace the drinks I just threw on the floor. My old man paid for my room and the train fare on his card, 'cos I couldn't even afford that. Life's just shit and I don't need you following me around to tell me it.' With that, he tripped on a tree root, as we had stumbled somewhat off course, and slid face first down a mossy bank, collecting a mouthful of pine needles on the way.

'Cunting fucking thing!' he croaked as he made his way back up the short 3 foot high incline, spitting the needles out as he went, his size 13 leather-soled brogues finding little purchase on its moist surface. Once settled, he suggested a walk around the block to clear our heads. So we continued up the drive and eventually made our way out onto the road, although you would never have guessed it as there were no headlights for as far as the eye could see.

We walked together a while, eventually coming upon an old small holding that was slightly set back from the road. You could still make out the orange glow from the dying fire within. It was now that Beaker returned in earnest to his 'everybody hates me 'cos I'm a worthless piece of shit' routine, a Mr Hyde that appears once in a while. He set off firstly with the verbal self-abuse. This was all too swiftly followed by the physical side. He stood in the middle of the road, drunkenly swinging punches at his own face. After a few that vaguely hit the spot he became even angrier at his inability to punish himself. I, however, came to the rescue.

'Stop being a twat, will you, I don't need this shit, I've got a speech to knock out tomorrow and I could do without you fucking what's left of the night up.'

'Great, so you're blaming me for fucking up the speech that you haven't even written yet now, are you?'

'No, I just mean...' and with that he set about hitting himself again. If it wasn't so sad, it would be an extremely comical image. I became bored with waiting, so landed him a large square fist to his left cheek. His eyes seemed to momentarily bulge as he froze with shock; he then rotated backwards about his heels until his cranium was one with the tarmac.

He lay in stunned silence for a moment, before clambering to his feet and dusting himself down.

'Thanks for that; you know, I kind of lose it sometimes. I feel better now, let's just head back, I think I've had enough fresh air for one night.'

It was not until we were about halfway back that it sunk in just how far we had actually walked. Beaker was lagging, so I drew to a halt next to a chain-link fence. I closed my eyes momentarily and waited for him to catch up.

'Fuck I'm an unfit bastard,' he wheezed.

'Are you talking about your marriage or your cardio-vulgar?'

'Ha bloody ha.'

With that he stood next to me, and leant back on the fence. After a 'Yeeaaaccchhh!' a twang and a rumble of bushes, I opened my eyes and he had completely disappeared. The dozy twonk had back-flipped over the flimsy excuse of a fence and bounced down a 30 foot railway siding. I squinted through the darkness, but could not make out his form. As his feeble moans wafted their way up, I decided that if I wanted to see my bed before sunrise, my only course of action was to drag him, kicking and screaming, back to level firma.

I made my way downward into the murk below, guided only by the pathetic whimpers of a drunken fool.

When I eventually met Beaker, he was wearing half a gorse hedge, but thankfully otherwise undamaged.

After dragging both my own weary body and Beaker's up what seemed like a sheer rock face, we were greeted by a torch.

The owner of said illumination was none other than Mr PC McPlod, accompanied by another McPlod in the panda car checking for missing persons with railway siding fascinations on the national computer.

'What on earth are you two laddies up to at this time in tha mornin?'

'Eeeeeerrrrr…'

Chapter 7

Wedding Bells

taking the joke just a little too far...

'Wake up wake up wake up, Daddy, there's everything to do and it's been light for ages. Come on, Mum's not getting out of bed at all, she says it's your turn to take me to breakfast, so come on Daddy, pleeeeease.'

Through my squinting eyes I registered that I was on the floor, a bare wooden floor at that. I was still wearing my dinner jacket, although it more closely resembled a combat jacket due to the remnants of railway siding ground into it. I felt exhausted, but still had yet to make a start on my speech. A glance towards the window confirmed it was indeed light, not surprising really as it had almost been dawn by the time we had found our way back to the castle, and that my son is most certainly impatient.

Brads was fully clothed (bless him) in back-to-front jeans, an evening shirt and slippers on the wrong feet. I rose slowly and took him by the hand, insisting we had a quick shower before going down.

After only a half-hour wait for the dining room to open at 7 a.m., we both went for the 'Big Guns Breakfast', consisting of everything one might find on a farmyard – save for the goose (and the donkey, I hoped).

The room steadily filled with guests for the big occasion. I nodded and smiled at mostly people I didn't know. They all, however, seemed to know me.

'That's him,' they said under muttered breath, 'look at the state of him, why on earth Ed couldn't find anyone decent to be his best man is beyond me!'

But they didn't know me; they hadn't a clue what I had up my sleeve. I'd show them.

'Daaaaad, what's this?' Brads was balancing a leathery discus with little white fatty spots all over it on the end of his knife.

'It's black pudding, kind of like a sausage made of blood, try it.'

With that, he kept the knife perpendicular, and twisted his neck around, as only a child would, to sample the new-found delicacy.

'Yeuuugcch.' He spat it straight back out, onto the floor.

'Pick that up, you rude little boy,' I barked.

'No way!' the response. Realising this was the wrong path to take, I tried again.

'Do you see that waitress over there, the one with the red hair all down her back?'

'Yes Daddy.'

'Well, she told me earlier that after supper tonight, all the boys and girls that have been good are going to the video room to watch *101 Dalmatians*. Those who are naughty or messy just get taken straight to bed.'

He pondered this a moment, then said, 'I've seen *101 Dalmatians* though.'

'Maybe I misheard; it could have been *102 Dalmatians*.'

'Oh, okay then,' he said innocently. With that he ducked under the table and retrieved the sodden half-chewed fatty lump.

Then a portly, ruddy-faced man entered the room, wearing full shooting tweeds and a deer stalker hat. He announced, 'All for the shoot must be assembled in the main lobby by 08:00 hours. Tardiness will not be tolerated, I warn you.'

With that, he turned and left. I then glanced at my son; he was sat with a clenched fist under his chin, elbow on table, pushing his beans around the plate with the fork in his free hand.

'I want to go outside,' he said.

'I thought you might, why don't you come on the shoot with me and the lads?' His face lit up like a thousand Christmases had come at once.

'Really Dad, really, can I, can I please?'

'I don't see why not, we just need to nip up and tell your mother, then that will be that.'

We assembled outside the castle; some were eager to bag their first bird, others just keen to escape their old bird for a few hours. After a swift round of sloe gins, presented to us on a silver tray, we were ready for the big adventure.

I lifted Brads into the back of the open top Land Rover. It was a large but rather worn example of late seventies engineering, with one rear light smashed, no rear seats, and a worryingly dented and scuffed roll bar that sported an assortment of spotlights in varying states of disrepair. He immediately dashed for the front, and set about climbing the mess of tubular steel framework that passed for a canopy frame.

'I say, who on earth let that little bugger run riot on my Landie,' barked the tweed-covered Major, swinging his shotgun around as if someone had shouted 'Pull!'

Everybody leapt for cover as I made a dash down the back of the vehicle, and rugby tackled my son to the ground.

'What's the matter with you lot; it's not as if it's loaded or anything.'

With that, he pointed the gun skyward and released the click of an empty barrel, shortly followed by the deafening crack of the second barrel, loaded as it now seemed.

'Christ! What daft bugger left one up my spout? Could have had some chap's head owff.'

Major Tweed then turned to clip his loader around the head, and after a swift boot to his behind, helped us finish loading up.

We trundled along the open road at a thankfully sedate pace, the Major turned on occasion to point out the odd landmark or battlefield, but we were all far too cold and uncomfortable to care. Besides, the roar of the knobbly tyres on the road surface rendered his ramblings almost inaudible. Brads turned to me and asked, 'Are we nearly there yet?'

How do all kids know this question? Why do they persistently ask it over and over? And did I used to do so when I was his age? I crouched down and opened my jacket; wrapping it around both of us, I engulfed him in a sea of quilted warmth. I smelled his hair, and then kissed his rosy cheeks. He then wiped his face with the back of his hand and repeated his monologue of, 'Are we nearly there yet?'

We veered off the road up a well-worn farm track, and followed it for what seemed like an age, eventually pulling up outside a small farmhouse. The Major hopped out, engine still running, and disappeared through the back door. He returned moments later accompanied by several men of varying sizes and ages who he introduced as the 'beaters'. We all squeezed up as they joined us in the back of the Land Rover. Laden now with about a dozen people, the vehicle bounced and slewed its way along the unmade muddy track. I was just about to ask the Major myself if we were nearly there yet when my prayers were answered. We pulled up in the corner of a field strewn with Day-Glo orange shrapnel, like an enormous dragon had vomited and lumbered off without clearing it up. The countryside's equivalent to graffiti, I guess. We all hopped out, one by one, me and Brads last.

'What's all that mess on the floor, Dad?'

'They, my son, are called clay pigeons.'

'Can they fly?'

'Well, sort of. Maybe if there aren't any real birds around today we might shoot those instead.'

'Real birds… shoot real birds. Why?' He screwed his face up and then slipped his hands into his pockets, hunching his shoulders as he did so.

A second Land Rover then arrived, also an open back type but laden with Labradors instead of people. The handler emerged from the driving seat and set about calming the overeager canines. He then returned to the cab and retrieved a small chocolate-coloured puppy. Brads was so excited, he immediately ran over and smothered the little dog in hugs and kisses, asking, 'Dad, Dad, can I take him home please, please Dad, can I, can I? Mum won't mind, will she? Pleeeease?'

The handler bent down and removed the dog from my son's grasp, explaining, 'Sorry, son, she's a working dog and this is her first shoot, so I don't want her to get all worked up and unpredictable. Her name is Jessie and you can take her for a walk when we're finished if you like.'

'Wow, thanks Mister.'

'Rod's the name actually, and that's okay. Just make sure you do exactly as your dad tells you today. These guns can be dangerous and we don't want any accidents now, do we.'

'No, Mr Rod, we don't,' Brads replied. I smiled and nodded my thanks, then left him to his dogs.

A short time later we all gathered at the front of the Major's Land Rover for our pre-shoot brief. He sat on the bonnet and ran through the structure of the day. Once finished, he then handed over to Rod for a swift lecture on safety.

'May I firstly point out to you all that as we are a little short-staffed today I will be both picking up and arranging the beaters, so taking of any ground game is strictly prohibited. Abide by these rules and we should all have a good day's shoot. Am I clear?'

The group raised a murmur of acknowledgment.

'Am I clear?' he repeated in a raised voice.

'YES!' we all replied, a little louder, in unison. He then turned to arrange his troops.

Once re-grouped around the back of the Land Rover we collected our guns. The Major handled what appeared to be an absolute masterpiece. The ornate engraving on the action, the forged dual hammers and the highly polished stock all combined with the sheer weight of it to give the appearance of a perfectly balanced tool, made by no less than an absolute master of his craft.

The Major then gathered us about 30 yards from the nearest foliage, and went on to explain that all of God's finest creatures would be flushed from this. All we had to do was murder – sorry, shoot them. Piece of cake.

Brads seemed to be getting bored.

'Dad, when are we going to get started?'

'Soon, mate, don't worry.'

The group made their way a little forward of the vehicles and waited patiently for the beaters to take their places.

The anticipation built, as one by one the beaters disappeared into the undergrowth.

Suddenly, with a deeply growing swell of noise and movement, the bushes came alive. The men were advancing on the birds, as one by one they broke from the cover of the trees, soaring skywards, fleeing the human enemy. With a cacophony of cracking shotguns they fell, one by one, like meteors to the ground.

Suddenly, above the roar of gunfire, the Major's voice rang out loud and clear.

'Rabbit!'

He swung his shotgun to ground level, dangerously close to the shrubs occupied by the beaters, and after a moment's sweeping aim, let rip with both barrels.

BANG...BANG!

The small creature twisted and writhed as its back legs were obviously shot to pieces but the front half was still racing.

'Dam the little blighter!'

Crack, whump whump. He ejected the spent cartridges, reloaded in a flash, took aim, and then paused.

'Little bugger...you wouldn't believe it, would you.'

He lowered his gun a few inches and squinted ahead. A look of astonishment grew across his face with the sudden stark realisation.

I heard Brad's scream, and out of the corner of my eye saw him dash towards the stricken animal. I dropped my weapon and launched myself in blind terror towards my sprinting son, whilst screaming, 'Cease fire! Cease fire!' as loudly as I could. Once I was within striking range I leaped forwards and pummelled him into the ground. He screamed hysterically, fighting and kicking to free my grasp, but I overpowered him and futilely tried to calm him. The gunfire ceased immediately, and the only sounds were the muffled screams of my child.

BANG! One final shot from the Major.

'For Christ's sake just stop, will you,' I angrily demanded, hugging my son as tightly as I could, partly through fear, but also to prevent him from hitting me any more.

After a few moments he calmed a little, and his anger developed into upset. He shivered and cried, whilst hugging me for all his worth.

He asked repeatedly for his mummy.

'What on earth do you lot think you are up to?' screamed a voice from the bushes. Rod then emerged, first tentatively, and then jogged over to the dead animal on the ground. After a quick inspection he gathered it up in his arms. As he did so my heart sank. Rod marched towards the assembled group with a face like thunder.

'Which one of you lowlifes shot my puppy then?'

'Dreadfully sorry, old chap, couldn't resist. Thought it was a rabbit, you know!'

'Well you'd best make a dam stew out of her then, hadn't you.'

He threw the dog in the Major's face, spattering all in close proximity with blood.

'Shoot's over, now just leave, the lot of you.' He turned to round up the rest of his beaters.

The ride back to the castle was almost surreal; we were all numb from both the shock and the cold as we wound our way through valleys and peaks. Nobody uttered a word.

The remainder of the day was spent walking in the grounds, eating unnecessarily and generally loafing. Unlike some of the others, I avoided the bar in preparation for the evening's onslaught of amber-coloured poison.

Whilst sitting alone in the garden, going over a few points for my dreaded best man speech, I heard the familiar voice of Claire.

'Don't...don't... I'm warning you, you'll get a smack on the bum if you do it again.' I saw her and Brads were at loggerheads, as he'd thought it was a great idea to kick the heads off the mushrooms that graced the shadier parts of the lawn. Claire, however, had thought otherwise. They came to rest on the bench I was occupying, and Claire nosed over my shoulder at the notes I had made.

'Bugger off will you, I'm trying to concentrate, I've only got an hour or so before we have to get ready.' I poked her in the ribs playfully and she took the hint. Once standing again, Brads asked, 'Dad, why did that horrible man just kill everything?'

'I will explain it all later, darling, run along with mum and I'll be in before you know it.'

'He was a stupid man, Daddy, and I wish he was dead.'

I raised my eyebrows and looked at Claire. She shot me a narrow-eyed sarcastic smile, as she scooped our son up, and over her shoulder.

I remained on the bench until it became too dark to see, and was just about to go inside when Tess appeared, fully made up, but not yet in her wedding dress. I sensed the need for a little final reassurance before she swore to her solemn oath of a lifetime's monogamy, so this I did with a joke and a pun.

Once back inside I stopped at the bar for a swift scotch, before returning upstairs for my final preparation.

Showered, shaven and shiny, we made our way down to the lounge, where the wedding guests were all gathered. Ed greeted me with an uncharacteristically formal handshake, leaning in towards me, asking if I was sure I still had the rings.

'No, you said you would keep them until I was on the train.'

'Yes, so where are they?'

'You've got them.'

'No, come on, don't fuck about, I gave them to you yesterday morning before I left for the airport.'

'You did? Oooooo fuck. I left them on the dashboard of the taxi I took to the station; it was one of those people carrier jobbies, piloted by an Indian.'

Ed's grip around my right hand became intolerable; he had started to glare, and began to display a hint of his canines before I eventually broke.

'Just kidding, they're here in my...my...err, shit, I really have lost them.'

I scrabbled through my pockets, but to no avail. Ed shot me the 'you'd better be kidding' look, although this time I wasn't.

'Err, I'll be right back.' I turned and dashed up the 18 foot wide stone staircase that led up to our floor. I found room 7 and opened the door.

The babysitter was sat reading Brads a bedtime story. He listened attentively whilst ignoring me. I scrabbled through my bag...no luck. I tried my jacket...likewise. Bedside drawers, jeans, everywhere. Still no luck.

Damn.

I sat and thought a while, trying to retrace my steps for the last 24 hours.

Then it came to me. When I purchased my train ticket at Paddington (you remember the one – coach 7, aisle 12, seat D), I had placed it for safe keeping in the top pocket of my shirt. Said pocket also happened to contain a clear plastic zip-top lock-type bag of approximately 2 square inch dimensions. Within it were, held securely, two rings, for the marrying of. I rushed to the drawer where the dirty clothes had been thrown and rummaged. I found the shirt with little effort, but sadly the pocket was bare. I retraced my steps again, this time in more detail.

Got it! I had a tenner in said top pocket. I removed it to buy the dozy old bat in coach 7, aisle 12, seat D, albeit the wrong train, a glass of fucking sherry. It was her fault again! I must have dropped the rings in the buffet carriage when I was paying for her bloody drink.

I vowed to hunt her down and kill her, simple as that. It shouldn't be that hard, I would just have to wait at Northampton railway station and she would turn up sooner or later, I was sure.

I returned to the more pressing problem of a pair of substitute rings. I walked back into the bedroom to ask the babysitter, but thought better of it. She was the prim and proper type who probably farts rose petals and smiles politely whilst sat on the loo. I thought it unlikely she would have any surplus metallic additions.

There was nothing else for it, I just had to go down and face the music. Halfway down the stairs, however, I noticed a somewhat solid-looking oak door wearing a gents' sign. I suddenly had an overwhelming urge to urinate, so I stepped inside. Once relieved, I turned to wash my hands. The taps were a rather ornate affair, great brass swan-necked tubes almost 2 inch diameter, finishing with what looked like half-opened daffodil heads where the water exited.

Upon turning the tap, I found myself suddenly soaked by the ridiculously high water pressure, forcing its way into and around the bowl of the sink. It ejected its way into my lap and over my shirt. As I struggled to close the taps I was struck with an idea.

I searched around under the sink for a stopcock, but to no avail, even tracing the pipes all the way back until they disappeared into the stone floor failed to reveal one. Bugger.

After a brief scout round, I found a broom.

'That'll do,' I spoke out loud. The echo of the stone walls made me jump. I then set about squashing the two water pipes against the wall, and used the broom as a kind of crowbar. On my first attempt I slipped and crashed to the ground, cracking my nose on the cold stone floor. My nose started to bleed.

I stumbled, dazed, into one of the stalls and unravelled about 20 feet of loo roll. It was soft, strong, and very, very painful.

Once the flow of blood had been quelled, I set about cutting off the water supply again, this time making sure that one foot was securely wedged under the sideboard, the other against the wall.

The pipes creaked and groaned as they were crushed together with the leverage that the broom handle offered. Eventually I thought they had deformed enough to stop the water flow. I then set about unscrewing the tops of the taps in search of my Holy Grail, the washers!

The water pressure was still a little high for the task in hand; as the taps were unwound I could feel the resistance building from the water beneath. It started to leak past the threads and down into the sink. Presuming it would be like unscrewing a bottle of Coke, one hiss and a bit of froth, I continued, unperturbed.

How wrong, how very, very wrong I was. As the last thread of the hot tap unwound I was treated to a sudden geyser of scalding hot water into my face, erupting from the now deformed, and hence pressurised, pipe. (Imagine, if you will, squeezing the end of a hosepipe to attain more pressure whilst rinsing off the Aston.) The room became soaked in an instant; the wayward jet of water rebounded off the ceiling and dissipated at high velocity around the entire room.

In a moment of panic, I scanned the room for any clues as to how I could reduce the spray.

The toilet. I swiftly removed the heavy porcelain lid from the cistern, and gripping it at one end, swung it like a baseball bat across the pipes. As the impact crushed them, it also smashed the cistern lid into thousands of tiny pieces. Instantly though, the water flow slowed to a slight dribble.

Flushed with my success, I then set about disassembling the cold tap.

* * * * *

'What the fuck happened to you, I thought you were just checking on your son,' spurts Sully, as I returned, dripping wet and slightly more than half-cut, in the ballroom where everyone was gathered.

'Problems with my tap dancing, I'll tell you later.'

I moved away swiftly; he raised an eyebrow as he returned to his previous conversation. There was something deeply disturbing about seeing a 25 stone football hooligan in a kilt, sipping delicately from a champagne flute, chatting politely to somebody's great aunt.

I arrived where I had left off. Ed looked at me and started to snigger, Claire frowned and Tess looked horrified.

'What on earth have you been up to?' Tess asked. I looked down at what had caused the sudden change of conversation, only to find a ream of bloodied loo roll hanging from my sodden sporran. My shirt was peppered with blood, which had now spread into pink streaks with the amount of water sprayed onto it from the wayward taps. In addition to this, the sleeve of my shirt had somehow been ripped, and wore a nice brown streak from my floor surfing. Add to this my nose, that had just started bleeding again, and the bruise that was beginning to blossom on my cheek. All achieved in only ten minutes. Not bad going really, even by Beaker's standards.

'You'll have to go up and change,' hissed Claire, in a sort of muted snarl.

'That would be a little tricky as I'm a bloke, and in being a bloke this means I don't carry 17 outfits for a weekend away like you lot do, so unless you have a party frock in size *fat bastard*, I'll be 'drowned ratting' it to the wedding.'

'You certainly won't,' she snapped and disappeared off to find the concierge.

We then settled into what began as a normal conversation. The tone then lowered a notch further when Glynn arrived, sporting an orange plaid suit and green patent brogues.

'Did I ever tell you the one about…?' he began, but I wandered off before hearing any more. I stumbled into Little Jack, all 6 ft 8 of him, and commented how it must be nice to be home.

'Aberdeen is a way north from here ya noo. It would be like asking a man from Cornwall if it's good to be back home as he sits in a pub in Dartford.'

'Yeah, point taken,' I replied. At that moment a bell sounded repeatedly until silence fell.

'Would the wedding guests all follow the bride and groom into the chapel now please,' requested the short but important-looking man, who was stood at the large double doors that led to the corridor, that in turn wound its way to the stairs, that then passed through the gallery that was adjacent to the lounge that joined the orangery, that then brought you to the staircase, via another lounge, that took you down the passageway that eventually led us to the wedding chapel.

I just hoped I wouldn't need a leak halfway through the service, or I'd be gone for hours trying to find my way back!

Claire returned with an overly frilly dress shirt. To call it ivory-coloured would be an insult to magnolia, so I must be straight with you.

It was butterscotch, with brown and gold frills.

I checked the collar, not only to confirm my suspicions that it was indeed three sizes too small, but also to see if Des O'Connor's nametag was stitched inside. It wasn't, but it might as well have been.

We all took our places in the small but cosy castle chapel. I stood next to Ed in pole position, and tried to ignore the diabolical gramophone-esque rendition of 'Here comes the bride' that warbled its way out of the pre-war speakers. The priest, suitably ancient, stumbled around in front of the altar nodding his head as he nattered away to himself, quite in a world of his own.

Tess eventually joined us at the sharp end of the congregation, and we waited a couple more minutes for the doddery old boy to gather his thoughts.

'Dearly beloved, we are gathered here today...' and so it went on. Half an hour later he requested the rings, and I must say, I did pause for a moment's reflection before producing the two brass washers from my still damp pocket and placing them on the red velvet cushion provided. Ed and I started sniggering, but Tess didn't quite get it. She leant over to me and whispered, 'No, Hazy, the rings.'

I looked at her with as straight a face as possible, and managed, 'No, seriously, these are the…'

The nasal snigger then erupted into a full-blown laughter fit. Tess was looking all around, still a bit confused. A shovel-sized hand then appeared on my shoulder, and a deep dark voice spoke to me in lowered tones, 'You'd best not fuck my daughter's wedding up, lad, or I fear you may regret it.'

Hint taken, I squared up, and presented the cushion bearing said washers to the priest. Tess was whispering to Ed, but he just shrugged and gave me a sly grin.

So I'm stood there at the front of the chapel looking like an extra from a sketch at the Edinburgh comedy festival; all I needed was a Tam-o-Shanter hat and a bottle of whisky (at least one – if not both of these would be appearing about my person in a wee while, I was sure) when I felt this drip on the end of my nose.

I sniffed.

It retreated.

I still had my hands outstretched as the reverend, in a world of his own, was yet to notice we had arrived at 'that' part of the ceremony.

Another drip; I tried to sniff again, but this time with less success, and was overcome with the irresistible urge to wipe my nose along the edge of the cushion. I held firm, but decided to try and support the cushion with just one hand underneath, so I could free the other in order to wipe my nose with the sleeve of my soggy jacket.

It was harder than I had anticipated. Every time I tried to take the weight in one hand, the sides drooped down and the washers – sorry, rings – began to slide off.

The drip was growing. I was so preoccupied with this little balancing act I failed to notice the priest had now come to his senses, and was beckoning me to raise the cushion higher so he could remove the wash…err, rings.

He coughed to draw some attention. This broke my concentration, and as I quickly looked up I was unable to quell the sneeze that erupted from my nose, showering the priest with a spectacular blast of snot and blood.

My hooter was then a tap once more; it spewed both clotted and freshly thinned blood onto the stone floor. The priest was completely oblivious to his new Technicolor coating and continued to recite the ceremony regardless. I sniffed, snorted and wiped my way through the next few minutes, but succumbed to the inevitable. I drew my shirt up from the waist, and stooped to blow, good and hard, the contents of my trumpet onto the shirt. This took a couple of attempts, and coupled with some yakking from my throat, drew a fairly universal cringe from the previously silent congregation. Once they settled, the blood-splattered priest continued.

'Do you, Edward Christopher Black, take…?'

'And do you, Teresa Elizabeth Ford, take…?'

So with the thrust of a washer, they were man and wife.

Chapter 8

Speech! Speech!

taking the joke just a little too far...

The reception was held in the Great Ballroom, and great it certainly was. With all the booze going on your room number, it was amazing how many people appeared to be staying the night with Gimp. He awoke the following morning to a £500 bar bill that nobody claimed responsibility for.

The drink flowed like there was no tomorrow (and for some, at least, they would see very little daylight hours of it) and as the sing-alongs started I thought it a top opportunity for my 'best man's speech' to break cover.

I drunkenly staggered to the main stage, managing to only fall twice whilst negotiating the few simple steps to the player's platform. I found, hidden away behind a curtain, a microphone. Slim, and stainless steel with an Afro on top, just like the ones on *Top of the Pops* in the seventies.

'BAAAPPPWWWBRR, TESTING TESTING, ONE TWO, NEEEAAAMMMWWWAAA.

The feedback whined as I stood too close to the speaker it was linked to. As the congregation dived for cover with hands placed firmly on their ears, I slowly got the hint and moved to the other side of the stage.

'Ladies and gentlemen, we are gathered here today...' (Christ almighty, did I sound like a priest or what? I staggered a little more.) 'to celebrate the coming together of our Ed and Tess, who we all know and love, especially when they throw the doors of their home open to us when the pubs have all booted us out.' A grand cheer followed, then silence.

'I would like to give a normal, witty and informed best man's speech now, but as I seem to be about as well informed as an ostrich, and as witty as an angry rat, I will stick to the tried and trusted route of making a fool out of not only myself, but the entire ensemble.

'I have known Ed for most of my life, although coming as he does from Edinburgh, and I from Surrey, I only really got to play the fool with him during term time at our boarding school, St George's College, in sunny Weybridge.

'This was halted in the fourth year, when we were both expelled for conducting our own chemistry experiment in the newly built sixth form study block. I will spare you the details, but to cut a long story to the quick, it involved the fire services of both Surrey and Hampshire, along with some chemicals experts from the Met to get our little mess under control.

'Uneducateable and unwanted, we ended up being accepted as day boys at a rather posh affair in Godalming. I fear the new Charterhouse Library bearing my father's name may have gone some way to sway the board's decision as to the acceptance of two wayward pyromaniacs. This meant that Ed was faced with either a 600-mile daily commute, or to kip down at my place during term time. No guessing which his parents opted for.

'Our friendship grew from strength to strength, forming an almost inseparable bond. Following school, we both joined the same accident repair company and were bodgers and fixers together for a while. We also both started racing motorcycles at the same time, but this is where our careers parted company. Ed was an instant winner, romping home in his first ever race some eight seconds ahead of the second place man – not me, I hasten to add, I was down in about 15th place I seem to recall.

'Whilst I then kept my hand to all things mechanical, Ed continued in his racing, eventually finding enough sponsors to turn professional at the ripe old age of 20.'

I rambled on for a while longer, outlining his career highs, and the slow climb to the premier class of motorcycling, Moto GP, where he now competes. I then moved on to the introduction of him and Tess, an event I staged one New Year's Eve when I accidentally on purpose invited them down to my family's Devon coastal cottage along with several other couples for a seaside celebration. The pair of them had been the only single people to arrive, however by the end of the festive period I was proud to announce that only couples had returned home.

I skimmed through the next few years of their life together, and noted a slight decline in the attentiveness of the audience. Clearing my throat loudly, just a bit too close to the microphone, causing at least one biddy to choke on her vol-au-vent, I then announced, 'Right everyone, just like the end of every good race meeting, it's time for the trophies to be given out.'

The now well-lubricated congregation all stared at me with quizzical looks on their faces. I gestured to Claire, who lugged a large blue sports bag onto the stage.

'Dive for cover everyone, it's a bomb!' shouted Beaker, who was having a Dublin flashback. As laughter filled the room I began my prize-giving.

'As you are all no doubt aware, ladies and gentlemen, the somewhat extended stag trip that took place in Dublin a few weeks ago did not pass without event. In fact, to be honest, there was not a single moment without something happening. Even in our sleep, we were awakened by either police officers looking for information as to our whereabouts the previous evening, or we were in fear of being hit by a flying muffin, care of our hosts. Heck, if you were really unlucky you may even be hit by a flying Beaker falling out of bed onto you. I am still haunted by the vision of Gimp's ritual talcing of his genitalia every morning from the top bunk, causing a pure white fog that hung in the air for hours. Mornings aside, the real trophies were earned in the trenches, after dark, where we bravely staggered from bar to bar, trying to out-do each other in many ways.

My first trophy goes to a man without whom Ed, I'm sure, would be a little fitter. For subservient behaviour at all times, even carrying Ed's Golf clubs from one end of town to the other. For being the biggest fan and groupie a rider could ever wish for, and for undertaking to be a general dog's body and slave for Ed to abuse, I give you the Gimp trophy!'

The Gimp award comprised of a mannequin's head that had been screwed to a piece of polished mahogany. The head, of course, was wearing a full leather gimp mask, resplendent with brightly polished brass zips, and yes, it was highly embarrassing going into a shop and buying it, I can assure you.

The chromium plaque read 'For services far exceeding the call of nature, the Gimpster award'. Gimp minced his way onto the stage and gave three overly exaggerated bows, followed by clutching his heart and beaming skywards on tiptoe, finishing with several kisses blown into the audience. Anyone would think he'd won an Oscar.

'My next award is issued to a couple who were inseparable during the weekend, who couldn't care less, and shared absolutely everything. And I do mean everything, from Big Macs to bed buddies, and hot dogs to old dogs; I give you the teamwork award!

I reach into the bag and retrieved another wooden-based trophy, this time the gold-plated plastic it adorned was that of two footballers attacking the same ball. Underneath this the plaque read 'The top tackle award, for perfect teamwork'.

'And the winners are...Ron and Gandhi!'

I saw across the room that Ron was already making his excuses and apologies to the fuming Mrs Ron. She appeared to be demanding an explanation that, quite frankly, was not forthcoming! Gandhi grabbed him by the arm and dragged him up to the stage.

'I will get you back for this, you bastard, make no mistake about that,' Gandhi threatened, his narrowed eyes betraying the true emotion he masked with a forced smile.

'Next, ladies and gentlemen, we have the Slipped Toupee award, that can go to none other than Glynn, for his extended research into follicle loss in Irish females.'

This also prompted a frown and plenty of questions from Mrs Glynn but he just ignored them and headed towards the stage to claim his trophy. He arrived in front of me and just muttered 'Bastard!' under his breath. I, of course, had the button on the microphone depressed, so his whispered insult was left echoing around the ornately decorated ceiling at about 200 decibels. I smiled. He glared. I moved on.

'And now, ladies and gentlemen, we bring ourselves to the pinnacle of stag performances. This award is not given lightly; it represents the absolute cutting edge of stag behaviour. For services to the entertainment of all present, above and beyond the call of duty. For being the only member of the party to decline food for fear of it diluting the alcohol for the entire trip. For being drunk beyond anyone's wildest dreams, or nightmares, during every waking hour. For being the only member of the party to be mugged. For being the only member of the party to be stabbed. For being the only member of the party to fall into a coal bunker. For being the only member of the party to be mistaken for a tramp, and refused entry to the hotel. For being the only member of the party to be beaten up by a cabbie. For being the only member of the party to be arrested. Finally, for being the only member of the party to be deported, penniless, and told never to return.

'I give you the Man of the Meeting award! Beaker, come and get it 'cos my God you've earned it.'

The Great Hall exploded in a crescendo of cheers and applause. Beaker made his way to the stage through the mêlée of people, many shaking his hand or patting him on the back.

He arrived at the base of the stairs and started to run up them, two steps at a time. This was his downfall (literally) as there were an odd number of stairs. He tried to clear the last three in a single bound, failing dismally as his toes caught the lip of the last step, which sent him crashing to the floor, face first. His pint glass scuttled across the floor and came to a rest at my feet. Beaker was up like a shot and bowing to the cheering crowd instantly.

He accepted the trophy, shook my hand and negotiated the downward flight with a little more care.

I left the stage to head for the bar, noticing out of one of the large ornate windows a Dyno-Rod 24-hour emergency plumbing van in the driveway. I turned to disappear into the crowd with only a slightly guilty smile gracing my face.

The evening rolled along with a predictable flow, Beaker got annihilated and ended up sleeping with the concierge's girlfriend, Sully got a little fatter, Glynn got a little louder, I got a little drunker, and Ed and Tess got a little one on the way!

Perfect.

Chapter 9

Kick Off!

taking the joke just a little too far...

We fast forward now to about a year ago.

I landed a top job in the Vertex World Endurance Championship team as first mechanic. This meant that not only did I get to travel the world for nowt, I actually got paid for the pleasure. Not having a formula one budget, however, meant lots of hard work, and overland travelling for all but the Japanese round.

I was not alone in this newly formed team, as they had poached several mechanics and data guys from other teams, most of whom I knew from around the paddock and some of whom you have already met on the Dublin excursion.

Ron was the fuel man. His task, 24 times a day, was to throw a pair of 3 inch diameter fuel hoses over his shoulder, then dump the nozzles into the spring-loaded twin fillers mounted in the fuel tank during the pit stops. The fuels would rush in at such a rate that it would take a mere six seconds to fill the 24 litre tank from empty.

Glynn was the data acquisition specialist. He was permanently wired to his laptop that contained, amongst other things, the largest database of emailed jokes and visual funnies in the world. Aside from entertaining the entire paddock with his constant gags and pranks, the Ulsterman records every lap time, every thou of tyre wear, every millimetre of suspension travel and every mistake the rider makes. The technology that exists in racing today is phenomenal.

When a rider would come in for a pit stop, Glynn was always there alongside Ron. Ron dumped the hoses into the fuel tank as Glynn plugged the data cable into his laptop. Fuel would go in, data would come out. Meanwhile I changed the front wheel for a fresh one, picked from the rack, pre-warmed and ready to go, whilst Gandhi, promoted to second mechanic, would slip in a new rear. The next rider would hop on, thumb the starter button and be howling up pit lane for his hour's stint a mere 30 seconds after the previous rider had come in. Clockwork.

Glynn would then retreat to the back of the garage and plot a series of graphs on the computer to analyse the performance of both bike and rider. You can't get away with anything these days; it even times the last pit stop.

Once the rider had recovered from his stint on the bike, he would join Glynn and Stevo (the crew chief) for a de-brief. The rider gave his opinion on how the bike was behaving, the computer then contradicted him and made him look stupid. Mind you, having not seen a computer that can get on a motorcycle and turn in a respectable lap time yet, the rider was usually cut some slack.

There were usually some girls on hand; Cassie the physio to massage a rider's punished limbs, or Kirsty and Julie who helped out with the catering side of things. There were even some female riders in a few of the other teams, but the mechanics profession remained somewhat male dominated.

Technology seemed to be un-employing the populous at an alarming rate. Even the lone time signallers that at one time sat upon the pit wall with a Heath Robinson illuminated sign box showing the rider his last lap time had been replaced by on-board dash systems displaying everything from current lap time to best lap, average lap, and indeed nearest lap dance bar, I'm sure, if you needed it!

The lap times were a much-discussed subject amongst riders. The outright lap record at any given circuit was broken year in, year out, with little technological advances to speak of other than the barriers set by the human mind. Typically a rider would break the record in practice, and then, amazingly, within the hour some four or five teams would claim to be within this time. Crazy.

It was off season, mid-September to be precise, and we had recently returned from the final round for our old team in the South of France at Circuit Paul Ricard, a mega fast track with a two-mile straight you could almost fall asleep on. No sooner had we left the ferry terminal back in good old Blighty, we were being headhunted by Vertex's crew chief, Stevo.

Stevo was a good old sort, hands like a bunch of bananas and broad shoulders to match. He was as straight as a guy rope and as solid as the concrete it was buried in. He was mid-fifties, from the heart of Hartford and started every sentence with 'I'll tell you…' or 'I've been in this game long enough to know that…'. Above all, he was a man you could rely on.

* * * * *

Five months later…two weeks before it happened.
A normal day at work was followed by a not so normal Friday night in the pub. Claire had gone to stay with her parents at their house on the south coast for the weekend. This was not unusual, as they were extremely close and mutually enjoyed a little family time together. I would usually join them after work on a Friday night, riding my bike down a favourite stretch of England's tarmac, the A283 towards Chichester; but as I had to work Saturday, coupled with the fact Claire

and I were getting on like a house on fire – during a fireman's strike, loaded with a leaky gas main and a thousand litres of petrol…well, you get the idea.

I left the house around six, hopped on my bike and just headed nowhere. After cruising in the Friday evening traffic I found myself winding my way towards Ascot and beyond.

The number of cars gradually thinned and my pace increased accordingly. Somewhere around Henley I turned back and hit the twisty B roads for home. This is something I fear that readers without any motorcycle experience will find hard to understand, riding for the sake of it. Getting away from all the stress and upheaval of our daily lives in order to just simply relax and be pleasantly distracted from anything else but the road ahead. Carving from corner to corner in a fluid motion. Bliss.

8 p.m.

I parked my bike around the back of Ed's house, and then made my way across the field towards the Crown. Once across said field I joined the familiar worn tread of the footpath that led me into the pub car park itself.

The place was absolutely rocking. I pushed my way to the bar, and ended up getting collared for a 30-quid round in the process.

'Ed's having an affair,' are the first words to greet me as I joined Tess at her table. She said it loud enough for the whole of Surrey to hear, had the DJ not been playing his shite techno so fucking loud.

The first thing that sprung into my head was, 'And your point is…? Surely you knew…everyone else did!'

Ed was a bit of a ladies' man; I for one was far from surprised to learn that either he had come clean, or he had been caught. It turned out, however, that the latter had prompted the former.

Whilst in a taxi cab earlier that afternoon, Ed's girlfriend had called to demand when he was leaving Tess to look after the newborn son he had apparently fathered during their illicit affair the previous year. This may not have caused such problems in the normal way, but Tess was sat right next to Ed when he took the call. It must have made for an eventful journey. (I'd love to have been the cabby!) The long and the short of it was, that Sandy, the mother of little Ed junior, was not accepting the brush-off. She rang him four times in what should have been a ten minute cab ride, shouting and screaming at him to dump his wife for the sake of the child he had left her with. The final call being in floods of tears, making it a little difficult for Ed to either hang up, or to console her given his immediate company.

He went for the latter, explaining to Sandy that he would leave Tess and move to Hampshire to make amends. All this with a virtually hysterical Tess sat next to him. Eventually she screamed herself hoarse, then took her head in her hands and just started sobbing. She never even saw it coming.

I drew a chair up next to her, and listened.

'It was horrible, horrible horrible horrible. Can't you go and talk to him, he'll listen to you.' I was at a loss for what to say. I scanned the bar and spotted Sully, Patrick and the man in question talking by the fruit machine. Ed, uncharacteristically, had his head dropped and was looking solemn. He was also swaying and using the machine more for balance than entertainment. He'd obviously hit the bottle with full gusto to help the evening slip past a little quicker.

'Go on…please, he always listens to you,' she broke my trance. I took a slug of golden throat charm followed by a full lungful of passive smoke, then headed towards the lads.

'Geeezaaaaahhhhh!' came Sully's greeting, followed by a bear hug and a couple of exaggerated jabs to my ribs. I returned the greeting by treading on his toes, twisting a nipple and giving him a dead leg.

'B'astaaard,' he protested, then conversation resumed.

'I'm at a loss for what to do. She's a lovely girl, but I don't know if I can just leave my kids. She's a better shag than Tess though, so I s'pose that counts for something.'

He's completely hammered.

'Anyone seen Coco? I'm busting for a line,' interrupted Patrick. Sully nodded towards the gents' with a raised eyebrow. The four of us trooped towards the little boys' room where Coco was holding court.

The toilets were quite spacious and Coco had managed to procure a table and two chairs from the main bar. A queue had formed around the room like that of a ladies', the only real difference being that the gents really were powdering their noses.

We hooked in at the back of the queue, and made our way slowly forwards. Once at the front, Ed, Sully and Patrick all do the hoover, but I declined.

'I've not touched the stuff since the stag do,' I say by way of an apology for turning down Coco's finest. Truth be told, I hadn't. With a new team and two young kids to look after (oops, yeah, forgot to tell you, Claire popped a little girl this year, marvellous!), you need your head to be somewhat square if you are going to get anywhere in life. Booze is a different matter of course…

I left the toilets with the sultans of snort in tow, and moved towards Ed in order to get a full run-down.

'What's going on, mate?'

'Fucked if I know. Sandy is giving me a hard time about her kid, saying it's mine an' all. Tess is doing her pieces; she's angry at me for the affair, furious about the kid, and absolutely livid with rage at the prospect of me leaving her to live with Sandy. She's completely lost it.'

'I do *not* fuckin' blame her.'

'I know, I know, it's my fault, but I really don't know what to do.'

'Stop being an arsehole, and stick with Tess, she is all you could ever want in a girl and she is the mother of your children. What more reason could you possibly need to stay with her and do the right thing?'

'I don't know, I feel as if I am falling in love with Sandy. All I ever think about is the next present I will buy her or when I am next going to see her. She's taken over my life and destroyed all my feelings for Tess.'

With that, his phone rang, and he was off in the corner whispering Sandy her sweet nothings and empty reassurances that would no doubt amount to just that. Back in the pub, I avoided eye contact with Tess and mooched around the other side of the bar for a while. This didn't last long, as I found myself one person short of a conversation. Tess sussed me, and was at my side within seconds.

'What did he say, what's he going to do?'

'I have absolutely no idea,' I responded, 'and nor does he,' I added. Tess looked sick with worry. She had downed at least three glasses of Pinot since my arrival some ten minutes earlier. The latter part of the evening drifted by with the predictable cycles of happiness, anger, love and hate that a terminally ill relationship suffers on its last legs.

As closing time loomed, they kissed and made up. I watched through the pub's leaded light bay window the pair of them staggering home, arm in arm over the field.

They probably even stopped for a shag. I, on the other hand…

Chapter 10

Beginning of the End

taking the joke just a little too far...

We arrived at Coco's around midnight. His traditionally well-stocked bar was brimming, as expected, at least until we arrived. Patrick poured himself a quadruple vodka, topped off with a dash of Red Bull, then set about rifling through the CD collection.

He settled for some Pink Floyd, and was no doubt comfortably numb by the time he'd melted into the sofa. Slouched with his arse two thirds of the way off the cushion and his shoulders hunched up by his neck, he looked half-asleep.

'What's all this namby pamby bollocks then?' Sully had arrived. From where I was stood, at the entrance to the conservatory, there was a total eclipse of the room as Sully's 20 stone frame careered past me. With a click and a whirr, followed by another click, and a spinning noise, the evening's entertainment was changed to something somewhat livelier.

James Brown 'getting on up!' and Beaker joined Sully for a dance 'alike a sexa macheeeen!' in the middle of Coco's living room. 'Get on upppaaahh!' I could tell it was going to end in tears, 'a get upppaahhh!' of laughter that was (piano solo...).

The pair of them were crashing around like a couple of bears in a tent, singing as loud as they could, knocking tables over – chairs, lamps, you name it, it got it.

Coco re-entered the room all sniffs and snuffles from a little cistern surfing, and started off on one.

'Come on, lads, you're trashing the place. It's not on, you know, I've got a lot of valuable gear in here.' With that the entire party burst into hysterics. The place is decorated with charity shop cast-offs, stolen from their doorways on Sunday evenings. The most valuable item in the entire room is the stereo, which he bought for 50 quid from John the Bank Robber (don't ask, I'll tell you all about him in good time, I promise) who, since his release, resided next door.

There followed a loud rap at the door. Someone answered it and in walked Ed.

'Boys! Thought I might find you all here!'

Coco's house is situated about a hundred metres from Ed's, so to his detriment far too much time was spent there. Ed went straight for the glass-topped coffee table, and with a gold Am-Ex card set about lining up some whiz.

Another rap at the door.

'Oh for fuck's sake, she does not know when to leave it!'

John the Bank Robber entered the room. Silence descended like lead. Someone even muted James Brown mid 'aahhh, AAHHH live in Ameerrr…'. It never ceases to amaze me how an inherently evil person can kill an atmosphere dead. Stone dead.

'Sorry mate, thought it was that nagging bitch.'

'It was, if your young wife was to whom you were referring?' Tess followed him into the room.

'I met John outside whilst looking for you, Ed, so he suggested we look in here.'

'Well whoopee fucking do, you've found me.'

John shot Ed an 'Oi you fucking runt, be polite whilst in my company' type of glare. You see, true to his name, John the Bank Robber is a mighty dodgy geezer. He may only stand 5 foot 8, but those deep-set evil eyes had seen suffering that only the brain behind them could justify. Always smartly dressed is John – Hugo Boss shirts and Armani jeans – but not too flashy mind; don't want to be attracting any unwanted attention now, do we? The only exception to this rule was his diamond-studded Rolex that hangs loosely from his left wrist. He claims not to have had time to get the strap adjusted since he had acquired it from someone who owed him some money. Rumour has it that when one of John's lads delivered said watch, it was still attached to the owner's wrist. The owner, however, was recovering in an Essex hospital. He, quite unsurprisingly, no longer plays golf, or the fiddle.

Tess joined Ed kneeling at the coffee table and tried to spark up a conversation.

'Don't fuckin' bother, just piss off and leave me alone will you,' was the disinterested response.

'We need to talk. I know you're upset and confused, so why can't we just go home and sort things out?'

'Upset and confused, are you having a laugh?' he replied. 'The only thing I'm upset about is how much time I wasted with you, and as for confused... Confused? Are you fucking serious? If you think I'm going to consider staying with my haggard old 40-something-year-old nagging wife to pass up the opportunity to go and live with a 21-year-old sex goddess, with legs as long as your memory and an arse tight enough to crack your nuts, you're even more stupid than you look.'

'I'm not 40 till next year,' she feebly replied as tears were rolling down her face.

'Stop yer fuckin' moaning and get back home.'

She remained slumped on the floor. Sully attempted to re-introduce James Brown to our ears, but only succeeded in scratching the CD and spilling a bottle of red onto the cream carpet. The Prodigy then took over with a swift rendition of

'Firestarter', followed by the rest of their *Fat of the Land* CD. As I waited for the violent strobe lighting to kick in, I was pacified by the intermittent glow of sporadic blue light.

'Oh fuck. The Old Bill have arrived.' Keith Flint was put on hold as all and sundry rushed around to hoover up what drugs were left on public display. Coco was buzzing around like a madman trying to cover his tracks. No, not the ones up his arms...

The blue light faded as the Old Bill drove off. We all gawped out of the window expecting them to turn back at any second, but they disappeared around the corner. False alarm, phew.

Fatboy Slim was then allowed to enter the room, as Gandhi changed the CD and cranked it to the max. Coco was fussing about the neighbours, but nobody seemed to care. John the Bank Robber had escaped out of the back door, and was over the fence before you could have said 'evenin' officer'.

Things then heated up a little. Tess had been laying in to Ed about his affair; this was just riling him further, and he looked ready to burst.

Within an extremely short period of time, everyone's character had become far more animated. Beaker grew ever more accident prone, burning his lips when he kissed a red-hot oven door for a laugh after the not so frozen pizzas had been removed. Gandhi, having missed the lower step out of the front door, had managed to face plant the concrete slab footpath spectacularly, grazing both his cheek and forehead in the process. Sully also, somewhat more carefully, had stepped outside and been caught by a neighbour urinating in their hedge. Patrick had been engrossed in a deep and meaningful conversation with Glynn, and I myself merely observed the action, taking it all in for future reference.

A short while later, home had beckoned, and we were all stood outside Coco's house. Ed and Tess's discussion had now evolved into a full-blown row though.

He had begun shaking her by the shoulders, shouting inches from her face. Tess, in tears again, seemed weaker by the second. The pair of them broke apart and she stumbled towards me, led by instinct but impaired by alcohol.

She collapsed into my arms, sobbing heavily. I felt awful, but what could I do? Ed had started to get really abusive; he charged towards us shouting and screaming, claiming she was a useless piece of shit, that she was crap in bed, and a terrible mother. Tess retaliated by slapping him around the face over my back, but this only served to fuel his anger.

With all the shouting and screaming that was going on, nobody even noticed John the Bank Robber exit his house, sawn-off shotgun in hand.

He thrust it squarely up Ed's nostrils, and politely appealed for quiet, as he was trying to get some sleep. Funnily enough, silence then befell Beverly Close.

* * * * *

I had started walking home, and was soon accompanied by Gandhi and Beaker, who both were headed in the same direction. We trudged our weary way over the fields that backed onto Coco's house, and then followed the river that wound its way back down to Shepperton. We parted company at about 4 a.m. I was turning left towards home and my companions were turning right towards Walton. We had reached an innocuous looking, but none the less famous, location. Possibly an even more famous location than the film studios themselves; you see, I was sat on a rather large felled tree trunk, well over a metre in diameter, taking a short breather, when it suddenly struck me that I was sat exactly where the great H G Wells must have once sat.

This was indeed the same stretch of river he described in his great masterpiece *The War of the Worlds* when the three-legged aliens that stood ten storeys high came charging down the Thames, blasting all in their way with their awesome laser heat ray.

He described in great detail the people fleeing from the river to escape being zapped; their frenzied panic created all manner of shouting and screaming. I closed my eyes and imagined the horrific mayhem that must have swirled around inside the head of Mr Wells.

I awoke with a start. The noise of the car horn as it screeched up to the roundabout a few yards away was enough to convince me I was being lazered by aliens. This waking state of complete panic had been enough to throw me completely off balance and send me tumbling backwards, off said tree trunk, and head-first into the floor.

Luckily the ground broke my fall. I clambered back over the trunk, and slowly realised it was getting light. My head was thumping, my mouth was as dry as an AA meeting and I now had an extremely sore neck.

Having sobered to the degree where I now realised it had not been such a good idea to have left Coco's the previous evening in only a shirt, I was now shivering due to the brisk chilly wind. I started to walk back home, thinking things couldn't get any worse.

Then it began to rain.

I arrived at chez Hayes feeling a little…err, hazy. Once I had unsuccessfully searched all my pockets for my keys, I remembered leaving them in my leather jacket. My thinking behind this had been that I wouldn't be stupid enough to walk home without it. Doh!

After a few moments' whirring of the old cogs in my sodden and slow head, I recalled hanging my jacket up in the pub, then – vaguely, mind – walking from the pub to Coco's in just my shirt. Stupidity, hypothermia and alcohol are all a lot more closely related than one may think. I was feeling so shit that even thinking hurt. Exhausted, dehydrated and numb with cold, I stared blankly at the impenetrable door.

I scoured the immediate undergrowth for something to pry the window open with, but after a pathetically short time, I gave up and looked to the rockery.

'Fuck it, who cares?' I muttered under my breath as I launched a rock the size of a basketball at the front window.

'AAAAAaaaaagggggghhhhh!' I screamed, as the rock completely missed the window, bounced off the sill, and careered backward into my shin.

'Fuck, fuck and double fucking fuck!' I shouted at the top of my voice, close to tears. I was even too tired to hop around on one leg. After a moment to regain my composure and inspect my now freshly bloodied limb, I summoned up the strength to try again.

I bent down, and collected up the unfeasibly heavy rock. With a few short breaths and almost all my strength I managed to raise it to my chin. I closed my eyes, gritted my teeth, and gave one last heroic effort to lift it above my head, letting out an almighty Neanderthal roar as the boulder was thrust from my grasp once again.

It wasn't until its forward motion had reached the critical point of no return that I had noticed the reflection of Claire's car in the Georgian bay window that was about to be destroyed.

I must have walked straight past it without noticing. Not only did I succeed in smashing a window, I also managed to completely decimate all 32 panes of glass, and the entire wooden framework that housed them, leaving a 4 foot square hole in the front of my house. Not stopping there, the flying boulder went straight through the glass-topped coffee table I had forgotten was on the other side of said window, and also smashed my PlayStation to pieces that was sat on top of it.

My son Brads was also, quite understandably, screaming like a demented cat, as he had awoken early, and was playing

Harry Potter and the Philosopher's Stone on the PlayStation when the unexpected 'Hazy Pisshead and the Alcoholic's Stone' had come thundering into the room.

He was covered from head to toe in powdered glass, plastic and wood. He scrabbled to his feet and sprinted across the room towards the door. I wanted to cry out that it was all alright, but my brain just couldn't fathom the correct sequence of muscle actions to achieve it, so I just stood there dumbfounded at my stupidity. All I wanted was to sleep.

Claire's thundering down the stairs screaming at me was enough to break my trance, but all I could manage was to say, 'Sorry, I thought you were still at the coast.'

'It fucking well rained so we came back, now get out of my sight, you absolute arsehole, before I get the police to remove you.'

I waited until they had both left the room before I climbed awkwardly through the window, slicing my hand open in the process, but not caring. I stumbled through the wrecked coffee table and collapsed onto the sofa.

With my eyes closed I was gone within seconds.

Chapter 11

A Night to Forget

taking the joke just a little too far...

The following week was no better. In an effort to avoid each other, we both busied ourselves at opposite ends of the house. I certainly had my work cut out, struggling to rebuild the wrecked window frame and getting the coffee table re-glazed. Claire fussed over the kids, and told them what a bad man I was whenever she thought I was within earshot. I ignored her and continued with my bodging.

Upon returning home from work every night she had usually eaten with the kids, so I was then left to make my own dinner once she was clear of the kitchen. I always made enough for two, but the other plate was rarely touched by anyone but me the following evening.

I then would go upstairs with the little terrors and read them stories in bed as their mum slumped herself in front of the telly and watched brain-dead soaps and sitcoms. We had even given up on the minor pleasantries of actually saying goodnight to each other as I had slept in the spare room for the past year.

It was a marriage only in name. The pattern had developed after an initial falling out of love. When you have lived with someone for 12 years it takes something special to keep it alive. That something special was no longer a resident at No 18 York Gardens, Shepperton.

I had started to work longer hours than strictly necessary, and in doing so had developed a raging thirst for the amber throat charm. I regularly stopped in at the Crown on my way home.

You know you drink too much when you walk into the pub and all of the staff know exactly what you drink. By the same token, you then know you are drinking way too much when they not only know what to serve you, they also know when to serve it.

A pint of freshly poured Stella was appearing on the bar moments before I entered. Day in, day out, always at five to seven. I know it sounds daft, but after a while I felt I had an obligation to go and collect my pint from the bar on my way home, otherwise it would only have gone to waste, now wouldn't it?

* * * * *

One week before it happened.
It was on one such night, exactly a week after my last journey to the dark side, that I found myself still propping the bar up at closing time. The evening had spun by with alarming speed; first I was nipping in for a quick one, next thing I had known I was being physically removed by Dave the Landlord.

Dave the Landlord, hmmm. If you happen to be perusing *The Oxford English Dictionary* one day, and find the page open at the letter B, you may notice a wee photograph of Dave, the silver-haired landlord there; it's next to the word 'Brickshithouse!'

You don't dare mess with Dave the Landlord, especially after 15 pints. The unfortunate thing being, following 15 pints is about the only time you ever would dare mess with Dave the Landlord. This, sadly, was one such night.

'Fuck off Dave, I haven't finished my pint,' I protested as he dragged me from my stool towards the door.

'I don't think that quarter of an inch at the bottom of your glass is going to make much difference with the amount you have already put away, so be a good lad and get out of my pub before I hurt you. I've got a wedding reception in here tomorrow and I could do without having to mop your blood off the carpet in the morning; and believe me, I will need to if you test my patience any further.'

Fighting talk, that was.

'Yeah?' I said, as I wrestled free of his grasp, and stood – sorry, swayed – in front of him with both fists clenched and my head rolling like a ship's compass.

I didn't see it and nor did I feel it, until 20 minutes later when I had regained consciousness.

Big Dave had broken my nose and soaked both my shirt and his carpet in my blood with just one punch. My face hurt, and I was in a strange kitchen.

'You alright there, buddy?' The familiar Belfast drawl of Mr Glynn.

'Fuck, man, what have you done to your kitchen, it looks great!'

'I'm surprised you can see it with your cheeks all puffed up over your eyes like that!'

I poked and prodded my face gingerly, only to find it was indeed a bit 'Elephant Man'. 'You should have seen the other guy,' I retorted, 'Cos I'm damned sure I didn't!'

Glynn chuckled, put a bottle of San Miguel in my hand, and suggested we join the others in the lounge. I traced the back of my hand along the wall as I walked in an effort to plot a straight course, but this failed miserably as I shoulder barged it at least three times on my way down the 10 ft long corridor.

'I swear I'm not going to drink tomorrow.'

We entered the lounge to find Maria, Glynn's wife, talking to a tearful Tess on the sofa. Ed had pushed her around a bit that evening, and been his usual, of late, drunken violent self. He had degraded her outside the pub again, calling her a thick, ugly, and useless wife. He had run her down further by saying she was too old, too fat and just too 'shit' to be with any longer. Most people would have dumped her by now, but he had been the martyr and kept her on, all of this in full public view. It was unimaginable how humiliated she must have been. Nobody had stopped him; they just shuffled their feet and looked away.

The sofa was large enough for three, so I perched myself at Maria's end and talked with Glynn, who nestled down into the single easy chair at a right angle to where I was sat.

About an hour of light conversation passed, Maria then retired upstairs and I called a cab. The controller informed me I would have the usual hour's wait that one can expect on a Friday night. Glynn also made his excuses and went to join his wife upstairs, leaving Tess and I alone on the sofa together.

'So why all this anger?' I asked.

'I don't know, I suppose he is at a loss as to what to do. He has to decide between his wife and kids, or his mistress and possibly his or someone else's offspring. It can't be easy, but I just wish he wouldn't be so aggressive the whole time. It's really upsetting the kids.'

'Has he done anything to them?'

'No, I'm sure he wouldn't touch them. He has been in a shitty mood with them all week, but then he's just been shitty full stop.'

'Well, if you ever think you might need to get out, you know, if it all gets too much, you can always come over to us. We have a spare room and could no doubt squeeze the three of you in there.'

'Thanks Hazy, but I hope this will just blow over and not get that far.' With that she lay down on the sofa, and rested her head on my lap. She was asleep moments later, leaving me to watch re-runs of *M*A*S*H** until I also nodded off.

'WAKE UP, WAKE UP! Christ, I'm covered. What the hell am I going to tell Ed?' My bleary head had begun to register both the slightest hint of daylight, and a mentally unstable female flapping around the room for no apparent reason. Just like home then.

'You've covered me in fucking blood, Ed knows we left the pub together after you were thumped, so he is just going to jump to the wrong conclusion and go absolutely mental.'

'Whoa, whoa, whoa, calm down will you.' Not easy, she was stood in front of the lounge mirror, and yes, my tap-like busted nose had been dripping warm claret from its tip, onto both her hair and her pink Burberry V-neck for several hours. She looked like the girl out of *Carrie*, and when I glanced down at myself, I saw that I also resembled an extra from 'that' beach invasion scene in *Saving Private Ryan.* Thankfully the sofa had survived unscathed.

'Fuck, what are we going to do?' I offered.

'Just walk me home, will you, I'll think of something on the way back.' I left her a hundred yards or so from her house, and watched until she disappeared inside, then whipped my mobile out of my pocket, and after checking the time (5.49 if you must be so nosey) called Star Cabs, the trusty knights in rusty Nissans.

Claire went mental. I must say though, in her defence, she did have a point: I smelt like a department store's cosmetics floor, care of Tess's overused bottle of Chanel N° 5; I looked like I had just been caught by the husband, care of Dave the Landlord; I tasted like a brewery, also care of Dave the Landlord; I appeared like a tramp, care of sleeping(ish) on Glynn's sofa; and I felt like a wreck, care of all of the above.

Bleary-eyed, blotchy-skinned and bursting of bladder, I ignored the onslaught of expletives and abuse that hit me as soon as the key was in the door and hid in the toilet for about half an hour.

I'd been a tosser, and although I knew it, I just didn't care. Claire had been making my life such hell for the main part of the week, I saw Friday night as a way of letting off steam without scalding anybody.

Until the next week, that was.

Chapter 12

The Point of No Return

taking the joke just a little too far...

Monday morning came and went, as did the afternoon. Before I knew it, I was sat on the riverbank in the Crown's beer garden contemplating where my life was going. If the white birds on the river were giving any clues, up the swanny would be my best guess. The rest of the week passed thankfully with little incident.

Tuesday I had been tasked with designing and making a faster refuelling rig for the pit stops. I set about trying to allow Mother Nature to work for me for once in a while. I figured I had walked home from the pub in the rain enough times, I felt she owed me a favour or two.

It suddenly struck me whilst daydreaming, thick-headed in the canteen, under the oppressive yellow hum of the cheap fluorescent tubes that were spaced just that bit too far apart to be considered adequate lighting.

I sat at my plastic table on my plastic chair sipping my plastic-tasting tea out of my plastic cup. As I drifted in and out of consciousness, I dreamt of a picture I had seen on the front cover of Time magazine. It depicted Arnold Schwarzenegger in one of his typical 'rich boy' poses: Hawaiian shirt bursting at the biceps, Rolex on wrist,

Havana in mouth, Lear jet at his side. Tanned, trim and confident.

I woke with a start, but couldn't remember the brilliant idea I had just had. Bollocks! I returned to the workshop, and continued to rack my brain for a way to make our fuel defy gravity and flow faster than anybody else's.

Pressure systems were banned, and the fuel tanks had a pair of spring-loaded fillers mounted inside that were each a maximum of 3 inch diameter, according to the regulations. What more could one do but feed them with a 3 inch pipe, I wondered?

I left work at five, exhausted. My brain had seized up hours before and all I could think of was escape. I left the building, donned my crash helmet and headed for the countryside.

I wound my way through housing estates and towns that in turn led to villages and farmland. Fleeing down the black ribbon of tarmac, leaving the problems of life in my wake. Past fields of cows and acres of plain rolling green England, I flew uninhibited, till suddenly it hit me again, the feeling of an idea bubbling under the surface, bursting to get out, but unable to recall what on earth it could be.

I drew to a halt in a lay-by somewhere near Reading. I removed my crash helmet, sat on a bank, and sucked a length of grass, just like the hillbillies do.

A few cars passed at a fairly hair-raising rate considering both the narrowness of the road and the height and density of the bordering hedgerows; these were followed by a lethargically lolloping tractor, towing a flat-bedded trailer upon which there sat several milk churns. It rattled and chugged past with the enthusiasm of a sloth with hiccups.

Ping! An idea formed. I closed my eyes and laid back to let all those creative juices flow straight to my brain. When none did, I sat up again and tried paying attention. What did Arnie Schwarzenegger and a milk churn have to do with a super-efficient fuel filler system, I wondered.

I hopped back on my bike and headed for the pub. After all, my pint would be getting lonely sat on the bar all by itself by now...

It wasn't till Friday that Arnie's milk churn really started to bug me. I had racked my sodden brain for hours trying to recall my brilliant idea. I'd tried everything from yoga and meditation to drinking a case of beer in the bath (more on that one later...) but nothing had stirred the old grey stuff with the correct velocity. I sat at my workbench for hours on end, helplessly looking at the array of fuel valves, couplings and catalogues. All of it just parts without a sum total. I simply couldn't improve on the system we had.

It had taken me a whole week to realise I was a failure. Something astute people can ascertain within only several syllables of meeting me, but then I suppose I did start from a slightly biased standpoint. Before I knew it Friday afternoon had arrived.

Three o'clock.

I glanced at the wall-mounted clock (again) to see it was only five minutes from where it was the last time I looked. I double-checked the time on my mobile phone, which corroborated that it had indeed appeared to have taken half an hour for five minutes to pass.

Four o'clock.

I mooched to the canteen for a cup of tea and a bun. I gazed out of the window into the wet car park, and was relieved that I had decided to take the car to work.

I admired the sleek lines of the black Porsche, and wondered if I would be able to keep up the repayments once we were divorced.

Four twenty-five.

I mooched back, and started toying with the valves on my bench again.

Four forty-five.

Still no inspiration

Five o'clock.

'Pub's open,' I thought to myself, 'wonder if I would be missed if I sloped out of the fire exit and got Gandhi to clock me out at six.'

Five ten.

Stevo came into the workshop.

'Hazy, have you changed the cams in the number one bike yet, 'cos we need to get it crated up for Spain tonight.'

My eyes fell closed in sympathy with my now dropped shoulders and sunken heart. I'd completely forgotten that the bikes needed final prep for their shipping on Saturday.

I burst into blue-arsed fly mode shouting orders at anyone that would listen, and plenty who wouldn't.

* * * * *

I dumped the Porsche at the far end of the Crown's ample car park at a disappointingly late nine o'clock. Having stopped at the offie en route, I had scored a case of Becks for a mere 15 quid (bargain!) and had been laying into them whilst driving. No sooner had I uttered the words, 'Pint of Stella please Dave,' Claire was on the phone massaging my ear in the least pleasant way possible.

'My...b...attery...oing...f...lat... C...all...ou...ater,' I stuttered into the phone, and then killed it immediately.

'Miserable fucking bitch.' I had just about had enough for the day and most certainly didn't need a bending of the proverbial listening device to further upset my evening. My pint had arrived with a perfect 3 millimetre cap of white foam. I held it to the light for just one second to savour its beauty, before downing it in one and ordering more of the same.

I mixed my way through the packed pub, stopping to relay my frustrating week to first Sully, then Glynn, finally coming to rest at a table occupied by Gandhi, Ed, Tess, Gimp and at the head, none other than Beaker.

I recall feeling a little light-headed with my speed of alcohol consumption, but couldn't have mistaken the frosty atmosphere at the table. Tess had her back to me and was confiding in Beaker. Gimp sat opposite Ed and was absorbing the aggressive manner in which he was being spoken to, nodding like an obedient puppy. Gandhi seemed oblivious, downing pints at a rate of knots. No guessing who I sat with then.

'Did you get the bike crated up ok then?' he asked.

'Yeah, but I notice you fucked off a bit sharpish when Stevo came in the workshop.'

Gandhi chuckled in response, and sank some more beer.

'This fast fuel rig is really doing my head in; I had this great idea for it when I was half-asleep in the canteen, but I'll be buggered if I can remember it. Home life is as calm and collected as the Hindenberg's last moments and to cap it all, I think I'm getting a cold.'

'What's up with Claire then, I thought things were improving?'

'Christ knows, she just ignores me most of the time, then all of a sudden she thinks about something to get pissed off about and flies at me all shouting and screaming, then snarling through gritted teeth with her fists clenched. All because I had forgotten to leave the milkman's money out, or made Brads tuna sandwiches instead of ham or something pathetic like that.'

Gandhi raised an eyebrow whilst polishing off his pint. Coco then joined us at the table, sniffing and twitching in his usual manner, before crouching down to have a quiet word.

'Tell Ed when he's finished with Gimp that I've scored some great crack, and it's not too steep either.'

'Fuck me, the day I've had that's music to my bent ears.'

'What, you mean you want some, Hazy? I thought you hadn't touched the stuff since Dublin.'

'No, but believe me when I tell you, I'm the most deserving customer you will meet this evening. My home life is a zoo. Work is, at best, described as depressing, and I was told today that my Uncle Ernie's become terminally ill, and probably won't last the week. I also feel like I've had my brain removed, kicked around a squash court, then baked in an oven and immersed in vinegar before being re-shaped with a chisel and some 40 grit wet and dry, so yes, Coco, if you would be so kind as to remove what little grasp I have on reality by way of a little Vim, or whatever else you have cut it with, and your grandest noseful of South America's finest, I would be much obliged.'

'Fuck me, if you feel that bad I'll front you up enough to stop a charging rhino.'

'Slow... I think enough to slow a wandering rhino would be sufficient. After all, you don't want to kill a paying customer, do you?'

'Lethargic rhinoceros it is then.' Coco tucked a folded triangle of tin foil into my breast pocket. A £50 then makes its way from my palm to his under the table.

'Thank you for shopping at Coco's and the Charlie factory, I hope you enjoy the ride!' he ruefully smiled as we parted company, the light glinting off a gold-capped incisor.

Whilst returning from the gents', pink cheeked and sniffing, I approached the table and noticed something quite odd about Tess's appearance. Maybe it was the lighting just playing tricks, but she looked as if she had lost her mirror whilst applying her make-up on a rollercoaster. Her eye shadow was both more than over generous and rather lop-sided. Her usually pale complexion was tainted with an overgenerous application of rouge, and as for the lipstick...

Buzzing from the recent hit, I pulled a stool up next to her to get the lowdown. I sipped my pint patiently as she finished with Beaker, then she turned to face me.

SHOCK is the only way I can describe the next few moments. I stopped drinking, but my glass stayed put on my lips. The whole pub seemed to hush as the tunnel vision directed my eyes to the multitude of bruises on Tess's face.

'What...how...shit! When did this happen?'

She looked at me timidly, clutching her hankie in both hands as if it was the only thing holding her together. Her eyes glazed over as she looked down at the dark and filthy carpet. She dabbed them with her hankie, then drew a deep breath through her congested nose.

'I opened the freezer door and a leg of lamb fell out and just caught the side of my face.'

She attempted a smile, but winced at the pain of using her bruised cheek muscles. I put my arm around her and gave her a hug.

Ed stood up suddenly. 'I'll leave you two lovebirds to it then; fuck this, I'm off. Don't expect me home.'

I was dumbstruck. The rest of the evening faded to a blur courtesy of Mr Coco and Dave the Landlord. Before I knew it I was stood outside Tess's house and she was inviting me in for a drink. As I was still capable of standing (just) and noticed a half-full bottle of wine in my hand, I thought it a perfectly acceptable plan.

I rooted through the fridge and found a couple of beers, then poured Tess a glass of Pinot, but she had gone straight to the freezer, and the bottle of vodka it housed. A dash of Red Bull later and we were sat on the sofa in the lounge. It was then I noticed that she had removed her make-up. There was a swirl of burgundy bruising around her left eye that gradually faded through some purples and yellows to a dense black near the puffy eyelid. Her right cheekbone was also raised and slightly discoloured. Her lips were all swollen and dark.

'So come on, tell me when all this happened.'

'You know how he's been for the last few weeks, being all shitty because he can't make his mind up. Well, when I came home on Saturday morning with your blood all over me he just lost control, accusing us of having an affair would you believe! He was shouting and screaming without a care for the kids or the neighbours. Then he started to lash out, knocking chairs over and violently shaking me. He banged the back of my head against the wall again and again, shouting and screaming millimetres from my face. By this time I was petrified; he had a real terror in his eyes and was just relentless in his attack. I just couldn't defend myself, it was horrible, Hazy, just horrible.'

She dropped her head for a moment, then looked up to the crisp white ceiling, and the Almighty who was a million miles above it, as she drew a deep breath and continued. 'I managed to scrabble to the kitchen to get something to defend myself with, but he just followed me and started punching and kicking me to the floor. You have no idea. I was so terrified. I thought he was going to kill me.'

The sides of my mouth were pointing down, pulling my whole body to the floor.

'He said he's gone to stay with Sandy this evening, so I don't expect to see him for a couple of days,' she continued, then leant in towards me and we kissed. It felt so natural, as if there was nothing wrong with it. We nestled down and got a little comfier, sliding easily on the leather three-seater. Our kissing became increasingly heated, tongues entwined with the power of passion. Her bra became surplus to requirements, so was removed with my trembling fingers, along with her T-shirt and jeans.

We drunkenly groped and fumbled in the dark for a while before Tess whispered, 'Come upstairs with me and make me feel loved again.'

'No, I mustn't. You know I'm married. I just can't do it.' I registered my own trousers and shirt were now missing, and wondered how that had happened without my noticing. Tess began to push her hips up towards mine, gyrating them rhythmically to arouse me further. My penis was throbbing like a pacemaker wired to the mains and was about to explode a few months worth of un-used man juice. I certainly did not need any further stimulation. When the pressure had become intolerable, I blurted, 'No, stop, this just isn't right.' We stopped. Instantly the moment seemed to have come and gone (unlike me!) so we snuggled down to a cuddle on the sofa, both finding comfort in each other, but discomfort in our damp, yet still worn underwear. We slept.

Chapter 13

What Joe Soap Saw...

taking the joke just a little too far...

Present day.
The Starbucks in Kingston upon Thames is situated above a book shop in the courtyard that used to be the old market square. It has the predictable array of wooden kitchen chairs stood sharply at the vaguely art deco round tables. The sofas and lounge chairs relax in the corners with their occupants sunken so deeply that they are unable to stretch to the low level table that's just out of reach.

Ed sits at one of the wooden tables, jigging his leg in anticipation. He fiddles with the serviette, then downs another latte. Joe is late. Not just ten minutes or so, but a whole hour. Ed tries his mobile again. 'Sorry, the mobile you are calling may be switched o…' He punches the terminate button with his thumb and throws the phone back on the table. After a moment, he struts over to the counter and orders (yet) another latte. On returning to his seat he checks his watch (again), the caffeine rush making him even more irritable.

After a further ten minutes of drawing patterns in the foam head of his coffee with the stirer, Joe finally arrives.

'Fuck, sorry Ed, d'frigin' traffic's backed up past Brooklyn. I mean Esher. Sorry, force of habit.'

'Hey Joe, so whaddya know.'

'Well Ed, it all kinda panned out like dis... Wait, let me grab a cwoooofee. I'll be right witcha.'

Joe returns a few moments later, clutching two piping hot espressos and a bag of assorted doughnuts and cakes. He delicately places them on the table, and then sets about removing his damp Mackintosh raincoat. He then shakes out his closed umbrella, much to the annoyance of the frowning old dragon on the next table, whilst looking around to check for eavesdroppers. Some might say he takes his role of private investigator just a little too far. He unbuttons his double-breasted pinstripe suit to retrieve the notebook he keeps nestled in his inside pocket, in order to accurately relay Tess's whereabouts the previous evening.

Licking his thumb, he flips through his horizontally spiral bound pad with deft efficiency, resting on a page headed 'Friday 18th'.

'I have you down here as leavin' d'Crown at what, ten-fifteen? I was sat at the edge of d'saloon bar near d'window, so nobody comes or goes without my noticin'. Your wife left d'pub at eleven tirty-seven, carrying a bottle of white wine and swaying visibly with a guy who was later identified by d'police as Paul Hayes.'

'Police? What the fuck do you mean, police?' Ed interrupts. Joe holds his hands in a mock surrender, and continues, 'Hey, don't go shootin' the messenger yet, I'll get to dat part in a minute. Dey walked – sorry – *staggered* back to your house taking turns to neck d'wine. Once on d'doorstep dey diverts d'eir attention to necking each other.'

Ed slams his fist on the table, causing a mostly empty cup to bounce to the floor. It didn't break.

'Damn!' he says through gritted teeth, 'I knew that fucking bitch was up to something, but I never dreamt it would be Hazy.'

'From d'ere,' Joe continues, 'd'ey mostly stayed in d'lounge, drew d'curtains after about, what, half an hour, give or take. I dug in for d'night, finding a hedge on d'other side of d'road, quite hollowed out with a convenient tree stump in d'middle to perch on. Perfect view of d'front of your house with no chance of gettin' seen.' Joe flicks over the page as Ed drains one of the espressos. He cringes as he reaches the gritty swill at the bottom of the cup. Joe then clears his throat and continues, 'D'lights stayed out till almost 5 a.m., den d'lounge, kitchen and bathroom all came on in rapid succession. Ten minutes after d'at, a beat-up lookin' Mr Hayes appeared from d'front door and walked over d'road, straight past me and across d'field opposite. I presumed he was off to get his car from d'pub car park so I waited at d'end of the road in my Sedan, obscured by d'five bar gate.'

Ed nods slowly as he envisages this all played out in his mind.

'As he drove past I pulled out t'follow. D'guy was driving like an A1 asshole. He was swerving from one side o d'road to d'other, narrowly missing the sidewalk. Eventually he hits a roundabout with his rear wheel and it nearly spins him clean off d'road, Christ knows how he saved it, but it didn't last long. We reached d'straight of d'Seven Hills Road and d'Porsche disappeared into the distance. D'next thing I sees is d'is pair of headlights twisting through the air, followed by d'tail lights. I knew he was in big trouble. When I arrived at d'scene he was stuck in his flaming car upside down and in a gaad daamn gorse hedge.'

'Should have fuckin' left him there,' grumbles Ed.

'Anyways, I dragged him clear. He's pretty shaken up and he collapsed as soon as he tried to stand. D'car exploded into a fireball so I call for d'paramedics and left as soon as I heard d'sirens.'

Joe takes a first glug of his now cold coffee. Ed stands to leave and throws a handful of £50 notes on the table and winks.

'Don't let them out of your sight, we'll talk again soon.'

Chapter 14

Ashes to Ashes

taking the joke just a little too far...

A few people come to visit me in hospital; mostly mates and my mum (bless her).

Claire refuses, so I spend the week without seeing the kids whilst my relevant organs and bones return to normality. Tess phones a couple of times, but she says it's awkward to visit. I foolishly believe her.

As I sit in my bed, the pain from my stomach is uncomfortable, but I stop pissing blood after a couple of days. The pain in my two broken fingers is severe, especially whilst trying to perform such menial tasks as peeling an orange, or turning the pages of a book. The pain from my ribs is excruciating, especially when some bastard makes me laugh, but the worst pain of all is in my soul. I know I have done wrong, stepped over that invisible line.

The guilt becomes overpowering and drives me insane whilst quiet and alone at night. I pray for forgiveness, for my marriage to recover and my passion to return for Claire, but it simply isn't there. My mind wanders from guilt to lust, then back to guilt as my consciousness returns.

I have only vague recollections of the night in question, and still don't know how far we actually went. It would be a bit of a slap in the face to ask Tess, so I fear the worst. This only seems to fuel my lust for her.

I was unconscious at the scene of the accident so the police were unable to breathalyse me, but the friendly doctor who treated me in A&E was kind enough to give them a specimen of my claret. Suffice to say if blood alcohol levels were an Olympic sport I would have carried home the gold. It isn't, so I now face a year or so on a pushbike.

Some more good news whilst holidaying in St Peter's orthopaedic ward is that my Uncle Ernie has passed away. In fulfilment of his last wishes the funeral is to take place on the Isle of Man where he had raced many times as a lad. His late wife always said that motorcycles would be the death of him, and in a cruel twist of fate…they were.

The Devil finally took him whilst he was getting off a traffic-clogged stationary bus in Croydon. A kid on a pizza moped was charging up the inside when Ernie decided it would be quicker to walk; he stepped from the bus and was promptly collected awkwardly onto pizza boy's front mudguard. Then, in a freak twist of fate, his flailing tie became entangled in the spinning front wheel, reeling his face in like it was on a high-speed fishing line. Messy.

The funeral had been booked for the following Monday, so my mum had arranged our ferry tickets for first thing that morning.

They released me on Friday afternoon, just in time for a swift one down the Crown then. I sit at the bar for a couple of hours wringing my celebrity status until it's dry, with tales of masterful car control and untold bravery. Truth is, I was fucked. At nine o'clock I called the knights in rusty Nissans.

I was home by half-past.

* * * * *

We head up the M6. Mum is driving as Dad witters away to himself in the passenger seat. Nobody's listening. The old boy is going a bit senile and his mind is fixed squarely in the distant past.

I sit slumped in the sumptuous beige leather, now grubby and cracked with age, that adorns the back seat of the Rolls Royce, with a vague but growing nausea. Was it the fact that I was about to enter my maker's house to confess all? Was it the fact that I hated sailing, and was nervous at even the thought of a turbulent crossing? Or was it in fact the dodgy prehistoric air conditioning that pumped from the circular chrome-finned vents in the dashboard which had indeed not been serviced since Elvis topped the charts? I try desperately not to think about the rife mildew and bacteria that call the car's air conditioning unit home. I wonder if it could just be the musty smell of 35 years worth of faded memories. I feel a rise of this morning's breakfast as another wave of nausea washes over me.

My phone suddenly springs to life in my trousers; I retrieve it after wrestling with my pocket for a moment and see a pixelated 'TESS MOBILE' on the display. I thumb the green button and ask her to call back in an hour. She sounds distraught, but what else can I do with the family so close and well within earshot?

We catch the boat at 9 a.m. and Tess calls back just as we are heading out of the harbour. The weather is shite; no sooner have we left the comfort of the sea wall, the old tub is tossing and rolling like a good'un.

'It's started again,' she says. I wonder if it was my nausea she is referring to as I deeply regret the bacon buttie I had consumed at the ferry terminal.

'He came home pissed from the pub last night and woke me up. I said I wasn't in the mood but he just forced me to do it.'

'Oh,' a truly inadequate response, I know, but I struggled to find the words to match the emotion.

'He beat me, and then raped me,' she said, now sobbing. At this point I thought it best to leave the table I was sharing with my mum and dad, and take a look out on deck. The horizon is rising and falling at such a rate I feel giddy even with my eyes shut. I find a vacant bench that is fairly secluded from the wind and listen.

'It started around midnight. He had been out with Sully and Coco so he was as high as a kite. He banged on the door because he couldn't find his key, even though it was in his fucking jeans pocket.' (I have, I must say, been guilty of the same myself from time to time, but on with the story…)

'He then started touching me up in the kitchen when I went to get a drink of water to take up to bed. I brushed him off, but he was so insistent. I didn't know what to do. He groped at my boobs from behind and started thrusting at me. I could feel his hard cock in my bum as he grabbed my shoulders and forced me around. He started telling me it's my duty as his wife to answer to his needs as he ripped my knickers from me, hurting me and cutting my skin. He then pulled his trousers down and fucked me over the kitchen sink.'

I am shocked into silence.

'Then, when he had finished he started getting violent, saying I'm an unfit mother and shit in bed. He slapped me around the face a few times, then kicked me to the floor. When I started crying all he could say was, "Stop that pathetic whinging, will ya," as he hit me again and again.'

I stare out to sea unable to respond. I vividly imagine the scene but cannot find the appropriate words of comfort to draw her mind away from it.

My life has just changed forever. We talk some more, but to be honest, I'm struggling. I promise to call her back after the funeral and then return to the table where my parents discuss the merits of the new Tesco superstore dumped in the middle of the old Brooklands racetrack.

My dad, it must be said, is a race-o-phobe. That is, he cannot understand why anybody would be even slightly interested in the art of racing either motor cars or motorcycles, to the extent that he has even cancelled his satellite television subscription as there is just too much motor racing on it.

The ferry docks early, and even though we're almost last off, we are still well ahead of schedule. Once clear of the terminal we plot a course for the church.

We arrive, despite a little scenic detour or two – due to the inadequate sign posts, or rather lack of them altogether to be more accurate – over an hour early, so we decide to head into downtown Douglas to find a bun shop for some tea and cakes before the main event. God has certainly got his sense of humour turned up to full blast as the wind races through the streets, turning brollies inside out and slamming doors shut repeatedly. The low sky is oppressively black as the rain pelts us with the vigour of a machine gun.

We take refuge inside 'Molly's Pantry', adding to the soaked and slippery polished wooden floor with our own spattering of water.

'Two sausage rolls, a pasty and three teas please.' The 'Molly' behind the counter scowls as if I had just ordered six petrol bombs, but makes herself busy with the tea urn anyway. We take a seat at a slightly too small table and chat away.

The hour passes swiftly and I take a quick peek out of the window as we stand to leave. Thankfully the weather has mellowed a touch and we all troop back to the Roller. This, of course, doesn't last as the wind picks up again to a howling gale in the time it takes us to walk the half-mile back to the car park.

As we approach the church, I see my cousin Bruce is having a tough time ferrying his three young daughters and pregnant wife from the Ford Galaxy to the large but welcoming oak doors of the House of God. His black umbrella has blown inside out and resembles a large comical crown.

Auntie Mary, the professional mourner who turns up to even the most distant relative's funeral, desperate for even the slightest look into the will, is of course present, as is her latest boyfriend, Derek. Derek is a jerk. His Elvis quiff is doing well in the battle with the hurricane force winds that beat across the broken tarmac of the church car park, aided no doubt with copious amounts of Dax Wax and half a tin of hairspray that struggle to hold it firm. He greets us with a handshake and a hug, uttering his condolences and looking solemn. I wouldn't mind, but the twat had never even met my uncle.

We move into the shelter of the church and are greeted to my surprise by the Glen Miller Band playing just audibly from the seemingly authentic nineteen-fifties speakers. We take a pew and I am quite taken aback with the size of the congregation. Amongst the hundred or so people gathered I spot seventies rock stars, racing legends from both car and motorcycle disciplines, television celebrities and a whole ream of family I had not seen in yonks.

Ernie's wife had died the previous year, after a long battle with cancer, and was also out here on the island. Her ashes had been spread in the grey mist of the mountains early one morning last December and now he was due to join her once again.

I am oblivious to the service as soon as it starts, just going through the motions. Stand, kneel, and sit. Stand, sit, and kneel again, all in a world of my own. The truth is I am so racked with guilt I find it impossible to do anything other than pray for my own forgiveness. Over and over in my mind I try to recall the night with Tess, becoming aroused when even the faintest of thoughts break from my fog-clouded memory. Over and over again the image would be overpowered with guilt for what we had done. But then, what had we done? I'm buggered if I know, other than the dreadful feeling I have welling up inside me is not likely to be completely unfounded. All this is spinning around in my head like the whirlwind outside. How can one feel guilty about something you are not sure you've done? I'm buggered if I know. (Oops, sorry Lord, forgot I was in church!)

Before I know it, the casket has gone and we are filing gently into the centre aisle to make our exit. The irony is, I now feel guilty because I have attended my uncle's funeral without even the slightest thought of him at all. I have spent the last hour selfishly concentrating on praying for my own salvation and forgiveness for the possible decimation of my wedding vows.

With the service concluded, the close family retire to the mountaintops to spread the ashes after a quick pit stop at the crematorium.

The après scorch party is mixed with laughter and tears as these events always are. It is held at Ernie's holiday home in the hills toward the centre of the island.

I head into the kitchen to see if I can lend a hand, where I find my Uncle Jack delicately placing some mini Cornish pasties onto a rather ornate looking Wedgewood-style server.

'It must have come as quite a shock, being your older brother an' all,' I offer.

'Naah, silly bugger was always going to go before me, be it tearing around on those bloody bikes or his appetite for aquatic danger. You know, he only learnt to scuba dive in his late fifties. I'm surprised he made it this far.'

I could see Jack's eyes begin to well up, so a change of subject was in order. 'Tess seems to be having a bit of a rough time of it at the moment, how's she getting on at work?'

'Oh, bearing up I suppose, old son. That bastard she married needs a right slap if you ask me. She came in the other day all upset...' Jack is beginning to become agitated. 'You know, more than she usually is after he's had a go at her.' He stops arranging the finger nibbles. 'And then I notice a couple of bruises and a swollen lip. Now it's not really my business, but if I see that little creep it would take an army of centurions to stop me from giving him a bloody good hiding.' Jack's eyes have narrowed, but he follows slowly in a softer voice, 'Friend of yours, isn't he?'

'Err *was*, was a friend of mine, Jack, *was*.' I rack my brain for a more productive subject.

'How's Little Jack?' I ask.

'Oh, fabulous!' Uncle Jack is smiling again, 'he's been like a dog with two dicks since we bought a container of stuff off of the Pinewood special effects department last week. Oh there's some real classics in there: motorbikes from *Tron*, a whole T-Rex torso from *Jurassic Park*, a rubber mannequin from *Frankenstein* and a whole host of stuff from the later *Carry On*s. You'll have to drop by and take a look.

I nod in agreement and scoop up the almost ready platter of nibbles whilst the going's good. I find myself in the lounge moments later, trapped in a corner by the vile breath coming from the incessant ramblings of a distantly related old biddy that I haven't seen since I was *this* big.

I divert her attention by waving and smiling to nobody in particular over her shoulder, then make a dash for freedom as she turns to see who it is.

I find my brother Bob in the hallway, and after some small talk and canapés I mooch out to Ernie's garage. The old wooden building is sited at the end of the garden, with a single door entrance leading to an immaculately clean but traditionally old-looking workshop. The double doors at the opposite end I presume open out onto the road. I close my eyes to imagine him sat at his bench, doors open and him glowing like a Ready Brek kid in the early morning sunshine, drawing on his pipe whilst tinkering away with a carburettor off one of his bikes, as the racers hurtle past just feet away during TT week. My trance is broken by his sister Elsie standing next to me.

'The weather has died right down now, why don't you take one of them out for a run? She gestures at the Vincent Black Shadow.

'I can't, Elsie, I don't think it's right,' I weakly protest, but before I know it I'm out on the road charging around the TT course, reliving the memories of my recently deceased uncle.

I return to the house a couple of hours later to find most folk have made their way home. I remove Ernie's leather jacket and hang it back on the peg next to the front door where it belongs.

We say our goodbyes and roll slowly down the crunchy gravel drive towards our homebound ferry. I ring Tess as soon as we board.

Chapter 15

Spain

taking the joke just a little too far...

The run to school seems a great deal jollier than in recent memory. Claire is still in bed nursing a hangover as I ready the kids for the start of another week. Brads and Lara behave impeccably, singing along to the left foot in, right foot out tape that winds its way through the van's crackly but adequate stereo.

I arrive just short of the school gates, in my usual spot, and make myself busy wasting time, rummaging around in the back for nothing in particular until I see a glint of sunlight flash off the bonnet of Tess's silver Audi. It's one of those new convertible jobs, like a TT only bigger.

She bounces up the kerb in front of me, then reverses back to almost kiss the front bumper. My heart rate rises to a cardo-killer thousand beats per minute. The doors fly open and Becky and Sarah jump to the pavement, greeting Brads and Lara with the animated excitement of a pair of lottery winners. Tess and I keep a discreet public distance, but are in full overkill with the exaggerated eye contact, to the point where I actually thump face first into a lamp post. Staggering backwards from the shock, I almost trip over another eager little uniformed soldier wearing a violin case and square spectacles, much to the delight of the kids who laugh as they think I have done it on purpose.

Tess flutters her eyelashes as she puts her fingers up to her mouth to hide her smirk at my clown-like misfortune.

We chat away as we walk, floating on an almost impossible high from each other's company. I love seeing her every morning, it makes the day just race by until our next brief encounter.

Ed has become ever more intolerable; he'd fly off the handle at the slightest provocation, and then storm out to make the short hike across the field to the Crown. He often returns after closing time, not just drunk, but angry, bitter and twisted. He usually starts by pushing her about a bit, and maybe a slap around the face. This, however, has recently developed into something far more evil, more vindictive, and ultimately, far more violent.

She tells me of how he had forced himself upon her on numerous occasions, using her like a cheap whore, degrading her afterwards with both insults and blows. He often spat on her after he had finished to further reduce her self-esteem.

She speaks of all this very matter-of-factly, even to the extent where it didn't seem to be really happening. The bruises, however, serve as a sharp reminder that the stories she told were as real as the discolouration of her perfect skin.

'You have to do something about it, can't you go and stay with your parents?' I ask.

'No chance, they live miles away. The kids have school and I need my job, especially if I'm going to leave him. Besides, I have to keep some normality in my life or I will end up having a nervous breakdown.'

I desperately fight the quite irresistible urge to hug her. I want to kiss her, love her, but above all I want her to be reassured that everything will be alright, that she will get through this and I will be there for her, to help her.

We reach the point where our paths split. I hold Brads and Lara's hands in mine and lead them down the corridor to their classrooms. Magically I am surrounded by brightly coloured masterpieces of 'what we did on our holiday' on crinkled paper from overeagerness with the saturation of watercolours. The vibrance of youth contrasting starkly with the yellowing age of the walls, bonded only by the spots of overused Blu Tack.

I kiss the cheeky little rogues goodbye, and after teacher peels Lara from my leg I make my way back outside. I reflect that I myself am not dissimilar to those walls of colour. I am, after all, not what I was on the outside and have recently begun to crumble away on the inside.

Tess is waiting for me in the main entrance lobby and we walk together back out towards the school gates. No sooner have I sparked the van into life, my mobile starts vibrating in my pocket, followed shortly by the ascending 'Always Look on the Bright Side of Life' Monty Python ring tone. 'STEVO MOBILE' the display proudly announces.

'Where the fuck are you?'

'Just dropping my kids off to school, I should be at work in about five min's, traffic permitting.'

'Well that won't do you a great deal of good now, will it? You were supposed to be in at half-six. We left at seven to catch the flight that you are about to miss, so I suggest you sort your shit out and book yourself on another plane.'

'Shit, Steve, I'm really sorry. With all the stuff going on at home at the moment I completely forgot about the test.' This was of course the completely wrong thing to say.

'FORGOT!' he bellows. 'You forgot about the fucking test! What the hell do you think you've been doing for the last two weeks, other than preparing the fucking bikes for the fucking test! Are we going to un-crate them in Spain this afternoon and discover you've forgotten to fucking build them?'

I cringe.

'Err…no Steve, I mean I forgot the flight was so early this morning.' I cringe lots, lots more, then make my excuses and hang up. I push speed dial for Gandhi's number. Two rings later, 'Hello.'

'Gandhi, mate, thank God you've not left yet.'

'Just about to go through now, where on earth are you, mate? Stevo's been going apeshit.'

'Yes, I know, he called me a second ago. Listen, can you do me a favour so large it would dwarf an Australian's beer cooler; book me on a later flight, then text me the details. I have to go home and pack a few things. See if you can get me on something like a 10.45 flight, I don't care what it costs, just book it, okay?'

'I'll see what I can do, you are a twat though.'

'Yeah, Thanks mate, I owe you one.'

'I think you mean *another* one.'

'Yeah, yeah… whatever. Shit! I almost forgot, I didn't do my lottery this week; it's a rollover so could you get me a ticket with five lucky dips before you go through and I'll square you up once I get to the Costa Del Crime; I'll see you at around lunchtime.' (Lunchtime in Chicago that is…)

The van protests as I sling it from side to side, swerving through the people carriers full of school kids peering out of misted-up windows. I dump it on the driveway next to the mangled and charred wreck that used to be my Porsche.

Inside the house, Claire seems surprised to see me. She still wears her dressing gown, but has made full progress with her make-up.

'Have you seen my passport?'

'Oh, off on holiday are we?' she sarcastically retorts.

'No, it's work. You remember, that little thing I need to do so you can sit in Starbucks all fucking day with your stuck-up buddies discussing *Eastenders* and the merits of Gucci handbags, without having to lift a perfectly fucking manicured finger to contribute towards. Now, have you seen my passport, yes or no?'

'It's wherever you have left it.' This, I must add, is her standard answer for anything to do with items mislaid about the house. She knows it is not only non-committal (that is, if she has indeed moved said searched-for item), but also extremely annoying. Nothing pleases her more than to watch me search the house top to bottom for something of which she knows the exact location.

Oddly, she finds it immediately and leaves it on the bottom stair.

'A fucking miracle, she's done something useful for once,' I mutter under my breath as I don my crash helmet whilst walking out to the garage to start my bike.

The revs are high as the automatic choke does its job, causing plumes of eco-death smoke to be thrust into the atmosphere.

After sliding on my rucksack and winding my fingers into the stiff winter gloves, I'm set for my dash to the airport.

I pull the clutch, engage first gear with the solid clunk of a cold gearbox, and depart. As I reach the end of the drive I am somewhat startled by a black Shogun almost swerving at me past the entrance.

Odd, I think Ed has a Shogun just like that...

I park my bike with the other motorcycles under the arrivals flyover, and then make the short dash to the departures level. Whilst running I check my phone for Gandhi's message.

'TWO NEW MESSAGES'. I scroll through to find them. The first is from 'GANDHI MOBILE'. I open it, and stand frozen to the spot.

'SORRY MATE, ALL FLIGHTS FULLY BOOKED. STEVO SAYS YOU'RE SACKED.'

I cannot fucking believe it. I fight the urge to throw my phone at a passing taxi.

'Bollocks!' I curse out loud, then check the next message 'GANDHI MOBILE'. What now?

'JUST KIDDING, FLIGHT BA217 @ 10.52.'

Bastard, I'll twat him one when I see him. After a five-minute search I find the lockers to stash my crash helmet and winter jacket.

Within the hour I am sat at my departure gate next to a fat bird with Shriek breath and a worrying taste for floral print dresses, whilst stood in decidedly chilly conditions. I just pray I don't have to sit next to her on the plane.

We arrive at Malaga Airport a little sweatier than we left Heathrow. I, of course, did get the seat allocated next to the fat floral pig, and as a result am now suffering from a lack of circulation in the entire left side of my body, due to her occupying not only her own seat, but also half of mine.

I had packed light, so avoided the luggage carousel fiasco and simply donned my rucksack before heading straight for the green channel exit.

As you have no doubt already guessed, with the way my luck has been running I got a tug from customs. After a thorough search of my bag and pockets brought them no arrestable goodies (yes, you guessed it…) they went for the full strip-search and internal examination up the tradesman's.

Ouch!

By the time I left the terminal, some two hours later, and added an hour for 'Spanish time' I had well and truly missed the first day's testing. I was in the shit (yet) again, so decided to head straight for the hotel. Sorry, correction, straight for the hotel's bar.

I sat in the back of 'Dario's' cab farting KY bubbles into my pants. This only partly masked the revolting smell of decaying kebabs and over usage of Old Spice that was home to Dario's motor.

Dario himself was a slightly older, mid-fifties, gent with slicked-back silver and black hair, a seventies-style green silk shirt, big collars and a playboy bunny on the breast pocket.

This was unbuttoned to mid-way down the chest to reveal a positive forest of black curly hair sprouting from his olive skin. I presume he was in a bit of a hurry this morning, and forgot the gold medallion.

His animated and psychotic driving has my knuckles white with fear as I grip the seat in terror. He shouts and swears at all other road users as he swerves his way through the traffic, then curses some more as he clips his mirror on an overhanging palm tree, leaving a burst of shattered glass in the air as we speed our way out of town.

We reach the notorious Marbella coast road in both good time, and surprisingly good shape. Here he picks the pace up to about 400 mph whilst talking to his wife (or lover) on his mobile phone and performing around 12 lane changes per minute.

This I can handle, but suddenly things get a little heated. Dario's female phone companion is giving him shit, showering him with large boulders of the stuff.

Dario's driving becomes so erratic that he has to abandon holding the phone in one hand and chooses to cradle it on his shoulder, tipping his head sideways to clamp it tightly in position. This inevitably hampers his driving skills, only being able to see the oncoming cars at 45° past the vertical. Not only this, but he now shows a new-found inability to operate the steering wheel with his head welded to his shoulder, which causes me much concern as the flashing headlights and wailing car horns only seem to fuel his anger.

Dario shouts and curses, showering the windscreen in spit as he does so. His arm movements become more and more extreme as he reaches frenzy point.

Eventually he removes the phone from his ear, and whilst holding it up in front of his face, screams a bombardment of Spanish obscenities at it, finally throwing it in disgust into the passenger foot well.

I breathe a sigh of relief and close my eyes. The pace drops and the atmosphere clears somewhat. Then...

Diddle-oo-do, diddle-oo-do, diddle-oo-do-duuuuur.

Diddle-oo-do, diddle-oo-do, diddle-oo-do-duuuuur.

Diddle-oo-do, diddle-oo-do, diddle-oo-do-duuuuur.

Dario stares at the foot well like it's going to come alive, takes a good look up the road, then makes a lunge for the phone.

He forgets he is still holding the steering wheel and the car veers dangerously to the right; thankfully there's only a sheer rock face to crash into, unlike the other side that sports a 50 foot drop to the jagged rocks that line the Med.

He is unsuccessful in his following attempts to retrieve the phone, so after the third try I foolishly offer my services.

I clamber head-first over the seat in front, using the front lip of it to pull myself forward, then stretch as far as I can, but I'm unable to quite reach the ringing phone. I edge forward a little further, but still to no avail.

SKREEEEECCCHHHHH!!!!! I am catapulted forwards, over the passenger seat and my back thumps the dashboard.

Dario had been so busy fretting about the retrieval of his phone, he failed to notice the traffic draw to a halt in front of us. He then applied a little more than the required pressure to the middle pedal, causing all four wheels to lock up in protest.

I compress into a heap in the front passenger foot well with the damn phone squashed against my ear, ringing loudly and vibrating like a cement mixer on a sheet of glass. Aside from that though, the thing that really starts me screaming and panicking is the big, hairy black rat I am now face-to-face with, that is hiding under the passenger seat.

I scrabble to get up, leaping over the headrest into the rear seat before Dario can utter a word. He looks at me quizzically, unable to understand.

I shout, 'RAT, RAT, there's a fucking dirty great RAT under the seat!' whilst pointing vigorously at the passenger seat.

The phone stops ringing.

Still stationary, Dario leans across the centre console and retrieves the phone first, checks whose call he just missed, and then goes after the rat.

He returns from under the seat a moment later swinging an ex-rat from its tail between his thumb and index finger.

'Oooooh, whiffey whiffey,' he exclaims as he waves his spare hand under his nose in a fanning motion. The rat had obviously passed away some time ago, so it is this, not stale kebab meat that is causing the rather noxious odour. Dario tosses the offending animal out of the car window, licks his fingers before wiping them on his shirt, and we continue on our way.

Shortly after we pass Puerto Banus we turn inland again, heading up a mountain road towards Granada. Dario is back on the blower giving it large; he shouts and screams at the phone without listening to the responses.

She hangs up on him, so he immediately re-dials. He begins to shout again, so she hangs up again. This happens another three times before she refuses to answer.

Dario curses and shouts some more, then throws the phone at the dashboard. Unfortunately, it rebounds off the air vent and makes a beeline straight for the 4 inch high porcelain figurine of Mary, Mother of Jesus, which is glued to the centre of said dashboard.

Mary smashes to a thousand pieces. Dario is aghast; he sits at the wheel of the speeding taxi unable to comprehend what has just happened. Suddenly he swerves violently to avoid going over a cliff edge, then grabs for his phone again. His concentration on the road is broken; he holds the phone in his lap with one hand, whilst negotiating the double hairpin bends with the other.

He's up to something, but I can't tell what, so I slide across the seat for a better view. Bastard! He is unable to keep an eye on the frequently turning and treacherous mountain road because the tosser is trying to type a fucking text message. He nearly has us off the road several more times before I decide enough is enough and lean over his shoulder to snatch it away from him. Although I take him by surprise, his reactions are quick and he puts up a good fight. It's not until the car wallops into an armco barrier, sending me careering into the front seat for the second time that journey, that he releases his grip on the phone. The car spins around and wallops boot first into the rockface of the cliff.

The force of the impact knocks Dario's head against the headrest, startling him. I was lucky enough to be in the passenger foot well at the time so emerged unscathed.

I get out and leave Dario and his lady friend to it. I continue my journey up the mountain road towards Jerez, with my rucksack on my back and a thumb in the breeze, hoping for a lift.

The dilapidated Renault driver (yes, both him and the car) drops me off at the end of the road leading up to the hotel.

'Haaaf a kilometre tops,' he informs me, but alas, he was short to the tune of about 2 miles. The sun may have set some time before I arrived in the Hotel Matador lobby, but it was still warm enough to work up a good sweat on my uphill hike.

I sign in and head straight to the bar for a swift sharpener (why on earth do they call it a sharpener, when all it does is blunt your senses a touch?) before I have to face the music that Stevo would be playing, no doubt at full volume.

A swift pint of San Miguel and two scotches later I am fit for anything. I check my room number on the key tag, then head off in search of it.

Whilst navigating the multitude of corridors, I spot a sign for the hotel's health club.

'Best take a look then,' I think to myself. After a brief stroll across a courtyard and through a quite fabulously ornate set of French doors I find myself being talked into a rather inviting looking cocktail by Corrina, the delightful young lady behind the fitness club's bar. She also produces a towel and gestures towards the sauna room.

'Well,' I thought, 'it will probably take me a while to drink this cocktail, so I may as well relax in the sauna whilst doing so.' I strip off and enter the steamy pine box. Twenty minutes later Corrina appears with another cocktail for me, this one featuring a green and pink umbrella, accompanied by a translucent blue plastic monkey swinging from the side of the glass. After a half-hearted refusal I swap the empty glass for the full one and glug away.

After about half an hour I'd had enough. I stand to leave, but immediately fall back on my arse. The combination of beer, scotch and a couple of 'Acapulco apeshits', or whatever they call them, and my head is well and truly spinning.

'Only one thing for it,' I think to myself and weave my way towards the pool for a quick dip to clear my head.

After a couple of lengths I tire of trying to keep my boxer shorts up and head back towards my sun lounger. Once dry, I gather my clothes and rucksack, then head back towards the rooms.

I bowl through the double doors that lead back to the corridor wearing nowt but a damp towel, only to crash head-first into Stevo.

'Fuck me, Hazy, what on earth are you up to now, this isn't supposed to be a friggin' holiday.'

'Yes, I know…err, sorry, I was just looking for my room, and…'

'Looking like a drowned rat, where on earth have you been?'

At that moment, Corrina burst through the double doors holding a pair of sodden white boxer shorts out in front of her. 'Please señor, you left these in my…err…how you say…in my steamy room!'

Stevo looks aghast. I look like a ghost.

'You had better come and see me in my room straight after you've tidied yourself up a bit,' he demands, then turns to leave. Corrina blushes and hands me the shorts before disappearing back from whence she had come.

The following day I'm the victim of much ridicule, Glynn and Gandhi being the prime culprits. We arrive at Circuito de Jerez at 8.30 the following morning. The bikes are still sat in the pit garages from the previous day's testing that Glynn continually points out I had been absent for. The riders suit up and are roaring down pit lane with the freshly warmed slicks pinging stones onto their undercarriage at 9 a.m. on the dot.

Jerez is a fiercely aggressive circuit, with plenty of ultra high-speed corners testing both the limits of the bike's adhesion and the rider's commitment. All three riders are slumped in loungers, showing signs of exhaustion by lunchtime. I head out to the back of the garage and call Tess.

No answer. Damn.

The afternoon is spent setting up the suspension and chassis geometry, which, being my particular field of expertise, means I get little rest until we are packed and ready to leave later in the evening.

We sign our hotel tab, get in the cab and Circuito de Jerez is history for another year.

* * * * *

Malaga airport is one that, I'm sure, over three quarters of the English public have visited at some point in their lives. As we draw closer I notice to my left a massive hospital. The sign at the gates proudly announces that it is the third largest hospital in Europe, but I can't help wonder if that's a good thing or a bad thing. Does this mean they expect regular air disasters? If so, then surely it's a bad thing. Then again, if they didn't have it and they did have regular air disasters, then what would they do?

I know, build an enormous hospital, just like th…i…s o…n…e…

Oh. I have now given myself a logical and conclusive explanation as to why this enormous hospital exists. Death, by aeroplane. I now also have a new-found distrust for airline pilots.

We check in, hang around and generally do the airport thing until our flight is called. Gate 27, miles away. Typical.

When we eventually board the plane, I slump down in my window seat, just fore of the wing and stare aimlessly out of the window at the slowly rotating fins inside the jet engine. My eyes hypnotically glaze over and I fight a losing battle with sleep, dreaming of a better life ahead, with Tess and all of our kids under one happy roof. How absurdly naive of me.

'GOT IT!!!!! I'VE FUCKING GOT IT!' I shout at the top of my voice. 'YESSSSS, you fucking beauty!' I exclaim as I kiss Sully on the head whilst pinching his cheeks with my thumb and forefinger.

'It's bloody simple, isn't it, all you need to do is take the rotating fins out of Arnie's Lear jet engine and put them in an inverted milk churn!' I exclaim with absolute delight. The rest of the passengers seem puzzled at best. I'm on my feet now, jumping with joy and singing, 'We Are the Champions' at the top of my voice when suddenly a loud booming voice comes over the Tannoy.

'Will sir please take his seat as we are about to take oooo…' And with that, the plane lurches forward at high velocity and catapults us into the sky.

Chapter 16

When Your Number's Up

taking the joke just a little too far...

Wednesday morning.
I arrive at work like Robin Hood with a bagful of swag. Gandhi and Sully have already begun to un-crate the bikes, but I just mooch past with a 'Get out of my way peasant' type of air about me. I march straight into Stevo's office and…

'You're late.'

'Yes, but Steve I've…'

'You're late. Do I always have to repeat myself when I am talking to you?'

'No, sorry, it won't happen again.'

'Bollocks it won't, anyway what do you want? I'm busy analysing the data from Spain.' I thrust some sketches I had been working on during the flight under his nose.

'What's this, some kind of turbocharger or something?'

'Got it in one. Forced induction, but without any mechanical pressure,' I exclaim, 'You see, Steve, it's that fast fuel rig I was telling you about; you know, the one I dreamt about but couldn't remember. Anyhow, the way it works is similar to a turbo, although instead of forcing air into an engine it forces fuel into the tank. As you know, a direct pressure system is outlawed by the rule book, but using my method, the fuel is accelerated by a series of carefully angled fins, held in a conical cage, that rotate as one on a row of bearings inside a circular funnel-shaped filler tank. As they rotate with the natural force of the fuel passing through them, the steepening pitch of each fin means that fuel accelerates faster the further down the fin it goes. This therefore creates a vacuum, which draws the following fuel down faster, which in turn rotates the fins faster, which in turn exponentially repeats the process over and over again. This means a tank that normally fills in five seconds will now be brimmed in just over two.'

'You're a fucking genius, Hazy, now pat yourself on the back and get back to work. I want a prototype by the end of the week.'

The door behind me opens, and in walks Glynn with another ream of data from the test. He smiles wryly in the presumption I have just been called in for a bollocking but I return with a sarcastic smile and head out towards the workshops. My phone does a swift buzz boogie in my trousers, and after enjoying the vibrating sensation for a moment I retrieve it from my pocket. I have a new message.

'TESS MOBILE'. I thumb the 'OK' button to open it.

'CAN YOU CALL, URGENT.'

I push 'MENU, CALL' and it connects automatically. Technology eh! She sobs on the end of the phone. I try to comfort her as quietly as possible, but she is really bad. We arrange to meet at lunchtime; the venue is a pub on the river next to Chertsey lock.

I enter the Boatman a couple of minutes early. To my surprise she is already there, sitting alone in the large conservatory overlooking the lock. The warming sun beams through the glass, and one could almost forget the chill of the fading winter outside. We order a pint of Stella and a jacket spud with chilli for me, a Diet Coke and chicken baguette for Tess.

After the first round of drinks I become conscious of my impending dungeon breath from the chilli, so whilst back at the bar I change my order to beans and cheese, hoping the ensuing flatulence wouldn't make itself known till I'm safely back at work.

We talk at length about our respective situations; but then, out of the blue, it comes like a napalm-loaded marriage proposal.

'Will you look after my kids and accept them as your own, you know, when we have our own house?'

The fork of food misses my mouth. As the prongs stab me in the cheek, it helps me to regain some distant grip on the reality of what has just been said, but before my brain can function my mouth starts digging me into a hole.

'Of course, I love them like they are my own flesh and blood,' I can hear myself saying, but it seems to be coming from somewhere other than my mouth. She stands, and heads for the ladies'. I am in shock – did I really just say that?

The electric buzz of our conversation once she returns causes the hour we have together to fly past at impossible speed. The subject is not broached again, but we have said all we needed to on the matter.

As we leave I put my arm around her waist. We walk to the car park slowly and it feels good to be together. No, it feels better than good, it feels perfect. We kiss and hug, then turn away, back to our monotonous miserable lives.

* * * * *

I arrive back at work 20 minutes late. Spotted, of course, by Stevo, whose glass-fronted office sits opposite the staff entrance. He lets the offence slide, but I feel acutely aware of the fact I'm skating on wafer-thin ice.

The rest of the day is spent in a kind of half-pissed state of after-lunch apathy. I mooch from workbench to workbench trying to look busy doing nothing.

'Beer off in 20 minutes,' Gandhi whispers under his breath as he walks past. I glance up at the clock on the wall to see with relief the hands pointing at 4.45. My body softens as I sense the relief of another day over, another day closer to the weekend. Another hour closer to the day I will leave Claire.

* * * * *

The Crown is unusually packed for a Wednesday. I greet both Ed and Gimp as I enter with Sully and Gandhi in tow, Glynn and Beaker following swiftly behind. The first round goes down a little too easily, and before we know it, the evening is upon us with a haze of numbed senses.

After more than a little flack for not buying a round yet, I stand at the deep mahogany bar with a £20 protruding from my fist. I notice the telly is on behind the bar. Strange, I think, as it's usually reserved just for the football on a Saturday, but stare vacantly at it all the same.

'And tonight's lucky winner of the Lotto rollover stands to win an estimated £18 million pounds,' squeaks the annoying Eamon Holmes into his microphone.

'Elsie, can we have the balls please,' he continues.

'With a voice like that, mate, I doubt you will ever have the balls,' smirks Gandhi, who appears at my shoulder. 'Come on then,' he continues, 'get your ticket out.'

I reach into my back pocket and retrieve the shabby pink scrap of paper that has accompanied my well-worn wallet halfway around Europe in the same jeans over the last couple of days.

The first ball out is number five. I check my ticket, to find that line three indeed starts with a number five. 'A third of the way to a tenner,' I think.

Dave the Landlord seems to be ignoring me. This pisses me off, because I actually pay the bastard's mortgage with what I spend in here in a week.

'Seventeen,' the dreary Irishman announces in his homo-inbred voice. I raise my eyebrows hopefully at Sarah, the perfectly proportioned angel behind the bar. She acknowledges with a smile, but moves on to serve the ageing tweed-wrapped git in the corner first.

'Eleven,' the telly announces. I check my ticket to see that whoopee fucking doo, I've won a tenner for three numbers on line three. I wait to get served; Dave disappears to change a barrel and Sarah is inundated with punters waving pictures of the queen.

'Seven,' mumbles its way out of the ancient nicotine stained TV set, as the little balls bounce their way into the history books of making thick people rich.

Dave returns from the cellar, but still ignores my best efforts at getting his attention.

'Nine.'

I raise my arm and wave an empty pint glass I find on the bar; Sarah takes it from my hand and immediately begins filling it with Stella. Not wanting to stem the flow, I resist the temptation to tell her it wasn't actually mine and hand it to a passing Beaker as soon as it's brimmed.

'Forty-five, and a bonus ball of twelve. That completes the numbers for this Wednesday's Lotto rollover.'

Flushed with the success of being served (eventually) by the gorgeous Sarah, and having scored a tenner on the Lotto I return to the table a new man.

'Whaddya win then, loser?' I ask Gandhi, who had helped me ferry the numerous beers back to the table.

'Fuck all, you?' he replies. Again I dig out my pink pounded parchment and smugly re-check my winnings.

'So, just to re-cap, tonight's winning numbers are, in numerical order, 5, 7, 9, 11, 17, 45 with a bonus ball of 12.

Early indications are that there is just one lucky winner of the jackpot.'

The hairs on my neck spring to life as an ice-cold shudder shoots down to my boots.

'Oh fuck, oh double fuck, oh fuck…fuck…f…u…c…k!'

I read the numbers again, then again, then yet again. I'm feeling pissed yet crave sobriety like never before. The numbers on my ticket match the numbers on the screen. THE NUMBERS ON MY TICKET MATCH THE NUMBERS ON THE SCREEN. FUCK! DOUBLE FUCK, I'VE WON THE FUCKING LOTTERY!!!!!

The elation runs through me like a waterfall. I cannot speak, I cannot move. Eighteen million excuses not to go to work tomorrow, 18 million reasons to leave Claire, 18 million reasons for my brain to explode! I can do anything I want, be anybody I want to be. I am invincible!

I order a round of tequila slammers for the whole pub, followed by a swift pint and a Baileys. The rest of the night stretches into a blur as the drinks are truly flowing and new-found friends appear quicker than ants at a sugar refinery.

By last bell I am well and truly blasted. I call every cab company in the phone book to order a coach to transport the entire pub to Stringfellows, but nobody's taking the booking. I guess my inebriated state is a little too obvious to be taken seriously. Eventually, I give up, and a few of us head to Glynn's for a nightcap.

* * * * *

I wake around eight., replenish the drained glass of water next to my bed, and after popping a couple of Aspirin, decide my head is absolutely mingin' so pop a further four in a vain effort to quell the thumping. I open the window; Claire and the kids are nowhere to be seen, so I lie back down for a moment. My tired swede finds the pillow just a little too inviting and sinks back into it for a little snooze. After all, there's no need to get up – I'm a millionaire, and millionaires do not get up before ten, or so I convince myself.

The next time my eyes make contact with the outside world is around eleven. I roll out of the bed and head for the shower. Even this is a magical experience, every droplet of water that bombards me sends a message to my nerves of re-hydration and replenishment. I feel a static glow of energy surround my body as I close my eyes and drink in the feeling of the super-human endorphins that now circulate my veins. I towel off and shave carefully in the narrow mirror before selecting the day's outfit from my mess of clothes that litter the bedroom floor.

Glancing up at the alarm clock, to see if it's midday yet, I'm suddenly struck with the horror that something is missing. Something pink, square, and extremely important. I leap across the tiny room and tear through the mess on my bedside table. Gone!

I clearly remember leaving the ticket next to the alarm clock when I retired some time earlier; I also remember it being there when I popped the Aspirin a couple of hours ago, but don't recall it there when I returned from the shower. Hmmm.

I check the rest of the house for bodies. I'm alone. Mind you, I doubt anyone with an £18 million ticket is going to hang around for long, so I poke my head out the window and look up the street. Nope, no multi-millionaires in sight.

I return to my room and begin a methodical search for the missing ticket. Oh, okay, I'm lying. I explode into a frenzy of tearing my room apart with little regard for anything in my way. Clothes, clocks, ornaments and kiddies' toys are all hurled onto the landing in my quest for the Holy Grail.

After 20 minutes, and in a moment of calm, a gust of wind from the still open window sends the little pink payslip fluttering out of the window. It must have been there, hiding amongst the junk on my bedside table all along. I stand and watch in disbelief as it dances through the air, then hovers a moment before disappearing below the windowsill. I drop Buzz Lightyear to the floor and race to the window. Looking out, I can see the ticket balanced precariously on a ledge some 6 ft below. I lunge out of the window but am hopelessly short of my goal. Thinking fast (a little difficult given the hangover) I tear the sheet from my bed and tie one half around my waist, the other half around the bed frame. After a swift Father, Son and Holy Ghost, I plunge out of the window head-first.

Damn, still a few inches short. I reach with all my might, but to no avail. Then, after the sudden realisation that I am still naked, I feel a tearing sensation. The sheet gives a little, and allows me to reach a little closer…another tear and I'm closer still… Suddenly the sheet gives another 8 in, sending me off balance and flailing after the ticket I have just dislodged from the ledge. I watch it float down like an autumn leaf, coming to rest on the front lawn.

Rrrriiippp! Another 6 in and I'm starting to worry. The width of sheet that suspends me is getting perilously thin; I rotate my body around and begin to scale the wall, back to the safety of the open window. Rrrrrriiiiipppppp! I give a desperate lunge as the strain on the sheet takes its toll, managing to secure just one handhold as the fabric gives way completely. I dangle from the window frame for a moment to regain some composure, before pulling with all my might to reach my other hand up to the safety of the open window frame. My bare feet scrabble and tear on the rendered pea shingle wall as I fight to reach the sill.

I clamber back into the room, gouging my belly button on the opener in the process, and fall to my knees momentarily, recovering from the effort.

'Shit! The ticket!' I cry out loud as I am sprung to my feet by my overeager legs as they whisk me down the stairs and along the hallway. I burst out of the front door and career head-first into the postman on the other side, tangling with both him and his bicycle that bring us all to the floor with a thud.

'What the blazes do you think you are up to, you madman?' he demands as he registers what has just happened. I look at him blankly as I scrabble to return vertical, clear my head with a swift shake, then charge towards the front lawn, where I thankfully retrieve my winning ticket.

After sinking to my knees with a mix of exhaustion, stress, despair and relief, I again remember I'm naked, and appear to have lost the torn piece of bedding I had been wearing as a rope. The postie cycles past me on the footpath, shaking his head; I don't bother trying to offer an explanation.

Elated with the successful retrieval of my ticket, I then return to the front door. The closed front door. The key to which is in the pocket of my jeans, upstairs. I think to call Claire's mobile, then quickly realise that my phone is also still sat upstairs in the bedroom.

I trundle around to the smashed bay window, forgetting I had secured it just a little too well with plywood and the new nail gun I had purchased last week for the job at B&Q.

'Hmmm, what now…another boulder?' I wonder. Best not, until I've fixed the carnage from the last one anyway. I scour the outside of the house for any means of entry. Remembering that my window is open, I decide my best course of action is to approach one of the neighbours. I recall there being a rather mature fig tree in the front of my neighbour's garden, so head for it in order to fashion a thong from the large leaves. This I fail to do miserably, as my thong making skills are dire at best, and end up using just one large leaf, held before my genitals.

Knock, knock, knock.

No answer.

After a few moments I turn to leave, but just as I do so a muffled voice emanates from the closed door.

'Who iz dare?' the weak but clearly German voice commands.

'It's Hazy, from next door,' I reply, 'I need to borrow a ladder as I've locked myself out.'

'Ahhh, you stupid boy, I vill open ze door in a moment.' A jangling of keys, locks and chains is audible for the next few moments, before the door sweeps open to reveal a short hunched man wearing brown carpet slippers, a sagging grey cardigan and a remarkable likeness to Albert Einstein.

'Jesus, or is it Adam? I always get my testaments in a tangle; I am Mister Schubert, from Stuttgart,' he announces with a smile, then turns to the Welsh dresser in his hallway and picks a Golden Delicious from the fruit bowl. 'Here, eat zis.' I take the gift from the elderly gent and take a large bite. He chuckles immediately and offers, 'Ahh, it must be Adam, ze temptation vas just a liiiiittle too much for you.'

The penny drops, unlike my fig leaf, and I smile politely at his humour.

'Vait here, I shall go and see vot I have in my shed zat may be of assistance to you.' He shuffles down his hallway and disappears out of the kitchen door. After what seems like an eternity he returns, still smiling, and nodding his head gently.

'Come, I have a ladder you can use, but zis is too heavy for me to carry, so you vill have to do zis for yourself.' I follow him through the faded memories that hang from his yellowed walls, out into his perfectly manicured garden.

'My passion,' he sighs as he sniffs a tiny flower from a hanging basket. I spot the ladder propped against the garden shed at the end of his little patch of paradise, and make my way back through the house with it, winning ticket clenched safely between my teeth. Once the hallway is safely negotiated

I leave via the front door, only to be confronted by a screaming school teacher with her gaggle of pupils, who are then whisked away as quickly as possible. Bemused by her actions, it takes a moment to realise that I had left my fig leaf in Mr Schubert's garden when I picked the ladder up.

Moments later and remarkably unscathed, I find myself back in my bedroom, clothed and ready to hand in my notice.

The van purrs its way across the car park of 'Team Vertex' towers and comes to rest by the staff entrance. I see Stevo through the glass doors, speaking loudly in French to someone via a crackly line on his mobile phone; I sit and wait for him to finish. Gandhi and Glynn then appear. After a swift nod to Stevo and a thumbs-up by return they come through the doors and head towards the van.

'We're off to get some lunch at the Crown, why don't you join us, you can give us a lift,' said Glynn cheekily. Stevo was still engrossed, so I agree to postpone my resignation another hour.

'Shit, mate, you're running on fumes,' Gandhi observes as we make our way out of the industrial estate. I spot a petrol station up ahead and clunk the indicator stalk left.

Sixty three pounds worth of unleaded later (well I have just won enough to buy Manchester; did you think I was going to be tight enough to only stick a tenner in?) and I join the queue in the plate-glass petropolis convenience store.

'Good afternoon, saab, and how are ve today?' asks the short tubby Indian gent behind the counter.

'On top of the world, mate; pump seven please.'

'Wow, you are certainly being very jolly cheery today, vat is making you so very happy? Oh, and dat vill be £63 as vell please saab.'

'Difficult to explain, my friend, but you could make me feel even better if you would be so kind as to check this for me

176

please.' I hand him both my credit card and the magical pink life-changing ticket, sniggering at the shock this little guy is going to get. I wait an eternity for the credit card to authorise, but can't keep the beaming smile off my face.

BLIP! He presses a few buttons on the Lotto machine, then raises his eyebrows before saying, 'Oh blimey, sir, you is being a very lucky vinner today. He beams a smile and waits for the machine to print out the winning chit.

'I have a very lucky shop you know, alvays vinners come to me,' he jokes, before pulling the chit free and making his way back over to the till. I hold my hand out expectantly for him to hand me the chit, but instead he hands me a £10 note.

'Ha, ha. Very funny,' I joke with him, then watch in horror as he tears up my ticket and throws it in the wastepaper basket.

'NOOOOO!!!!! I scream as I leap over the counter, barging him to the floor and scrabbling inside the bin for the remains of my golden future. I stuff the hundreds of scraps of pink paper from a month of discarded winners' chits into my pockets before turning to punch the Indian in the face.

'You stupid bastard, that's my winning ticket, it's the fucking jackpot, you brainless idiot, what have you done!'

I stand in a fury and begin to kick him repeatedly as he tries to rise. Gandhi and Glynn are at my side within moments, dragging me back down the aisle kicking and lashing out in a hysterical frenzy. They manage to get me into the back of the van and pin me to the floor. I fight with all my might as they restrain me, but it's futile. They have overpowered me.

'Calm down, calm down will you, it was just a joke,' shouts Glynn over my rantings. 'The Lotto ticket wasn't real, it's a wind-up.'

I continue to fight and scream, oblivious. It takes a good five minutes before I'm exhausted, and resign myself to listening to my captors.

'We recorded last week's Lotto draw, then got you a ticket with those numbers on for this week's draw. The show you watched in the Crown was a recording, not live. We had Dave put it on when you arrived. None of us could believe you fell for it so completely. Check your ticket, look at the date, and the fact that it's not actually a lucky dip. We chose the numbers on purpose. It's just a fluke that you won a tenner.'

The muscles in my body release their tension as I melt into the carpeted floor of the van's interior. I'd been had, good and proper.

'Take it as the lads' little payback for your best man's speech at Ed's wedding.'

'You utter, utter bastards. I am going to so get you back for this.'

Chapter 17

Meeting Frankenstein

taking the joke just a little too far...

As if by magic, spring has sprung. I have begun spending far more time at work than is strictly necessary, to such an extent that I even fall asleep at my desk from time to time, usually after everyone has gone home. The trouble is I am absolutely sick of my home life, so seek to avoid Claire as much as possible. It has also become a little too obvious between Tess and I down at the Crown, so I literally have nowhere else to go. I guess this is how being an alcoholic starts.

I regularly find myself waiting until everybody has left work for the day, so as I can sneak out to the off licence in the nearby Byfleet village for an eight pack of Stella. If that isn't enough, I also find myself drinking tins of Coke during the day. This may not appear too strange on the surface, but the key difference being that unlike the rest of the staff, mine are half-full of vodka.

I had a close call only two weeks into this new-found habit, when Glynn picked up my tin.

'Mind if I take a slug?' he asked. I reacted by grabbing it off him with such force he staggered back three paces, flabbergasted.

'I have a cold coming, don't really want to give it to you now, do I?' I said by way of an apology. Lesson learnt. After that extremely narrow escape I've made sure everyone is aware that I am suffering from an impending flu virus by coughing, shivering and pretending to blow my nose at any given opportunity. This works perfectly; nobody comes within ten feet of me, let alone asks to drink from the same can. To be sure, they have even made me put an elastic band around the tin I am drinking from to ensure nobody picks it up by accident.

'Marvellous,' I thought to myself. 'Why didn't I think of that?'

I have now discovered the true beauty of the elastic banded drinking vessel, out of habit more than conscious effort though. Every night on my way home from work (if it's still open, that is) I stop in at the Crown for a swift several. As a matter of course now, whenever anybody hands me a drink I immediately mark it as my territory by placing an elastic band around it. This, I have now discovered, is a great aid to actually holding the glass.

After about 12 pints of Stella, you tend to relax your grip slightly on what you are holding; the tensioned elastic band both grips the surface of the glass, and acts as a stop for your alcoholically anaesthetised hand, therefore preventing it slipping further downward and out of your grasp. The down side to this is the fact that God probably installed the lack of grip syndrome all alcoholics face as a kind of safety valve. If you are indeed so pissed you keep dropping your pint on the floor, then either the landlord is going to stop serving you or you will run out of money before you drink yourself into a coma. If, however, the elastic band enables you to keep hold of your pint whilst completely wankered, you stand a far higher chance of killing yourself from overdrinking.

There's a lesson to be learnt here. Never accept a lift home from a man who has an elastic band around his pint glass.

Conversely, if you find yourself getting into the habit of putting an elastic band around your own pint glass, it's time to start worrying.

* * * * *

A couple of weeks fly by, things begin to cool down and the season is looming closer by the day. Work seems to be going well and I have managed to see Tess almost every other day, what with school runs and pub visits etcetera.

The team is due to go for a spot of pre-season testing at Donnington Park race circuit in Derby, creating just the opportunity I have been waiting for to lure Tess away for a dirty weekend. I call her mobile, but to my surprise my Uncle Jack answers the phone.

'Err, hi Jack.'

'No thanks, we cannot abide terrorists here, you'll have to offer your services elsewhere, my boy!' He can never resist that one, but I must admit it threw me a little this time, expecting to hear Tess's perky tones.

'It wasn't a question, Uncle Jack, it was a statement. Anyway how's life in the special effects department then?'

'Can't complain really, as no bugger ever listens when you do. We're currently making a few animatronic dancing penguins for a beer advert. You know this game, never a dull moment.'

I smile at the thought of Jack tweaking the flipper movements on his 3 foot high friend with the aid of a long reach number two screwdriver in its armpit – sorry flipperpit – when Tess's voice suddenly breaks my trance.

'Come and meet me for lunch, one o'clock at the studios. Got to go, my fibreglass resin's going off and I'm halfway through a beak.'

With that she was gone. I glance up at the wall clock, only to be depressed that it is only half-past nine. I have a whole three and a half hours to wait until I can tell her about next weekend, and those hours drag past as if the air is filled with lead.

* * * * *

I pull up to the clipboard Nazi's plastic bubble hut as the barrier rises, without me even having to stop. I am well aware that with the recent regularity of my visits he must know my van by now, but he usually stops me anyhow, just for the sake of it.

I park up at the front of the workshops and make a dash through the light rain and biting wind to the shelter of the foyer.

Nobody there.

I proceed with caution through some wreckage from the *Titanic*, then dodge past the palm trees and mortars of an old *Vietnam* set, to finally be greeted by the open expanse of the main workshop.

The ceiling must be at least 20 ft high, and now with the lifesized sperm whale gone that I remember from earlier visits, the true vastness of the place is evident (not that you can tuck a lifesized whale away just anywhere, but you get what I mean!).

I stand in awe at the hive of activity that is laid out before me. A man is sat at a desk airbrushing the pink veins into a collection of mock human brains, another is fitting an eyeball into a swamp monster's head whilst a rather twitchy-looking girl checks the movement of its torso using a rather complicated-looking remote control device. This somewhat hampers the bloke's eyeball fitting process, but I sense there's a certain urgency in their work so leave them to it.

I find Tess and the Jacks amongst a cluster of penguins at the far end of the building. Big Jack stands to greet me with a firm shake of the hand, followed by a slap on the back. Little Jack nods, smiles, then throws his eyes up at another strict deadline rapidly approaching.

Tess pops up from where she was crouched, putting the finishing touches to a pair of flippers, and kisses me square on the lips.

I'm quite taken aback by this public show of affection, but all around seem engrossed in their work so it passes without comment or notice. We turn to leave, and I'm suddenly struck by a looming presence a few feet above our heads.

Quite how I had missed it upon my arrival I will never know, but not 5 ft above us, there it is! Strung from each limb by rusted chains hangs the dead body of one Robert De Niro, clothed in the respective outfit worn during the film *Mary Shelley's Frankenstein*. I'm instantly drawn to the figure, checking out its every detail.

I am, I admit, a bit of a De Niro fan, but an idea so sinister, yet so comic begins to formulate in the most creative side of my old grey matter that I just have to stop and smile, as my brain runs ten to the dozen.

Telling you now would just ruin the surprise, but suffice to say that a dead body, Robert De Niro, a roll of carpet, a shovel and a wayward Beaker are all to feature in my prankster's plan for revenge.

For lunch I had booked a little bistro called Charlotte's in Shepperton town. A rather smart, yet unfussy sort of place you feel at home in the moment you sink into the soft leather loungers that adorn the bar, whilst you wait for your table to be readied.

We dine on oysters and fillet steak, the latter proving a little too rich with its peppercorn sauce for my usual lunchtime appetite. I'm sure the chef's dog enjoyed it though. We sit opposite each other, staring into one another's eyes, though I can't help plotting my prank over and over again in my mind. Tess continually asks if I'm okay, and if there is something bothering me, but all I can do is beam her the widest grin as I plot my evil plan.

Chapter 18

Testing, Testing

taking the joke just a little too far...

The fast filler system was working a treat. I had evolved it from a straight turbine to a perforated turbine, to a slotted turbine, then a wrinkled turbine and eventually, after days of testing, I settled on a forwardly angled fin, set at 26.3° increasing to 53° throughout its overall length, giving optimum pressure into the fuel drum.

The drum itself comprises of a cylinder 600 mm high by 300 mm in diameter. The lower section is then attached to a conical shape, leading to the pair of 3 inch diameter hoses that, during pit stops, join the fuel tank in perfect harmony.

My turbine vacuum system has halved the time spent on refuelling, this meaning a three second advantage every hour, which then obviously leads to a 72-second advantage over other teams over race distance. This equates to nearly a lap in hand by the end of the race which means the other teams will need to up their lap times by around 2% from the off just to stay even. Fabulous!

We arrive at Donnington Park racetrack early on the Thursday morning. Surprisingly, things couldn't have gone better. By lunchtime we are halfway through the workload, with another day and a half to go. Stevo insists we do some practice wheel and brake pad changes after each component is tested. Glynn has his stopwatch running for every one of them, typing the info into his laptop and recording every detail for future reference.

Tess rings around three o'clock to check we are still on for the following evening. Everything's rosy, for once.

We return to our hotel a little after five as the dwindling light had stopped play, that and the fact we were all starving as we had worked through lunch. After a shit, shower and dash of Calvin I was in the bar ordering steak and chips with a splat of side salad, although I didn't fancy the black peppercorn sauce this time around. After grub came a couple of pints, followed by a swift tequila. By ten o'clock I was ready for the sack. A couple of the lads drift off up the road in the vain hope of snaring some local talent, but I just head upstairs and lie in bed, awash with thoughts of the upcoming weekend.

We finish testing by two o'clock the following day, then head north into Nottingham for a beer and a letch. Once there, we storm a Mexican bar, order some munchies and set about the urgent task of a little heavy drinking. A couple of pints in, and the food turns up. It always amazes me that, without fail, some plank orders the nachos. Five quid for a plate of crisps with a bit of cheese on should be an arrestable offence in my book. (Hang on a tick, this is my book – so damn it, arrest that man!)

Food done and four pints sunk, it's time for the mob to disband. Stevo hops into his Oxford blue Range Rover and roars up the cobbled street. The rest of the team bid their farewells and leave me to it in the bar.

I have had to be a little careful here, as half the team drink down the Crown. Knowledge of my imminent guest would be a shot in the foot so large that it would have taken my kneecap off. I thought it prudent to say that my brother Bob was attending a sky-diving course nearby and I had arranged to travel back with him.

So here I sit, pint in one hand, phone in the other at the bar. I speed dial Tess's number without the usual caution as I know she is alone in her car, and hopefully not too far away by now.

'I'll call you back,' was her immediate response. The phone goes dead. I presume she's either negotiating a roundabout or in a petrol station, and will call back soon.

Ten minutes slowly pass and still no call. A rather stunning young blonde sits at the bar next to me and glances my way with a smile. She looks at her empty wine glass and asks me how I'm doing.

'Great, err…I'm waiting for someone, so if you don't mind…' I turn my back to her and thumb Tess a text message.

'I'M IN NOTTINGHAM, HOW FAR AWAY R U?'

I wait for a reply. After a couple of min's without one I turn back to face the bar. The blonde Doris is still sat there, but with a full glass now and her purse on the bar.

'Listen, I'm sorry for not buying you a drink, but I'm waiting for my girlfriend. She is supposed to be meeting me somewhere in town and I can't get hold of her to tell her exactly where.'

'Don't worry, the night is still young,' she replies with a flutter of her overglooped eyelashes. She must only just been in her twenties and wears a breathtakingly perfect figure. If I kick myself in later life for not seizing certain opportunities, I'm sure this will be one of them. We make light conversation and she leaves after a couple of drinks. I glance at my watch; a whole hour has passed since I had sent the text to Tess. She still hadn't replied. I try calling her, but the automated message states that her phone was switched off. I send another text.

'WHERE R U? I'M GETTING CONCERNED.'

Another hour and a further four pints later I eventually receive an answer from Tess.

'PROBLEMS @ HOME, I'LL CALL U L8R.'

Marvellous, stood up 200 miles from home, without a fucking car. Perfect! Now where on earth has that little blonde number disappeared off to then...

It's nine o'clock by the time Tess calls me back. I am wedged into a packed Irish bar called Brannigan's somewhere in the maze of the city.

'Hang on a second,' I shout as I fight my way towards the door, and the tranquillity it promises beyond. Once outside I can hear her a little more clearly.

'What's the matter? I thought it was all arranged?' I blurt drunkenly into the phone.

'He's been an absolute nightmare. He tried to force me off the road earlier and has just completely lost control. I had to get out, so I'm sat in a lay-by on the dual carriageway near the M25 junction at Chertsey.'

'Are you alright?'

'Yes, I suppose so, a little shaken maybe, but I'm still functioning.'

'Good, well get on the motorway and call me when you are near Nottingham.'

'Nottingham, what on earth are you doing there? I thought you were meant to be in Derby.'

'Long story, I'll tell you when you get here.' I head back into the wall of music and order another pint.

Chapter 19

Soap Gets The Slip

taking the joke just a little too far...

Joe Soap selects first and pulls out of the long lay-by neither indicating nor turning his lights on until the Audi he pursues is safely into the second lane and indicating right towards the main M25 junction.

He flicks on only his sidelights as the road is illuminated by an orange glow, remaining in the slow lane until Tess disappears onto the roundabout and down the slip road leading to the motorway. The traffic is light and they make good progress, reaching the M1 in just over 30 minutes.

Joe keeps his distance, but knows that he needn't to be too careful. Even the most observant of people are quite unlikely to notice a tail at night on a motorway, let alone a stressed-out emotional wreck on her way to meet a mysterious partner five counties away in light rain with steamed-up windows.

Joe reclines in the sumptuous leather seat and calls Ed shortly after they join the M1, just to update him. The conversation is short, but not without a brief display of emotion from the recipient.

Tess notices an orange light glowing on the dashboard. The fuel range of the Audi is good, but in her heightened emotional state, she immediately worries if she will make it to Toddington services before the tank runs dry. She slows the car to a pace of 60 miles per hour and pulls across to the slow lane. Joe responds by falling back a little further, unable to figure out why her speed has dropped by a third, but remains a fixed distance from his target.

A large lorry pulls between them, and a steadily increasing incline now forces their pace to drop nearer 55. The spray from its rear wheels is distracting, but Joe knows that with 12 miles till the next junction Tess has nowhere to go.

He waits a few moments, then checks his mirror before moving into the second lane. After passing the juggernaut he notices Tess has picked up her speed somewhat and is now a fair distance ahead. A sharp bit of right foot later and he is comfortably back within striking distance.

This happens several times over the next few miles, and a pattern develops of Joe waiting a few moments before charging back up to the back of the Audi, only to retreat again in a concertina fashion. The Eddie Stobart lorry was to be his downfall though. As Joe draws alongside it to pass, he notices a distinct lack of silver Audi in the slow lane ahead. He hits the gas, thinking she had sped off again, but the grim reality quickly hits him as he glances into his mirror and sees the services that the lorry had obscured during his overtaking manoeuvre.

'Damn it, I do not fuckin' believe it.' Joe pulls into the hard shoulder and waits.

Tess draws up to pump 12, switches off the engine and just sits with her head in her hands, bawling her eyes out.

Tap, tap, tap. Someone is at her window, a plump black woman in a 'Welcome Break' uniform. Her wild and crazy hair is tamed only by the 2 inch wide lime green sweatband that grips a tuft of it on the top of her head.

'Are you okay in dere lady? You've been 'ere for a quarter of an hour widout ya movin'.'

Tess tries to lower the window, stabbing the switch with increasing vigour and frustration until she finally realises the ignition is off. She turns the key, depresses the switch and lets Delores, as the nametag informs her, know that she is fine and will be on her way soon.

'Nonsense my girl, park your car up out of dem peoples way an' I'm gonna make you a nice strong cuppa coffee. We can'd 'ave you rollin' around da place all upset an' all can we?' Tess gives a little smile. Then, warmed by Delores's show of compassion, moves the Audi to a parking spot around the side of the building. They sit and talk in the staff room that's hidden behind the counter whilst Eddie, the spotty teenager, attends to the bank of flashing lights and buttons that control the pumps.

* * * * *

Joe checks his watch again. Where on earth could she be? Half an hour has passed since he lost sight of her and he's starting to worry. Is there a commercial entrance at the back of the service area that Tess might have used? Joe scrabbles under the seat in search of his map to see if that might offer any information.

He flicks to page 27, where he traces his finger up the blue stripe of the M1 to locate Toddington services. Unfortunately for Joe, the scale of the map is such that it is impossible to tell. He throws it back into the foot well and lights up another cigarette.

* * * * *

Tess thanks Delores for her sympathetic ear and warming coffee, then makes her way back to the car. She swings around and parks back where she had done previously, but this time with somewhat more composure. Forty-five pounds worth of unleaded later and she's heading back down the slip ramp towards the motorway.

* * * * *

Joe has reached bursting point. He's held it in for far too long and his belly is starting to really ache. He un-clips his seat belt and jogs around to the other side of the car in the now torrential rain.

Unzip. Peeeeeeeeeeeee. Tuck, zippp.

Flash! A silver Audi speeds past in the fast lane.

Flash! Another one identical in the middle lane.

'Fuck, fuck, fuck, fuck, fuck!' Joe scrabbles around the back of the car, slipping and sliding on the wet road, then flumps into the driver's seat. He sparks the car into life and speeds off in hot pursuit. The driving rain makes it nearly impossible to make out the shape of the cars ahead, let alone their number plates.

Two junctions later, one of the silver Audis turn off. Joe decides to follow. It isn't for nearly a mile though, that he manages to get close enough to read the car's registration plate.

It is, of course, the wrong one. Tess is still munching the miles to Nottingham whilst Joe has now resigned himself to turning around and starting his long depressing drive home.

Chapter 20

Nottingham

taking the joke just a little too far...

By midnight I had bounced from bar to bar and drunk myself sober, at least that's what it feels like under the buzz of streetlights that line the main square. This is, of course, providing you presume sober people fall down flights of stairs, trip over dustbins, then vomit on public statues.

Tess calls and I guide her in as best as I can in my pathetic state, shivering amongst my grim concrete surroundings.

Once inside the warmth of her car we cruise the streets for accommodation, eventually finding a Hilton on the outskirts of town. We check in in silence, both of us numb.

Sleep comes almost instantly in the double bed, arm in arm, offering each other comfort and security in the otherwise uncertain lives we now lead.

I wake earlier than I expected and call room service for a pair of full Englishes. The polite but clipped tone of the woman who answers my call informs me that as we had not pre-ordered the night before it would be around ten o'clock before we could be served.

'Wonderful, I'd love a lie in,' I exclaim, but the woman doesn't seem to share my enthusiasm.

'Ten o'clock it is then, sir.' A harsh click informs me the line has gone dead. I roll back into bed and give Tess a long lingering kiss on the lips. This, not surprisingly, wakes her.

'Don't… I need to get my head together. Wake me when breakfast gets here.'

I lie on my side of the bed clutching the duvet, wondering where my life is heading.

Knock knock knock!

I wake with a start.

Knock knock knock!

After taking a moment to register my surroundings, I remember ordering food. Good plan.

I remember wandering around Nottingham talking to complete strangers. Not a good plan. Best of all I remember to put a towel around my waist before I answer the door. Extremely good plan. The waiter dumps the tray of goodies on the desk and leaves swiftly, without even hovering for a tip. I turn to notice Tess's naked body sprawled out on the bed; the poor lad must have been a bit shy!

I can feel the towel rise a little with a sudden rush of blood to the wee soldier. Tess stirs and heads straight for the bathroom.

A gargle, a flush and a bathrobe later, she joins me at the table for fried farmyard.

We check out around half-eleven and head into town. Nottingham has certainly lost its glow of affection in the stark morning's weak sunlight. The white and grey buildings reflect pain and discomfort into my hungover eyes, care of the ale houses that are now innocently serving coffee to the millions of inner city shoppers that have descended in order to buy a chromium toothbrush stand or a bamboo carpet slipper holder from Shabbytat or the like. The melee of bodies is almost unbearable.

We sit and have a 'lovely cup of tea' in a piazza by a park, then decide to go 'full tourist' starting at Nottingham Castle. The usual delights of re-hashed suits of armour and talking mannequins greet us on our tour through the ages, but to be honest I am far more interested in my immediate company than any of my surroundings. Unfortunately though, she seems a little too pre-occupied to enjoy the attention. I find myself standing unnecessarily close, just to breathe the heady smell of her perfume. I walk a few paces behind just to study her figure, and when not doing this I snake my arm around her waist to just feel her body next to mine.

From there we head to the somewhat extortionately priced Robin Hood exhibition, which, I must say he would have been proud of. Daylight robbery 'n' all that. We then flit from restaurant to bar, before Tess finally announces, 'I need to get home; I cannot stand to leave the kids with him any longer.' I know exactly what she means, so agree to return home immediately to sunny Surrey.

Chapter 21

The Test Drive
taking the joke just a little too far...

The rain lashes at us from an angle approaching horizontal, the black and uninviting sky that hangs above us feels as oppressive as an SS uniform in a synagogue.

It's Sunday, March the 19th, 10 a.m. but the light is so sparse the eye could easily fool the brain into thinking it is nearer dusk.

Tess and Ed walk ahead of us, dragging their offspring along the wide soaked pavement as if they were wearing manacles around their ankles. I huddle little Lara to my chest against the belting 30 mph wind as we make our way up London's Cromwell Road towards the extremely impressive, ornately chiselled stone arches that welcome us to the sanctuary of the Natural History Museum.

Once inside, and past the rigmarole of the anti-terrorist searches, we battle our way to the cloakrooms through the mass of humanity that clogs the entrance hall, in order to stash our soggy outer skins.

'Dad, Dad, can we see the T-Rex, Dad, can we please, pleeease, pleeeeease Dad?'

'Of course we can, Brads. We just need to get ourselves a little straight first; where's your sister gone?'

A quick scan of the immediate area reveals she has gone walkabout. My heart rate increases drastically as a flush of heat rises from my now hollow feeling stomach to my throbbing head. Claire is nowhere to be seen, so I grab Brads' hand and drag him at high velocity around the immediate area. I spot Tess walking with her 2 foot high protégé Sarah towards the toilets.

'Lara, have you seen Lara? She's gone missing.' We're jostled by a flock of German tourists, and before I know it Brads has escaped my grip and also made a run for it.

I cannot believe it, here five minutes and I seem to have lost my entire family without even seeing one friggin' dinosaur. Tess returns without Sarah.

'Don't tell me you've lost Sarah now.'

'No, Ed has taken the girls off to see the Diplodocus, any luck with Lara yet?'

'Does it look like it?' I snap, then think better of it and follow it up with, 'No, sorry. I am terrified, can you help me look for them?'

'Them? Have you managed to lose the pair of them now?' I look at her with the best pathetic loser face I can muster, then we split in opposite directions to search. After a couple of minutes that drag like hours, I manage to cover the entire entrance hall and a few of the galleries that adjoin it, but to no avail. I find Tess again but my nerves are shot to pieces.

'I have an idea!' I rush to the security guards at the entrance.

'Have any of you seen a boy and a girl come through here?'

'About 4000 so far this morning, sir, you may find a little more accuracy in your description may aid our memories somewhat though.'

I resist – just – the temptation to grab the nearest blunt instrument and pummel this sarcastic jumped-up police force failure low-life twat into the floor until my energy is spent, and return with a heavily breathed, 'They are both blonde, the boy is four, the girl is two, and they have gone missing.'

'Clothes, sir?'

'Yes of course they are fucking clothed, haven't you seen the weather!' I bark, realising the stupidity of my answer as I do so, but the stress burns me like a branding iron.

'Yes sir, I appreciate they may well be clothed as it is a bit nippy out, but I meant in what fashion are they clothed.'

'Yes, sorry, sorry. I think he was wearing a red football shirt and...' (come on, think, *think)* 'err, she usually wears pink, I suppose. No wait, did she have her red dress on, or was it the light blue cardigan, oh fuck it I don't know, have you seen them or not?'

'I really couldn't say sir, with your vague description it could be any number of them.'

'Oh for fuck's sake!' I throw my eyes up in desperation and turn to head back into the throng, soon bumping into Ed and the girls who are stood next to a rather large tree trunk of a leg bone, looking up.

'It's a Diplodocus!' shrills Becky.

'What?' I quizzically look down at her. She points up at the ceiling. Before me is a 30 foot high dinosaur stretching the entire length of the room. If I have failed to notice a prehistoric skeleton the size of three double-decker buses in the room, I wonder what chance would I possibly have of finding two small children. Whilst looking up at the head of said large herbivore, I notice a cheeky little face in a red football shirt poking over the balcony of the first floor.

'Gotcha!'

I sprint to the stone staircase. Seeing this, Brads obviously assumes it's a game as he then disappears in a flash. I reach the top of the staircase a little short of breath and catch sight of him running off between Cro-Magnon man and a Neanderthal that bears a striking resemblance to Gandhi.

I am in hot pursuit. He ducks under a sabre tooth tiger, then disappears again. I pace the whole floor in search of clues, but none are forthcoming. I glance over the balcony to the floor below in an effort to use my high vantage point to search for Lara. Still no luck.

Half an hour passes, and I am now frantic. I have sprinted through the entire museum, I am sweating like a rapist and my lungs are on fire. I collapse on the floor next to a pillar on the second floor, amongst a mock Iron Age village.

I hear giggling.

'Those little buggers, where on earth are they?' I leap to my feet and rush from one mud hut to another, upending wooden beds and tables as I go. I can still hear giggling.

I stand very still and listen, straining my ear in an effort to ascertain from where it is coming. I then walk slowly towards the noise. A pair of Swedish students drift past, talking loudly with animated hand gestures. I turn and snarl at them, 'Will you shut up, I'm trying to listen!' They move away both swiftly and silently, repeatedly glancing over their shoulders. The giggling is now intermingled with 'Ssshhh!!!' noises from Brads, which only serves to fuel Lara's laughter. Eventually I see a red reflection on the polished grey stone floor, which I presume is Brads' football shirt, under an upturned circular wicker boat. I grab the edge of the boat and spin it over. Lo and behold the pair of them are sat cross-legged in the middle, laughing uncontrollably.

'What on earth are you playing at? We've been looking for you three for nearly an hour,' the voice behind me demands. It's Claire. Elation, anger, relief and shock all rush through my body at once, confusing my tiny mind and rendering it incapable of forming any kind of answer.

'We've been waiting to go and get some lunch, Ed's kids have gotten grouchy and I'm not exactly impressed. Call yourself a father? Look at Brads and Lara, they're starving.'

With that, she scoops Lara up and heads off towards the restaurant.

'Bit close for comfort,' I think to myself as I take Brads by the hand and meander down the corridor after Claire.

Stepping out of the lift into the atrium that is home to the restaurant queue, I'm immediately faced with a mass of tourists, all eager to devour as much grub as is available. Ed, Tess and Claire are all standing near the back. Brads and Lara are soon being entertained by Becky, and Sarah is asleep on Tess's shoulder.

'Fuck this queuing bollocks, I'm starving,' states Ed, taking Becky by the hand as he stomps to the front of the queue. They disappear out of sight around a corner and never return. Tess shrugs, and then offers, 'Once his blood sugar levels drop there's no stopping him. Becky's the same.'

I nearly add that Claire must suffer likewise, but thought better of it as she's well within earshot.

By the time I sit down, on a 30 quid lighter wallet I hasten to add, Ed and Becky are on desert at a table near the servery. Claire has opted to sit with them, whilst I share with Tess and the rest of the kids at a large table on the back wall.

Claire eats quickly, then saunters off with Ed. Becky joins us with the remains of a large slice of chocolate cake, that stains both her teeth and cheeks as she plods her way through it.

So now the test drive begins; you didn't think it was a car, did you? Once stuffed full of lasagne, chips, hot dogs, coke and cake, the blended families of Hayes and Black move into the next phase of furthering their knowledge of the evolutionary path of mankind. In other words, we burp and leave the refectory, then drift from hall to hall laughing, joking and losing ourselves in the wonder of being one big happy family.

Lara rides on Becky's back like a rucksack and insists on pointing out all the really important stuff like dung beetles, dodos and sharks whilst Brads runs about the place with a smile so bright it could illuminate the world. Baby Sarah just giggles and coos at all the things she can't possibly understand. It was a perfect afternoon.

By four o'clock we find ourselves in the cafeteria on the ground floor for some tea and biccies. Once finished, an announcement over the PA system informs us that the museum is to close in ten minutes.

We make our way to the cloakroom to retrieve our jackets, where, upon doing so I note that both Ed and Claire's have already been taken, apparently some time earlier. We wait for them in the foyer as long as we can, but at five o'clock the security guards grow increasingly impatient and continually ask us to move outside.

We rush the kids through the rain to Claire's car, a Golf GTI, and cram ourselves in. But with two adults and four kids there just aren't enough seat belts to go round. I make a mental note to buy a car large enough to adequately house all of our children with the upcoming migration of nests in mind as the rain pelts ever harder, thumping on the sunroof like a Tommy gun. Not only that, but by the look of the sky we are about to be joined by a chorus of thunder and lightning. The murmurs are distant, but growing closer by the second.

The kids grow restless, and start to become agitated. I am suddenly aware through the dank musty smell of drenched clothes of a drip, drip, drip on my shoulder. The sunroof is leaking. Not only on me, but also on Tess's lap. Great.

The tension expands within the airtight cabin to bursting point. Brad begins bickering with Becky. This swiftly develops into poking and pushing, which in turn provokes a reaction of scratching and pinching, before exploding into a ball of punching, thumping, kicking and screaming. Sarah, in the middle of it, begins to ball her eyes out and Lara is now doing her best to climb over the front seat in order to avoid the conflict altogether. This proves disastrous, a misplaced jab from Brad's finger to Becky's ribs lands squarely in Lara's eye and all hell breaks loose.

The mayhem subsides after a few moments, with the promise of impending sweets if everyone behaves, but I have the distinct feeling it won't last. We are just preparing to set off when in the distance I can vaguely make out through the sodden windscreen Ed and Claire, who are heading our way, sharing an umbrella whilst playing the fool and splashing each other in the puddles.

'Test drive over,' I mutter, then resign myself to the fact that Claire has returned to drag my life back down to where it was this morning. Bummer.

Chapter 22

Starbucks Revisited

taking the joke just a little too far...

Joe Soap stubs his cigarette in the ashtray that makes the centrepiece of the low glass coffee table.

'Well, I did as you asked, but to be honest dere was nothin'' you might call kinda incriminating, as such.'

'Go on.' Ed listens intently.

'Well, I caught up witchyou guys as you entered d'museum. Jeeessshhh what a klutz this Hazy character is, short-sighted like a bat in d'midday sun. I mean, Jeesh, he wasn't standing 3 ft from his kids when he goes and gives dis Oscar winning performance as d'distraught father whose had his gaddamned kids abducted. He runs around d'place all outta control, tearin' his hair out 'n' stressin' big time. He first asks your wife as she is taking one of your kids to the latrine. Then, as you know, he later moves on to ask you a few questions by the Diplodocus. From dere, I must admit, he went a little schitz on me, running all over. I found it easier to track d'kids, as I knew he'd find 'em, eventually. I struck lucky on d'second floor about a half an hour later. Brads and...err, Laura, is it?'

'Lara,' Ed corrects.

'Lara, sorry. Brads and Lara are just about to disappear down d'fire escape when I intervene and suggest dey go hide under an upturned boat, not 10 ft from where their father was wearily looking for dem. Then this broad, Claire, that you are…err…'

'And?' Ed sternly interrupts.

'Yeah this broad Claire enters d'picture and lets rip at dis Hazy character, full guns blazing if you get my drift.'

Ed nods and takes a sip from his espresso.

'Anyways, after I follow dem to d'restaurant they do a split. Again, as you knows, because you was wid her.'

Ed sparks a cigarette, draws a deep lung of death, then glugs the remains of his coffee as the smoke releases slowly from his nose. Joe does likewise.

'So dis Hazy and your wife are getting all communal with the kids at d'same table, then take off to see the rest o' d'exhibits. A tail was easy, what wid all the kids in tow, and I saw nut'n of interest until dey all squashed into a small VW off d'Gloucester Road.'

'What, is that it? Is there nothing else you can give me to nail this bastard?'

'Nada.'

Ed looks agitated.

'This is bollocks, I'm paying you good money to get an angle on Hazy and all you can come up with is this shit?'

'Ed, I can't tell you shit he ain't doin', I'm tellin' ya what I saw, straight up.'

'This is fucking bollocks,' Ed says as he stands, throwing eight £50 notes onto the table, as Joe thinks better of mentioning his cock-up on the motorway.

'You watch them like a hawk, you understand, like a fucking hawk.'

Chapter 23

Brooklands

taking the joke just a little too far...

As Tess's birthday rapidly approaches, I thankfully manage to blag the day off. We decide to meet for lunch at one of our usual haunts, and I hand her her present.

She loves it, of course. It's a silver Gucci watch, square faced with a single, but not insubstantial clear crystal rock marking the 12. This is complimented by a pink leather strap, with the clasp also sporting a few shiny diamonds. Said timepiece has set me back no less than two and a half grand, but she's worth every penny, and a little more.

The little more turned out to be a whole lot more when I would eventually get the finance agreement through the post a month or so later, sent to my mum's of course. What do you think I am, stupid?

Best not answer that.

She's to have a dinner party in celebration at the old Brooklands museum. This has been arranged well in advance, but true to form, Claire pulls a flanker on me at the last minute.

'We've got friends coming over tonight, so any notions you may have had about seeing your wanker mates at the museum have been put on ice, so don't go disappearing.'

Fanfuckingtastic. I quickly thumb a text message to Tess, then ring Gandhi to see if he and his missus would skip the Brooklands do and bail me out at home.

Sorted.

Ten to eight and Gandhi turns up with his missus, Jane, just in time for cocktails. Claire's buddies have shown up early, and are digging in to my scotch collection without permission.

'Gandhi and Jane, let me introduce Terry and Emma.'

'Hi.'

'Hi,' is the extent of their conversation, things are already that obviously tense. My mobile bleeps, it's a text from Patrick.

We continue the small talk for a while, and then move into the dining room for the feast. My phone bleeps again, it's Patrick again.

'WHAT THE FUCK R U UP 2, GIZ A CALL.' I ignore it and proceed with the evening. Around eleven o'clock my mobile springs to life with its 'Always Look on the Bright Side of Life' Month Python ring tone.

'PATRICK MOBILE' the display informs me. I press the little floating green phone symbol to instantly connect me.

'You sly old fucker,' he says.

'What, what on earth are you talking about?' I retort.

'Oooo, the sheriff has got to come and have a word with you, my boy. Been out Robin' hood, or humpin' good I wonder?'

'What the fuck are you on about?'

'Oh I think you know what I mean, taking married women out on the razz on a Friday night, followed by a quiet night in a hotel nearby for a little recuperation, yeah right. You dirty old bastard, you've been shagging her rotten for ages.'

I really don't need this at the dinner table, especially with Claire and her buddies within earshot.

'Where are you?' I ask.

'At the museum with your girlfriend and her husband…you remember, the bloke for whom you were best man.'

This throws me momentarily. I try to imagine them all wearing black tie, surrounded by dinosaurs, then remember it's the motor museum they are at, not the Natural History.

'No, I mean what part of the museum, you twat.'
'The gents', why?'
'Use your fucking brain.'
I hang up, then switch the phone to silent.

* * * * *

Back at the museum…
Patrick tuts, flips his phone shut, then checks himself in the mirror before returning to the party.

The third cubicle from the end then swings open and out walks Sully.

* * * * *

Back home…
Starters consumed, and it's time to move on. The rack of lamb has been in for almost an hour. Despite regular protests that it must be well and truly dead by now, Claire had decided that it needed a further half-hour to 'crisp it off'. 'Decifuckingmate it' I would have said, but ho hum, I'm only the stupid husband, so a further half-hour it gets.

I carve the carcass a full hour later, as the spuds had somehow been overlooked and the broccoli was still stood in stone cold water. Too many cooks maybe? Just no sober ones, more like. We eat – or chew to death should I say – the 'rock of lamb' dinner, and as we do so my phone repeatedly vibrates with several missed calls.

Just as desert is served, my favourite, a 'Betty Crocker' vanilla sponge cake with chocolate frosting, the house phone springs to life.

I quickly stand to answer it, but Claire beats me to it. I snatch it from her grasp, much to her disgust, and listen intently.

'You trying to avoid me?' come Patrick's dulcet tones.

'No, we're just eating dinner, can't this wait?'

'Time rests not for the wicked,' he retorts.

'Fuck off, Patrick, you self-righteous twat.' I hang up, but a moment later the phone rings again.

'Just leave it, it's Patrick and he's out of his mind,' I say, but with silence having fallen on the table, the shrill of the phone invades the atmosphere like the Lancaster bombers surrounding the caller.

'I'll just get that, it may be important,' states Claire as she rises from the table to answer it.

'No, I insist,' as we both race to the phone. Only by me yanking the flex from the wall do I silence it as Claire answers it.

'What the fuck are you doing?' she demands.

'Sorry, it was ruining the evening,' I say pathetically. She scowls at me and we both sit back down.

'Come on, you two, put your toys back in the pram and behave yourselves... Easter tomorrow,' Gandhi says, as if this makes everything alright.

* * * * *

Back at Brooklands...
Things were going just as badly. Ed is going into hyper-drive with the amount of coke he's been stuffing up his nose, also drinking vodka and orange with far more emphasis on the vodka, from pint glasses.

Tess is getting ever friendlier with Patrick, and noticing this, Ed strides across the dance floor to where they are dancing, only to plant a full blown five knuckle welcome onto Patrick's nose, followed by a slap around the face for Tess.

Patrick's nose explodes in a fountain of claret as his knees buckle with shock. He lands in a clump on the floor. Tess turns her head and simply looks humiliated. She leaves the room at a brisk pace, and fishes in her handbag for her mobile.

Once outside in the crisp sobering air, she repeatedly dials my number, but without success.

Then she tries the house phone, only to find the same, and eventually gives up. She takes refuge in the dark doorway to one of the old hangars. After a short while Patrick appears with Sully. They seem to be arguing, but Tess is just too far away to make it out. Sully curses and swears at Patrick, then returns inside. Patrick then dials several phone numbers without success, but finally one gets through...

* * * * * *

Claire's mobile begins to ring in the kitchen. Fortunately I am stood next to it, and 'accidentally' nudge it into the sink full of washing up. It warbles to its death as it disappears from view through the murk of the lamb fat and washing up foam below.

Chapter 24

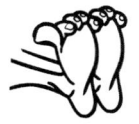

The Plot

taking the joke just a little too far...

In the ensuing couple of weeks, Patrick drops off the radar. He obviously regrets his words, so decides to keep out of striking distance for a while. Ed is avoiding me, and Tess will only talk to me if there are other people around. She's also stopped answering her phone.

What could I have possibly done?

Best not answer that one either.

We have become extremely busy at work, as the first round of the championship is due to commence the coming weekend at Le Mans. The trucks are loaded by Tuesday evening and we head out towards Dover before six in the evening. I take command in the driver's seat of one of them, with Beaker as co-pilot and Ron in the window seat, whilst Gandhi drives the other truck housing Glynn and Sully.

Once on board the ferry, we dine care of Harry Ramsden, and drink care of a Belgian bird called Stella.

The short boat ride is over in a flash and we hit the 'N' roads just outside Calais. Ron hops into the back to grab some sleep, and I wait until I can hear his snoring before I begin relaying my plan to Beaker.

'Who is the most solid, reliable, dependable person you know? The kind of person that would always put himself out to help, no questions, just get on with it no matter what?'

'Err, you I guess, Hazy, as it's you that's asking. Is this a trick question?'

'No. Why did you just answer my question with a question?'

'I didn't, why are you asking me?'

'See, you're doing it again.'

'How could I be?'

'And again! Can you stop asking fucking questions?'

'Why, what's wrong with questions?'

'STOP IT YOU FUCKING TWAT AND LISTEN!'

'Why's that then?'

'Shut the fuck up and I'll tell you.'

Beaker makes an overanimated gesture of zipping his mouth shut.

'Right, let's start again – who is the most solid, reliable, dependable person you know, the kind of person that would always put himself out to help, no questions, just get on with it no matter what?'

'You're asking questions again, that's not fair.'

'Oh I give up!' I say, exasperated, and stare out into the blackness in front of us.

'Gandhi.'

'Where?' replies Beaker.

'No you fucking idiot, Gandhi is the most solid reliable dependable person we know. He would, would he not, come and collect you at four o'clock in the morning on a damp Tuesday if your car had broken down on the M6.'

'Yeah, I suppose so,' mumbles Beaker in response.

'He would also, I think you will agree, lend you a hand to do a really shitty job like re-lining a cesspit, or replacing a broken sewer pipe.'

'Yes, yes, yes. Where on earth are you going with this, Hazy?'

'Remember, no questions,' I say, holding a finger up like a school teacher. Beaker throws his eyes up and shoves his foot on the dash as he reclines in the seat, baseball cap now lowered over his eyes.

'We both know that to say he likes a bit of a drink is a somewhat mammoth understatement. Admittedly you make him look like a complete amateur, but he does possess certain fishlike qualities.'

'Ooooi, watch it you,' Beaker returns with a wry grin.

'Do you think,' I continue, 'a man of his amazing credentials, and given a liberal lubricating with some of the golden throat charm, may be persuaded, given the correct circumstances, of course, to help you dispose of a dead body?'

Beaker bolts upright, sending his baseball cap flying. He glares at me in confused disbelief at what his ears have just witnessed.

'A body as in…a…dead…body?'

'There you go, asking questions again,' I dryly retort.

'What do you fucking expect, you tosser, you've just asked me to be an accomplice to disposing of a dead fucking body, and not only happy with that, you want to drag Gandhi down with me. All this whilst you, no doubt, keep a squeaky clean 100-yard distance from the whole fiasco. Are you fucking mental or something? In fact, more to the point, who the fuck have you killed?'

'Robert De Nero.'

Beaker is stunned into complete silence; he sits in the cab drawing long controlled breaths as the beads of sweat roll swiftly down his forehead. The look of shock on his face is enough to scare Scooby Doo.

'Listen,' I say, 'Calm down and breathe normally. It's a prank I have been working on.'

'You fucking tosser, you really had me going there.'

A smile grows its way across my face as I continue, 'Last time I was at the studios seeing my Uncle Jack (best ploy I thought) I noticed a mannequin of Robert De Niro hanging from the rafters above where he and Tess were working on some animatronic penguins. Said body was from a Frankenstein movie, so it was all bloody and gruesome. It looked as if it had been run over or something. This image, as you can imagine, set the old grey cogs whirring into overload. I've come up with a stonking idea, but I need your help.'

'Go on,' says Beaker.

'All right, but you must swear to me you won't mention this to anyone.' Beaker nods. 'Right, here's the plan: I have already asked Little Jack if I could borrow De Niro for this gag, but he turned me down flat. He said my Uncle Jack would fire him for less, and despite my best assurances he was having none of it. This leaves us with Tess; she's the only other person I know with a set of keys to the workshop. I gave her a brief rundown and she says she's in. I've yet to firm up a day of execution with Tess, but it will run something like this:

'We will no doubt be able to slope off slightly early after work, even if we have to stay till five-thirty it shouldn't be a drama. I will have already pinched Gandhi's car keys at lunchtime to ensure I keep full control.

'After a quick staged search for said keys I will drag him off to the Crown for a few of jars to get him warmed up, hopefully keeping him there for a couple of hours to make sure he's well on his way. I will then drop him home and let Jane force feed him a further six or so cans, not that he will need much forcing. Again, she's in on the prank and is more than willing to stitch him up in the name of a good laugh.

'Tess reckons the Jacks will have left the building by seven, so we should be safe to head over there by eight. We will pick up your car and head to the studios.'

'My car, what on earth do you want to use that rusty piece of shit for?'

'Exactly, your rusty piece of shit is exactly what we need. Anyway, do you ever stop asking questions?'

'Sorry, go on.'

'So we dump your dented and blood-spattered car in the lane around the back of the studios and scale the chain-link fence.'

'Whoa, whoa, whoa, hang on a minute. My Volvo doesn't have a mark on it, what's all this blood and dents talk?'

'Fuck off, Beaker, it's a shitter, you said so yourself not two seconds ago. How much did you pay for it?'

'That's not the point.'

'Come on, how much does it owe you?'

Beaker mumbles a figure into his chest.

'Sorry, I didn't quite catch that.'

He mumbles again, a little louder but still inaudibly over the roar of the tyres.

'Come on, speak up, man,' I demand.

'Alright, 250 quid,' he says in a raised voice, resigning himself to the fact I won't let it go.

'Right, like I said, it's a shitter.'

'It still doesn't have any dents in it.'

'It will have, dear boy, but just one to corroborate your story.'

'What the fuck are you on about, find somebody else's car. I'm losing interest in this by the second.'

'I will give you 100 quid to fix the dent afterwards.'

'No, no fucking way, the bodywork is spotless.'

'What about the dent you put in the rear quarter when you punted the flowerpot outside the Crown last week?'

Beaker looks sheepishly at the floor then offers, 'Not unless you fix the dodgy rear light as well then.'

'Fuck it, all right. I'll fix the dodgy rear light as well,' I say, 'now do we have a deal?'

'Yeah, s'pose so, this had better be worth it.'

I lean across, holding the steering wheel with my knee, and with a shake of hands our fate is sealed.

'Right,' I start, 'so we make our way to the prosthetics department to meet Tess, who should be there waiting for us. We then proceed through the rigging store and across the covered courtyard that houses the tropical plants. This in turn leads us to the gun shop. We walk along the alley next to it, which brings us out next to the rear entrance of the main special effects building. Tess will have pocketed the key to the back door at the end of her working day, therefore ensuring us access to the room that houses Mr De Niro's body without a single security camera laying eyes on us.'

'So we are kidnapping Robert De Niro. Are you fucking mad, we could all go to prison for that.' Beaker appears to be regretting the deal already, but I continue undeterred.

'Calm down will you, one cannot be prosecuted for kidnapping a mannequin, we are simply borrowing him.'

'What about breaking and entering then, I don't want that on my rap sheet thank you very much.'

'Trust me. We will not be breaking and entering. We have a key, remember. And if the shit does hit the fan, we will have Tess with us who is perfectly entitled to be there. She might get a bollocking from Uncle Jack, but that's about it so don't worry, I've got everything sorted.'

'You still haven't told me about the blood.'

'I'm just coming to that, my friend; have some patience.' With that a motorway service station looms into view. Intermittent amber flashing illuminates our faces as I head for the fluorescently lit forecourt in order to recharge both the fuel tank and our caffeine levels.

Ron stirs as the litres of diesel flow into the tank below him. He appears out of the side door of the truck and stretches with a yawn and a little shiver.

'What time is it?'

'One o'clock,' I reply. Ron then wanders towards the main building for a little hunting and gathering.

Once brimmed, I follow and do likewise. The vastness of choice at French motorway service stations never ceases to amaze me. The number of combinations of ham and cheese they manage to stuff into baguettes, morning rolls, croissants, sandwiches, toasties, croque monseurs, pizza breads, paninis, and even more friggin' bread-ettes is astounding. I wonder if the French would starve if they ever ran out of pigs and cows. Probably not, come to think of it, as there's always goats' cheese, and I doubt they would ever run out of frogs or snails. Anyway, I try to dispose of the thought of a goats' cheese and snail tart with a side order of frog's legs, and get on with selecting my midnight feast.

Gandhi and the other crew also stop for diesel. After a quick banter we hit the road again.

This time out we play follow the leader as the other blue and silver Vertex truck throws up a fine mist of spray from the light rain shower we have just had. Ron is perched between us now, and devours two hot dogs, with the emphasis on dog I fear, a tin of Coke and two bags of crisps. After a belch of truly record-breaking volume and duration he proceeds to stuff an entire Snickers bar into his mouth, chewing only twice before swallowing. Another belch, another yawn, and he disappears into the back again for some more shut-eye.

Beaker gets comfortable again, then enquires, 'So, go on then, tell us more…'

He's on the hook! I put my finger to my lips to silence him and wait until I can hear snoring from the back…

'Right, where were we?'

'Abducting Robert De Niro,' Beaker answers.

'Right, we sneak the body out of the studios and dump it into the boot of your car. There will be a roll of carpet in the back, in which we can wrap De Niro, so as Gandhi can't get too close a look. Tess will then walk out of the front gate, as usual, and head towards the off-site car park. She gets into her car and heads home. We then lie low for a couple of hours, and at around eleven we head towards Gandhi's place.

Jane is set to put a sleeping pill into one of his beers, then put all the clocks forward a few hours as soon as he nods off. This way he will be a bit dozy and think it's the middle of the night.

As we enter Gandhi's road, we can pause to scuff the front wing of your car along the inner wall of the railway bridge, then I will produce the small bottle of blood that I will have obtained earlier from the butcher's. Don't worry, I used to go to school with one of the lads that works there so we should be sorted on that. Said claret will then be liberally splattered over the bonnet and windscreen to add to the realism.

I will then get a bottle of scotch and douse your shirt in it. You will need to take a couple of swigs yourself to get it on your breath, but only, and I repeat ONLY a couple of swigs for effect. I can't have you reeling around pissed or you will be a liability. Understand?'

No reply.

'Understand?' I reiterate.

'Yeah, I suppose so.'

'Anyway, I will then jump into the back seat with a camcorder and film the whole event.'

'What event is that?'

'The massive test of loyalty and conscience we are going to give Mr Gandhi.'

'Oh, okay.'

'You will then drive up to his front door, parking deliberately haphazardly, and leaving an indicator on with the engine still running. Then, carrying a shovel you will charge up to his front door, and in a fake drunken stupor, describe to him the horrendous accident you have just had, running over and killing an innocent bystander. You need to convince him that he has to help you bury the body so as to dispose of the evidence. Drag him, if you must, out into the road and show him the corpse in the boot. He is bound to believe you, and it would be great to see if in his own drunk and confused state he is willing to help you dispose of a dead body. His reaction will be priceless and I will have it all on film. We can rip the piss out of him for years to come on this one. See, I told you I'd get the bastard back for the sodding Lotto gag!'

Beaker's grin has grown from ear to ear.

'You are an evil bastard, but I do love your sick sense of humour.'

He gives me five and we continue chatting about the fine details until we eventually reach the circuit.

Chapter 25

Le Mans

taking the joke just a little too far...

In the early hours of Wednesday morning, the welcome sight of a vastly illuminated Le Mans circuit looms into view. Once in the paddock I manoeuvre the truck so as the rear roller-shutter door is directly opposite the roller-shutter of pit number six, which is to be our home for the next few days.

The rest of the lads in the other truck draw up in front of us. Gradually we all emerge from our varying states of near sleep to begin the build-up of our camp. The vast marquee is erected for the all important sponsor's hospitality, and the catering equipment is then nestled away out of sight behind a partition wall. This whole caper takes the crew a good couple of hours to complete, so by the time 4 a.m. rolls around we are all ready to hit the hay. The unloading of the bikes and myriad of spares can wait until morning.

I roll into my bunk, chilled to the bone, as the spring warmth that was promised by the weak daytime sunshine has certainly ebbed away, only to offer a misty and frost covered morning in replacement.

Seven o'clock beckons, the crew are awake and I am last to rise. We breakfast on croissants and jam, with a little crispy bacon and cheese on the side, before unloading the bikes and furnishing the pit garage. The walls are suddenly awash with all manner of tools, stands, instruments and computerised wizardry. An Aladdin's cave of techno-mechanical marvels, all in the name of a faster lap time.

Pit lane opens at midday for practice. No drama, no pressure, just turn a few laps and get some data. How wrong.

Enter Christiano Migliorini of Naples. The team's newest, brightest and most expensive star is to be fielded alongside the team regulars, Dave and Richard, the team's riders from last season. In true Latin temperament, however, by first knockings this morning he has managed to irritate half the paddock by parking his hotel sized motorhome so obnoxiously as to achieve no less than 12 complaints to the organiser's office before 10 a.m.

He then, after having an argument with his stunning 'Miss Brazil finalist' girlfriend, managed to twist his ankle whilst descending the steps of said motor hotel, causing a bit of a swell and a sprain. The consequence being that he, after waving his overly legal and extremely complicated contract under Stevo's nose, was refusing to ride.

This obviously left us a rider short. After a swift team meeting in the circuit cafe over 'road-tar' consistency espressos, it was decided that I was to ride.

I had, after all, done some pre-season testing in the saddle, and was the only other member of the team to hold the required F I M international licence, having raced myself in a privateer team only two years previously.

We organise the crew so Gandhi steps up to front wheel changes, Beaker rears, and the rest of the team as they were. Beaker's position of general mechanic is now open to negotiation with the rest of the crew, so we all just agree to muck in.

Dave, the number one rider, is out first. He pits after ten laps for some minor adjustments and is back on circuit within minutes. He runs for a further 50 minutes at race pace, then pits for a rider change.

Glynn plugs in and downloads as Richard hops on. We practice a front and rear wheel change as we are now on slightly unfamiliar ground staff-wise, but everything falls into place with Rich back out on circuit within a minute.

With data analysed and tyre wear gauged, Rich is left to lap for 35 minutes before the signaller shows him the 'IN' board. He acknowledges with a nod as he howls past at over 100 mph, then charges up pit lane a lap later.

Another wheel change practiced and this time a new set of front brake pads to bed in. This means six laps and in again. The team do this to match the pads to the discs, so as they are ready to use, as the inevitable wear and tear destroys them after only a few hours' racing. Six laps later Rich pits again and the bedded pads are whipped out in lieu of another fresh set. This process is repeated twice more, then it's my turn.

I stand in the warmth of the sun futilely trying to bring my body up to a temperature where it won't shiver quite so much. When stamping my feet and rubbing my arms appear to have no effect whatsoever, I resign myself to the fact it must be just a case of nerves more than temperature. My dry mouth and constant clock watching seem to confirm this, so I simply resign myself to shivering. With eyes closed I try to recount my way around the circuit over and over again, but there seem to be some gaps in my memory. Not a good plan when you are about to be let loose on a quarter of a million pounds worth of race bike, with 50 other demented hooligans doing likewise that would as soon kill you as look at you.

The final 'IN' board is hung over pit wall to a streak of blue and silver, signalling only another two minutes' mental preparation before I'm chin down and all guns blazing. Gandhi, with a raised eyebrow and a crooked smile, and Beaker both arrive at my side clutching their respective wheels. Steam rises from the shiny new slicks into the cold air, showing they have just been peeled from their baking hot tyre warmers.

Rich appears in what seems like only seconds. The crew fly into action with twirling spanners and galloping fuel. The brake pads are changed again, confirmed by Stevo who grabs my arm and shouts, barley audibly, over the raucous sound of whizzing air tools and revving engines, 'Pads, you're on new pads and rubber, so go easy for a couple of laps.'

'I'm incapable of doing anything other than taking it easy with the mess my brain's in at the moment,' I silently think as I nod my head behind the black Perspex visor of my helmet. Stevo slaps me on the back just a little too hard which sends me careering towards the bike, Ron retracts the fuel filler, working spectacularly I may add, as I mount up and stab the starter.

A whirr and a clunk follow as I toe the bike into gear, then I'm cruising up the pit lane towards the exit onto the circuit at the mandatory 30 mph.

Once I clear the shelter of pit wall, the twistgrip is opened fully, releasing 180 brake horsepower to the rear tyre that squirms and spins in protest, then grips to cause the front wheel to rise violently, taking me quite by surprise. I feather the throttle to keep it in some semblance of control and snick up another gear to mellow the power hit. NEEEEEOOOOOWWWW... NEEEEEOOOOOWWWW. Two flashes of colour blast past me in close formation, almost brushing my elbow as they disappear around the upcoming corner at a seemingly impossible velocity.

I feel lost and vulnerable as I try to drag my unwilling brain from its depressive state into 'fit and feisty racing superstar' mode as I negotiate the vaguely familiar racetrack.

'Sort your shit out! Concentrate, you twat!' I shout inside my crash helmet, then shake my head in an effort to clear it.

The corners come and go, and within a handful of laps I'm shown the 'IN' board.

'Oh fuck, I can't have been riding that badly, could I? That's it, I'm fired I know it, lapping at the pace of a granddad has cost me my job. Fuck it.'

A swift cool-down lap and I pull into pit lane, spotting Stevo, with arms folded across his chest, waiting outside our pit amongst a sea of mechanics to deliver the bad news.

The slow trawl towards the pit is agonising, my head awash with paranoia. My momentum ceases as I arrive at the line marked outside our garage, within seconds a fresh set of brake pads are thrown in, and Stevo leans in towards me. 'Six laps to bed new pads, not eight. I should *not* have to remind *you* of that as you're supposed to be the fucking head mechanic. Your lap times are improving so stay out for the rest of the session and get some practice.'

I find my rhythm faster this time, and 20 minutes later I'm lapping at a respectable, if not record breaking pace.

By mid-session I feel we need to make some adjustments to the handling. I pit with 20 minutes of the session left and bark my muffled instructions to Gandhi through the chin piece of my crash helmet, 'A coupe of clicks less on the rebound damping, and give me five mill extra ride height on the rear.'

A twirl of spanners ensue, and I am out again within five long minutes. The adjustments seem to have helped, so I lap for a further ten minutes, then pit again to experiment further.

'Give me three mill more offset at the front, as I could still do with a little more turn in at the end of the main straight.'

This, it transpires, was a bad move. The once precise steering surgical instrument has now become a liability, shaking its head angrily as the balance has been tipped a little too far. I pit again with five minutes left in the session to change back to where we were.

I snatch the last couple of laps in my session to finish the day fourth fastest, reasonable I suppose as we were bedding pads and just generally setting things up. Stevo seems up-beat, so the team retire a happy clan.

Thursday morning arrives a little too swiftly for my liking. I had spent a couple of hours in the bar of a neighbouring hotel, in order to avoid any prying eyes that may report me for drinking on duty, as it were, and greet the dawn with a little less enthusiasm than the sunset a few hours earlier. The day is spent tyre testing and bedding in the qualifying brake pads. These are a softer compound that give, as many condom packets advertise, more performance with improved feel. The downside (which said condom packet would certainly not want to advertise) is greatly reduced longevity.

The Dunlop rep appears at eleven o'clock to take our order for race tyres. Dave, Rich and I gather in Stevo's office along with Glynn and Mr Dunlop for a swift powwow on available compounds to test throughout the remainder of sessions.

With tyre compounds chosen for slick, intermediate and wet tyres we call it a day at half-four and prepare the bike for this evening's night qualifying.

I hate night qualifying, plain and simple. Why on earth would any sane human being charge around a racetrack risking life and limb when they can't even see as far as the next corner? Buggered if I know either. It's all down to mathematics, see. As any great mathematician will proudly tell you, life, the universe and everything is all just a case of putting the right numbers in the right sequence. This is of course true when racing motorcycles. We use a system of counting our way around a circuit, to have a 'map' as it were for the track in our heads. During daylight laps I will cross the start/finish line and start my own mental clock:

One…two…three…four… Brake, turn, power.

One…two…three… Brake, turn, power.

One…two… Turn, power, chicane.

One…two…three…four…five…six… (long straight this one, isn't it!) …seven… Brake like fuck!!!!!!

You get the idea.

The sun drops from view, and I make some final preparations for my session. Thankfully it's still dry, despite a little low cloud cover, but I'm sure it's nowt to worry about. Rich is first out, posting a second fastest time on only his eighth lap, then pits after his half-hour session finishes to swap with Dave, who's out second.

By the time Dave re-appears in pit lane the clouds look as if they've dropped to 80 ft and have grown dark and menacing. I mount up, thumb the starter and head out on track.

A feeling of isolation surrounds me as I charge through the night, tucked neatly behind the low windscreen watching the thousands of insects, momentarily illuminated by the powerful halogen headlights, before exploding on the Perspex bubble in front of me. It's like a scene from *Star Wars* as the Millennium Falcon goes into hyper-drive:

…six…seven… Brake.

I cross the line for the umpteenth time and will my session to end.

… Brake, turn, power.

One…two…three… Rain… Slick… Tyres!!!

…four…six…three…Shit! Brake, brake harder…tarmac…slide…gravel…sky…grass…sky…grass…darkness…motionless…medic.

I come around in the back of an ambulance. The French doctor has a syringe in the crook of my elbow and is pushing some treacle-consistency fluid into my arm. He smiles in a way I find less comforting than his previously blank expression so I lie back and close my eyes again.

* * * * *

Friday.

I wake around ten, and pad to the bathroom of my hotel suite. The mirror offers me no indication as to why my head thumps so much, but slowly my mind registers the previous evening's crash. I remember being discharged from the medical centre, but still have no recollection of my journey back to the hotel. After a couple of Aspirins and some croissants, care of room service, I catch a cab back to the circuit.

'Sorry Stevo, I don't quite know what happened. I lost count, then next thing I know I've got Doctor Death pumping shit into my arm.'

'Don't sweat, Hazy, the bike in front of you burst its radiator and took half the field down. Slicks don't perform well on a soaked track as you well know. The good news is that both Team Pace and Abacus both went down as well, so it didn't alter the standings drastically. Get some fluids down you and get ready to go out first after lunch, we have a race to win.'

I agree, grudgingly, as I'm still feeling a little shaky, and make my way to the back of the pit garage where I find Cassie, backlit by the midday sun, as she stands framed in the doorway.

'I don't think anyone has ever looked more like an angel, Miss Cass, than you do. Take me out the back and beat me up, right here, right now.'

'If I didn't know you better, Mister Hayes, I may well have taken that the wrong way. See me in my tent in five minutes,' she replies with a smile.

I hobble over to her awning and lie face-down on the massage table, my head finding the hole just a little too small as the fluff from its towelling cover irritates my nose. Within moments of Cassie's hands gliding over my strained muscles, relief is secreted in a numb buzz over my entire body. I lie in silence, falling into a distant trance as my pain seems to literally melt away into the table below.

I stumble, slightly dazed, back into the pit garage an hour later. The bike is fuelled and ready to go, the pit a blur of activity as the crew make their final preparations for the last qualifying session. I swing my leg over the saddle, carefully press the starter button, clunk it into first gear and head out down pit lane.

After a somewhat rusty start, I find my form and we finish the day's qualifying in third spot on the grid. Fabulous! And certainly not bad for two 'proper' riders and a mechanic in the seat.

The teams ahead of us are the French squad of Team Pace, defending their honour in their homeland, and Abacus, a top-level Chinese team that employs European riders on Japanese machinery. A formidable force of affluent efficiency.

* * * * *

Saturday morning pierces its way through the hotel room's curtains at around 6 a.m., forcing me from my cosy dream-filled slumber into the harsh brutality of the real world. Today is, of course, race day, and the nerves never get any easier. After a swift visit to the bathroom, my stomach still churns like a cement mixer with half a load of readymix on board. I shower and shave, then check my gear one last time before heading down to the lobby for seven.

The team are scattered around the place, identifiable by their starch stiffened blue and grey Vertex pit shirts. I think we all look more like a darts team than a world championship motorcycle squad, and I would far rather have a trendy sponsor like Fat Face or FCUK supply the team's clothing, but the powers that be prefer sharp collars and contrasting coloured epaulettes, so that's what we get.

Once at the circuit, I join Dave and Richard for a tactics talk in Stevo's motor home. I'm elected to start, having set the fastest time yesterday. (It must have been the bump on the head!) This is usually the case as the fastest rider can gain the most ground in the first hour and give the team a bit of a cushion.

Morning warm-up goes without incident, and by one o'clock we are left with little to do other than fit the fresh tyres and brake pads for the start of the race, as always, at three o'clock.

The race is started traditionally by all of the riders lining up on the grass verge opposite the pits, whilst the number two rider holds the bike upright on the other side of the track, closest to the pit wall. When the flag drops, the riders sprint across the circuit, hop onto their bikes, and then charge down to the first corner in a spectacular mêlée of colour and noise.

The ensuing mess usually involves a few broken dreams, by way of a few broken bones. The track is only so wide, and 40 motorcycles into one corner just doesn't go. Not all at once, anyhow.

The sun has warmed the chill from the March air and I actually feel a bit hot for the first time all weekend. My leathers feel tight, but my boots loose as I overanalyse everything possible that could go wrong over the next 24 hours. I see Dave holding the bike at the other side of the track, squatting down behind it to give my leg a free swing over the seat. The clock above the starters gantry says two fifty-eight, but takes an age to clunk its way around to two fifty-nine.

My muscles are like bow strings, taught at the prospect of letting rip. My brain is so totally focussed at the slightest movement of the starters hand that it feels like I can smell the sweat emanating from his pores some 50 yards away.

I am a catapult, stretched to its breaking strain. The 60-something gent, wearing a handlebar moustache and tweed jacket, then raises the red white and blue striped flag high above his head.

We all wait, bursting with anticipation.

Nerves.

I check the straps on my gloves (again).

Tension.

I check the visor on my crash helmet (yet again).

I refuse to break the trance, staring at Mr Starter for even the slightest movement of the flag.

He raises his left hand in a ridiculously over theatrical way and stretches it out to pull his jacket sleeve clear of his wrist watch.

He eyes the timepiece with a squinting frown as he struggles to read the hands due to the sun's reflection on its face.

Slowly he turns away from the sun in order to offer his watch some shade.

His eyebrows rise suddenly, his head sweeps up to survey the track, and he drops the flag vigorously to commence the mayhem. There is, as always, an eerie silence that hangs in the air at the start of an endurance race. The flag has dropped, but there is still comparative silence – a void.

We sprint from one side of the track to the other, almost in slow motion. Our steeds await, yet there's a strange feeling of an unstoppable event you are witness to, but with no control whatsoever as to the outcome. A muted avalanche.

The aural spectacle collides head-on with the visual as the riders reach their bikes, and with a deft swing of the leg they are on their way.

The raucous explosion of horsepower and cheers is akin to the cry of a thousand Vikings charging into battle.

I cannot believe it, my start is perfect, and I pass both Pace and Abacus almost immediately to take the lead into the first corner with ease.

'How the hell did I do that?' I wonder, as I get my head down and ride harder than I have ever dared before in order to keep the position for at least one lap. I pass the pits still leading and brake hard into the first corner again.

I cannot believe the sound that follows me like a Mexican wave around the circuit; people are waving flags and cheering so loudly. It spurs me on to ride even harder.

Next lap around my pit crew show me a '+1' on my pit board, meaning I am one second ahead of the second place rider. I glance down at the digital display of the on-board computer that Glynn designed; it is showing me both my current lap time, and a performance meter that tells me via various beacons around the circuit if I am faster or slower than the last lap at any given point by way of a red and green bar graph on the dashboard.

A few laps later I'm shown a +2, then a 3, 4, 5, and by the end of my first hour we have seven seconds on the Team Pace guys.

I pit at one hour eight minutes for a re-fuel and rider change. Team Pace are doing likewise, but due to the fast fuel rig I designed, Dave leaves the pits a whole ten seconds ahead of the competition.

I, it must be said, am on a roll, for once! Dave holds station for his first 30 minutes, then really puts the hammer down to pull a whole minute's lead on the pursuers by the end of the second hour.

Richard then takes the helm at the next pit stop and sets a scorching pace from the off, smashing the lap record on his 12th lap and gaining a three-minute lead by the end of his session.

I bet by now you are all expecting me to change our dominance for disaster, but on this occasion we poke fate in the eye with a shitty stick and come out on top.

We conquer the other teams at Le Mans to the delightful tune of three laps at the end, and we're the first team to win the prestigious event for Team Vertex in no less then 12 years. Needless to say, I get so pissed on Sunday evening that we have to stop over a further night as I am still too inebriated to drive until Monday afternoon.

Chapter 26

Playtime

taking the joke just a little too far...

I return to work on Wednesday, still sore from the weekend's efforts. All of the bikes have been unloaded and are swiftly being prepared for the next round of the championship, held at Spa-Francorchamps. The Belgian circuit is an awesome ribbon of perfect tarmac that twists and winds its way, falling and rising like a seductive temptress, daring you to race faster and faster through the maze of the Ardennes forest. It's certainly the highlight of the season for both riders and crew; some even say the best circuit in the world.

Christiano makes an appearance at lunchtime to assure Stevo that he will be fit to ride, but this is yet to be seen. What's painfully clear, however, is despite my valiant efforts the previous weekend, riding is no longer an option for me. The top brass at Vertex had promised sponsors big names in the seat in response to the big cheques they had written. A fluke win by a has-been mechanic was interesting, no doubt, but sadly not in the contract they had signed.

The shine from my previous weekend's victory has also begun to tarnish. Steadily the week reverts to its usual 'get pissed to avoid thinking too deeply or going home' routine. Again I find myself staying at work later than strictly necessary, with only my 'special' Coke can to keep me company. I then regularly stagger into the Crown, only to be slung out by Dave the Landlord at slinging out time, and crawl back to my van in order to drive home.

The Porsche is still a wreck and I'm having a great deal of hassle with the insurance company, possibly due to the level of blood they found in my alcohol stream. Claire has been as offensive as ever, locking the front door so I can't get in, or disappearing and leaving me with the kids at the drop of a hat.

I'm depressed.

I find myself doing the weekly shopping, cleaning and childcare whilst trying to hold down a decent social life – sorry, I mean job. Strangely Claire seems to know far too much of what's going on at the Crown. There must be a spy in our midst, but I'm yet to discover who.

On a Friday, mid-April, my suspicions are tweaked somewhat further. I bowl into the house uncharacteristically early at seven o'clock, in order to shitshowerandshave for the evening's performance of drinking until I'm unconscious down at the Crown.

I enter the house, kiss and hug my two little angels, then give them each a lolly and a toy. Brad's is an 'Action Man Urban Extreme', complete with ninja death stars kamikaze head band and a rather large automatic weapon. Lara gets a 'Barbie Uptown Girl', complete with poodle, more 'bling' jewellery than 'Mr T' and mobile phone (what kind of message are we trying to give our kids, I wonder?) This succeeds in the receipt of a rather acidic scowl from Claire. She disappears upstairs, then moments later the front door slams with a 'back in a min.'

Before I even have the door fully open again I snatch a glimpse of her car tail lights disappearing out of the end of the driveway. The 'min' I later learn is somewhat longer than expected.

By eight I'm getting a little restless. Nine I'm pissed off. Ten brings anger and at eleven o'clock, as the time bell rings across the land, it turns to rage. The fucking bitch had destroyed my evening.

I cannot help feeling a pang of guilt though, as I retrieve my children from the seemingly monochrome sofa where they both lie. The television flickers from the video tape that ran out hours before, and I carry them to bed. At midnight I give up and head upstairs to bed myself, the spare room I hasten to add.

The weekend that follows is its usual blend of silence, tutting and snatching, with a little eye rolling and exaggerated frowning thrown in for good measure. By midday Sunday I can't take it any longer and scoop the kids into the van.

With a twist of the key we're off for a little peace by way of the local playground. I stop in at the mini-mart grocery store in Weybridge to score some beer, but it's not until I arrive at the playground that I realise just how awful it will look for me to be getting pissed in a kids' playground before driving them home.

Nothing for it then, camouflage is the order of the day. Brown paper bags are just 'so tramp', so I rifle around in the back of the van for a suitable container, but none is forthcoming. I don't fancy an empty oil can, and the 20 litre jerry can, although new and unused, would no doubt look far worse than a beer can.

As I swing the rear doors closed I suddenly catch a glimpse of the orange water bottle fastened to the rusty heap of a bicycle I keep in the back of my van, just in case I'm so pissed I can't even operate a key and need alternative transport.

This, of course, is pure optimism. If I had indeed had so much to drink I was actually incapable of driving (I had long since given up worrying about the law) I would no doubt find said bipedular mode of transportation a pain in the arse as it would be taking up the space in the van I would no doubt need for sleeping.

I pop the black plastic lid, and with a hiss of stale air I sweep my head quickly to one side. The reek from the fungus inside is revolting, but with little else to use I have no choice but to improvise. I bravely take a peek inside, but it looks every bit as bad as it smells.

After a little further rummaging I find a rag and some spirit wipe, citrus scented. Mmm, yummy.

A swift de-contamination follows, then I glug the beer into the plastic receptacle, pop the lid on, and draw the nobly teat up and into my mouth, in order to imbibe a fresh mouthful of crisp, chilled beer.

Nothing... I suck a little harder but still nothing. Raising the bottle to my eye still leaves me curious as to the blockage. I then replace it in my mouth, suck as hard as I can, and squeezed with all my might... Pop, skkkrrrssssshhhhh gag gag.

The mouldy cud of rotting shit that was blocking the orifice jettisons its way into the back of my throat, followed by a blast of beer that causes me to gag repeatedly in a near vomit induced hunch. I spit the offending article from my mouth, then crouch down to inspect it. With my eyes still watering I pick up the small black pellet of fungus and flick it into a nearby hedge.

I've been so preoccupied with my little task I had completely forgotten about the children. I close the rear doors and walk around to the cab. Gone! My hair leaps on end as I imagine the worst. I leave the van and sprint to the park gate. A quick scour, however, finds them safe and sound, playing on the vulgar red, yellow and blue coloured climbing frame.

I enter the play area and sit alone at one of the many benches. The kids all seem to be enjoying themselves and the adults appear glad of the break, either nestled behind their broadsheet newspapers or mums chatting about avocados and curtains.

I then get the urge, you know, the 'had a sip of beer and need another one' type. I grope inside my jacket and retrieve the plastic bottle, pop the cap, and successfully draw another refreshing mouthful of beer – bliss.

The rest of the bottle is downed within minutes, then refilled behind a tree with one of the beer cans I had secreted about my person earlier.

On my third journey to the tree I notice one of the other dads from school. I smile and raise my eyebrows in acknowledgment. He does likewise. I return to the relative safety of my bench and slouch back with my legs out straight in front of me, crossed at the ankles.

The beer buzz starts to grow. I close my eyes and imagine a warmer climate. Coincidently as I do so the sun makes an unexpected, yet nonetheless welcome appearance. It warms my bones and sends me off into a wonderful daydream…

'HI, I'M TOBY, JESSICA'S DAD, PLEASED TO MAKE YOUR ACQUAINTANCE.'

A rather 'Hooray Henry' type of voice booms far too loudly and far too close for comfort. I squint my eyes open a couple of millimetres and see the dad with his hand outstretched, dressed in a well-used Barbour jacket, white Arran roll neck and sparkly new Timberland boots. I bet the twat drives a metallic green Range Rover with a '51% vote to keep hunting' sticker in the back. The tosser probably has a major difficulty swatting flies, let alone killing a beast of the forest, and while I'm on the subject, this 51%, where the fuck did they go to vote for the right to hunt down and rip to shreds God's innocent creatures; buggered if I was ever invited to go and vote. Come to think about it, were you? I doubt it.

Anyway, back to Toby.

'Oh yeah, hi, I'm Hazy, Paul Hayes that is,' I reply as disinterestedly as I possibly can. After a brief and decidedly one-sided conversation about the weather and the rugby, he gets the hint and clears off, back to his perch on the other side of the playground.

A quick look confirms that Brads and Lara are still playing happily, so with eyes closed I begin to slowly slip back into my magical dream world again...

Just as the topless Hawaiian masseuse is about to set to work on my lower regions whilst I relax on the white powder sand of a beach somewhere tropical, I am dragged instantly from my slumber by Brads shouting, 'Dad, Dad, Lara's stuck on the climbing frame.' After initial sun blindness from opening my eyes too quickly, the purples reds and blacks colour balance themselves slowly back to the dull British greys blues and greens that our pleasant land is so famous for.

There is, however, an odd swaying red image that I struggle to focus on in my direct field of vision. Then, as it becomes clear, I leap from my seat and sprint to the climbing frame ahead. Lara has fallen from the highest point, and having snagged the hood of her coat on a protruding piece of said climbing frame is now dangling precariously from the neck.

'LARA!' I scream at the top of my voice as I career through the sand pit, sending infants flying in all directions. Parents turn their heads towards me in disbelief, jaws falling open with eyes like saucers.

My daughter appears to be dead. She had been rendered unconscious with the sudden jolt, and all her muscles instantly sagged as if the life itself has been drawn from them. As I unhook her hood from the protruding frame, I can see a dark crimson bruise appearing around her throat; the coat has acted like a noose.

I pull her into my chest and hug her with all my might. This, it transpires, was not such a smart move. The effort of me running across the playground has shaken the plastic beer bottle to near bursting point; this, coupled with a little compression from my overzealous hugging, results in an explosion of beer all over the pair of us. We're soaked head to toe, and stink of a stale brewery.

Toby was first on the scene. 'My gosh, old boy, are you both alright?' he inquires, swiftly followed by, 'My God, is that beer I can smell. You're drunk, I'm going to report you to the authorities.'

I clench my fist and thump Toby square on the nose, full connection, lots of blood. He staggers back, then falls on his arse. His once-white knitwear is now streaked pink as he shakes his head in an effort to re-grasp reality.

I turn my attention back to Lara who has begun crying and showing animated signs of disgust with her fists. This, of course, is a good thing, as it proves she is, in fact, not dead.

The beer has exploded all over my shirt and jumper, it has even reached my hair that was now standing on end with both the stress and the sticky liquid assistance.

Toby retreats, walking briskly towards the exit, and drags his two small children by their anorak sleeves towards the Range Rover. All the other parents keep a discreet distance and avoid eye contact with me, as it's now clear that Lara is fine, if a little shaken.

My return home brings another blazing row with it, although this time Claire does actually have a valid point to argue. We battle tooth and nail anyhow, culminating in me throwing a saucepan at the wall.

She then performs her new trick and disappears, leaving me to bath and bed the little darlings. Brads goes off unusually easily, but Lara is still a little shaken from the day's events. It takes several readings of *Angelina Ballerina Goes to the Opera* and a swift few pages of *What Do People Do All Day* before she eventually settles. Claire had left on foot, so her car is still sat outside.

A quick zap from the key fob and the interior light slowly glows into life. Once inside, I spot a screwed-up cinema ticket for the 9 p.m. showing of *The Time Traveller's Wife* from the previous Friday night at Staines Cinema. Interesting...

I rummage some more but only come up with some used chewing gum and several cardboard Starbucks coffee cups. My suspicions are tweaked, it must be said, and I shall have to keep a tighter focus to my observations of both Ed and Claire's pastimes from now on.

Monday morning finds me hot under the collar. Not only are the kids being a complete and utter pain in the arse, fighting, name calling and generally acting like their mother (who happens to be upstairs asleep with another raging hangover). The van is as also as dead as Dodi's chauffeur. I try in vain to start the old dog but it's having none of it. There's nothing else for it, I'll have to take Claire's Golf.

I load Brads and Lara into the back, packed lunches on the passenger seat, and we're off. As the school gates come into sight, I note that some fat, fake-tanned, leopard skin Lycra-clad hussy, with a bleach blond perm, is extracting her offspring from a new Mercedes 4x4 pavement crusher, finished in metallic Bordeaux Burgundy (like the face of her fat accountant-type husband after a swift session with his secretary, no doubt) that happens to be in my usual parking slot.

I manage to find an alternative, parking nose-first up against a wall, next to the gate of a private road that's a mere stone's throw from the school's entrance. I extract the children and hang around for a moment to see if Tess is going to roll up.

When she doesn't, I swiftly run the kids across the road and into their classrooms. It isn't until I return to the car that I notice something odd.

Ed's black Shogun is parked across the back, blocking the car in to such a degree it was obviously done on purpose. I walk up and unlock the driver's door of the Golf, noticing there's a Daffodil under the windscreen wiper blade. I get in, after removing the offending article, and wait.

I see Ed saunter across the road from the school wearing a size ten cock-sure smile. This, however, turns to puzzlement when he draws a little closer and clocks it's me, not Claire, in the driver's seat.

He swiftly hops into the 4x4 and sparks it into life. I pull out after him and follow the Mitsubishi down through Weybridge High Street and beyond.

The glow of brake lights increases as we settle into a pace just ahead of walking. Lurching forward, he could only make one car's distance on me as we filter our way through the rush hour traffic. Upon reaching the log jammed dual carriageway that heads out towards Brooklands, I seize the opportunity to draw alongside. Ed pretends not to notice me. After a few short stabs on the horn he glances over and feigns surprise as he rolls his window down.

'My God, I didn't recognise you in that car, where's the van?'

'Fucking bollocks he didn't recognise me,' I think.

'Dead battery,' I reply.

'You on your way to work?' he enquires.

'Yeah, what are you doing headed this way?'

'Got a meeting with some of the heads of Vertex this morning, you know, just trying to sort some contract shit out, nothing serious.'

We slowly edge our way to Vertex towers, then go our separate ways once inside. Work whizzes by for once, and I find myself in the Crown before I know it. The evening is mostly spent chatting with Tess and Glynn, as Ed is ignoring us altogether. Beaker enters the pub around ten, and try as I might I cannot seem to drag him away from the bar in order to discuss the upcoming prank. The evening ends in the usual row between Ed and Tess outside the pub, and I make my weary way home, pissed again!

A couple of days later, about a week before we set off for Belgium, I manage to speak to Tess for longer than the usual ten minutes and set up a night out; she seems a lot more upbeat than usual, and I look forward with great anticipation to our secret rendezvous.

We meet, as arranged, on Tuesday at nine in a small wine bar called Gaspers in Esher High Street. The décor is tired and the customers sparse, so it serves our purpose perfectly. Sitting on the back wall with only a slim candle stuffed into a wax-sodden rosé wine bottle for illumination, I order a pint of Stella whilst Tess chooses a glass of house red.

Table service…nice, must come here more often. Once over the usual euphoria of seeing each other, we nestle down into a normal conversation, the result being a mutual raising of eyebrows as the truth unfolds.

As I explain the reason for my absence the preceding Friday, a few too many coincidences become ever more apparent. At seven-thirty (whilst Claire was upstairs) Ed had received a phone call on his mobile in the pub. At ten to eight (the time Claire left the house) he disappeared out the back door of said pub, not to return until the following morning.

Claire had returned home some time between five o'clock (when I passed out) and seven o'clock (when the kids woke me up again.)

Suspicious, what do you think? Ed's explanation had been a fairly non-credible, 'I fell asleep in the car, down by the river, thinking,' whilst Claire's was a little more to the point, with a swift, 'Fuck off, it's none of your business.'

We surmised that they had spent the night together. Time traveller's wife followed by somebody else's, but it was no great loss to either of us.

I then suggest that we meet up the night that I was supposed to be driving the truck over to Spa, opting to stay in a posh hotel on the south coast instead of a slog for hours behind the wheel.

I had managed to collar Beaker at work and arrange for he and Ron to take it in turns through the overnight stint in the truck, enabling me to take my bike, thus allowing me the time to leave a whole 12 hours later.

I arrange to meet Tess for a swift dirty night at the Hilton in Bournemouth on the Tuesday, allowing me enough time to wake early on Wednesday morning to catch the 7 a.m. Dover-Calais ferry.

The preceding Monday, however, arrives with bad news. Christiano has aggravated his ankle injury whilst playing tennis with one of his film star mates. He therefore would, despite his promises, not be joining us at Spa. To compound this, I get a text message from Tess mid-morning announcing, 'ED @ SPA'.

This, as I'm sure you can gather, is not good news. I wonder what team he would be riding for, and why. Surely his Grand Prix schedule would preclude him from such forays into alternative championships, but as the day wore on the full horror of the upcoming weekend was to unravel itself.

At 4 p.m. Stevo calls a crisis meeting. He announces that due to injury and contractual difficulties Christiano would not be joining us at Spa Francorchamps, or indeed for the rest of the season. His place will be taken by a far brighter star, who has recently fallen to a slightly lower playing field, by the name of Ed Black.

Stevo goes on to further explain that due to circumstances beyond Vertex's control, Ed has been dropped from the premier Grand Prix class of racing and would thus be a little short of work this weekend. My heart sinks like an anchor to the seabed.

The team let out a great cheer as I silently cringe at the thought of sleeping with his wife the night before working with him in the team.

'That's racing' could, I suppose, suffice as an excuse, but it eats away at my sense of honesty and loyalty. I feel like shit.

Didn't stop me going to Bournemouth though.

* * * * *

I sit with my back to the restaurant that's obviously catering for the 'obnoxious stuck up twat in a Bentley, paid for by Daddy' annual general meeting.

The snorts, scoffs and hurrahs from the Ruperts and Tarquins are beginning to grate on my previously optimistic mood. Tess is half an hour late, but this is no great surprise as her time keeping is usually about as accurate as my recollection of how much I had drunk the night before.

The bar of the Bournemouth Hilton is as one might expect. You could be anywhere in the world, in a Hilton bar.

By 8 p.m. she was an hour late. I'm starting to slump in my chair as the fifth pint was winding its way into my soul. Traffic must be bad, I tell myself. By eight-thirty I call her mobile.

Switched off, bollocks.

By nine o'clock I know I have been stood up, but remain optimistic until the end of my eighth pint.

By ten I don't care – pints, that is, not o'clock. Time can go fuck itself. I sway and stumble my way to my room.

I sprawl out on the bed and regret not eating.

My stomach gently turns, as only one does that has had its hunger quelled by beer. I resist the urge to vomit, and stick my head under the tap in the bathroom for a full ten minutes. It feels refreshing, if a little chilly.

I wake around six with a storming head. I take a shower, dress, and am sat at breakfast by six forty-five.

Egg, bacon and a banger later, I find myself back in my room under the covers fighting the reality of daylight.

I wake again at eight, munch five Nurofen Plus, then head towards Dover in a state of numb half-consciousness.

Chapter 27

Spa Francorchamps

taking the joke just a little too far...

I try in vain to sleep on the boat, and we dock by the time I manage to get comfortable. I feel a great deal better than I had first thing, but that's not really saying a great deal.

Off the ferry, turn left-ish, and head for the pine trees. I make good progress on my bike, but by lunchtime I begin to notice a slight vibration through the handlebars of my usually silent Honda Fireblade. This puzzles me more than worries me, so I carry on regardless.

By four o'clock I'm within sniffing distance of the forest. As I enter the myriad of spruces my nostrils come alive with the fresh smell of toilet disinfectant and anti-biological floor cleaner. I wonder if the natives pined for (sorry, I couldn't resist) 'Inner London smog' scented cleaning products?

My ears are treated to the chiming of Coldplay's 'Clocks' by way of my MP3's headphones as the shadows stretch across the ever-winding roads, rendering them almost dark save for the shafts of light to penetrate the slight openings in the near absolute cover of the evergreen trees around me.

It is, truly, a magical experience. Belting along at over 100 miles per hour without a care in the world, other than the several thousand in the back of my mind, but best not spoil the moment, eh.

The road opens up on occasion to give the most wonderful panoramic view of treetops, streams and ravines, before diving back down into the depths of the green and black pine tunnels below; it's an absolute rollercoaster of emotion to truly make all the senses scream at once.

As I enter the final town of my journey, I'm greeted by locals who line the road, clapping and cheering all the race-goers, welcoming us by offering plastic cups of orange juice, or fruit buns and pain au chocolate set out at the side of the road on decorators' wallpapering tables and the like.

I feel a real warmth in the reception we receive, like we make a difference to their otherwise uneventful lives. It also makes a massive difference to my own stressful, and overcomplicated life.

My God! I feel great for a change!

I find Garage 12 hidden cunningly between numbers 11 and 13. The large blue and sliver Vertex trucks give it away. Parked parallel to each other, as usual, with an awning spread between them. I park my Honda out of sight (wouldn't do for a Vertex mechanic to endorse another brand, now would it?) and enter the pits.

Dusk has fallen, and I had missed the afternoon's testing. I knew Stevo would be mighty pissed, but I stroll in with the optimism of a certain Cassius Clay.

'You useless bastard, where the hell do you think you've been for the last 12 hours. You were given a privileged position in this bloody team because I was led to believe you could be relied on, but the only message you have sent me since you walked into my fucking office is cunt Cunt CUNT! So what on earth is your excuse for acting like a CUNT today?'

See, I told you Stevo would be pissed.

'Err, how did testing go?'

'Testing, TESTING, the only thing that's been tested is my fucking patience with a cunt like you on the team.'

Stevo retires to the back of the garage and takes a seat at Glynn's desk to analyse the afternoon's data. Sully is doing his best not to crack up laughing, Gandhi likewise, but Beaker is in hysterics, hiding behind the wheel rack. I now feel like shit, I know Stevo is right. I have indeed acted like a cunt since the start of the season and it is plain for all to see. I feel an overbearing cloud of depression descending onto my shoulders.

I check the schedule on the notice board and see that we are in the early nighttime qualifying session. Bollocks!

I rally the troops and sort who is to do the wheel changes if need be. The brake pads have all been bedded and the slicks all scrubbed to remove the shiny moulding film.

We're set; at least I think we are. The clouds race across the night sky at such a rate that it couldn't possibly rain. The session commences with the moon illuminating the circuit like a giant spotlight, following each and every rider, keeping them safe for their session aboard.

Our first rider, Rich, blasts out of the pits to put us in eighth place within six minutes. The pace heats up somewhat by mid-session, and we finish in 11th.

Not good for a factory team. Stevo swims through the pits like a great white, ready to tear somebody's head off.

Dave is out next, with a fresh set of qualifying slicks beneath him. He knows he only has ten laps to post a good time before they 'go off' and relegate him to a cruising lap back into the pits.

He scorches out of pit lane, and on his second flying lap posts a time good enough to place us third. Cheers all round… Until the tyre goes off, that is; his initially fabulous lap time is gradually eroded away by the other factory teams that had saved their fancy rubber till the last few minutes of the session. This drops us back down to eighth. Then, like Buzz fucking Lightyear, Ed appears out of the light fog. His figure is illuminated by the pit lighting, mimicking a smoke and mirrors style super hero's entrance. He leaps onto the bike and disappears up pit lane before they have even called his session.

Moments later he is out lapping the circuit at near lap record pace – in the dark! We reside on pole position for the duration of the evening, and look forward to re-enforcing our command on the proceedings during the following day's daylight qualifying.

Friday morning finds us still firmly in pole position as the opposition struggle to get within a second of our qualifying time. Some teams even struggle to match Ed's nighttime session, let alone his daytime pace.

By the end of qualifying at 4 p.m., it's set. We start from the number one slot on Saturday at three o'clock, for 24 hours of madness, mayhem and sleep deprivation. The Friday night is spent with the riders going over tactics and strategies with Stevo. The mechanics huddle around me, looking for inspiration and guidance for the gruelling race ahead – fools!

Ed had succeeded in avoiding me in anything other than a fully rushed professional capacity, but I know he feels the tension as strongly as I do.

* * * * *

On Saturday morning, around 8 a.m. and under a clear blue sky, I personally check the bike for any defects. I go over it with a fine toothcomb to look for potential failures, possible problems, or even just slight discomforts for the riders. I find none. We've done a good job.

As midday arrives, some of the team members appear to have their usual jitters and insecurities. These, however, are quelled any time the qualifying sheet is pointed out that shows us nearly half a second ahead of the competition. I too have the jitters, but not relating to the race. Tess hasn't called all weekend, and I dread that she will at any time when Ed is within earshot. The tension is getting to me; I can't sit still and I find myself checking my phone for text messages every couple of minutes. I decide to go for a wander around the paddock.

After 20 minutes or so I grow a little bored, so decide a swift sharpener is in order. Belgium, for those who don't know, is the home of Stella Artois, so as the great Caesar probably once said, 'When in Rome…' The Stella bar was situated a short walk up the Eau Rouge hill. In order to reach it, and the 'eau amber' I craved, I need to leave the pits via a pedestrian tunnel under the main straight, and out into the scary world of the general public. I squeeze past the 18 stone security guard who obscures the gate and disappear into the sea of race goers.

By the time I've reached 'camp Stella' I have well and truly worked up a thirst. It may only be late spring, but I am certainly a touch warm under the collar after my hike up a tourist-covered hill.

'Two glasses of Stella please, love.'

'Eight euros please, zir.' After a double-take at the price, my hand finds its way to the bottom of my pocket to retrieve some cash.

'Oooh fabulous! Is one of those naughty little things for me?' I swing round in an instant to see a Cheshire cat faced Beaker at my shoulder.

'Err, I suppose so, what on earth are you doing here? Two more Stellas please, love.' I hand over another pound of flesh, and then we both take a seat at a litter strewn picnic table that overlooks the circuit.

'I saw you hovering around the pits, so decided to join you. By the time I had caught up to you, you were disappearing down the exit tunnel, so I thought I'd see what you were up to.' We then sit in reflective silence for a moment.

'What time is it, mate?' I ask.

'Half-twelve, loads of time. You having another?'

'Do you really need to ask?'

'Four Stellas it is then.' Beaker disappears back into the crowd as I amuse myself with trying to spot the most ridiculous looking race fan. There are plenty of mullets and handlebar moustaches to choose from, the all too frequent sighting of skin-tight denim or Lycra on overweight German or Dutch head bangers with their national flag draped across their shoulders, ingrained with stale beer and dirt from sleeping rough the previous night. Then I see him, Gerhardt, or so I instantly name him. He wins hands down. I cannot decide the country of origin, due to his mismatch of clothing and, dare I say it, style. He wears, beneath his mint green leather lederhosen, a faded, yellowy-brown stained 'Spanish Grand Prix 1982' T-shirt, sporting mustard and ketchup scars from at least five different years. His slightly too small peaked baseball cap wears the Playboy bunny proudly on its pink front, and has 'Sex instructor, first lesson free' embroidered in chrome on the peak. The hat, it appears, is only mildly less amusing than what lies beneath. He removes the headgear almost on cue and scratches the crown of his shiny pink head – expelling fleas and head lice, no doubt – that is devoid of any hair whatsoever at the top. This is made up for, though, by the mass of unwashed locks that cascade down his back, from the ears down, to a scraggly end near his bum. Some in plaits, some dyed red or purple, the majority though, just left fallow.

Beaker arrives back with the beer; I raise my eyebrows with a cheeky smile, tipping my head towards said character. Beaker erupts in laughter, almost spilling the entire contents of the plastic glasses. He eventually, after a moment or two, settles down and just sniggers from time to time.

A while later I ask Beaker the time again.

'Only half-twelve,' comes the reply.

'Shit, time's dragging today, I just want this race over with.' I notice a slight slur in my voice as I talk, so decide to limit myself to just two more beers.

'How's things with Tess?' he asks. I, instantly on the defensive, reply, 'What do you mean, there's nothing going on you know.'

Beaker looks at me quizzically. 'What, you've called it off?'

'It was never on! What makes you think there is anything going on between me and Tess?'

'You told me.'

'No I didn't!'

'Yes you did! The prank, you know, with Gandhi and Robert De Niro – the blood and everything.'

My body sags with the realisation. Oh, *that* thing going on.

'Err, fine. I'll keep you posted.' I breathe a massive lungful of relief and make a sharp exit. The queue for the bar has grown to a record-breaking length, but the appetite for a further buzz outweighs the laziness brought on by the beer consumed so far. After what seems like two days I eventually reach the head of the pack.

'Four Stellas please, mate,' I shout over the din of race engines charging up the hill.

'Eh? Ssspeak uppa. I canna hear you overa tha motabikesss,' the Spanish looking chap behind the bar replies, waving his hands at his ears.

'I said…' Oh shit, the penny has just dropped all the way to the basement, taking the colour from my face as it went. I fight my way back through the crowd to meet Beaker, who is also white with panic and throwing Europeans out of his way at will as he barrels towards me.

'What the fuck is the time?' I demand. Beaker glances down at his rising hand to reveal the watch face fixed steady at half past twelve.

'Fuck it! The battery must have died.' He removes the offending item from his wrist and lobs it into the air. I grab a passer-by's arm and try to look at the time; he retaliates by snatching it away and punches me squarely on the nose.

'Get your own bloody watch,' the burly Australian commands as he turns and continues on his way. Beaker manages to grab a look at somebody else's and shouts, 'Ten to three! Fuck!' We sprint as best we can through the throng of people, arriving back at the tunnel just as the security guard is clicking the lock shut for the start of the race.

'Too late, guys, the warm-up lap has already started.'

'Please, you have to let us in, we are needed for the start, we're part of a factory team,' I plead.

'Sorry, too late. You can try going up to the organiser's office on the other side of the circuit, or wait until the race is over, the choice is yours.'

'It's a 24-hour race, you twat, we'll be on our way home when the fucking race is over. I demand you let us in.'

'Sorr...'

Thwack!

The security officer falls to the ground like a sack of spuds. Beaker is stood next to me holding a fence post. He smiles with a demented grin, and then stoops to frisk the guard for his keys.

Once inside, we make our way to the Vertex camp as quickly as possible. We sneak in the back door unnoticed and try to blend in.

'Where the fuck have you two been? Stevo's been doing his pieces,' Gandhi inquires as we make our way to the front of the pit garage.

'Long story, where's he now?' Gandhi points out towards the pit wall where the timekeepers and pit board signallers

251

stand. Stevo snaps the button down on the stopwatch he holds as Ed flies past at record-breaking pace. After a brief conflab with Kirsty, the pit board girl, he turns to face us, then starts heading in our direction. Oh shit.

He enters the garage, and merely whispers in my ear, 'Don't fuck up again this weekend, we need another good result and that's only achievable if we all pull together. Heads will roll if we don't finish here leading the championship, so have a word with Beaker when you get a moment, as I hold you personally responsible for the entire crew this weekend. And let me remind you, it won't be my head that's rolling.'

With point well and truly taken, I breathe a sigh of relief and head out to the track where the bikes are beginning to line up on the grid. Dave waits in his leathers at the pole position slot for Ed to appear from his warm-up laps on the bike, whilst Rich stands with his back to the action chatting to one of the gorgeous brolly dollies, looking full rock star of course, in his designer jeans, Hugo Boss skin-tight T-shirt and Armani shades.

As usual, the riders all line the grass verge that is opposite the pits, their steeds waiting expectantly. Dave holds the bike as Ed limbers up on the other side of the track.

Before I know it the flag has dropped, and the stampede towards the first corner is well underway. Ed, of course, makes the perfect textbook start and flies through 'Eau Rouge' (a particularly scary uphill off-camber left-right bend, taken at well past 120 mph for the brave) leading the pack. We all watch the other riders follow as he makes it just look far too easy.

Waiting for the leader to appear from 'La Source' hairpin, back onto the start-finish straight for the first time is always a tense time, but we are relieved to see Ed a full half-second ahead of the Pace team, who are nestled down in second place.

After five laps Ed has a one-second cushion.

After the first half-hour he has stretched it to 22 seconds, and by the first hour we are nearly a full minute ahead.

Ed pits on time; we change riders, wheels and brake pads in the time it takes to say 'it'.

We are the best.

Rich holds the lead for the whole of his session, dropping it by half to only a 30-second advantage. Again, my super efficient quick filler soon returns this to a full minute with the next pit stop and we begin Dave's first session confident of a repeat victory. Two and a half hours into the race, I make my way to the back of the garage to discuss with Stevo the tactics for wheel changes and general race strategy for the remainder of the daylight sessions.

No sooner have I sat at his desk, my phone starts to ring. The display announces 'TESS MOBILE'.

Just as I depress the red 'END' button a hand rests on my shoulder. I glance up to see Ed standing behind me. I gulp.

'Sorry, Stevo, you were saying…' I pathetically mumble.

'Team Pace are right on our tail, and the rest of the pack have closed right in on us, we are going to pull Dave in a little early so as to give Ed maximum time on the bike and hopefully pull out a bit of a cushion. We are also going to switch tyres for a slightly softer compound, so as to allow Ed the luxury of going hard in the first half of his session. This will hopefully faze the other teams a little as they see our lead growing quickly. I can't stress enough how critical this next pit stop is.'

'Righto Steve,' I say, and then stand to leave. Ed blocks my way momentarily, and there is an awkward silence as I squeeze past him whilst making eye contact with his shoes in the tiny makeshift office.

My phone buzzes in my pocket informing me of a text message from Tess, 'CALL ME, URGENT.' I thumb a swift reply, 'LATER.' Ed appears at the front of the pit garage, now wearing full leathers, and talks to Stevo through the mouthpiece of his crash helmet.

My mobile buzzes with another message from Tess, 'NOW, CALL NOW, IMPORTANT!' I press delete, then look left out of the pit garage and up the track to see Dave in the distance, doing the requisite 30 mph pit lane speed. He is only seconds away. I shout instructions to motivate the lads and get them in place for the pit stop.

Dave is 20 yards away, Ed walks up to the pit lane and is no further than 6 ft away from me, ignoring my existence.

My fucking phone rings.

I hit the delete button and it stops. No sooner have I done this, than it starts to ring again.

Ed stares at me. I pluck the phone from my pocket and check the caller ID.

'TESS MOBILE'. I apprehensively press the green button, but before I can say a word she blurts, 'Ed knows all about Nottingham.' I am stunned, I don't know what to do, my mind is swimming.

Confront?

Apologise?

Delay?

Deny?

Run?

Change the wheel on the bike that has just arrived at 200 miles per hour?

I am in a daze, the team are shouting and waving their hands at me but I find it hard to comprehend what I should be doing.

'Change the fucking wheel!' Ed demands as he thumps me on the shoulder. I let go of the phone with shock and it falls to the floor, smashing into a dozen pieces.

Dropping to my knees I set about removing the wheel. I am all fingers and thumbs; I drop the spindle, put the wheel in backwards and find it impossible to find the right combination of push, twist, screw to safely re-house said hoop. All the time I imagine Tess yakking in my ear about how Ed is going to kill me. I glance up to meet his glare bearing down on me. I look him straight in the eye whilst single-handedly losing the race for both him and the team.

My brain is shot to pieces. I finally achieve the right combination of nuts, bolts and screws with a little help from Gandhi, and a lot of 'what the fuck are you doing?' type shouting from the rest of the team.

Ed shoots down the pit lane, after running over what's left of my phone, shaking his head and giving me the wanker sign with his left hand.

'You're sacked.' Stevo is stood beside me. All I can muster is a slight rise of the eyebrows and I collect my tools and head back into the flickering fluorescent buzz of the pit garage.

Ed is out-knocking second after second from the leader's gap. Stevo finds me in the back of the garage, sat in a fold-up chair with my head in my hands.

'One more like that and I will personally kick your arse out of this pit lane, are we clear?'

'Yes Steve, I'm sorry. It won't happen again.'

Ed finishes his session in fourth position. Not ideal, but better than the seventh place my fumbling wheel change had relegated us to.

By mid-way through Richard's second session I have managed to rebuild my phone into a working concoction of gaffer tape and solder. It's not pretty, but I've got three bars of signal, so after immediately scanning the area for any sign of Ed I set about calling Tess.

Answerphone. Bollocks. I hang up.

It's a whole four hours before Tess returns my call. Thankfully Ed has just gone out for another stint in the saddle so I am relatively relaxed about talking to her. She's been crying.

I try to comfort her, but Ed has threatened to kill her, and sadly she believes him. I think I do too, what a fucking mess.

After about ten minutes she calms herself, but her voice is still pretty shaky.

'I don't know how he could have found out, who have you told?'

'Nobody,' I answer, then continue, 'but Patrick seemed to know all about it the other night; he rang me when you and Ed were at Brooklands.'

'He wouldn't say anything though, surely?'

'I don't know, Tess, it wasn't me who told him in the first place.'

'I know, I'm sorry; it just came out the other night when he came back to our place after the pub. Nobody else was there, not even Ed.'

'Well, I have kept it completely to myself, love, so I guess you're the one to blame on that one.' We talk some more, but draw no conclusions other than Patrick was in some way involved and Ed is mighty pissed off. It also strikes me that with Ed and Claire's new-found fondness for each other, she would no doubt be fuming when I return to sunny Blighty.

To cut a long race short, we finished in third place. This was partly due to a wrong tyre choice during a five in the morning drizzle shower, but of course everyone blamed me for the fucked-up wheel change at the beginning of the race, so I was public enemy number one.

Even Glynn was ignoring me. The traditional après race booze-up was a little lack-lustre to say the least. Only Stevo and the three riders turned up to collect their trophies; the rest of us loaded the trucks and prepared for the off.

It was starting to get dark by the time we were set, and in order to travel as lightly as possible I opted to leave my overstretched rucksack and panniers in the truck, enabling me to make a swift dash for the early ferry unencumbered by luggage.

Shortly after leaving the circuit, however, there is a noticeable drop in temperature. My crash helmet begins to mist up slightly, but I carry on regardless. I tell myself it is only going to be dank whilst in the forest.

The vibration through the handlebars that I had felt on my outward journey seems worse than before, but I figure I'm just noticing it more because I'm cold and tired.

The twisting roads of the Ardennes, whilst delightful on the way here, are now playing tricks on my weary eyes. I continually dab the brakes or flinch as I imagine things scurrying across my path. The daylight has faded to zero and my headlight (or is that my brain) is most certainly not as bright as I would like.

The tiredness is really getting to me. The mechanics usually take it in turns to get a couple of hours' kip during the night, but I hadn't slept at all due to my stressing over the Ed and Tess incident. Something I now deeply regret, in more ways than just one.

I settle into a mind-numbing rhythm, humming to myself as the batteries in my personal stereo have gone almost as flat as my enthusiasm, whilst I wind my way home. Then, all of a sudden, a loud noise like a roulette wheel makes itself known:

Rat…tat…tat…tat…tat…tat…tat…tat…Whhrrrrrrr…silence…

My engine explodes its guts all over me. The searingly hot oil bursts through my jeans and screams pain into my right leg. An engine component flies out of the side of the bike and rips through my trainer, taking half of the nail off my big toe.

The agony must be excruciating, but to be honest, I am so tired and fed up I can't even be bothered to register it. I roll to a stop and let the bike fall on its side in my disgust. Removing my now fully fogged-up crash helmet, I drop it to the ground and sit on a grassy bank that borders the road. After a few moments it starts to rain.

Now, more than anything I crave a cigarette. I had given up the wicked weed ten years ago, but right here, right now, that's all I want. A fag.

I let go the tension held in my muscles and lie back. The rain falls harder, onto my face and over my cheeks, disguising the tears that roll from my sad tired eyes.

I sleep.

* * * * *

'Monsieur! Monsieur!' I wake with a start to find French truck driver bent over me, holding me by my lapels and shaking me violently left and right. He's a slight man with an enormous hooked nose, beneath which sits a dimly glowing cigarette perched between two wispy thin lips. I reach up and grab the cigarette, stuffing it in my mouth and draw on the now neon glowing cherry of fire like my life depends on it.

I cough and choke violently, convulsing into the foetal position, then begin yakking like a mule. The Frenchman stands suddenly and takes a couple of steps back. He looks somewhat puzzled, then runs back to his truck and speeds off before I can explain.

Bollocks.

It's a whole hour before anybody else stops, this time it's a tattooed bull of a man called Ramon, from Barcelona. He doesn't speak a word of English, but gets the gist when I show him my ferry ticket. Unfortunately the cows in the back show their disapproval of sharing their travelling quarters with a dead motorcycle by covering it in excrement as we speed towards Calais. By the time Ramon helps me drag it off the back of the truck it is well and truly looking like a shit-heap.

It takes a couple of hours to find an English trucker going in my direction willing to take me and the bike, but I repay Basil the long haul driver of an empty furniture removals lorry by way of a hot meal and a case of Fosters. He drops me off at junction ten of the M25 just before sunrise.

'Sorry, mate, I can't take you any nearer as I'm due back at the Heathrow depot within the next half-hour, good luck.'

'Thanks for the lift, I appreciate it.' The air brakes 'whoosh' and with a scrunch of gears Basil is gone. It's a three-mile push back home, but with a swollen toe I figure it will seem more like ten. Don't you just hate it when the bloody birds start singing when it's not even fully light yet?

Chapter 28

Bath Bong

taking the joke just a little too far...

I almost collapse with relief and exhaustion as I cross the threshold of the thankfully empty Number 18.

With the bike dumped outside the garage I opt for a little self-indulgence before putting it away. The scrambled egg on toast slips down a treat with the help of a dash of ketchup and a nice cup of tea.

Next, personal hygiene. After 48 long hours in the same clothes there's nothing for it but a red-hot steamer, the ultimate way to enjoy a bath. I scour the kitchen for a large bowl and a deeply dished roasting tray, then to the garage for a length of one quarter-inch diameter rubber hose.

Into the bowl I pour six cans of Stella, then said bowl I place onto the roasting tray. This I fill with ice to keep the beer chilled, then take it upstairs and place it next to the bath. The taps screech a little as they turn, but give a good flow of steaming hot stuff almost immediately.

After stripping off and hopping in, I pour a generous helping of muscle soak bubble bath in along with some moisturising oil and lavender.

Bliss.

I lie back and adjust the taps with my toes, so as the hot is pouring a little more than the cold, but only at the same rate as the overflow hole is letting it out; this way I can enjoy a steadily increasing temperature whilst keeping a constant level. Now the rubber hose comes into play. I clench one end between my teeth, and then dangle the other into the bowl of beer. I purse my lips and suck, with enough vacuum to start the siphon going. Slowly it delivers a constant flow of lovely chilled beer to my coarse dry throat.

The aromatic steam fills my nose, clearing my head of congestion. Tension leaves my body as if my very soul is rising above it. My mind slowly leaves the world behind as the alcohol finds its way through the maze of my grey matter.

I pass out, and dream vividly of lying on the deck of a yacht in some distant paradise, the hypnotic lapping of the sea against the bough... The gentle breeze...

Sleep...
S l e e p...
S l e e p......

AAAAAGGGGGHHHHH!!!!!

F-F-F-F r r e e e e z i n n g g g g c-c-c-c o o o l l l d d d!

My whole body wakes, numb and shivering to the point of convulsing. The bath water has spewed over the side to such a degree that not only is the bathroom totally flooded, but I can see it running down the stairs. The beer bowl is empty, and my head attacked with such a sharp pain I have to check it for axe wounds or bullet holes. My entire skin is not only prune-like in texture but also bright purple with cold.

The tap is still pumping out water, but freezing cold and at a fair rate of knots. I leap from the icy depths and grab my towel from the radiator.

Wet – bollocks!

The end of the formerly dry item was touching the ground, so when the great flood passed, on its way to the landing, the towel drew the water up like blotting paper. Cursing, I splash my way into the spare room and grab a fresh one from the linen cupboard.

Once dry and clothed, sans socks of course, I venture downstairs, noticing there are no electrical items working. No lights, no flashing time on the video that's never been set, no hum from the fridge... just dripping. The room seems darker than I remember – a trick of the light, or just a fuzzy head? Sadly neither.

I look up and notice the stain on the ceiling that runs from one end of the room to the other, turning at the edges and creeping a good 12 inches down the lounge walls.

Smoke damage, oh dear, time to hide in the kitchen.

* * * * *

The familiar jangle of keys in the front door draws me back out of my daydream. I throw the remains of the now cold mug of coffee the neighbour made me down my throat and go to face the music.

'Hazy...Hazy...what the hell has been going on, it smells like you've been barbecuing in a sauna. Why is the ceiling black, and the floor, what in God's name have you done to the floor? Get in here right now, you tosser, and explain this lot!'

I tentatively poke my head around the kitchen door.

'Weeeell...' I pause, trying to think of the best way forward.

'Well, well what? What the fuck have you done to our house?'

'Nothing, honestly, I was in the bath and it all just happened around me.'

'What, what just happened around you; I see fire and floods, but what actually happened?'

'Well, there is some good news, but also a hell of a lot of bad news.'

Claire rolls her eyes and sits on the arm of the soot-stained sofa. The kids charge in through the front door, and straight back out into the garden via the kitchen door.

'I've had a complete disaster of a weekend, it started wi...'

Claire swiftly raises her hand into an open palmed type of stop sign, then with her eyes closed and through gritted teeth snarls, 'The house, just the house, what have you *done* to the house.'

'For fuck's sake, I was coming to that. The bath I fell asleep in somehow overflowed, this soaked through the floor and down into the fuse box on the utility room wall, which in turn caused an electrical short, which started the fire.'

Claire looks at the floor and slowly shakes her head.

'The good news is, that whilst the fire was raging in the utility room, the water was gathering above it in the joists. When the weight of this overcame the soaked plasterboard fixings the whole ceiling came down, extinguishing the fire before it had a chance to spread any further. Stroke of luck, I'd say!'

'Stroke of luck, stroke of fucking luck, are you out of your tiny little mind. I had all my dry cleaning in that utility room – my Jaeger coat and Chanel cocktail dress – and you have the audacity to say, stroke of fucking luck. You make me sick!'

Claire launches off the sofa and violently attacks me with her fists, some of them actually hurt as well!

'Get out, get out of my fucking house you pig, I want a divorce. We should have got one years ago, now get out!'

After a swift gathering of my stuff into a rucksack I step out onto the driveway. I look to my left where my cow-dung covered motorbike is leaning pathetically against the garage, dead and dirty. Beyond that I survey the charred remains of my once beautiful Porsche, now a useless wreck waiting for the scrap men to come.

The rear door of the still immobile van opens with an oilless groan and I dig out my pushbike.

As I leave Number 18 York gardens I give it a last look. The destroyed window frame still wears its scars from the rockery boulder, it's now held together with a tarpaulin and rusty nails. The front door sits ajar, and sports a new black soot-coloured fan rising from where the smoke has escaped and stained the paintwork, and all the windows have steamed up from the damp carpet. What a hell hole.

I wouldn't have regretted leaving if I hadn't noticed Brads and Lara waving slowly as they peer out of their bedroom window. I blow them a kiss and turn to leave.

As I pedal away the tears begin to fall once more as I start to cry.

Chapter 29

Gravity

taking the joke just a little too far...

I sit with my back to the door, so don't see him enter.

'Two pints of Stella please, Dave.' I turn towards the voice; Beaker shoots me a deranged smile then joins me at my table.

'Doctor Stella, I presume.'

'Yeah, s'pose so,' I reply.

'Christ, you're happy, did your gerbil die or something?'

'No, Claire threw me out, I'm staying at my brother Bob's flat till things sort themselves out.'

'But it's your house, she can't do that?'

'I flooded it, then set fire to it. At least the flood put the flames out.'

'Get a grip, man, you're talking gibberish.'

'No, honestly, I just want to drown my sorrows. Thanks for the beer.'

'Fuck off, they're both mine! Sorry – only kidding.'

I raise a half-arsed smile and revert back to my ten-yard stare.

'So, your quick filler system was certainly doing the business at Spa.'

'Yeah, I guess it went some way to recovering the lost time due to the fucked-up wheel change.'

'Bollocks, it was all down to a wrong tyre choice in the night and we all know it.'

'Try telling Stevo that.'

Beaker shrugs in response, then takes a sip of his freshly poured pint.

'So tell me, how does this fuel rig you designed work then?'

I search for an excuse to change the subject but none is forthcoming. 'Well, there are spiral veins that are welded to a cage clockwise inside the conical shaped tank, set at such a pitch that they actually speed the fuel's natural rotation and increase the gravitational pull on the liquid downwards.'

Beaker ponders this for a while, and then draws a conclusion. 'Let me get this right, the earth rotates and creates gravity.'

'Yes.'

'The gravity pulls all things inwards, towards its core.'

'And…'

'So when we travel to Japan and Australia next week – that are, as I'm sure you're aware, south of the equator – using the old plug hole theory, does this mean that instead of speeding the flow of liquid, your veins will actually interfere with the natural direction of the earth's draw, causing untold turbulence and mayhem inside your filler system, ultimately culminating in the fuel fighting gravity as opposed to flowing with it? I'm no expert, but had you actually thought of that?'

'Fuck!' I drop my head even further down, nearly head-butting the pint glass.

'I take that as a no then, do I?' Beaker smiles compassionately and adds, 'Bit of a shit they crated it up for Japan today then, otherwise you could have changed it.'

We drain our pints and I head back to the bar.

'So, when do you think you'll be free to do this prank on Gandhi?' I ask, focussing on this as the only positive thing to distract me from my other thoughts.

Beaker takes a sip from his fresh pint, and ponders the question. 'Monday.'

'Are you sure about that?' I ask.

'Yeah, sure. Why's that?'

'Because there's only about three hours of Monday left.'

'Fuck, better get a move on then!'

'No, we haven't warned Tess or Jane, let's leave it till tomorrow.'

'Tomorrow it is then.'

We 'chink' glasses and consume more and more beer, until Dave the Landlord slings us out.

Chapter 30

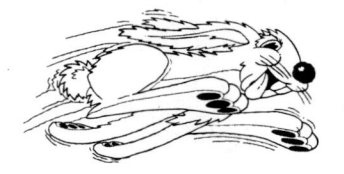

Bunny Love

taking the joke just a little too far...

I wake to the sight of a thousand Teletubbies – red, yellow, green and purple Teletubbies – spread over an expanse of pure white wallpaper.

I'm in agony.

Not sure which is worse, the pain in my head from the copious amount of ale consumed the previous evening, or the pain in my back, as I have spent the night in a bed that is only 4 foot long and hemmed in by several thousand soft toys and Barbie dolls. I struggle awkwardly to remove myself from the pink-duveted torture chamber, swinging my legs around. As I sit up straight I whack my tender head on the overhanging rail for the 'Princess Portia' bed vale, also in pink, of course.

I hop down from the bed and land on the remains of a Lego dinosaur. The sharp plastic edges, whilst digging into my feet, are vying for space within my internal pain threshold with both my head and my back.

Breakfast is a swift bowl of cornflakes on the living room sofa, alone, as my brother is not yet in the land of the living. Since his divorce he has taken to rising at ten o'clock and scraping by, just to make ends meet.

I leave the flat around eight, arriving at work by half-past. After a team meeting at nine we're left to sort our loose ends before the 'big off' to the other side of the world a week Wednesday.

By eleven o'clock I have begun to grow impatient, swiping Gandhi's keys whilst he's off making the coffee. This goes smoothly enough, but with the thought of him quizzing as to their whereabouts, I feel the need to summon a little Dutch courage from a certain Mr Jack Daniels, who I find hiding under my workbench.

I ring Tess at lunchtime to run through the full plan again; she seems to have the grasp of it, but asks far more questions than is warranted for her minor role in this prank of pranks. By two o'clock I begin to relax in the comfort that the stage is set.

At five past I am summoned to Stevo's office. I enter and sit down on the swivel chair in front of him, trying not to sway as the whisky starts to buzz around in my head. The weighty stress in the air subsides as the chair creaks to break the silence.

'As you are no doubt aware, Hazy, the team has been far from its usual well-oiled machine this month.'

'Yes, you could say there have been some hiccups, Steve, but where exactly do you think the finger of blame could be pointing?'

'Squarely at you, you prat, or I wouldn't be wasting my breath firing you.'

'Firing me, why?'

'Yes, firing you! We employed Ed Black to win the championship for us; we employ you to make that possible. The tension between you two is clear; the fiasco of a wheel change at Spa last week highlighted that a little too publicly. Not only that, but it has been brought to my attention that you are hiding alcohol under your workbench – this I find totally unacceptable,' Stevo continues, red-faced now and leaning forward a little more aggressively. 'To top it all, I learned today from overhearing a conversation with a couple of your colleagues, that the filler system you designed is destined to fail in Japan because of the adverse rotational force in the Southern Hemisphere. You are a liability, Hazy, and I just can't have that in a factory team. I'm sorry but you've got to go. It's company policy to give you a month's pay, but due to the dangerous nature of the sport you are not allowed to work it, so you are suspended with immediate effect, then released from contract exactly one month from today. You will leave the building immediately and hand in all keys and passes to Sally at the front desk, are we clear?'

'Err, no, not really. So you're firing me because I don't get on with Ed?'

'No, I'm firing you because you have too many issues to deal with at the moment, you're world is a fucking mess and you couldn't concentrate if your life depended on it, let alone a rider's, now get out of my office before I get upset and have you thrown out.'

The Crown beckons like never before, but first I have the little task of obtaining some blood for tonight's practical joke. Good job I've been fired or I might have struggled to find the time. Only problem now is, my only form of transport is a pushbike. At least I won't get done for drink driving!

I pedal the length of Weybridge High Street in search of the butcher's that Chris, my old school friend, works at. All I can find though, are coffee bars and overpriced ladies' hair salons. I stop and ask an elderly looking gent, as he's sure to know.

'Do you know where the butcher's has gone please, mate?'

'Now then, young man, are you referring to the late Mr Gladstone's place? I served with him in the war you know, lovely chap, such a shame. Survived the Hun, but had one of his testicles bitten off by that wretched dog he insisted on keeping. It happened when he got home that night in 1983 or was it '4… it all gets so foggy you know. I told him time and time again, as did Agnes, but…'

'Sorry to have troubled you, mate.' I manage to get in somewhat edgeways as I turn on my heel, or should that be wheel, and beat a swift retreat. One thing has become painfully obvious: after several passes up and down, there are certainly no butcher's shops in the High Street. Closest I can come to it is the meat counter in the supermarket at the far end.

I lean my bike up against the steel railing next to the trolley park and head inside.

'You can't just leave that there, sir. Health and Safety would have a fit if an officer were to see it sticking out into the public walkway like that. You need to put it over there, sir, in the cycle rack we have provided at no extra cost to the customer,' a dictatorial type in a green uniform informs me.

'I'll only be a tick, I've just got to get some blood.'

'Blood, sir, oh no, we don't handle donations here, sir. They are over in the town hall today from four o'clock. Didn't you read the posters?'

'No, I don't want to give blood, I only want to take some.'

'Take, take, take…I don't know, people today,' he says, shaking his head. 'You still can't leave your bike there, sir.'

His disapproving frown says it all. I turn tail and push it over to the bike rack, parking it nose-first amongst the kids' BMXs and grown-ups' million-pound mountain bikes.

The conceited grin on the doorman makes me want to punch him, but I could do without being arrested today so I just return a sarcastic smile. Finding the butcher's counter was a piece of cake; it was next to the patisserie (why do they insist on giving them French names?). I explain my strange request to the lad behind the counter. He explains that the meats are all drained of blood at the abattoir before delivery to the squeaky-clean supermarket shelves.

'Don't you just have a bit, I'm really desperate; couldn't you just wring out a couple of out-of-date steaks or something?'

He gives me a puzzled look before disappearing off to get the manager, who promptly asks me to leave under the supervision of Mr Conceited Doorman. I retrieve my bike once outside again, and after a few wobbly pedals glance back to the green figure, who is still grinning as I flick two fingers up at him over my shoulder. Damn it, what next.

I make my way to the park, finding an empty bench upon which to perch and ponder. It doesn't take long, a scurrying from the bushes followed by a couple of jostling squirrels set the cogs back into motion.

'Got it!' I exclaim, and stand to do a little jig on the spot. Just then my phone rings, and Beaker's voice blurts from the earpiece, 'I've got to be quick, just nipped out for a fag, Gandhi will no doubt join me any second.'

'What's up?'

'Nothing, I just wondered if you've scored any Dracula juice yet.'

'Funny you should ask. I was slung out of Waitrose a few minutes ago by some miserable bastard, but since seeing a couple of rodents having a punch-up in the park I've come up with an alternative plan.'

'A cunning plan?'

'Oh yes, a cunning plan indeed. A rabbit, I'm going to buy a rabbit.'

'I thought you were slung out of Waitrose.'

'I was, but I plan on getting a live one from the pet shop in Addlestone, then slit its throat at the crucial moment to spurt blood over the front of the car!'

'Christ! You can't do that, it's sick.'

'No it's not, we slaughter thousands of animals every day for food and clothing, what difference does one more make?'

'Quite a lot to the cute flopsy-eared bunny I should think.'

'Don't be so soft, if your conscience is that strong you can sling it on the barbie when we've finished instead of buying a kebab. See you in the Crown at six.' I hang up and hop on my bike in search of Flopsy, the unwitting martyr.

Addlestone High Street is only four miles away, or so I thought, but on the rusty heap of junk I'm using for transport it may as well be the far side of China. Squeak buzz, squeak buzz, squeak buzz, the bike protests as I pedal into the headwind of the dual carriageway. The tyre is rubbing on the mudguard and the brakes are dragging sporadically as the buckled wheels turn just a little slower than I would like for the amount of effort I'm putting in. A damp sweat begins to grow across my back and I find myself short of breath. Eventually I reach the roundabout at the end, and coast down the gentle slope into the parade of slightly dilapidated shops.

The 'ding ding' of an overhead brass bell welcomes me into the sprawling mess that is home to the most sad and manky creatures this side of a vivisection laboratory.

Frenzied scurrying and squawking accompany my every footstep, as deeper into the pet's prison I go. A small but cheery man appears from behind a sliding screen that separates this din from his humble living accommodation in the rear.

'Hello, sir, and what can I be helping sir with today. A bag of feed possibly, or a 6 ft alligator, sir. What is it to be, I wonder; don't worry about me, sir, just a little joke of mine, haven't really got any feed!'

He laughs to himself at this no doubt massively overused line and sets about feverishly sweeping away the brown pellets and straw strewn across the counter top with a dustpan and brush.

'Can I grab one of those rabbits in the hutch by the window please.'

'A rabbit, how wonderful, sir. Will you be calling it… Starsky, you know, as it spends most of its time in a…hutch, sir?' Again the laugh escapes from his larynx, and I can't wait to get out of this idiot's shop.

'Any of them will do, what about that one in the corner?'

'Oh the Polish Dwarf, sir, very popular that one, sir, sold three this month already. How about this little chap, sir, it's a Dutch – breed that is, not nationality. Great with kids, so soft and cuddly. Then there's of course the Red-eyed Himalayan with its fabulous black and white coat, but they tend to be…'

'No you idiot, the big one in the corner,' I interject, just a little too aggressively.

'Oh, sorry sir. That one, it's not really what you want is it, sir? It's a Belgian Hare you know, as you can see he has a fabulous reddish brown coat and those powerful long legs are just magnificent, aren't they sir!'

'Come on, how much is it?'

'He, sir, he is £52.'

'Fifty fucking quid for a poxy rabbit!'

'Well sir if you are going to be rude I shan't let you take any of them. I take great pride in whom I pass my animals on to.'

'Shame you don't take a bit more pride in the rubbish tip you live in then,' I quietly mutter to myself, then delve into my pocket and thrust two twenties and a ten on the counter.

'Call it fifty quid and we've got a deal.'

'And would sir like to buy some feed?'

'No, I don't think that will be necessary, thanks all the same.'

'But sir, he's bound to be hungry in the morning. And they do get a little feisty when their little tummies are rumbling.'

'Not where he's going, mate, he won't be feisty or famished I can assure you.'

The shopkeeper unfolds a flat-pack cardboard hutch for Starsky and pops him inside.

'There we are, sir, all snuggled up and ready to go.'

I head outside and strap the box to the handlebars.

Once back in Weybridge (a damned sight quicker with the wind behind me, I can tell you!) I check the clock on the church steeple just as it chimes three-thirty. The High Street is awash with colour as 3-ft high people carrying school bags and hockey sticks flood the pavement. I pause a second as I can hear a faint but familiar noise, 'Dad...Dad...over here, Dad.' I scan the crowd and pick out Lara's beaming face as she runs towards me, arms outstretched, with her golden hair in perfect pigtails. She grabs my leg and squeezes it till it goes numb. I crouch down and cuddle her back. I feel as if I'll explode with emotion at the joy of seeing her.

'Have you had a good day at school, darling?' I enquire.

'What's in the box, Daddy?' She makes her way around to the front of my bike and peeks inside.

'Daddy! You've bought me a bunny rabbit, wow! Lydia, Lydia look at my new rabbit!' A horde of small people then swoop in on me and I am surrounded by oohs and aahs as Lara shows her entire class the feisty hare.

It's too late. Bollocks. It doesn't take long before 'Ol' Big Chief Face like Thunder' arrives.

'What on earth do you think you're doing?' snarls Claire. It's the first time we'd spoken since she threw me out. 'You have destroyed both my and their lives in the last couple of months, and now you're trying to buy back favour with your own kids, who despise you, by giving them ridiculous presents. You're sick, Hazy, sick. You really do need to see a psychiatrist, you fucking weirdo.' She turns her attention towards Lara now, 'Come on, darling, we need to go and get Brads.'

'But Mum, Mum, we need to take my bunny!'

Claire scowls at me as she rips the cardboard box from the handlebars. 'Not funny, you arsehole, not funny at all.'

I shrug in submission, 'His name's Starsky,' I call after them, as Lara steals a smiling glance back over her shoulder before they disappear into the crowd.

'Oh Christ, where the hell am I going to get my blood from now,' I groan, just a little too loudly, earning me a strange look from a passer-by and a tap on the shoulder from the priest that is stood behind me.

'Young man…'

'Ever so sorry padre, I didn't mean to take the Lord's name in vain.'

'Oh don't worry about that, my child, a swift couple of Hail Mary's should sort that one out for you. I mean only to comment that there is a session in the church hall today for blood donors, so if you are a little anaemic I'm sure they'll be able to either sort you out, or at least point you in the right direction.'

A miracle! All I have to do is turn up and mooch around until the opportunity arises to swipe a pint, then off to meet Beaker.

'Thanks, Father, I owe you big time.'

I hop upon my bike once more and head for the church hall. I cannot see any way in other than the main entrance. I park my bike around the back, next to the fire escape and head inside.

'Good afternoon, young man, have you donated before?' the rather imposing-looking nurse enquires as I enter the foyer.

'Yeah,' I reply, 'I'm sure I gave you lot a couple of quid at Christmas.'

'No, sir, *blood*. Have you donated blood before?'

It drains from my face, I glance down to check there isn't a red puddle at my feet. 'Err, no. I…err…am only here to have a look around, you know, get the feel for it, in case I want to donate next time.' I hadn't thought of an alibi for being here and it shows. The nurse slaps a worn but colourful folder into my hands, and with her arm around my back, guides me into the waiting area.

'Your name is…?' the nurse enquires.

'Hayes, Paul Hayes. Why?'

She raises her eyebrows and says, just loud enough for everyone to hear, 'Don't worry, Mr Hayes, we all have our reservations the first time we donate, but you have to remember that you are doing a wonderful thing; you might this very day be saving a newborn baby's life, or ensuring your own survival should you be mown down by a reckless driver upon your departure.'

I almost assure her this will be highly unlikely as I know Beaker's whereabouts, but think better of it. One of the other donors starts to clap. Then another, and then another. Before long half of the occupants of the room are giving me congratulations and shaking my hand. What can I do? I have to go through with it. I sit in silence once the hullabaloo subsides and dread the upcoming draining of my arm.

I fill in the form I am given, and with a trembling hand, give it back to the nurse, who flashes me a smile of reassurance that borders on sarcastic.

'Paul Hayes,' crackles over the inadequate Tannoy. I may have missed it altogether had I not been listening intently with absolute dread. I take my seat opposite an Asian doctor who asks me, amongst other things, if I had had anal sex in the last six months. I answer in the negative, which prompts him to stick a needle in my finger to draw some red stuff. A small squirt shoots into a bottle, making me feel quite strange at the sight. The doctor then quickly stems the flow with a tissue.

'Press this for a moment and the bleeding will cease.'

'That wasn't so bad, I expected you to take a bit more than that though,' I say. 'Can I go now?'

The doctor smiles, 'No, Mr Hayes, this is only to determine your blood group. Please take a seat and you will be called in due course.'

I stand and return to my seat, hoping nobody else heard my dumb comment, and in doing so catch a look into the main hall. Beds have been set up all over the place. It looks like a film set where they convert the school gym into a makeshift hospital when there's a nuclear radiation leak or an incurable plague to contain. One thing's for sure, I do *not* want to go in there and join them. I hastily change direction and make my way back out to the foyer.

'The toilets are that way, Mr Hayes,' the intimidating nurse guarding the door states, pointing back to from whence I had come. I turn, defeated, without even a word of objection, and sit back in my seat.

Whilst perusing the colourful folder I realise that I am actually doing something decent for a change. The text explains how thousands of people are saved from the clutches of death every day by something as simple as a pint of my blood. I smile with a little satisfaction and decide to ask the little bleeder who bleeds me to knock me out a spare half-pint for the prank, once I have donated my first pint that is. I scan the room for familiar faces, and my eyes rest on a gorgeous-looking dark-blonde-haired girl in the back row. I recognise her, I just can't think where from. I gaze for a little too long, as she meets it with a small smile, and then embarrassingly looks back down at her folder. I know her, I'm sure, I just can't place where from.

Time drags by, and half an hour passes before the Tannoy crackles back into life, summoning me into the war zone to be drained.

PING! It comes to me as I stand; 'Keira Knightley!' The girl in the back row blushes, then looks at the floor as I realise I have let my thoughts escape through my big mouth. I hurry past, now also embarrassed at pointing her out to everyone in the room, and enter the main hall. From the sight I expect to hear wailing and crying, but everyone seems quite up-beat. 'Can't be that bad then,' I think to myself as I'm shown my bed by Kevin, my greasy-haired little bleeder for the day.

'Hello, sir,' he says in a nasal drone of a voice, 'when you are comfortable I will insert a small needle into the main artery in your arm, then allow you to bleed for a few moments. Are you left or right handed, sir?'

'Right, why?'

'Oh we usually bleed the less used arm as it may sting mildly afterwards, sir.'

'Would you be so kind,' I ask, 'as to stick another sack on after I've given the NHS their bit, as I need about half a pint of my own.'

'Oh no, sir, couldn't possibly do that. You will feel a little giddy as it is with a pint missing, so to draw another half-pint would mean you would have an unacceptably low amount of blood in your system. This would result in dizziness, weakness and generally poor judgment. You would feel almost drunk, sir.'

'Excellent, take three pints then,' I quip, but it is lost on Kevin, who just goes about his work without further comment.

Before long I have a flow of claret from my left arm topping up the nation's needy. I roll a piece of tubular plastic back and forth in my palm to help prevent pins and needles (other than the fookin' enormous needle hanging out of my arm that is…). Kevin returns, placing a tuft of medi-wipe in the crook of my elbow to stem the flow, as he withdraws the tube from my arm.

'Place a little pressure here, sir, and feel free to help yourself to tea and biscuits once you feel able.'

'Feel able?' I ask as I swing my legs down from the bed and sit up swiftly, only to find I am indeed a little light-headed. A minute or so passes, and I seem to feel straight enough to make it safely across the room without having to stop and join the blue rinse brigade, who have all congregating around the tea urn. As I make my way to the door I notice all the bags of blood are being carefully labelled and packed into white polystyrene cool boxes. I'm tempted to swipe one, but the crucifix bearing down on me from the wall above is enough of a jolt to my conscience.

Once outside I am fortified by the crisp fresh air, but I'm sadly still lacking in my quest for Dracula's tipple.

My phone rings, it's my brother, Bob.

'Hello, mate...eh?...what?...sorry, mate, I can't hear a thing.' I hang up. The phone jumps to life again, but still no signal. The third time it rings I have moved far enough away from the building to achieve a couple of bars on my screen.

'Where are you, mate?' he asks.

'At the church hall, giving some blood.'

'Bollocks, I meant to go down myself, but I'm still stuck in Bristol. Anyway, do you think you could nip into the Kingston office and pick up any post that's there. I won't be back for a couple of days and I need you to fax a letter to me that should have arrived this morning.'

'Err, not today, I have some pressing matters I need to resolve. You don't know where I can get a half-pint of blood from, do you?'

'Well, you're at a donor session, haven't they got any spare?'

'No, already asked them to bleed me off an extra bit but they weren't having it. I then contemplated swiping what I had donated, but my conscience got the better of me.'

'Well go in and pretend to be me then. Once they start you going, just pull the needle out and leg it. You won't have any conscience issues because you've already given them all they are allowed to take, and after all, it is your blood you are leaving with, so you're not actually stealing it.'

'You're a fucking genius!' A smile grows across my pallid face.

'Here we are...' there's a rustling noise on the line as Bob opens his wallet, 'right, my donor number is: 00399854782, registered at my flat.'

'Brilliant, I'll try to get your post in the morning. See ya.' I thumb the little red terminate key with a 'blip'.

I make my way back to the hall, but in doing so catch my reflection in one of the windows.

'Bugger.' I have a wad of white medi-wipe strapped to my arm. I take a peek to see if a scab has formed, but this only serves to resume the flow. I strap it back in place and head towards the High Street to find a disguise.

* * * * *

I return an hour later sporting a new, slightly less conspicuous, arm dressing, a Fat Face hoody and freshly cropped hair. I approach the front desk with some trepidation, convinced of discovery any moment, but breathe a sigh of relief when the nurse buys the 'It was my twin brother here earlier' line and hands me the now all too familiar information folder. (Besides, what on earth would any normal person be doing, acting as an impostor in order to give more blood than they are actually allowed to?) I sit in the queue, as before, and daydream until it's time for a little more bleeding.

Mandy is the nice young nurse that shows me to my bed, and whizzes through the procedure as only someone who really has 'done it a thousand times before' can. Before I know it I am lying on my back, rolling the plastic tube back and forth again, but this time in my right hand.

I crane my neck around to see the bag swiftly filling, and decide just before the halfway mark that we should have enough. I cringe at the thought of yanking the tube from my arm, so decide to pull it from the bag instead. This I do by squeezing the tube with the thumb and forefinger of my right hand, whilst giving it a sharp upward tug, out of the bag, with my left. A few drips hit the floor, forming a small puddle, but nowt to worry about. I then set about un-hooking the bag from its stand. My arms throb with their recent draining, but both seem to be functioning properly. Carefully I slide the bag up and over the chrome arm onto which it is impaled and look around for some way to plug the hole.

'What seems to be the problem, Mr Hayes?' I'm startled to hear. The nurse from the front desk is at my shoulder with a face like a slapped arse.

It takes me by such a surprise that my only instinct is to run. As my legs leap down from the bed, their feet meet with the purple pool of blood below, causing a slip and a slide as my weight is capsized. I crash to the floor with a giddy head, and in doing so both release my pinched grip on the tube, causing the re-activation of flow from my arm, and also land on the unsealed bag of blood, sending jets from their small orifices streaming over the entire room. It's carnage. The blood-soaked woman on the bed next to me starts screaming hysterically, the man next to her shouts to the nurse that his Ralph Lauren shirt has been ruined, the teenage hippy opposite seems to have lapsed into a wide-eyed coma and is frothing at the mouth with shock as the nurse called Mandy runs around covered in blood splats trying hopelessly to calm everyone. I make a dash for the fire door, but progress is hampered, crashing from one bed to another as the blood loss is now taking its toll on my balance. I burst through the door to the sound of the automatic alarm system firing up and glance back at the mayhem as the sprinklers burst into life.

Once outside, I somehow manage to mount my bicycle and make it out of the churchyard and back onto the High Street before falling off it again. People gawp and rush to my aid, no wonder really as I look like I've just been run over by a petrol tanker, but I don't have time for their concerns and re-mount to make headway towards Bob's flat, stopping briefly to tie a knot in the tube and poke the end back into the bag.

I fall off six more times on my way back.

Chapter 31

The Ball Begins to Roll

taking the joke just a little too far...

In dazed confusion I head towards the Crown, stopping briefly again at chez Fat Face for yet another set of unsoiled clothes. Shortly after five, Beaker turns up at the pub with Gandhi.

'We would have been here sooner, but Gandhi the prat has lost his keys,' quips Beaker as he rests a round of drinks on the table.

'You look like shit, what the hell have you been up to?'

'A long story involving a rabbit, a priest and a nurse, but I shan't go into it now, best save it till we're really plastered, cheers!' I take another sip from my pint, and feel the rush as my alcohol to diminished blood supply ratio surges for the worst.

As the poison works its way through my weakened body, the concept of time evaporates. After three more pints we all appear to be slurring. I glance at my watch, it isn't even seven yet.

'Another pint anyone?' enquires Beaker.

'Don't you have to drive tonight?' I retort with a swift kick under the table.

'Yeah, I've only had a couple; I'll be fine,' he answers, with a frown. I raise a single eyebrow in disgust, but can't come on too strong or Gandhi might suss something's afoot.

Two pints later and we're all too pissed to care. Suddenly, buzz buzz, I have a text message.

'TESS MOBILE'. I open it…

'CAN'T LEAVE DOOR OPEN, KEYS @ MY HOUSE FROM 8.' This thumps a nerve.

'Beaker, shouldn't you be giving Gandhi a lift home by now?' This was accompanied by another swift kick under the table.

'Err, yeah, alright bloke, I'll be back in two shakes of a rat's ringpiece.' Beaker and Gandhi down their pints and head for the door. I order pint number six from the fabulous Sarah, and wait for the return of Mister Beaker.

* * * * *

People come and go, some just sit at the bar, roll-up in one hand, stout in the other, putting the world to rights. I watch the shadows stretch across the lawned rear garden that eventually gives way to the inevitable darkness. I don't know how long I've waited, having forgotten what time they'd left. All I know is that the beer is working nicely.

'If he's not back by half-eight I'll call the whole thing off,' the voice in my head informs me. My eyes then glance to the clock behind the bar to confirm it is actually eight thirty-seven.

'Damn, better make it nine. If he's not here by nine I'll definitely call it off.'

Car headlights sporadically illuminate the overhead beams as they pull into and out of the car park, each set I hope will be Beaker's.

Solemnly I celebrate the passing of nine o'clock with a vodka shot and another pint. I can relax now; it can wait till another time. Halfway through composing an abortive text message to Tess, a single headlight beam dances across the ceiling.

'Motorbike,' I think, and strain to look out of the window. 'Too late,' as it disappears around the side of the building before I can catch a glance.

Moments later Beaker rolls in, barging into an obese woman perched on a rather worried barstool, sending her gin and tonic flying, and narrowly missing her elephant skin handbag sat on the floor below. Apologies accepted and he sways his way over to thump himself down on the seat opposite me.

'Right, bloke, we all set?'

'No, I'm calling it off, we're both too pissed and it's far too late.'

'You told me it had to be dark; besides, it's not that late is it?'

'No, you prat, I said we had to be at Gandhi's by nightfall so as he couldn't see the body properly. It's gotten too late I say.'

'Err, you might be right there, but it's too late to go back, not too late to go forward, as I've already done the car. After I dropped Gandhi off, I was on my way to Coco's place to try and score some weed to chill me out a bit. Halfway there I realised he lived at the end of Tess's road, so I would be going there later with you anyway. I swung into a cul-de-sac to turn around and lo and behold a fucking wall jumped out and twatted the front of my car in.'

'Hence the single headlight.'

'Yeah, how do you know that?'

'I thought it was a bike coming in, I expected to see Glynn or Patrick holding a crash helmet.'

'Oh, yeah, I see what you mean. Anyway, Gandhi is out of his scull by now; Jane handed him the tin of beer with the sleeping pills in while I was there just to make sure he drank it, and if he sees my car tomorrow with the damage, it makes the whole plot less credible if we do it later on.'

'Mmm, you're right I suppose, but no more drinking. You were only meant to be acting pissed, and you're a little too convincing for my liking.'

Chapter 32

Settling In

taking the joke just a little too far...

Joe Soap sits quietly in his little hedge hideaway. It's quite a home from home these days; he has his digital camera poised to record any extra-marital activity, the tripod aiming it squarely through Ed's front window. His flask is topped with tomato soup, and the tree stump he uses for a stool now sports a generous cushion. He wonders just how many hours he has sat there, or indeed how many more there are to come.

Boredom had set in hours ago. He idly thumbs the keypad of his mobile phone, trying first an orange background with blue letters, then blue with yellow. Neither do it for Joe so he returns the screen to its dour grey with blue.

Suddenly he perks up at the squeal of brakes, followed by a scuffing noise, as if someone has grazed a kerb.

A one-eyed Volvo lollops into the road. Joe ducks when the headlight sweeps through the hedge as Beaker swings the car around to park in Tess's driveway.

Joe spots Beaker and Hazy, then quickly tap, tap, taps a text message to Ed, informing him of the predicted guests…

Chapter 33

Game On!

taking the joke just a little too far...

We arrive at Tess's house a little after ten. Ed has gone out and left her with the kids, so sadly she's unable to join us on the Shepperton raid.

We sit in her kitchen as I run through the geography of the studios with her once again, just to be certain. Beaker disappears into the lounge in search of the telly.

With pen and paper, the two of us sketch out a floor plan of the studios. Once confident of our direction, I kiss Tess on the cheek, and then pick up the workshop key as I make my way to the lounge.

'WHAT THE FUCK ARE YOU DOING?' I demand.

'Just a little pick me up, it won't do any harm.' Beaker stands up from the coffee table, sniffing the remnants of white powder from his nose. I take the large but half-empty tumbler of Scotch from his hand and thump him on the shoulder.

'Fucking grow up will you, this is serious.'

'Sorry, Hazy, I thought it was just a prank.'

This throws me somewhat, as it is.

'Yeah, you're right. Sorry for thumping you, I'm just a bit wound up today, you know. Anyway, I thought you didn't go to Coco's?'

'Well, after I twatted the car, I was so stressed I couldn't wait, so I went there anyway. D'you want a spliff to chill out?'

'No I don't want a sodding spliff. Let's just get this over with, shall we?'

* * * * *

We cruise down Shepperton High Street. I don't know who's in a worse state – me, Beaker, or the car he is supposedly piloting. He's so pissed by now he even has one hand over his left eye to reduce the double vision. How on earth we haven't been pulled over yet I will never know.

We find a secluded parking spot at the back of the studios, next to the chain-link fence we need to scale. One look at the barbed wire on top of it has me searching the car's tool kit for a pair of wire cutters. Moments later a hole is snipped in said fence with the car's Fisher Price pliers. I go first, slipping on the damp grass, followed by Beaker, who falls flat on his back within 10 steps of entering.

We make the short dash across the lawn to the rear of the rigging shed. Once under the cover of shadows I unfold the map to get my bearings. Ahead and to the left is the prosthetics department, our original rendezvous with Tess, so to the right of us should be the covered courtyard.

We enter the rigging shop through a fire exit on the back wall. The whole building is timber, reeking of linseed oil and hemp. It smells a bit like some flats I've lived in, but best not go into that one just now. We thread our way through the maze of rope and masts, eventually finding our exit at the opposite end of the warehouse.

Beaker is obviously restraining himself as he sniggers quietly and limits himself to just the one 'Aye aye Cap'n!'

I push the solid oak door and it opens with a creak, the pitch heightening the further it swings. This reveals a glow of blue moonlight that illuminates the courtyard through its glass roof. Tropical palm trees flood the cobbled enclosure with a sprawl of vines and other unlikely foliage, all potted and ready for an instant jungle scene. The effect is so real I find myself frequently checking my shoulders for large hairy spiders. I glance back to check Beaker is still up to speed, and give him a reassuring nod.

Next up is the gun shop, thankfully they don't keep real ones so we find the door unlocked. We start at the Flintlock end and travel through time like Doctor Emmett Brown's De-Lorean passing Napoleonic war tools, a few cannons from Trafalgar, Messrs Smith and Wesson, a few Enfields, Gatling guns, Bren guns, Lugers, Colt 45s, M16s and an array of hand-held automatic weapons. We eventually discover our exit just to the left of the *Starship Troopers*' Photon mega blasters.

'Freeze motherfucker an' empty yo' wallet, nigger!' I turn on my heel to see Beaker pointing a hand-gun at 45° and his left hand clenched in a fist with his little and index fingers pointing downward, in a rap star stylie.

He bursts out laughing as I snatch the rubber weapon from him.

'Will you pack it in, you're going to get us caught!' I hiss under my breath. He dips his head to one side like a naughty schoolboy and does a Benny Hill-esque salute.

'Yes boss, I'za gonna be a good slave from now on, you'll see, please don't put dem chains back on though, I'za beggin' ya, boss.'

'Will you cut it out!' I implore.

There's a short dash we have to make in order to bridge the gap between the gun shop and the back door of the special effects building. This we have to time perfectly as there is a sweeping camera that Tess has warned me about, whose duty it is to cover this open area. I scroll through to find the stopwatch function on my phone, then click the go button as soon as it points sufficiently away.

Sixteen seconds. That is how long we've got to drag Mr De Niro from one door to the other without any chance of being spotted.

I give Beaker the nod, and we ready ourselves to beat the camera. Once it sweeps past, we're off. I punch the start button to time the operation on my phone again as we go.

The dash is easy, but now the hard part. Fumbling with sweaty hands, I struggle to get the key in the slot. The bunch slides from my grasp and I drop them into the dirt below. We both bend to pick them up, banging heads as we do so.

'Fuck it, abort… ABORT!'

We dash back into the cover of the shadows cast by the gun shop. After holding fire a moment to catch our breath, I realise those seven pints were definitely a bad idea as my head is spinning like a top.

I spot the keys glistening under the spotlight as the camera sweeps past again.

'Right, this time let me sort the keys. You stand clear until the door's open, okay?' Beaker grins inanely, and I wonder how much coke he has actually stuffed up his nose. Too late to worry about it now though, I suppose.

I zero the stopwatch again and make another dash for it, this time all goes to plan and we are inside within nine seconds. Perfect.

The back door opens into the kitchen; we both take a quick drink of water from the tap as the beer buzz is slowly being replaced by a dehydrated head thump. Leaving Beaker behind, I make my way tentatively through a flock of fibreglass flamingos (or fling-gos as Brads calls them) and head towards Little Jack's office.

The original scene from the film has Kenneth Brannagh, the mad Dr Frankenstein, hoisting the monstrous Robert De Niro from a large copper drum by way of a large chain attached to a wooden pulley system. The scene is dark and creepy, save for the constant flashes of electricity, lightning and sporadic moonlight from the racing clouds through the high windows in his ancient laboratory. The scene laid out before me is not dissimilar: dark, creepy and rather alien.

There are part-built animatronic animals, human limbs and full torsos strewn about everywhere. I bump into a standing grizzly bear and let out a yelp. This, and the creepy illumination from the floodlights outside really conspire to put the willies up me.

Once over at Jack's office I take a peek in to see what he's been up to. There's an R2-D2 with its front panel removed and a mass of wires spewing from it in front of his desk. C-3P0's head is also present, but no more evidence of the effeminate robot is apparent.

Glancing up, I can see my goal. De Niro is right where he should be, hanging from the rafters by his chains. I squint as my eye tracks the source of his suspension, and find the pulley behind a burgundy-coloured velvet curtain.

Thankfully the chain winch has a crank handle in it, so I immediately set to work.

'Skreeeeechhhhh' the moving parts complain loudly as it's turned, so progress is painfully slow. Ten minutes pass like an hour, but eventually he is down and we have our corpse.

Just as I am about to call for Beaker to give me a hand lifting him, I freeze! I can hear the rattle of keys in the front door. The deadbolt unlocks with a heavy clunk. I dash behind the curtain as the door swings open and in strolls Uncle Jack.

Sweating profusely, I notice my hands are clenched in tight fists as my jaw aches with the tension it carries.

After a painful few moments I hear the distinctive rattle of a loose-fitting window in Uncle Jack's office door as it swings to a close. The muted sounds of an argument with somebody on the other side of the Atlantic then ensue for the next 20 minutes. Hoping Beaker has sussed what is going on, I daren't look out to see if I can see him in the kitchen. I don't need to though, because in a moment of relative silence I can hear the lazy sod snoring.

Moments later Uncle Jack's office door swings open and bangs against something solid, causing the thin glass to shudder again. He stands for several moments breathing deeply, trying to relax.

He pulls a roll-up from behind his ear, re-licks the join and pops it into his mouth. The familiar clunk, strike, crackle of his vintage brass Zippo lighter fills the air, and is soon accompanied by the raw smell of un-burnt lighter fuel.

Drawing his first breath through the glowing bud of tobacco he rolls his head back with his eyes shut. He holds the toxin in his lungs for an eternity before slowly exhaling a thin jet of grey smoke through tight rounded lips, punctuating it with a perfect smoke ring.

As his eyes slowly open, head still back, a look of horror spreads across his face as he glares at the bare rafters.

'What on earth has been going on here then?' he mutters under his breath, clearly audible in the cavernous room.

The echo of his wooden-heeled shoes marching briskly towards me on the heavily varnished floor fills me with such dread I can feel my heart sink past my testicles.

He stops, inches short of the curtain and sinks down onto one knee, over De Niro's body. He runs his hands over the mannequin to check nothing's damaged, then shakes his head.

I can barely breathe, he's so close I'm sure he will hear my heart thumping.

'Bloody work experience kids, I'll have the little toerag marched off the premises for this tomorrow.'

Jack stands, pulls his waistcoat taught, and then walks somewhat more sedately towards the entrance.

I almost lose control of my bladder as the welcome wave of relief flows through me when the door shuts firmly behind him. I dash to the kitchen to find Beaker lying flat out on a counter top, the tiny bulges of his closed eyes swivelling manically in their sockets. Whatever his drink and drug addled brain was dreaming about, it was far from relaxing!

I touch his arm and he bolts upright with a start, eyes wide and glaring.

'Fuck, fuck, I just dreamt…err…um… Bollocks, I can't remember. It was mad though, I remember that much.'

'Yeah right, let's dance, we don't have long.'

'Okay, boss, you lead, but mind my toes.' He pisses himself laughing for a moment. I leave him to it and head back to Mr De Niro. Once we have carried said body to the back door, I glance through the window to accurately gauge when the camera has safely swept past us.

'On the count of three we sprint like mad, okay? One… two…three!' Bursting through the door, we perform a push-me-pull-you kind of lollop across the yard, Beaker stumbles, but recovers well without a fall. We dump the body in the shadows and pause to catch our breath.

Tracing our footsteps back the way we came proves to be somewhat harder than anticipated. We persevere though, only dropping him once as I catch my foot on some rope in the rigging shop. This brings all three of us to the ground, but thankfully without injury.

With only the slippery sprint across the lawn to go I feel a sense of achievement already growing inside me; that or my bladder is full to bursting point.

We make the dash and slip through the chain-link fence with no further drama. Now the body is safely in the boot, we walk around to the front and get in. Beaker fumbles in his pockets then shoots me a pathetic wounded rabbit look.

'Go on then, tell me you've lost the sodding keys.'
'I've lost the sodding keys… Sorry Hazy.'
'How did you open the car then?'
'The locks are a bit dodgy so I never bother.'
'Wonderful… You stay put; I'll go back and look for them.'

I retrace our steps once again, this time slowly though, using the light from the screen of my mobile phone as a makeshift torch.

Twenty minutes later and I successfully locate them in the gun shop, sat on the bench where he had picked up the rubber pistol.

Briskly I make my way back, but stop, stunned at Beaker's stupidity as the car looms into view.

'What the fuck have you done?' I demand.
'What?'
'What do you mean "What?", the fucking blood all over the front of the car, that's what.'
'You told me we had to cover the bonnet in blood to make it more realistic; you even put the bag of it in the glove box.'
'Yes, yes I know. I meant when we were outside Gandhi's house, you idiot. Now we have to drive six miles down the road with you pissed as a parrot, carrying a small Colombian's chemistry set in your pocket, with only half the lights on your blood-splattered car working and a stolen corpse in the boot at two o'clock in the morning! Don't you think we might look a *little* fucking suspicious?'

Beaker shrugs and replies, 'Err, it's nearer nine miles actually.'

'No it isn't, it's six to Gandhi's house – if that.'

'Err, no. Nearer nine I'd say when we go back via Tess's house. I forgot to put the carpet in the boot, so it's still on her front lawn.'

'Christ, Beaker, all you had to do is one little job and you even fuck that up, don't you.' I close my eyes and let out a deep sigh. 'Alright then, mate, best we head back to Tess's.'

The Volvo surges forward as Beaker plants his right foot to the floor. We swerve our way back, sunk deep in the black leather seats with the windows down and the stereo quietly pouring out Robbie Williams' 'Me and my monkey'. It seems strangely apt, given the mental agility of my driver.

'Fancy a beer?' Beaker enquires as the safety of Tess's road looms ahead.

'Why the hell not,' I find myself saying, 'we've managed to get this far with you as drunk as a lord, so one more can't hurt. Where have you hidden them?'

'Err, under your seat I think, in a Tesco's bag.' I bend forward and delve in the dark as the clunk tick, clunk tick, clunk tick of the indicator tells me we are now turning into Tess's road.

I grab couple of cans and offer Beaker one. He glances over and says, 'Crack the top for us, can you, I'm trying to keep the rudder straight.'

With that I dig my nail under the ring and pull. Cha-kssssshhhhh. The froth explodes in my face as it bursts over both of us. I hope it will settle, but it just keeps on coming. I wave it at Beaker, unsuccessfully trying to keep the wayward white stuff from soaking me any further. Beaker lunges for the now slippery can, knocking it clean out of my hand and straight into my lap. I try to stand, my head hits the roof and I recoil down, knocking the beer into the foot well.

The can is now spinning like a Catherine wheel and erupting jets of amber fluid everywhere, even onto the windscreen!

With Tess's house now only feet away I bend down to retrieve the offending article, losing my balance as Beaker swings the car wide to perform a U-turn. I knock into him, causing a momentary loss of control. The beer-soaked steering wheel spins left and he has no hope of stopping it, then the dashboard rushes up to thump me in the face as the car mounts the kerb.

Beaker grabs at the wheel to regain control, with his foot finding the wrong pedal in an effort to stop, punching the accelerator hard to the floor.

We career along the grass verge for a few feet, then through a large bush with a worryingly solid thump; a large object smashes into the windscreen, leaving behind a spider's web of cracks, and a crimson hue to our vision.

Beaker finds the brake pedal and rams it into the carpet. The large object is thrown forward, off the bonnet and disappears down in front of the car.

I manage to pull my head up from under the dashboard and sit with Beaker in stunned silence.

'Oh fuck.'

'Yeah, oh very fuck,' I reply.

'Do you think he's dead?'

'Who?' I ask.

'The bloke who has just smashed his face into our windscreen.'

My head is all aswim from the copious amount of beer, the lack of blood and the impact with the dashboard.

'Come again, did you just say someone's face smashed into the windscreen?'

'Yeah, ugly fucker he was, wearing a long coat I think.'

'Oh very, very VERY fuck!' I reply numbly.

'Yeah, oh fuck indeed. You wait here, I'll go and check him out,' says Beaker. There's steam rising from the ruptured radiator, but the engine is still running. I watch numbly through the blood-red streaked and broken windscreen as the wipers judder across it intermittently.

Beaker grabs under the arms of the body and drags him past my window. All I can see of his face is just pure red flesh, dripping with blood. Beaker makes his way around to the boot, and with a click and a whoosh it is open.

He struggles somewhat, but before long Joe Soap is dumped in the back of the car next to Mr De Niro.

I am frozen, slumped in my seat, unable to think straight. I just watch as Beaker goes back to the now flattened bush and gathers up some stuff.

'Fuck me, digital camera, trilby hat and even a flask of soup,' he comments upon his return.

'Let's just get out of here before the Old Bill arrives,' I suggest.

'Got to shift the body, you know, evidence an' all,' Beaker replies, and after a moment's silence selects first and trawls across the road into Tess's driveway.

'Who is it?' comes the familiar feminine voice from behind the locked door that has been knocked for ten minutes solid.

'Santa fucking Claus, who'd you think?' comes my grouchy reply. The door sweeps open and in we go.

'What on earth took you so long?'

'Well, this could be a long story, but let me do some editing. Beaker was late, got pissed, crashed the car – twice – killed someone then dumped the body in the back of said car with a kidnapped Frankenstein monster. Any questions?'

Tess falls silent. She can't quite take it all in, but senses from my tone I'm not kidding. I head into the lounge where Beaker's tumbler of scotch is still sitting on the table. I down it in one and pour another, then another. The burn in my throat feels good, the buzz in my head even better.

I drop back into the comfort of the leather sofa and sit in quiet mental mayhem. After some time Tess comes in and sits next to me, her arm snakes its way around my shoulders and I feel suddenly dozy. I close my eyes and begin drifting to a better place.

'Fuck me, Hazy, take a look at this.' Beaker stands with a notebook in one hand and a mobile phone in the other.

'This bloke is a private eye, he's been tailing Tess for months, texting Ed with regular updates. Look here, the last one he sent was earlier this evening, informing Ed that we had been here visiting.'

I rub my face and try to think.

'What the hell are we going to do? If we go to the police, they are bound to know he was following us. Ed will see to that, just to get me out of the way.'

Beaker looks pensive.

'What about the prank?'

'Are you off your fucking head! We've just fucking killed someone!' I reply. 'You have a sodding dead body in your car, and you want to know if we are going to continue with a goddamn prank!'

'No, no, no,' Beaker says, shaking his beetroot-coloured head. 'We continue with the prank as planned, but use the real body; that way Gandhi can help us get rid of it.'

'What! Have you gone totally and utterly fucking insane? You're suggesting we just dispose of the body and pretend it never happened?'

'Err, yeah. So far as I can see it beats rotting in prison for the next 20 years.'

I try to mull this over but my mind fails to make any sense of the situation. I look to Tess for help but she just shrugs.

'Fuck it,' I resign with a heavy breath, 'go on then, I guess we've got nothing left to lose. If we hand the body in we'll go inside for manslaughter anyway.'

'I'd better go and sort the car out then, and I guess we'll be needing two rolls of carpet now,' Beaker says as he stands in the doorway.

'I've only got one, rug that is, and that's the one you took earlier. It was a wedding present from my Aunt Gloria.

She has a lovely flat overlooking the sea in Worthing,' Tess quietly mumbles. I think her brain is slowly shutting down so I comfort her on the sofa as Beaker heads out to cut Aunt Gloria's carpet in half.

Chapter 34

Gandhi's

taking the joke just a little too far...

The chewing gum sealing the leaky radiator seems to be holding, the makeshift rear light may not be quite so convincing.

I had taped a kid's rear bicycle light in the orifice that used to house the tail-light, and done likewise at the front. A brace of cable ties stitch the bumper and grille together, but little could be done about the windscreen.

As we hit the road towards Gandhi's house I amuse myself with the notion that the mutant Volvo indeed resembles its originally intended cargo of one Dr Frankenstein's monster.

Only the hum of electricity pylons and the amber glow of flickering streetlights welcome us to Pelham Walk.

We pull up at number 27, both drawing a deep breath before we step outside. It takes quite a while for Jane to come to the door.

'What time do you call this? He'll be sober again any minute.' We make our apologies and avoid the subject of the real stiff in the boot.

'I'll go and see if I can get him up. Ere, I thought it was only meant to be Beaker, don't you have a camera to be waving around or something?'

'Change of plan,' we both reply in unison.

She disappears upstairs as we step into the hall.

'What the fuck is this all about then. It'd better be good or I'll twat the pair of you.'

'We need a favour…a, like, massive one.'

Gandhi shakes his head.

Beaker then says, 'I think we need to go and sit down.'

Gandhi gives an impatient sarcastic smile then sways his way to the living room.

'So, come on then, what is so important you have to drag me out of my pit at this unearthly hour?'

I start, 'Morning is exactly our problem, Ooooh fuck, where on earth do I begin… We devised this prank.'

'You, *you* devised this prank,' Beaker interrupts, 'don't go inferring I am doing anything other than trying to get you out of the shit hole you've put us both in.'

'What the fuck does it matter, you're the one that killed him,' I snap back.

'Whoa, whoa, whoa, killed who? What the hell are you two going on about?'

'Alright alright, I persuaded Beaker to help me steal a mannequin from Shepperton Studios…'

And so it went on.

'…So we need you to help bury the body.'

'What, the Frankenstein or the real one? Come on, you two. You are out of your minds if you think I am going to help you dispose of a corpse.'

'The trouble is,' I continue, 'Beaker has strained a muscle in his back, so he can't dig. I am crap and unfit at the best of times, and it will be light in two hours, so without you we're fucked.'

Gandhi shakes his head.

Jane had been listening from the doorway, and to our surprise adds, 'Go on, you should help them out, really, after all that's what friendship is all about, isn't it?'

We all stare at Gandhi with wounded puppy eyes, albeit with black rings around them. He ponders for an agonisingly long time, then, 'Oh fuck it, go on then. You grab the shovels from the garage whilst I go and get dressed. You have no concept of how much you owe me for this.'

As soon as he has disappeared upstairs Jane shoots me a massive grin and says, 'Go on, where've you hidden the camera, you little rascal?'

It then dawns on me that she still thinks it's a prank – how amusing!

She'll kill me when she finds out though!

Chapter 35

A Bridge Too Far

taking the joke just a little too far...

The three of us climb into the Volvo and head out in search of some desolate wasteland; not easy in a suburb like Weybridge, I can assure you.

'What about the Chertsey Meads?' offers Beaker.

'Naah, too popular for dog walkers and the like; he'll be discovered far too soon,' I reply.

'How about St Anne's Hill?' tries Gandhi, but Beaker shoots him down immediately.

'If you think I'm lugging a corpse up there with my dodgy back you've another think coming. I say we should stay low, maybe find some marshland or something; hide the stench, you know.'

'There's always the derelict power station on Desborough Island?' Gandhi prompts.

'Yeah, on the river just up stream of the Crown,' I add.

'Perfect,' concurs Beaker.

* * * * *

Now, for those unfamiliar with the local geography, I shall expand a little. Desborough Island is a small stretch of land in the middle of the Thames, about a mile from Weybridge town. It can only be accessed by one of the two parallel bridges that connect it to the mainland. One bridge flows traffic onto the island, the other off it. These bridges are set about a half-mile apart, the total length of this chunk of land.

The island is home to a rugby club, a couple of rather large houses and the aforementioned disused power station. There is also a lover's lane car park that is these days used purely as a gay pick-up joint. We all seem to be fairly certain that at this time in the morning we can carry on undisturbed.

We approach the first bridge after about ten minutes of driving in silence. Beaker flicks the indicator and we roll onto the bridge. Once on the island, the old power station looms ahead of us looking as creepy as a derelict mansion in an old horror movie. I would love to tell you there is thunder and lightning cascading from the skies to add to the drama, but it's spring, so it isn't.

We do, however, have both Frankenstein and a real dead body in the car, so I guess there's enough drama going on inside without adding to it.

The lolloping mutant Volvo draws slowly up to the enormous industrial building. The moonlight's now fading as the sun nudges its way ever closer to the horizon. Thankfully, the security at the old site is somewhat depleted. You would hardly need a crack SAS team to overcome the chain-link fence that now stands where the multiple layers of barbed wire and impenetrable tight mesh fences once stood when the place was still active. We stop under the cover of a willow and set about our tasks in relative silence. Beaker and Gandhi retrieve the pick, shovel and spade from the rear of the car whilst I set about snipping a hole in the chain-link.

Once within the grounds, we make our way through the brambles to a small clearing. The dark shadows cast by the nearby dour grey walls offer a welcome cover to our criminal activity.

'Go on then, Rambo,' offers Gandhi as he hands me the spade. I pathetically stab at the rock-solid ground, doing little more than scratching the surface.

'Fuck me, Hazy, this isn't a knitting class,' Beaker starts, 'put a bit of backbone into it.'

'You try then, it's like bloody concrete.' I throw the spade at Beaker's feet. He stares at me blankly.

'We don't have any option, we must work together or we're fucked, so put your handbags down, girls, and get out of the way,' Gandhi commands, then continues, 'I'll break the ground with the pick, then you two clowns can shovel it to the side. That way you'll hardly break into a sweat or chip a precious fingernail, okay?'

'Okay,' we reply in unison. The vast-shouldered Gandhi then pulls the pick above his head, before violently swinging it downward into the solid ground.

Chink, chink, chink. The swing of the pick increases into a steady rhythm. After breaking the clay-rich soil in a man-sized rectangle, Gandhi gestures for us to begin. I bend over and start shovelling. Beaker does likewise next to me, but as he is left-handed and I am right, we just succeed in bumping into each other awkwardly, eventually drawing to a stop when Beaker yells in pain after I inadvertently thump the shovel into his hip.

'For fuck's sake, you two, can't you even do that without a fucking drama?' barks an agitated Gandhi. 'Just take it in turns, will you.'

I then continue on my own scratch-shoo, scratch-shoo, as the dirt is displaced from the slowly growing hole. Once cleared, Gandhi gets to work with the pick again to break the ground a further few inches down. Beaker then sets about his turn, shovelling the loosened clay and rock from Joe Soap's impromptu grave.

An hour passes. I exhaustedly swing the shovel to my side, but then lose my balance and collapse to the floor. My breathing is laboured and my head giddy with the effort. The grave is still only 10 inches deep, the going has been impossibly hard and we've just reached a large piece of concrete.

'Fuck this, we're not going to make it before sunrise,' Beaker states, 'we've at least a couple of hours worth of digging left and I've had it, I can't lift another load. Mutually we all agree that it's futile and 'red card' the idea.

Deflated, we return to the car and cruise around to the lover's lane car park. We pull up to mull over our severe lack of options as Beaker sparks up a spliff.

Moments later the car is thick with smoke and renewed optimism. We decide unanimously to dump the body in the river. Beaker fires the engine into life and we cruise down to the exit bridge.

* * * * *

'Fuck this, there isn't any cover here. If anyone comes along the main road we'll stick out like a cock in a nun's shower.'

Beaker nods in agreement of Gandhi's suggestion and looks to me for an alternative.

'What about the other bridge, the one we've just crossed to get onto the island?' I suggest. We all glance upstream. There is far more foliage shielding it from the road, so without further ado we make our way back.

The tyre squelches as it bumps up the kerb. I can feel the soft thud of the rim hitting concrete as the tyre feels underinflated. I pray the off-road excursion of earlier hadn't given us a slow puncture.

Gandhi pops the rear open and starts lugging the body out, Beaker assists as I walk a few yards back towards the road to keep lookout. I cup my hands and blow into them. It seems suddenly cold.

Watching the two clowns struggle to get the roll of carpet over the edge of the bridge would seem comical if it wasn't so damned serious. In a split second though, my face turns from mild amusement to absolute horror.

As the carpet is bundled over the edge, I get just the quickest of flash of the occupant's foot – naked foot.

The world closes in around me as my head spins wildly in a blur of thoughts.

'Nooooo, you fucking idiots, that's the wrong one!' I shout as I run back to where they are stood.

'You absolute tossers, you've thrown Robert DefuckingNiro in the river, not the dead fucking body!'

Beaker and Gandhi just look at each other in disbelief.

'Jack will have me in a roll of carpet over this bridge if I don't get De Niro back tonight. Get that body in the river,' I say, pointing at the corpse in the car, 'I'm going after Frankenstein.'

With that, I move a couple of paces back and take a running leap onto the side of the iron bridge. I hesitate a moment, then draw a deep lungful of freshly chilled as I fall forward through the air.

The words 'what on earth am I doing' flash through my mind just prior to my impact with the icy river, but I have little time to answer my inner voice as the current carries me swiftly away. I gasp for breath and fight to stay buoyant in the churning, swirling water; it takes all my effort to keep afloat.

Once settled I can see my target floating ahead. I hear the splash behind me as the second roll of carpet hits the water, but survival instincts dictate that my attention is a little too tied up to turn and look.

I swim like mad to try and catch up. With the speed that the water is flowing, it feels as if I am moving at 50 miles per hour. Slowly I make ground on De Niro, aiming to catch him by the time we get to the next bridge. With the sky now clear, the moon's reflection in the water illuminates my way.

As I draw closer to the bridge, a car pulls onto it and stops mid-way. I am spinning and rolling, unable to keep a tight course, but I'm aware enough to know that it is indeed a police car observing my progress.

Panic overrides me as I swim frantically towards the roll of carpet in front, hoping I can dismiss the one following me as pure coincidence, and 'nothing to do with me at all, really Officer, I haven't killed anyone tonight, honest Officer.'

Before I know it there's a spotlight trained on me and some big mouth with a loud hailer telling me to swim to the side.

'You fucking try it in a strong current like this, you tosser!' I gargle as the river swirls around my head with turbulent force, occasionally dipping me under as I try to catch up to Mr De Niro. The swell surges to take us under the bridge, pushing relentlessly towards Weybridge.

I clamber fully onto the carpet, and hug it face-down to catch my breath. The stench of wet shag pile filling my lungs is acrid enough to rival that of the real dead body a few metres behind me.

'It's a good job this Frankenstein's made of rubber, not used body parts, or the bugger would have sunk by now,' I mutter to myself, and then look behind to check progress of the other carpet in my flotilla. It's still there, bobbing along behind me. I will it to sink, but it still seems buoyant.

The current slows a little as we round a corner, the water flattens out and I find myself moving almost serenely, as the banks grow farther apart and the trees that line them morph into bricks and mortar.

The back garden of the Crown comes into view a little further along. I start kicking my legs, guiding us towards it.

The cold attacks me to such a degree that I have almost forgotten about the two policemen and concentrate on my achingly numb body instead.

The pushing current brings us gently to a stop as we bump up the bank that edges the beer garden. I stagger from the water, shivering and convulsing as I attempt to drag the roll of carpet onto dry land. Then watch in horror as the other roll of carpet housing one Mr Soap also washes up on the bank about 30 feet further along.

'Bugger it,' I exclaim, wondering where Beaker and Gandhi have gotten to. I decide to ensure the safety of the mannequin before tackling the body, so begin heaving it out of the river. My wet trainers slip and slide as they struggle to find purchase on the slick mossy bank. I then sink deeply in the muddy silt that lines the river and lose a shoe to the soft mud. I try every way I can possibly think of to shift the carpet from its sludgy tomb, but fail miserably. I collapse, having exhausted my already depleted body and lie on my side, eyes closed, for what seems like an age before I hear footsteps approaching.

'Beaker, thank God. Sling that stiff back in the drink and let's get home, I'm knackered.'

'Err, would you kindly tell me what on earth you are doing, sir?'

Chapter 36

The Cell

taking the joke just a little too far...

I come to, draped between an armless plastic chair and the cheap steel-framed laminate chipboard table in the interrogation room.

A name to strike fear into even the innocent who find themselves within its fluorescent lit walls, let alone a man caught red-handed trying to bundle a stolen mannequin and carpeted corpse into the River Thames.

I idly spin the empty plastic water cup on the table, awaiting the arrival of my duty solicitor. The energy my body once held is now so depleted, it's hard to ascertain whether the loud hum is coming from the lighting or just inside my head.

The chair is adequate, but not comfortable; my prospects bleak at best. Clunk jangle clunk...skrrrrch.

The heavy door opens slowly and in walk the pair of arresting officers. The younger, broad-shouldered one speaks first.

'I am Officer Conroy and this is Officer Beale. Mr Paul Hayes, you have been arrested for the murder of a Mr Joseph Soap on the morning of Wednesday, May the 28th, 2008. Do you understand fully the grave nature of this charge, and the implications it carries with it?'

'Err, yeah, I s'pose so. Life imprisonment and no walks in the park for a while, I guess.'

'Mister Hayes, it has already been a long night, sarcasm will not help either mine or my partner's patience, so knock it off before we are forced to get our truncheons and beat the living shit out of you.'

'Wooooo, tease me big boy.'

Thud.

The truncheon impacts my shoulder with extreme violence, numbing the skin immediately whilst sending an army of alarm bells up my neck to explode into my head. I scream with pain as I collapse off my chair and collide with the concrete floor face-first, causing my nose to burst a crescent of crimson blood over my bare chest. 'Where has my shirt gone,' I wonder.

I lie whimpering with pain and exhaustion as I watch the boots of the officers walk around me, one of which buries itself swiftly into my stomach, causing me to double up in pain. Coughing and choking, I'm dragged by the shoulders back up onto the chair. I sit forward, head dipped submissively as the lecture begins. I have given up without even a returned punch. I feel at such a low ebb that even a feather could fell me. I need blood – straight, un-poisoned with cocaine or alcohol, claret. Pure and simple, but none seems forthcoming. The shorter, slightly heavier built officer then starts.

'So, this Joe Soap that you have beaten to death, he was a friend of mine, a good friend. How does that make you feel?'

I think about this a while, and opt for an honest answer.

'Shit,' I reply.

'So you admit beating him to death?'

'No, no, I didn't say anything of the kind. Stop putting words into my mouth.'

Officer Beale then continues, 'Could you please then explain to us, Mister Hayes, how you came to be floating down the Thames with a rubber mannequin in one roll of carpet and the body of the now deceased Mr Soap in another, identical roll of carpet?'

'Coincidence?' I pathetically offer, but this just earns me another slap. An hour passes, maybe two, it's hard to tell in a small room with no windows or clocks. I have avoided the subject and given as many evasive answers as I possibly can, but finally the officers tire of my lethargic un-cooperative state.

I am ground down to the base of my mettle, my body aches, my head thumps and my dry mouth has the tang of old fish skin. I just want this whole nightmare to end, but I know admitting to murder is wrong; that and the prospect of going away for a long, long time hardens my resolve.

'Fuck this, Beale, maybe we should show this little shit what he's done. Show him the result of his mindless violence and who he has hurt as a result of it. Yeah, let's teach this little shit a lesson.'

Beale shoots Conroy an inquisitive look.

'Down to the morgue, let's take him down and show him Joe Soap – Joe Soap's body…dead body. Stiff and drained of life, ready for embalming, and make this tosser look into Joe's dead eyes and see if that shakes his fucking memory as to how he fucking killed him.'

They both look at each other, then walk slowly towards me…

Chapter 37

The Morgue

taking the joke just a little too far...

The squeak of their Doctor Martens' boots is the only intrusion to break the silence of the bleached corridor.

Beale walks ahead of me, Conroy behind. My sweaty hands tingle with pins and needles as the overtight cuffs dig into my wrists, restricting the circulation. My nose fills with the dull aroma of disinfectant, adding to my disorientation.

The walls seem to be closing in on me as we near the end of the corridor. A bright light comes from beyond the twin portholed swing doors ahead. This, combined with the stainless steel kick plates that cover their lower half, makes the entrance resemble an evil, skull-like face. Beale shoves the door open with such force the hinges strain to remain in the wall. The room beyond is both bright and clinically white.

To my left there is a body with an obvious head wound, the top half of the covering sheet is sodden and drips with blood. A burgundy pool has formed on the previously scrubbed clean white floor tiles beneath his trolley. To my right rest a pair of comparatively un-dramatic corpses. Both are dressed in plain white sheets and appear to be on operating tables.

Beale checks the brown paper luggage tag fastened to the big toe of one of the corpses in the centre of the room, then draws back the covering sheet to reveal the pale drained face of my victim – sorry, Beaker's victim. (My God! They've even convinced me I did it!)

Conroy grips my arm and whispers through gritted teeth, 'Now, you little fuck, you can see what you've done. Smell the vile embalming fluid that Joe Soap will soon have pumped into his dead, decaying body. Feel his clammy skin as it withers away, and rots to a putrid mush as the maggots start to form and devour his rotting flesh. Inhale the rancid stench as he loses control of his muscles and all the shit and piss oozes from him like a geriatric without a colostomy bag. Go on, smell it, feel it, look at what you have done, you sick fucker, LOOK!'

Conroy grabs me by the back of the head and thrusts me in the direction of Joe Soap's face; he holds me millimetres away, our noses almost touching. I cringe and wince as the tears start forming in my eyes. I am overcome with emotion and the warm spread of liquid down my left leg tells me that I too have lost full control of my body. My legs start to weaken and my hands shake violently, then BAM! Joe's bright blue eyes burst open, as the smile on his face explodes with the words, 'SUCKERRRRR!! Jeez, we sure got you there, boy!'

My legs instantly buckle beneath me with shock as I collapse unconsciously to the floor.

Bastards!

Chapter 38

Aftermath

taking the joke just a little too far...

It was all Gandhi's doing, of course. The crafty bugger had been trying to plot a prank on me in revenge for my best man's speech for years, so when I mentioned the proposed escapade to Beaker whilst driving to Le Mans, it offered him the perfect opportunity. Ed joined in when he heard the rumours and Joe seemed the perfect scapegoat, after all he was being paid anyway...

Gandhi and Glynn's Lotto thing had just been an interim measure to let me think I had got away lightly.

Ed and Tess remain separated, as do Claire and I. Tess tells me that the reason I cannot remember much about the night I spent on the sofa with her is because there isn't much to remember. I fell asleep, pissed, before anything happened. She then just played along for the attention. Stevo has offered me a slot on next year's team, on the promise that I have cleaned my act up, and we are all due to meet at the Crown for a drink tonight; in fact I'm already there.

'Uncle Jack! How are you doing, mate. Listen, sorry about De Niro, but I just couldn't resist.'

'Don't worry, old son, I would have done the same in my day, I can tell you! Anyway, are you not going to get this old fella a drink then?'

I gesture to Sarah behind the bar for a pint of Bombadier, when a familiar smiling face appears at Jack's side. I smile back.

'Oh my God, I'm so sorry for embarrassing you the other day, I was having a hell of a time. Let me tell you all about it over a bottle of champagne.'

'That would be a perfect end to the most disastrous day!' she replies.

'Sorry for being so rude and not introducing you,' interjects Jack, 'have you met the fabulous Keira Knightly before then?'

The end… Or is it just the beginning…

DESTDENIED

Sample Chapter

The Tour guide ushers us towards the relic of a coach we're due to call home for the next few or hours. The waft of stale sixties air envelops me as the doors whoosh open inches from my nose. I place a trusting hand onto the tubular chrome hand rail, but feel it flex just a little too much for my liking. The rust around the welds serve as a warning for any who put even the lightest faith in its ability to do its simple job. I open my grip and use the door frame for leverage instead. The driver turns his head towards me with a mixed gold and gapped smile as his teeth appear to be in varying stages of disrepair.

'Welcome aboard my friend, follow your ways to back of coach and make comfortable, ok?'

'Thanks mate.' I return with an amused face as I climb the couple of steps into this retro time machine, then make my way along the passageway past the filthy seats that shamefully wear an acid casualty designed swirl of burgundy and green paisley velvet. Wendy and I opt for a place three quarters of the way down, and sit in hopeful anticipation as to what the day might hold.

The coach fills quickly, and after a short welcoming speech through the diabolically inadequate audio system by Raymond, our effeminate tour guide, we chug our way out of the city walls and into the open countryside.

After only a few minutes of driving, I notice how rapidly the scenery changes from city to suburb, then outskirted scattered buildings blend into desolate wasteland just moments later. The empty road ahead of us has neither junctions nor road markings, the few random points of reference marking the gaps between sandy expanses are simply the odd burst of marijuana plants or a few stork nest set in the occasional dehydrated tree.

'Sod breaking down out here.' I mutter to myself as the relentless sun beats through the grimy window, before returning to the *'Perfect Home'* magazine I had bought in a newsagent whilst we were still in Gibraltar.

After half an hour I begin to feel a touch light headed. The combination of dodgy Moroccan roads, dodgy Moroccan fare, and reading whilst on the move have conspired against my brain and sent it swimming. I note, however, with amusement how the roles in the modern world have truly been gripped by sexual polarity. Whilst I sit studying colour combinations for our hallway, and kitchen styles for the refurb we plan to begin some time in the near future, Wendy sits reading a book whose cover features a strapping lad with a pair of taught buttocks clad in nowt but a pair of elastic white jodhpurs. Boys choosing wallpaper whilst girls read pornography, how did that happen with nobody noticing? Closing my eyes, I try to ignore the discomfort of the glass that serves as my heads harsh pillow.

I rouse some time later with a fuzzy swede. The heat of the midday sun has taken its toll now, and my swollen tongue gasps for a drop or two of crystal cool water. Delving into my rucksack, I retrieve a bottle of disappointingly lukewarm refreshment that serves as merely adequate at best, although my parched throat welcomes the re-hydration and softens in response.

'Jeez, what time is it?' I ask Wendy. She grabs my wrist, and in an over dramatic way brings my arm to within an inch of my nose, saying;

'I don't know Mr. Wolf, let's find out shall we? Oooh! The big hand is almost at the twelve, and the intsy wincy little pinky is looking straight at the two, so I'd guess it must be around two in the morning, wouldn't you say? No! Scrap that, it's blaringly hot and the sun is above us, make that two in the afternoon.'

'Thanks love, two would have been sufficient.'

'So look at your own watch next time Romeo.'

'Yeah, okay, point taken. Man do I feel fuzzy, how much longer do we have to endure this manky rat den for?'

'Probably only another hour or so, we're just reaching the base of the mountain now.' I look longingly at the thin dress, draped across her perfect shoulders as my eyes wander down further to her full...

'Stop staring at my tits will you, I'm horny enough as it is, without you eyeing me up at every opportunity, you're like a bloody rabbit.' Wendy shoots me one of her heart melting grins, and right on cue, my heart melts. I quietly skulk back to my interior design journal, with a smile to my face that truly ignites the soul. Christ, I am so lucky!

The coach unexpectedly veers to the right, I lollop onto Wendy's shoulder;

'Hey tiger, thought we were going to wait till later,' she whispers enticingly. I rouse, and glance up to meet those vivid eyes, that draw me in for a deep, deep kiss.

BANG! The rear of the coach clips a rocky outcrop in the road, and sends the back end hopping abruptly across the narrow mountain path. I instantly draw my attention to the window, and note for the first time that we have indeed climbed some way up, and are now threading our way along a seemingly treacherous stretch of road. The twists and turns fall ever tighter, yet the drivers speed appears ever constant. I begin to feel the root of deep concern growing in the pit of my stomach.

With the coach slewing and sliding beneath us, I stare out of the window with growing anxiety, and watch as the dust and shards of grey rock spill over the cliff edge from the worn and overworked tyres. The drop is increasing, and the jagged rocks seem ever more deadly as the road width depletes to almost a single track. Wendy's face pales as a growing look of concern spreads across it. Her freckled brow furrows as a grimace appears with every twist and turn, the drivers control becomes increasingly reckless, and the passengers become more and more agitated. I start to sweat, then notice that I've begun to turn the ring on my right hand with the first three fingers of my left hand. The greater the increase in speed of the coach, the faster the ring is spun on my finger.

Then, a sense of relief spreads throughout the interior. The road opens up again, and everyone takes a deep breath before relaxing back into their previously paused conversations. I close my eyes once more and loll onto Wendy's shoulder,

'Bugger off will you, I'm reading.' She pushes me away forcefully, so I take the hint and find the familiar, if somewhat uncomfortable window my pillow once again.

*****

Crack! I'm awoken with an explosion of pain from the front of my face, as my nose impacts with the back of the seat I have been thrown against at great velocity. A lunge to the left, followed by one to the right has my head thumping into the window, leaving a smear of blood. I cannot decipher what is happening; the world is just in a spin around me, set to the terrified screams of all inside. We are mid crash, but the sequence of events appear to be happening in such slow motion. The wail of car horns outside, the screech of burning tyres that frantically fight for grip, and my realisation that with the coach sliding sideways at our current speed and trajectory, we will tip over the edge of the cliff in a fraction of a second's time. I grasp my hands together in a moment of panicked prayer, only to find the world dramatically slowing to a stop.

I open my eyes, I hadn't even realised that I had closed them, but must have done in the sheer panic, and look in awe at the frozen world around me. Glancing down at my tightly clenched hands, the thumb, fore and second fingers of my left hand are all clasped tightly around the ring on my right, squeezing the three sapphires simultaneously. I release my grip, and then notice the tension I am also carrying in both my shoulders and jaw. One by one I slowly release the pressure from my taut, aching muscles. Curiosity invades my mind like never before, I notice that everything around me is held in a state of suspended animation yet I alone am free to move. How can this be? I wonder. The dust particles hang in the air in front of my face, and I look to my side, jumping with fright as I see Wendy's face is fixed in a tortured scream. I reach out to touch it, still soft skinned, but the muscles of her face have contracted into hard sub-skin knots, just as mine were only a moment ago. I stroke her hair, it moves with the softest of touches, but reacts like an astronaut's might, bobbing and floating in a vacuum without the aid of gravity to keep it in check. This disturbs the dust particles in the air around me, and I begin to wonder what else I can affect in this surreal world.

'Everything.' Comes the bold reply. Startled, I look around for the source of the voice. Shocked, I see none other than an aged Michael Caine standing in the aisle wearing a blue boiler suit. I blink my eyes and shake my head in an effort to clear my mind enough fathom what the hell is going on.

'You're about to die old son, but I guess you knew that when the coach tipped its arse end over a three hundred foot cliff edge.'

'I don't understand.' I pathetically offer.

'No, you lot never do. That's where I come in though, to act as a sort of guide to help explain a few things, get you on the right track so to speak.'

'But…' Caine holds his hand up in an open palmed stop sign.

'Let me introduce myself, you've probably heard of me; Guardian of the Gate is my official title, and one I quite like actually, but most just call me by my more popular name, Saint Peter.'

'So I'm dead?'

'Well, not yet. Given a couple more seconds and you certainly would have been. Smashed, crushed and then burned alive in the wreckage. A horrible way to go I must admit, I hate it when we get the burned alive ones, they stink the place out for weeks.'

'Heaven?'

'Yes of course it's bloody Heaven, where else do you think I'm Guardian of the Gate, down there with… *Him*?'

'You swore!'

'Yes of course I bloody swore, I swear all the bloody time. I'm Michael bloody Caine, haven't you seen any of my films? And no *"Only meant to blow the bloody gates off"* jokes whilst I'm on the subject either!'

'I thought you said you were Saint Peter, are you lying as well?'

'No I'm not bloody lying. It's all a matter of perception.'

'Perception?'

'Yes, perception. Let me explain: Suppose you were walking along a pavement, the sun was out for the first time that March, and you came across a half eaten burger, in a half opened wrapper sat directly in the middle of the path in front of you. What would you do? My guess is that you would cuss at the kids that had discarded it and walk on without a second thought. Now imagine that same half eaten burger sat innocently in the path of ten starving and shivering men who had slept rough for five days, running towards the only form of nutrition they have seen in almost a week. Imagine, as they fight and jostle over such a precious source of food. It's obviously of a far higher value now, therefore their perception of it is somewhat different to yours wouldn't you say?'

'Yeah, I suppose so, but what the hell has this got to do with you being both a famous seventies actor and the guardian of the gate?'

'Perception, my old fruit. The thing is, once you get up here, you can't take your body with you, so everyone sees you the way that their mind perceives that they *should* see you, be it litter or nutrition, warm or cold, Michael Caine or Saddam Hussain. You are seeing me as I was in that old film with the Minis in Italy, where the coach tips over the edge of a cliff at the end. You obviously identify that character with the saviour who is going to dig you out of this shit hole you seem to be firmly wedged in. It's your own personal image of who is going to save you. Comprende?

'Err, yeah I suppose so, but how are you going to save me though?'

'I'm not.'

'You're not?'

'No, I'm not my old son.'

'Fuck.'

'Now look who's swearing.'

'Do you fucking blame me? I'm just about to plummet down a three hundred foot cliff, smashing, crushing and burning myself to a hellish oblivion, and you have the audacity to berate me for my fucking language!'

'A hellish oblivion can be arranged my old son, but from what I've seen of it, I certainly wouldn't recommend it. Let me help you out a little here, take a deep breath and listen a moment, 'cos I think this could be important to you:'

'You have on your finger a ring, and yes, ornate though it might be, innocent it most certainly isn't. In your hand is the power to change the world, the destiny of all around you and possibly the future of the planet you lot call home. It has graced the hand of many before you, and will also be passed to many after you, provided you don't really fuck up and lose it or something. It cannot be destroyed, it cannot be replaced, and it certainly cannot be imitated. It is the original eternity ring.'

'Eternity?' I question.

'Yes Jack, eternity. However that doesn't mean the bearer lives forever, it just means the ring will, so don't go getting your hopes up.'

'Oh. So what happens now?'

'Oh yes, sorry, where was I? The ring bearer, that's you by the way, will have it passed to him, or her, you've got to be so fucking P.C. these days it dries me up, by the previous ring bearer once his or *her* ninety second privileges have been exhausted.'

'What the fuck are you talking about?' I interject.

'Are you going to shut up and let me bloody finish or what?'

'Yes, sorry, continue.'

'Anyway, your ninety second privileges start now, as you have used the ring to summon them by depressing all three stones at once. This is the signal to the universe that you need time to halt. What this also means, is you have been given three time slots in which to reverse time and re-assess your decisions or actions. Time in the real world stands still, you can take as long as you like to suss the situation and do whatever you need to, to put it right. Some tossers have taken weeks, months or even bloody years to decide what to do. The downside to this is that time doesn't stop for the bearer, you'll age at your normal rate. You must have heard of people that seemingly deteriorate or go grey overnight, they aren't freaks, they're just previous ring bearers who've agonised for years in their frozen world for the right decision to make, only to return, seemingly only thirty seconds earlier, as the old men they had become during their indecision. My only advice to you is this; make your decisions with your gut, it is usually right. Agonising over your options in the consciousness of your mind has never worked, so don't be tempted to prove the exception. It doesn't work, believe me.'

'So let me get this right, I have eternity to decide what happened thirty seconds ago?'

'No, you have the rest of your natural life span to decide what you would be better doing thirty seconds ago than you already did, but best not die of old age before you make a decision.'

'Right, so how do you propose I get myself out of this shithole then? And with that, Michael Caine smiles and simply fades into the ether.

Great.

I run through the words I've just heard over and over again, still making little sense of them. I can't even remember my own name with the mess that my brain is in, let alone what happened thirty seconds ago. *Get out*, is my first instinct. A wise one at that me thinks. Trust your gut he said, and as I have no desire for my guts to be sprawled down the side of a rockface, I see this as a good option. I draw my knees up, place them on the seat, and hop over Wendy into the aisle. Upon reaching the front, I try to open the doors, but they are stuck fast. Ahh, pneumatic. I find the release switch on the dashboard a moment later, wincing at the vile stench coming from the inanimate driver that I have to lean across in order to depress it. Nothing, I press it again, still nothing. No power, I conclude. Damm. I make my way back down the coach, looking for the emergency exit. Relieved, I see it about three quarters of the way down on the right hand side. There is a mother and child obscuring my access to it, so thinking quickly I gently lift the child into another seat, then return for the mother. She, it transpires, has never heard of Weight Watchers. I tug and heave at her grossly overweight carcass, her light floral dress tearing with the effort as she slumps and slips from my grasp. I eventually get her into a headlock and drag her, face first, into the aisle.

The window whooshes as it glides up out of my way by its horizontal overhead hinge. I leap from the coach, finding the dry ground a little farther than I anticipate, and jar my back in the process. After a moment of discomfort I jog over to the safety of the undamaged Armco barrier a little way back down the road. I glance over its edge to remind myself of just how lucky I truly am. I turn, face the coach, and clasp my ring in my three fingers, ready to apply the required pressure for the spectacle I am about to begin.

I stop, overwhelmed at my own selfishness. Surely there's something I could do for the rest of the passengers. My thoughts then spring to the overweight woman I had so much trouble shifting. Wouldn't want to try and oik her out of the window. Hmm, this presents a problem. I shake my head in an effort to stimulate its contents. I can see what Caine meant now, I could vacillate on this for hours, getting older in the process. What are the implications, I wonder, of saving a group of tourists to continue their lives as normal, albeit with altered destinies, as opposed to me not intervening with the natural order and allowing them to plummet to their graves? There could be a mass murderer on board, and my interrupting this chain of events could have catastrophic consequences. I recall reading of the doctor who saved a rather famous patient of his from the affliction of peritonitis, deadly if left untreated, only to have a guilt and remorse filled existence a few years later, once his patient recovered to become one of the most powerful men in history. Adolph Hitler was just another cut and stitch job to the surgeon at the time. I decide to let the coach plummet.

Wendy, what about Wendy? I can't let her perish aboard the coach, now can I? My hands fall to my side as I walk back to the stricken vehicle.

For information visit:
www.haghughes.com or www.penpress.co.uk